LONDON INDEPENDEN
RISING STARS & P
5TH ANNIVERSARY
ANTHOLOGY
SHORT STORY – FLASH FICTION - POETRY

LISP
LONDON
INDEPENDENT
STORY PRIZE
2023

First published in Great Britain
by the London Independent Story Prize, 2023
e.info: entry@londonindependentstoryprize.co.uk
www.londonindependentstoryprize.co.uk
Follow us on Twitter and Instagram @Londonisp
www.facebook.com/LIStoryPrize

978-1-7384671-1-2
British Library Cataloguing-in-Publication Data
A catalogue record of this book is available from
the British Library.

Edited by Ozge Gozturk
Cover art by Samantha Sanderson-Marshall,
Smash Design and Illustrations

LISP
LONDON
INDEPENDENT
STORY PRIZE

Table of Contents

Introduction

London Independent Story Prize (LISP) is a not-for-profit organisation founded by storytellers for storytellers. LISP aims to nurture brave voices and create sustainable networking opportunities for writers and filmmakers. Our purpose is to build a community that embraces multicultural differences, bold voices, unique writers, and extraordinary artistic approaches to storytelling.

The stories compiled in this anthology were selected from the LISP 2023 competition. Aligning with LISP's core strategies, these stories are not proofread, edited or polished by professional editors and proofreaders. We acknowledge that language skills, such as grammar and spelling, are linked to access to education. Therefore, LISP does not seek excellence in those elements but values the distinct voice of the writer, the originality of the stories and braveness in the storytelling techniques the most.

Enjoy reading these fantastic stories and poems.

Foreword, Jessica Andrews

Writing gives us the power to tell our own stories on our own terms. It allows us to unravel the twisted knot of memories, sensations, emotions and images inside of us, unpicking loose threads. It is particularly potent for those of us who do not hold much power in reality, or who often feel voiceless. We can narrate life the way that we see it, asking our readers to unpeel their own skin and consider the world from our perspective.

We push elements of ourselves into our characters and send them into the unknown. We smell their sweat and notice the dark circles beneath their eyes, registering their shaking fingers as they fiddle with their phones or light their cigarettes, noticing the coffee growing cold in their takeaway cups. We watch them stumble and falter, wrought with impossible dreams.

We let them try new things and seek connection, making mistakes and acting carelessly as they run headfirst into joy, grasping at brief, gleaming moments of pleasure. Through our characters, we gain a deeper understanding of the business of living, which can teach us compassion for ourselves and each other. To look carefully at something deems it worthy of attention, and to write about a person, place or experience gives it significance, asking other people to see it too.

Stories are tools we can use to carve out space in the world and the work in this anthology is testament to that. Each writer asks us to step into their narrative, to stop for a moment amid the clamour around us and pull off our masks, or try on new faces. They ask us to be open to new connections, knowledge, challenges or confrontations. They invite us to inhabit these temporary spaces, to feel the texture of their language and see the world anew.

Jessica Andrews, November 2023

LONDON INDEPENDENT STORY PRIZE 2023 RISING STARS

In Absentia, Francesca Duffield

In Absentia

The alien pulse
of the ceiling fan,
and the metallic gasp of the insect spray,
were all that remained
of my belated lullaby,
among the ceaseless croak of cicadas

in the endless night stretched behind
my closed eyelids
all I could see
was red
red dirt roads
dirty red, like the blood that flowed between us,
and white walls stained
with red
dust, or blood,
I couldn't tell,
through tinted glass,
gliding inside the chilled car,
and you, wearing aviator shades,
that changed the colour of the veldt
and made you into
a cheap tv villain,

but mainly, most importantly
hid your eyes

Dhal in South East London, Truly Johnston

Dhal in South East London

I am weaving a tapestry;
a fleshy heart root and sinuous web
of laterals for structural support.
I gather the matter
from my bone marrow
and forge it anew – for her.

I hand-stitch fraying fibres of tales,
and tailor the matted mycelium of
frame of mind and favourite food.
I curate the best bits of me
and sew them into her mettle;
to nourish her tall, strong and true.

Intimate idioms and hallowed histories;
streets, names, stories and feasts:
the time her Granmy saw a ghost in her bedroom;
me, a toddler, lost in Trafalgar Square;
her Dad's tooth-in-the-forehead rugby scar;
how we waited / and waited

Warm drift of coconut milk in dhal;
curdled call of our chicken's egg song;
the dark, malty pubs of South East London
where we gigged when nights were still long;
anniversaries of our dead and lost.
In all this, how we sequestered her name.

I wear the mantle of maker and keeper,
homespun and sported before and beyond me.
Shaping, containing and pinning personhood

through time-taming photos printed in books
and ghost-voiced tapes in loft-lidded boxes;
an intermedia anchor in place and truth.

When those inevitable words reach her -
said with curiosity or callousness, '*where are you from*?'
She will taste this tangled tapestry beneath her gums,
judge their worth to see her shape
and tug her threads of light and shade.
I have sown her story.

He I, Emily Tsang

He I

How do I feel about you?
Like a mariner at sea
Tilting against the deadening beam
In the waning light
A pale hook pierces
Dull wounds on my hands
How do I feel about you?
Like the midnight breeze
Skimming down my curtains
Ruffling up my sheet
In sleep my dreams seep through
My pillow heaves
Like you they conquer
Like tears they shimmer

How should I feel about you?
Your eyes sparkle a thousand words
I think of the seashell flung through my window
Landing in a bed of cottons underneath
It fell like a comet coming home
And there in crystal light sails
An incandescent glow

What is there to feel about you?
My cocoons were tampered
You were a glaring shade of red
Heat boils down my vacant spine
In your smile silk sings.

Driven, Michael Salander

Driven

Sometimes, in the dead of night,
a car pulls up outside.
The engine is turned off,
a car door opens
and somebody gets out.
The front door of a house opens
and slams shut again.
That makes sense.
Or…
The front door of a house opens
and slams shut.
A car door opens
and somebody gets in.
The engine is turned on,
the car drives away.
That makes sense.

But then there are other times.

A car pulls up outside.
The engine is turned off
and then silence,
a silence that seems to go on forever.
Nobody gets out,
what the hell are they doing?
Or…
The front door of a house opens
and slams shut.
Somebody gets into a car.
You wait for the engine to start,
but there is only the same endless silence.

Eventually, you drift off to sleep.

It's the harsh daylight that awakens you.
There's a crick in your neck.
You're half frozen,
and it's only then that you realise
you are still wearing your seatbelt.

PAIN, Danielle Todd

PAIN

it seems difficult to talk to oneself as much as poetry does
and withhold
from a storied word like *pain*.   blurred stacks of wetness
park up
on your brow. You are assigned,   (salted)
in my tidal pool. yesterday, I flung apples
from my arrow – beat my way beneath habit and floorboards
to the rim of a nightly terror, inching a thumb of
cream into a coffee cup.
Apples for apples,
I heaved with the naming of
everything. I wore a golden net over my face.
I catalogued minutes by their sound. Terra.   I wanted
to tell you something, but I never want to speak of ghosts again.
level light streams in through the window and We pierce
the feeling with names. *Mediterranean.*
a piece of string dipped in wax, encrusted
in tourists' brains.

Two Boys

i.m. Alan Kurdi, September 2015

Sand –
in your hair, in your eyes –
invasive grains. A new shoreline
gathering in cupped palms, water
drizzling from fingertips puckered with cold.
Tiny insects in a tender swarm:
you salvage, lay them out,
the seriousness of three years on your face.

The seriousness of three years on your face.
You, salvaged, laid out,
tiny insect in a tender swarm:
drizzling from fingertips puckered with cold;
gathering, in cupped palms, water,
invasive grains. A new shoreline
in your hair; in your eyes,
sand.

'Harrison Ford 8 is not to be trusted', Andrew Philip Boulton

'Harrison Ford 8 is not to be trusted'

It was the early eighties and everything good in the cinema had a Harrison Ford in it. I'd been hired by the studios in '81 to make more Harrison Fords – a joint venture between Warner and Paramount, the first they'd attempted since that bad business with Burt Lancaster. They'd decided there weren't enough Harrison Fords to make all the Harrison Ford movies they wanted to make so they called me. I made eight new Harrison Fords and gave them seven. The final Harrison Ford went a little wrong. It's like when you're making scones and you give the last of the dough to a child and she rolls it into an asteroid or a gorilla foot, but you bake it anyway because you're curious to see what it'll make. Harrison Ford (v8) was my asteroid gorilla foot. He wasn't terrible. He mostly looked like Harrison Ford, but there was a stain on his front tooth that looked like a harp. The studios wouldn't have taken him like that, so I did. I brought him home and introduced him to my wife and my daughter. He was very charming, as all the Harrison Fords in those days had to be. When he drank water, his ears shrank a little, which I hoped wasn't happening with the others. He was almost a friend, in a way. By Christmas, my wife had fallen in love with him and was asking me to leave. She got Harrison Ford to tell me. He sat me down, on a couch the colour of a butchered heart, and gave me the news. I didn't say anything, I just sat there with my secret Harrison Ford and imagined myself small enough to play music on the harp in his teeth.

Without Warning, Birds Fall

Above a desolate northern marsh, soaring starlings sweep the mauving heavens. Small, fluid flocks, making the most of the shortest day, swarming from all directions faster and faster. Driven by some invisible force, they part and join with great purpose.

High above the Meatpacking District, on New Year's Eve
I'm mesmerised by their mobius twists, their seamless shape-shifting…black ink smudge…
a giant's teardrop…heart…speech bubble…

The smooth-headed maestro, loved for his energy and wit
My all-seeing, all-knowing species can map – even replicate – a starling murmuration, but software cannot explain what their flocking means, how it feels to be in that moment.
Relying on machines to communicate, I try to make meaning, overlook signs, miss alarms.
I wonder at these perfectly synchronised small birds.
Thousands, too quick-witted to collide,
each knowing what the other intended.
I cannot fly.

The broad-smiling shaman, who made clubbers dance
Without warning, the birds fall, dark leaves upon the holm, the vacated, dimming sky and their baffling avian ballet delivering stark proof of nature's transience.
Sombre, I trudge past the burnished reeds.

The Englishman lies silent and still on the king-size hotel bed
I trace old railway lines long eclipsed by silver birches, knowing that nothing is perfect, nothing is finished, knowing that nothing lasts.
For too many new years, I've traipsed after happiness, been left duped and burdened by broken, cast-iron resolutions. Today, I have seen through her false promise.

Security break down his door too late, he will never fly home…
Everything changes, everything is mortal. Knowing this hiatus will pass, knowing that light and warmth will return, I will ignore the lure of that Judas Sheep. Impermanence means that anything is possible.

This year-end, skydancing starlings are cleaved to my heart. Under the stalling solstice sun, I resolve: make no more resolutions.

Murmuration, Sarah Masters

Murmuration

We creep around the house like ghost hunters, the dog and me. I lay my palm over the salt sweet dip of the sofa, still warm; Jessie finds a wisp of your grapefruit shampoo. I check my phone, rub my thumb over your smooth cheek, your windcurled hair.

Upstairs, your bedroom door stands open, the 'keep out' sign redundant, your walls a constellation of sticky dots that we don't know how to read. Jessie leaps on the duvet, scrubs with her back paws, but it's empty as a cloud. I tug a dust-smothered sweatshirt from under the chest of drawers, sit on the floor, my back against the radiator, drape it around Jessie and me.

We sleep, though it's mid-afternoon. Your text wakes us: 'Arrived, room nice, met other students.' I send a kiss.

I conjure up the bounce of voices, the blue spark of your energy. I turn on the radio, then I turn it off and cook in silence, letting my thoughts bubble and dissipate. I feed Jessie at the table, knowing you'd tell me off.

We take a late walk, Jessie lurching through the barley, like she's swimming butterfly stroke. She flops by my feet, and we watch the rose-striped sunset. Out of nowhere a dark haze collects, separates, swirls. We're under it, Jessie and me, just staring as it shakes the sky like a million shivering leaves. You'd point and pull at me if you were here. You'd tell me what it means that the swallows are early, and why they fly in this formation. But you're not here, and I listen to the murmuration, and watch it, and me and Jessie, we're okay not knowing more, and we're not lonely. We know all we need to know: that they'll return, and so will you.

LOOK AT ALL THE PLACES

The stalwart bulk of the kitchen door. Solid, the estate agent said when he showed you around, knocking on wood.

Yes, solid. Like the newel of the banisters or the oak-topped sideboard or the dining room mantelpiece.

Or sharp. Like the alpine apex of the iron, the chrome handle of the microwave, the knifing corner of the glass coffee table.

Complicit all, they stand accusing.

So . . . you can hear your friend Jan saying – irritably – what's the problem? He's gone, isn't he? You've survived, haven't you? You're safe. Better than safe. You're financially secure, you had a good lawyer who got you a barring order, and a divorce settlement that includes the house. And the kids.

She's right. The kids don't talk about him in that fearful way they used to, quickly looking over their shoulders and lowering their voices before smuggling their urgent morse to you. They don't talk about him at all. The ugly wound in the air that used to sit around him has closed up and has left only a gnarled seam.

And yet, late at night – battle time – when the kids are asleep in the very peace of the house that has been so hard won, you feel uneasy.

The hard surfaces emanate dangerously as if they might chest up to you and do you damage. Or they stand back and whisper like a Greek chorus.

Coward!

Look at all the places your head has kissed.

Decomposition, AJ Morris

Decomposition

The floorboards creaked as I stood up and looked to Muse, reminiscing on the dance I'd just performed with my brush across the canvas.

How stroke after stroke, flourishing flourish, and each sporadic splatter inspired a brush change. How my stomach rolled to life while the small smushes with my fan brush kept me from tarnishing the pale walls.

Looking around, I kept mental note of where I'd touch up the piece with Liquitex white and a detail brush. Others where, as the blood dried up in the heat, unfortunately, a red acrylic would suffice.

My mouth twitched and I twiddled the brush I held around in my fingers. I felt Muse's eyes on me as I shifted my weight, towards the canvas, as if it murmured *–closer*.

I could only completely wash my hands off this, be *proud* of my art once I'd disposed of the body.

I thought back to my very short plan. I primed my canvas. I wore gloves. Just like before. But now? As heat poured through the window, as I sweat profusely, and suddenly inhaled the sticky, metallic air around us – regret surpassed the adrenaline.

I dropped into a squat beside the canvas, quickly adjusting my footing for balance. I could already see the body in rigor.

My mouth twitched again as a wave of warmth rose through my limbs. I looked to the window, slightly blinded by the sun and back at Muse.

He smiled lightly at me as he pulled a phone from his pocket to take the photo.

His soft, pride-filled expression always said it all. He got me this far, but this part was my problem.

"Good luck, darling." He murmured as he peeled away from the wall and left us in the room. Another vignette for the collection.

Quiet life pie, Emma Burnett

Quiet life pie

In t'autum, when t'berries down t'road are ripe and ready fer picking, yer can mooch up t'old field and fill yer boots. Them berries is perfect fer a crumble.
Yer'll have to push through t'hedge to reach t'old field, up in the arse end of bugger-me-why-would-anyone-live-up-here-north-o'nowt.

What yer need

- Pick loads o'them reyt good bramble berries, save bother o'going twice
- Stain yer fingers purple on t'soft fat fruit
- Some flour
- Some butter
- Some sugar
- Fair bit o'brandy

What ter do

Rinse them berries gently so's not to crush them. Mix them with some sugar, add mebe a bit o'vanilla if yer've got it, an 'efty splash of brandy.
Take a sip o't'brandy.
Save the mithering. Take a sip o't'brandy.
Crumble's easy. Mix equal amounts of t'flour, butter, and sugar. Add some oats, mebe an 'andful of crushed walnuts. Mix everything together 'til it's pebbles in yer fingers.
Smear butter on yer fingers, rub them around the edges of t'pie dish, then tip in t'filling. Lick them off. Check if t'brandy's still good.
Pooer the crumble on top. It'll bake a crispy brown atop, stay soft below.

Mix one o’t’berries into a bit o’brandy. Gives it a grant flavour, it does.
Stop to cook summat fer tea. Mek sure it’s what ’e wants.
When tea’s nearly ready, put t’crumble in t’oven at an ’undred and eighty degrees fer forty minutes. Crumble’ll be ready ten minutes afor tea, time to cool off a mite.
After tea, scoop out t’warm crumble and serve it up wi’cream and put a bowl afor ’im.
Watch ’im shovel half t’serving into his mouth and swallow it down without so much as a single solitary chew, swallow it down whole so’s ’e can get back to whatever ’e was saying before you went and interrupted.

Dauntless, Rebecca Douglas

Dauntless

My birth-giver discovered I had travelled and unfurled the set of knives used for her mille-feuille of cuts. Broome or the Gold Coast or Hobart would've been worthy of scolding (or scalding), but Berlin and Salzburg and Venice were unforgiveable. Who would tend to her festering necessities? Not her sister, who betrayed her all those years ago by finally uncoupling the gravy train and evicting her. The sister, who tried to give her a free holiday to Perth to visit their brother. The birth-giver could not afford it anyway – she couldn't, she couldn't, she could never. Others were convicted of crimes of pleasure, not passion. A vacay here, a sojourn there, and they might be dangerously close to achieving escape velocity. Words were dissected for hints of holidays and if detected, if proven guilty, retribution was exacted a week after their slinking back to the proper time zone. Then the birth-giver would smugly take a trip, one to hospital. Gastrointestinal distress, agonising back pain – a question mark in illness form, invisible to untrained eyes. 'I wouldn't want to be a burden,' she says with her mouth but not those orbs and falls into unwrinkled sleep.

Spits and Pieces

Each time he opened his mouth, another piece would fall out. Small at first, in the bathroom sink every other morning. He kept them all, assigning them each to a bag. Plastic sealed, in case they grew, then inside a box. After the thirty fourth fragment, he tipped them out onto the kitchen table, throwing aside the fruit, watching the pieces slide around the bottom of the bowl. Two fit together, then three, then five. Next day he got back from work via the hardware store, one hand lining up streams of hot glue whilst the other dug into the back of his mouth, rooting around behind his molars. That was when they started to get bigger. First the size of a fingernail, jagged, like a whole crown had dislodged itself. Then, at dinner with a friend, he'd spat out a shard the width of a razor blade, the filigree of blue ink visible under gravy and potato clods.

And then. Months, years? He couldn't remember how long it'd been. It wasn't quite perfect. Hairline cracks, pieces he'd probably swallowed. They were only coming every so often now, so he'd found himself willing to show it to others. Gathered in the kitchen, next to some dessicated fruit, he spun it under the steady halogen light. A couple had turned their heads, pointed out a gap here and there. A few asked what it had looked like when it was whole.

What did that mean? Didn't everybody make them like that?

The White Scarf, Annie Bien

The White Scarf

I've never told anyone this before, but when I first saw Tsering with the scarf stuffed down his throat, his face and body contorted, I thought he was teasing me, I wanted him to stop always teasing me. Then his face, all of him looked stuck, he didn't blink, something was wrong and Ama-la grabbed me and covered my eyes. You can't unsee something gone wrong, and I knew. My brother was gone. I wondered, will I never hear Ama-la say, "Your brother Tsering…" with a smile on her face? Ama-la's arms covered me as she wailed, like the yak cried when it was killed. I hope no one will ever cram a scarf cram down my throat. I said mantras for Tsering, Apa-la taught, *Om mani padme hum, Om mani padme hum…* I could not unhear Ama-la's wailing. Would she only call his name and never mine? He was her eldest. A reincarnation just like me. He just gave his first teaching. She was so proud of him. So was Apa-la. I didn't know if Apa-la would wail and cry like Ama-la. He was silent. His mouth opened. I felt invisible. I had seen a goose shot by an arrow once. I had cried, that life was ended by someone who didn't care about the goose. I wanted to cry. But I didn't. Yet. Because Tsering was supposed to get up and laugh. Ama-la, and Apa became silent. To let him leave. To let peace come. I crept back and lay down next to him, just like every night. He lay flat, legs together, like a statue. Then, I felt a breath on a winter night. Tsering slipped out of his body and held me. The next day the vultures would be invited to his Sky Burial. I cried.

The Apolyptic Columnist, Marc D O Brien

The Apolyptic Columnist

Many years ago, I almost did not cash my sandy dusty chips while trapped in the desert theater filled with isolated electrical lights headlining heavenly creature appetizer bites. Instead after reviewing winnings, I bought into affordable living quarters, perfectly fitting my creative writing needs. An honest investment until the area felt a sizable shock knocking itself off the vacation paradise pedestal designed by previous generations.

"Did everyone leave our magical rural metropolis?" I defended my artistic professional ground obtained before the debatable cinema choreographed global destruction, "the sinkhole prompt, only was a pitched television show."

Rising, watching my automobile emerge from the underground, I tipped the valet attendant, a young gentleman trying to survive the same horrendous condition dropped upon society due to a decades long political strife. Returning home, stomach filled with trayful touristy treats that soothed my inner soul, I decided to complete the afternoon, enjoying selfish imaginative images then communicating observations using the keyboard.

Arriving at the destination, a wonderful social investment but today's reality scripted the property as a cold setting waiting for cameras to shoot. Bypassing the refrigerator stuffed with international dishes I discovered the hideaway office oasis. Taking a seat, I peered out the window to the pool boiling in anger.

Lounging tabloid still gripped, a skeleton representing the tease talent once a vital fixture to the land I call 'the domesticated dwelling.' "Your right," I pondered, "my past actions, needed to be more aggressive back then, if I only reported that single detail, maybe, just maybe the occupant relaxing outside, my daughter, might still have flesh."

Watching the water inside the aquatic spa form tiny bubbles I powered up the computer and wrote another science fiction chapter explaining firsthand results editorializing 'when two superpowers play catch, using their nuclear arms.'

Point and shoot

Green pill, red pill, white pills: done. For now.

Rain trickled down the still-black window. Thirty minutes before he could even make a cup of tea. These new white pills. What was he supposed to do for half an hour?

What Rob did – what he used to do – no one did any more. Not that it was difficult, or required any particular skill. It was just … an approach … a way of fixing the world. Not mending it, he didn't mean that. More like setting, crystallizing, the way photographers used darkroom chemicals to fix an image that would otherwise smear softly under your thumb.

No one did that any more.

Point and shoot. That's what they called simple cameras, ones any fool could use. Before cameras were all mobile phones anyway.

Point and shoot.

That wasn't it, either. Photography. That wasn't what he was talking about. It was just …

It was time enough. He warmed the pot, swirling the water before tipping it out into the sink. The small pot; no use for the big one, now. He spooned loose leaves – one, one-and-a-half teaspoons – and re-boiled the kettle.

It wasn't hard. It was just not wanted.

Not Wanted On Voyage. Where had that come from?

He saw her, sometimes, still, heard her more often: a voice, distinct, brooking no misunderstanding – that was Carol, all right – from a room he had just left.

He poured a mug of tea, cut two thick slices and dropped them into the toaster that could take four. The condemned man. The words came, now. The condemned man ate a hearty breakfast, that's what they always said. Sixty years since anybody hanged, but still, they said it.

Tea, toast. What else? Butter – the doctor wouldn't like that. Fuck him. Marmalade. Ditto, he supposed. It was always going to be something, wasn't it? The difference was that Rob knew what, precisely. A bit of fat and sugar wouldn't alter that.

You didn't have to see a GP any more, didn't have to look them in the eye. Repeat prescriptions. Two months' supply, just click on your phone and collect it from the pharmacy. They'd deliver, but he preferred the walk. Even on days like this, with the rain spitting in yesterday's puddles. He was slow, but so what? You could shave a week or two each time: no one counted. The woman in the chemist's was usually friendly, if there wasn't a queue. She never asked to see his card, the one for free prescriptions because he had a lifelong condition. She said he was in their system, and little by little his stockpile grew.

Lifelong could cover a multitude of sins.

They had agreed, he and Carol: they would help each other, if it came to that. They would fix it for each other.

Alistair was behind the bar at the Prince of Denmark, which he wasn't always, not at lunchtime. He nodded to Rob while scraping the head off a Guinness for another customer. Young lad. Hair like pissed-on snow, with a tuft sticking up where a fringe should be. Rob hadn't seen him in the Prince before. He took his Guinness over to a table by the window, shrugged off a small rucksack and a padded coat. That was all right. Alistair had to get new customers somehow.

"Christ sake, Rob. Not on the bar." Alistair was pointing at the paper bag. It was white with big green crosses either side. "Anyone would think you're dealing."

Rob laughed. "Who to? Tintin over there?" All the same, he took the bag off the bar and squeezed it into his overcoat pocket. He felt the cardboard packets give way under the pressure.

He used to think he'd pulverize them – Carol's spice grinder would be just the job – and dissolve the powder. Tie a tourniquet around his arm and – bang! Point and shoot.

That was stupid, though. Too much TV. Where would he get a big enough syringe? He'd want a turkey baster.

They hadn't exactly agreed. He'd offered, and Carol had said all right, if it ever came to it, maybe just to shut him up, stop him talking while she tried to watch TV.

Alistair was pouring his pint now. "How's things?"

"Oh, you know."

Things were much the same. Which was surely the point of things. Stability. Also: getting in the fucking way.

Alistair reached between the pumps to place the pint in front of him. "You want a short with that?"

He could wash them down with whisky. No, not whisky – too much of that would make him sick. Which wouldn't help. A really nice bottle of wine, perhaps? It wasn't like he'd have anything better to spend his money on. Champagne'd be too fizzy. He giggled, as if he'd been drinking already. He shook his head. If beer made you queer and whisky made you frisky what was it wine did?

Wine made you fine, that was it.

Fine.

Point and shoot.

"No," he said. "You're all right."

He handed over a fiver, told Alistair to drop the change in the bottle. Not that there'd be much. Good job he wasn't trying to drink himself to death.

"There's a paper there," Alistair said. "If you're bored."

"Thanks."

Bored. That was about the truth of it. Was he in severe pain? No. Had the doctors given him six months to live? No, more's the pity. If he had that he could go to Switzerland. If he had that and the money.

He took the paper and his pint over to a table across from where the young lad with the hair was wiping off a Guinness moustache with his sweatshirt sleeve.

The paper turned out to be the *Daily Express*. He wasn't that bored. Rob laughed to himself again. A little chuckle, but out loud. He should get a grip of that, he thought, before people went thinking he was happy.

"Something funny?"

It was Tintin. His voice was flat, hard to read. He surely wasn't trying to pick a fight? It was eleven a.m., there was only the two of them. Alistair had disappeared wherever barmen go when they aren't actually behind the bar. Daylight leaked through the window behind the young man's head.

"In the paper? Something funny?"

There was something funny about the way he was pushing this, Rob thought. Funny in the head.

"No," he said.

"Only you laughed."

"It's a free country."

It wasn't, but so what? It was just another of those things people said. Carol said. Like the condemned man's hearty breakfast. It didn't matter if it wasn't true. It was just a way of telling Tintin to fuck off without telling him to fuck off. Only the young man didn't seem to understand this, because he was picking up his empty glass and walking over. Which probably wasn't good. He held out his free hand.

"I'm Michael."

Not good, okay, but probably not dangerous. Apart from the hair, he looked pretty normal. Tall. Skinny, under the shapeless sweatshirt. Good bones, Carol would have said. Something funny about the eyes, though.

Rob ignored the hand. "The thing is, Michael, we don't do that round here."

"Here?"

Rob shrugged, indicating the Prince. London. England. Anywhere, really. It was the same the whole world over, far as he knew. You didn't just walk over, stick out your paw and say hello. Why not? Well, because you might get stabbed, for starters.

No, that wasn't it. Look at him. Rob wasn't going to stab anybody, was he? This guy Michael must see that. It was just … you didn't.

Michael said, "What are you drinking?"

They didn't seem to move, the eyes. That was it.

"No, you're all right, thanks."

Michael sat down, pointed at Rob's glass. "I mean, what is that?"

Rob looked at his own glass. "Bitter."

"Bitter?"

"Best."

Michael laughed. "Why is it best?"

Rob shrugged. "That's what they call it."

"Is there a worst bitter?"

There must be, Rob thought. He'd had a few contenders in his time. He said, "You're not from here, are you?"

"I am from Bergen. In Norway."

So that was it. There wasn't an accent Rob could detect. But just that ... flatness he'd noticed from the off. As if the words weren't quite alive, or real.

"You speak very good English."

"Thank you. You also."

What? Did the guy think he was some kind of foreigner, too? Was that why he'd come over?

"To the manner born, me."

"Ha, ha. Very good. Because this pub is the Prince of Denmark, yes?"

"I'm sorry?"

"*Hamlet.* We read Shakespeare in school."

"Right. Me too." School was a long time ago, but yes, he had read *Hamlet.* And – the other one? – *Twelfth Night?*

"Of course, Fortinbras is Norwegian. Perhaps that's why."

Rob knew he shouldn't, but he had to ask. "Who's Fortinbras?"

Michael looked at him for a moment, perhaps trying to tell if he was joking.

"School was a long time ago," Rob conceded.

"Go, bid the soldiers shoot."

"What?"

Was that some kind of threat?

"The last words of the play, remember? Like, a salute. Fortinbras is the one who turns up and takes over when everybody else is dead."

"Result."

Michael grinned. "Readiness is all. Hamlet's father had killed Fortinbras' father, so perhaps it is only fair."

Rob said, "I think I'll have that pint after all."

Go bid the soldiers shoot? He'd thought it was some kind of threat.

"I didn't offer, but okay. Best bitter?" Michael spoke as if ordering a foreign delicacy he didn't quite trust. But also as if he knew it, and was mocking himself. The way Rob had once asked for *cheval?* in Belgium and Carol had laughed. Try anything once. Mocking me, too, though, Rob thought. Michael, not Carol. Carol had just been laughing.

"And a short one with it."

"A what?"

Finally, something the Norwegian know-all didn't know. "A whisky."

"A whisky and a beer?"

"Live dangerously. As they say."

"Live every day as if it were your last?"

Christ, thought Rob. He'd almost forgotten.

"That's really not a good idea."

Tomorrow was another day. Which was the fucking problem. Why he was where he was.

"No," said Michael. "I think not, too."

It was still raining. At Rob's house, they hung their dripping overcoats in the hall. He showed Michael the spare room where he could dump his stuff and where, tonight, he could sleep. Tomorrow would be another day. He could take his pick then.

"The sofa folds out," Rob said.

"It's from IKEA. My parents have this bed at home."

"Right."

What else was he supposed to say? Comparing notes on Swedish furniture wasn't exactly living dangerously.

"Bathroom's there. Sort yourself out, then I'll get some lunch together."

First he had to take his pills. He wasn't usually so long in the Prince and he was an hour overdue. Not that it mattered, now. Just habit, wasn't it? No, it wasn't. His blood pressure could drop through the floor while his mood shot through the ceiling. He couldn't afford to be wobbly.

Go bid the soldiers shoot.

Point and shoot.

Any fool.

Rob swallowed his lunchtime pills, finishing off one of the blue-backed blister packs. No problem. He'd picked up more that morning, along with everything else.

Downstairs in the hall, his coat hung next to Michael's, two small pools of water on the vinyl floor beneath them just about to merge. He remembered standing at the bar, crushing the chemist's bag into the left-hand pocket. It wasn't there. There was nothing there. Nothing in the right-hand pocket, either. Shit.

Michael? Could Michael have nicked them?

No.

Why not?

He didn't know why not. It just ... it wasn't Michael.

Re-create the scene. The last known movements of all his drugs. At the bar, pills in left pocket, pint in right hand. Over to the table. He'd hung the coat over the back of his chair. That was it. Must have fallen out then. Must have. There was no point going back or calling Alistair. The pub had filled up by the time they left. Any drugs on the floor, they'd be long gone. Warfarin. Rennies. Diazepam. Didn't matter what.

He'd have to re-order. Surely they'd notice that? He'd have to explain, to phone the surgery. Which was pretty much impossible these days. Even if he went in, he wouldn't see the doctor. They'd leave a message; it would be a couple of days before he could collect them from the pharmacy.

He had his stockpile, though he didn't like dipping into it.

Another couple of days? He'd be all right. You couldn't live every day as if it were your last. That way you'd never start a book, or get the groceries in. Rob wasn't much of a reader. All his bills were paid.

Would Michael stay? He'd never planned on having Michael here. He'd always thought it would be Carol.

Point and shoot.

Any fool could do it.

Go bid the soldiers shoot.

He liked the sound of that. Someone to pick up the pieces.

He started making lunch.

Semi-Presence

He tries to lure her out with the smell of baking. As if she'll fall for that, it's a soft blanket that wraps around her where she hides. No need to come out. Today he's chosen cinnamon buns, and he hums while he bakes. The past few weeks, the cabinets and fridge door have filled with post-it notes. 'REMEMBER: Talk to Ella!!' And he has remembered, only she doesn't want to hear it.

"I just want to speak, Ella." He calls from the corridor with the steaming tray in his hands.

Next to the post-it notes is a handwritten inventory of missing items she's collected and squirrelled away.

1. Suit jacket.
2. Ornamental carousel horse.
3. A framed photo of my mother.
4. Dustpan from a dustpan and brush.
5. Paperweight.
6. Plant pot- plant removed.
7. A video camera.

"I've tried Ella, I really have but, it's time for me to move on. I'm sorry... it's… This isn't working. I can't live like this. It's so lonely."

His words jolt through her, and she feels herself come into focus so abruptly that she's almost sick. She's lying next to the cat on the bedroom carpet. The cat levitate-jumps in shock at her sudden appearance and darts out into the hallway. He pushes open the door and finds her lying there staring fiercely up at him, one side of her body sunk into the floorboards.

"Ella?" He sits beside her and reaches for her hand. She pulls herself back into fade and sinks completely under the floor. Lonely! She thinks, lonely? You can't begin to understand what loneliness is, coming home trailing the day's voices, conversations perking up your body like caffeine.

That night, a whole chorus of half-rememberings appear. Their vague forms hover in her mind like mourners over a wet hole in the ground, spilling words like clods of earth.
"Many years ago, you danced naked in front of the mirror. You left your curtains open. Saw a man in the street watching you."
"What did he want?"
"To touch you,"
She allows their voices to wash over her under the floor. A few feet away, he sleeps soundly in their bed.

She didn't choose this. Who would? One day, she woke up feeling odd and couldn't shake it. She tried to carry on as usual, but she kept losing things, keys, thoughts, memories, her solidity. It felt as if her body was part of the air and she'd soon join its soft currents. By the end of the month, her hands were pixelated holograms from a cheesy Sci Fi film. Stress said Google. Maybe anxiety. Maybe working too hard. Maybe cancer. Maybe her thyroid, or her adrenals or the menopause or a neurological disorder. 'It will go away by itself' was her mantra, but it didn't. The doctor told her she was the picture of perfect health. Had she considered antidepressants? Therapy?

Then she stumbled across an article, or more accurately, half an article, written by a woman who became what she coined as a full 'Semi-Presence' before she completed it. Her sister had added this footnote and under that came the comments. Women's voices from all over the globe joining in agitated desperation. Tears of recognition had welled in her eyes. She typed her own comment, then lost her nerve and deleted it. When she went back online a few days later, she couldn't find the page again.

Days pass by fast-slow. She can still sense her body ageing even though she no longer fully inhabits space. She's learnt to blend in with her surroundings, taking on the pattern and colour of wallpaper and upholstery. In the early stages, before she knew how to do this, he found her crouched in corners, under tables or in the small spaces between furniture, cradling a faded arm or leg. Sometimes she controls it, mostly she can't. Some days are worse than others. Her substance, her relationship to solid matter, changes day to day in a way that she finds hard to track. Nights are always uncomfortable, studded with visitations and awakenings. You couldn't call it sleep, what she does now, just a deeper kind of fog. She loses hours, days, weeks, slouched on the couch or tucked away into the comforting darkness of a cupboard.

He builds an over-sized mousetrap. Knowing she can't yet slide through dense metals; he buys an old steel trunk and sets it up in the living room as a coffee table. He fills it with blankets and spare cushions, knowing she will want to squeeze herself into it and curl into the soft layers. Which she does. He lets her get used to it for a few days. One morning, she hears the latch on the lid clang and the click of a lock. She pushes up and meets resistance, realises what he's done, hears his footsteps rush off to work. She panics. It takes five hours of battering her body against the sides to sink through. The worst five hours of her life, she is searing all over, knows more of her is gone. He gets home only fifteen minutes after her escape. She watches him slide the trunk across the carpet into the corridor and hears the front door slam. She could still be in there, fighting the pillows as he took her god knows where.

When it first started, he said he didn't care, said he wanted to stay here through it all, that he sensed her even when he couldn't see her. He sees her eyes, shaped like setting suns, now a violent green, appear to float in the walls and furniture, blinking in and out like the Cheshire cat. He said that was enough. Then, as it got worse, he kept forgetting she was there. She'd tap or scrape to remind him, but he didn't knock back. Now, he'll go to sit on a chair she's in and she has to dart away or sink through it, which hurts like hell.

She refuses to be forced from her home.

He wakes to find a video playing on his laptop, a closeup of his face while he sleeps. He looks freaked out, so she keeps doing it; him changing in the bedroom; him brushing his teeth. He starts a frenzied search for hidden cameras, trying to figure out how she's doing it. He sees a red light blinking out from a crack in the floorboards, next to it, her eyes. "Stop!" he punches the wall, "Stop, stop, stop!"

In retaliation for the camera, he leaves every window open for a week. She hides trembling under the stairs. She comes out to steal his personal documents and though it takes all her courage to go near the windows; she lines them up on the sill in the rain. When he comes home, they have blown out into the garden and lie in soggy, ink-stained heaps. She has tried to go outside three times since the onset. None were a success. Attempt one, a gust of wind nearly took her. Two, she sank halfway out before being hit by a noise, such a clamouring, bone rattling din, she was sure her head would explode. She pulled herself back in and ran for cover. The last time she stuffed her ears with cotton wool and lined her pockets with tins, but as soon as she stepped out, she regretted it. Everything had become hyper-real. Things loomed, crisp and plastic looking. She didn't try again.

"I've met someone." His face is a fist. "Someone beautiful and solid."

The blood rushes to her head, filling her ears with a roaring. That night, she topples his computer. It smashes as it hits the ground. Next, she begins on his framed certificates and qualifications hung in the office, each one crashing from the walls and shattering. If she's going to be a ghost, she'll be a poltergeist.

"Many people loved you." The words of the half-remembering root her to the spot. It's baby face moonlike in front of her closed eyes.

"They stood in a circle, their hands inked with your name."

"Where are they now?"

She primarily eats fruit. It's the easiest. He left her bowls full in each room, extravagantly colourful fruits, unexpected and delightful flavours to ease the monotony. This gradually dwindled to one remaining bowl, bananas and apples on repeat. After the computer, he stops altogether. The bowl in the kitchen is empty. So, he remembers her enough to starve her. She tries other things; a nibble of cornflake, a lick of jam, a bite of cheese, but everything else makes it worse; the pain and disintegration.

"Can you make him hear you too?" She asks the foggy, spindly body of a half-remembering.
"Who?"
"Him!" She gestures towards the sofa where the man has fallen asleep. It ignores her and begins.
"There was a golden day. You stood on the edge of a barge and jumped into the water. You stumbled upon a figure playing guitar under trees fat with green. A picnic with three heads pressed close together on the blanket."
She loves this one. She closes her eyes and lets the sun appear behind them.

Some people believe she's dead already, that because the Semi-Present are like ghosts, they are ghosts. The lack of subtlety is astounding. She still eats, she still breathes, that it's not the way others might eat or breathe doesn't mean that she isn't living.

A few days later, the fruit bowl is full again, grapes, pears and a mango, her favourite. She is so hungry she darts towards it, catches herself. Why would he fill it now?
She bends to sniff the fruit, prods it, puts her ear to their skins. Something's not right. It's torture. She's desperate to bite into juicy flesh. Instead, she picks up the bunch of grapes and plucks them one by one off the stem, placing them across the surfaces of the kitchen. She puts the pears on the cushions of the sofa and the mango on his pillow.

On his return, he finds the fruit spread out. She watches his face, the confusion, then disappointment, then anger, again. He is always rigid with it these days.
"Fine. Don't eat!" he slams the door on his way back out.

She prefers it when he's here. She's not so invisible. He seems to be the only living person left who remembers her, the only one who still sometimes sees her. He stays out more and more, goes to dinner parties, pubs, shops, cinemas, anything that keeps him from having to come home. Lately, he's been absent whole nights for weeks; a new lover.

When he doesn't return that night, she shoves her hands into the toaster. She wants to feel something, but today she's insubstantial and receives only a comforting warmth, which will do. She lays her head on the chopping board; the crumbs pressing into her awareness, crumbs are friendly, discarded from what was once whole, like her. One grape is staring at her. She tries to stare it down, but in the end, she gives in and pops it into her mouth. The taste is off. There's a chemical buzz on her tongue. The next thing she knows, she is opening her eyes in the darkness.

"We were worried,"
She starts. For the first time, the voice of the half-remembering seems to come from outside of her.
"Where am I?"
"You're in the wall. You couldn't hear us for hours."
She can't breathe. She's never sunk completely into a wall.
"How?" But she finds she can answer herself. "The fruit. He's drugged the fruit."
"We can't stay."
Then she's alone. The weight of concrete pressing into her. He drugged her! She tries to move and can't. "OK. Keep calm. You've faced worse." She murmurs into the wall and tries to move again. Moves her hand a fraction. Slowly, in the full darkness, she presses it through, then her head, but when her eyes get free, she's looking at an unfamiliar room. A woman

sits on a couch with a child in a school uniform perched between her knees, picking at a bowl of porridge while her hair is brushed. Seeing them is so dazzling, so shocking, that she cries out. The girl hears her! Sees her forehead, green eyes and disembodied hand protruding out of the wall and screams. The woman must see something too, because she jumps into action, pummelling Ella's face with the hairbrush. Her body pulls back in pain and shock, and she lands in her own living-room where she lays breathless and crushed, tears prick, but she resists. Each time she lets them come, it's awful for days. The sound of a laugh, a woman's laugh, freezes her. There is no strength to stand. She stops her breath to listen, a sing-song voice drifts from the kitchen, a deeper tone in reply, the smell of toast and coffee. He brought her here. The lover. She must have stayed the night.

When he returns from work that evening, she's still in the same spot. He heads straight to the kitchen to make his dinner. Soon she hears the office door slam, the sound of the TV, then he goes to bed. Slowly, she gets up and goes to watch him sleeping; he looks so peaceful, so beautiful.

"Small children crowded you at a party. They put their hands into your bag, grabbing at you, trying to find sweets. When they had taken everything, they ran away in every direction."

"Like a school of fish?"

"Like piranhas." Answers a half-remembering with glittering, mischievous eyes.

"And me, did I have a child?"

When the half-rememberings are gone, she lies on the bed beside him and resolutely tries to solidify her fingers. At two am, she's conjured a thick mist. She reaches out to stroke his face. He stirs, and she moves her body closer to his, slides her hand onto his chest. He sighs and turns towards her. Opening his eyes, he recoils in shock at the sight of her green setting suns, the touch of her mist hand, but then he softens.

"Ella," He whispers and puts his palm over her knuckles. The warmth of it, the hum of his palm, the sigh of his skin submerges her whole body in liquid wax. Her hand comes into full focus and the focus spreads up her arm, to her chest and face.
"Ella," He repeats, stroking her wrist, reaching to touch her cheek. She leans in and kisses him. It's strange. It's underwater with a mouth full of popping candy. He kisses her back.
"This is all I want. This is all I ever wanted."
But you'll only have me whole, she thinks.
"If you bring her here again, I'll haunt her." The effort of speaking drains her substance. His hand falls through her face and onto the pillow and he lets out a small shocked "Oh!"

The house fills with boxes. She keeps shoving her head inside them to listen to the packed-up objects of their now lost life. She doesn't remember their significance, but she likes the way they sound. He's leaving to live with the sing-song woman, the unabridged woman. The piles diminish. She struggles to collect a few tokens before they are gone, but she can't grab hold of solid matter anymore.

"The house is yours for as long as you need it, Ella." he repeats, in case she's unable to hear him. He is so proud of his reasonable generosity. What's an empty house? It's only rooms, rooms for her to disappear into. He's leaving nothing he doesn't value; minimal furniture, just a few boxes of broken things, superfluous bits, ornaments he thinks are ugly. He's even taken the cat. How will he know when she has truly and finally vanished? Will he check on her? She doubts it.
"This is goodbye, Ella." He sits on the carpeted stairs. "I'm sorry it came to this." It sounds like he means it, but then he always does. She watches through the crack of the door as he leaves. Then he's gone.

Time is worse, much worse, without him. Everything blurs, minutes turn to murmurings. It's as if she is being spread out across the surfaces, ethereal marmite on toast, ghost on walls. The world is a talkative thing, and at last she's listening. Sometimes it feels like she's the warm water in a bath, sometimes it's banishment, a twitching agony that splits her, her body wants to withdraw in all directions, dismember itself or dis-remember. Often, she wishes she would just disintegrate.

It could be weeks, or months, since he left when the first one arrives. There is an unidentifiable sighing near the front door. It draws her towards the avoided edges of the house. She sees a woman panting on the welcome rug, sprawled out in worn floral pyjamas. She looks up at her with brilliant blue eyes.

"You can see me."

"Yes,"

"Yes?" the woman stares, open-mouthed.

"Yes." Ella holds out her hand. The woman actually grasps it.

They look at each other in astonishment. The relief is pain. They pull each other nearer, trying not to cry. They stay close for a long time, letting the sensation of each other's body sink down like silt in water.

Haven, Elizabeth Hewes

Haven

This story took place in a bath.

The bathtub in question was slightly too narrow for the large-bottomed person I had become. It was designed for a delicate French *derrière* — a pair buttocks that could perch elegantly on a *Bistrot* chair while their beautifully-groomed owner lunched on nothing but coffee and cigarettes. My behind betrayed my passion for cheese. I had recently relinquished all restraint as a wave of misery engulfed me. I now consumed cheese at all official mealtimes and nibbled it between. At the peak of my distressed cheese-eating, I developed a parallel and equal passion for bath-wallowing, so my slim French bath was now a snug fit.

It was not a glamorous bath.

Squeezed between two walls of what resembled a compact cupboard, there was only a narrow passage beside the tub to allow for a sideways shuffle up to the tap-end. It was also a relatively short bath—it was not quite a sit-down-tub, but my limbs refused to fold into it. So, as I wallowed, my feet chilled on the cracked tiles half-way up the wall above the taps. Limescale and dirt from previous occupants' feet had stained the bottom of the bath, leaving mottled patches. The grey blotches resisted scrubbing, despite my desperate application of vinegar, lemons, and an array of chemicals. My bath looked grubby. Always.

But it had atmosphere.

A cold draft from the outdoor stairwell in the apartment block whistled through the painted metal grill by my head, bringing with it the sounds and smells of four floors of other people's lives: tramping, laughing, confiding, flirting, fighting, hacking, coughing, spitting and smoking.

Books fell into the bath; and so did towels. A phone was retrieved undamaged twice and then drowned on its third dousing. Plastic ducks came and went. One squeaked and another lit up and flashed when floating on water; but in the end the squeaky duck fell silent, and the flashy one started to swim squiffy and eventually lurched into a bin. The lip of the bath also held drinks: water, Earl Grey, Lapsang Souchong, jasmine tea, peppermint tea, red wine, white wine, and glasses of steamy gin and tonic with bubble-coated slices of lemon.

That bath was my sanctuary for twelve years.

Over those years, I looked down at the same breasts, stomach and legs. But as I flick back through those images now, I see many different bodies, many different women, and none of them is me.

At my youngest, I was a woman full of enthusiasm and sexual confidence. There I lay, soaking in hope and plans for a family. Over the following years my stomach slowly sagged with the realisation that something was wrong. Time and again, I washed away memories of intrusive medical examinations, swept up bubbles to hide myself from view. Later, my finger traces the pink starlike scars of exploratory surgery. The results revealed a mash of minor problems which added up to one bigger one. So, almost inevitably, a swollen landscape of hormone-distended flesh came next. The skin on my stomach grew dappled with scudding violet-black IVF bruises, tender bumps, and red puncture dots. The waistband of my jeans left long-lasting painful red creases on its mottled, swollen canvas.

I miscarried a tiny speck at Christmas and bled through my jeans for new year. Miles away from home, I sluiced blood away with icy water and then spent a humiliating pyjama-clad evening with friends, longing for the sanctuary of my hot bath behind the closed door of my own locked apartment.

After that, I often laid a wet flannel over my battered stomach, wrapping it close in warm mortification. Half-swaddling half-shroud. I kept doing that until my last hope died.

Six months after we decided to stop IVF and accept that we would never have a family, I fell pregnant naturally. My gynaecologist called it a miracle and it felt miraculous. I was light and dizzy and stopped soaking in hot water and stood in the tub to take showers instead. At ten weeks, I saw my baby's tiny legs and arms kicking and dancing on a fuzzy screen and listened to its racing heartbeat.

Two weeks later, at the routine twelve-week scan, the frozen foetus rocked on the floor of my womb, dead.

Ten days later I returned to my bath to soak in failure: IVF failure, miracle baby failure, my body's failures, and my personal failures. All that failure soaked into the water, rose in the steam, and condensed on the walls, spelling shame. Shame permeated my skin, my thoughts, my soul.

When the prune-sized foetus died and was scraped out of my womb, the hospital gave me a week to recover. I told myself that I would take that week for mourning and then I would be fine.

I went back to work and was fine.

I was really fine.

I was fine, really.

Then suddenly, one Monday, I was not fine at all. I splintered and shattered.

I did not work on Mondays and on that Monday, several weeks after the curettage, I woke up weeping and cried all day. I could not stop. Tears ran down my face as I got dressed, my face dripped as I chopped vegetables, and I wept as I washed up. My eyes leaked while I read, and I cried into my bath.

The rest of the week wept by. Whenever I was alone, I cried: I cried and cooked; I cried and translated. When my English students left the room, I went to the toilet and let the backlog of tears wash down my face. Then I wiped them off, flushed them away, breathed, braced, and went back for more.

I forced myself to be normal when others were around, but normal was exhausting. I closed my door on the world at night and crumpled. I usually collapsed into my bath.

I could not sleep, but I was constantly exhausted. When I did sleep, I clenched my teeth and ground them so hard that I woke up with a headache. My mind could not focus or grasp anything. My memory was fragile whisps. I mixed up words, names and languages. I brought my phone to my own lessons so I that could search for the answers to my students' questions because I could not find the answers myself.

In the evenings, I was rehearsing for *Romeo and Juliet,* but I could not hold onto my lines. One Sunday I sat for two hours with the script, repeating, repeating, repeating. When I stood up the words slid away, leaving my mind blank.

My partner watched me limping through my life. He stood at my elbow, waiting to catch me as I swayed. He put out his arms to hold me, but I pushed him away. I wavered and dithered alone through my dark days. I could feel his eyes on me. I could feel his concern, but he seemed unreachably far away.

A fortnight after I disintegrated, he had to go to Paris and Lille for a week for work. He wanted to cancel and, when I said no, he insisted that he would make a six-hour round trip mid-week to come home for a day. I could not allow that, so I conjured a smile from the depths of desolation and refused. I told him to go away for the whole week, see friends, escape, live.

That was, perhaps, when the climax of this story truly began.

As soon as he left, I knew that I had made a horrible mistake. Friday slipped further and further away from me, and I had no idea how to get to it. It seemed unreachable. As though manifesting my frozen panic, my neck seized up and would not straighten or turn. I held my head like a wounded bird.

Monday and Tuesday passed somehow. Friends called but I let my phone ring to voicemail. I curled on the sofa and soaked in the bath. Tears coursed.

I made it to Wednesday.

Wednesday was a bank holiday and a friend's birthday. I was invited to drinks with people I barely knew, and I had to go. I needed to go. If I did not go 'people' might find out that I was broken and my shame would be public, my failure complete. So, I had a bath, dressed, dried my hair, painted my face, and put on music. I flung myself into ritual. I threw myself as high as I could and wobbled out on stilts of illusory joy.

I remember arriving at the bar and looking through the windows at the golden lights, black marble, and elegant strangers. It looked like the scene from a movie. I took a deep breath and plunged inside. My face floated a mile away from my soul, wearing someone else's smile.

I drank glass after glass of wine until the world shimmered. I talked, joked, danced and fell. I was helped up and I laughed and danced again, like a puppet tethered to jerking strings. When the bar closed, a kind woman looped an arm through mine and steered me through the dark streets to my door. She seemed worried about my climbing the four flights of stairs on my own. I could not understand why. I wanted to walk her home after she had walked me home. I remember trying to make the point.

I must have given in eventually and made my way upstairs because that is where I woke up, dizzy, with a dry mouth and headache. There was a half-empty bowl of chilli on the floor by my bed, so I must have tried to eat. Yesterday's clothes trailed from bathroom to bedroom, so I must have tried to wash.

When I woke up, tears were falling.

I checked my schedule but then realised that I could not work, so I called in sick and cancelled my day. I rang the doctor's surgery for an emergency appointment instead (about my frozen neck), climbed into the bath, and cried.

Tears were still slipping down my cheeks later as I sat in the waiting room. I wiped them away and pretended I was invisible. The other sick people and their relatives looked away whenever I raised my eyes.

My doctor at the time had a pony-tail, vegan shoes and time did not concern him. Seconds, minutes and hours were his gift to his patients. I once waited until three hours for an appointment because the person who went in before me just needed to talk, so, I felt safe coming to see him today, now.

I was taken aback when brisk young locum greeted me in his office.

'How are you?' she asked.

'Fine,' I lied, my voice cracking. I started to sob.

She gaped.

She pushed a box of tissues across the desk, turned to her monitor, and peered at me out of the sides of her eyes like a nervous horse.

'I'm sorry. I'm fine. Actually, my neck hurts, but I'll be fine. I'm sorry, I'm just crying because I can't have… and… I was pregnant… but...'

What was I saying?

I gulped, back-tracked and tried to make sense. The IVF, the miracle, the dead foetus and my partner's trip tumbled out of me and across the desk in a mangled mess.

'How is your neck now?' she asked, delicately picking out my medical excuse and revealing it for the sham it was.

'I'm not sure. I think it still hurts but I actually drank so much last night, I can't really tell,' my foolish mouth gibbered without permission.

'Do you often drink alone?'

It was clear what she thought of me. A vision flashed into my head of a version of me sprawled across a kitchen table swigging gin alone.

'Oh no! I wasn't alone, I was in a bar!'

Her eyebrows shot up. 'Hmm. A bar?'

'Yes. With friends.'

'Friends?'

Her incredulity painted a vivid picture of a different me hanging off a bar stool confiding in a drunken stranger. The idea made me laugh. Now I was laughing and crying at once and I could see from her face that I needed to exert some control.

'Yes. Really. I was with friends.' I tried to make my face stay still and the damned tears stop falling.

A pause.

'It was a birthday,' I added.

More disbelieving nodding.

Then she went through the list. And, I think it was then that I became aware of exactly what I must really look like, drunken barfly or not, I had become a woman who could not stop crying, who admitted to being so drunk she could not be sure if her neck hurt or not.

Did I drink? (Not that much.) Was I sleeping? (Not really.) Could I concentrate? (No.) How was my memory? (Terrible.) Did I cry much? (No. Yes. Maybe six hours a day.) Was I eating? (Yes. Cheese.) Suicidal thoughts? (No. Not really.) Was there anyone at home? (Yes. But he was away just now). Her face told me clearly that my partner's temporary absence sounded permanent to her. She thought he had left me, or perhaps that I had made him up.

She proposed to sign me off work for a month and suggested anti-depressants and a therapist. I panicked. It sounded terrifying. Without work, I saw a structure-less abyss stretching before me. What would I do with those blank days? What would I have left that I could I cling on to?

I refused. Besides, I did not need anti-depressants. I would feel better soon. Probably by Monday.

We haggled.

Finally, she agreed to sign me off up to the weekend and backed down on the anti-depressants and the therapist. She made me promise to come back if I had suicidal thoughts. I watched her type something in my file with deliberate keystrokes. I imagined an enormous red 'RISK' in flashing lights popping up in my notes the next time I came to see vegan pony-tail doctor man. What would he think?

I went home with my sick note and spent two restless, tear-streaked days moving from kitchen to sofa, from bedroom to bath. I flipped from book to radio, from internet to film, from pottering to inertia. I could not do anything, but I could not do nothing either. I could not settle, I hurt whichever way I sat.

On the Friday evening I ran another un-soothing bath and sank into it. There was a clenched fist in my chest, my breath snagged, and my heart writhed. The endless tears were still streaming down my cheeks, mingling with the steam and bath oils. I was so bored of crying, so fed up with feeling so hopeless, but I felt powerless to escape my pool of pain.

Then, several hours too early, I heard footsteps that I recognised leaping up the stairs, two or three at a time. The key crunched and the front door stuck, jerked free and shuddered shut again. Shoes landed. Keys jangled and dropped. He called out. I could hear him checking the bedroom, the kitchen.

His face appeared round the door and his eyes met mine. For a moment, he hung there, suspended, torn between the world out there and me. Then he came inside, closed the door, and dropped his bag and coat by the sink. He hunkered down in the narrow shuffling gap between the wall and the bath and trailed one hand into the water to find mine.

He asked me what was wrong.

I told him it was nothing and everything. I did not know why any longer. I did not know how to be alive and could not imagine any way of living. I did not know *why*.

I do not remember what he said (nonsense I expect), but he stayed there with me, tucked beside the bath.

As my fingers gripped his, the shattered pieces inside me found something to cling on to. A tiny flame of hope, or love, licked away some of my tears, loosened the fist in my chest and I found I could breathe.

In that moment, I discovered that my haven was a grotty French bathtub with my hand in his. I was still very broken, but I was home.

The Stranger

Iris Mackie lit the candle and watched the oily smoke curl upwards, carrying her prayer to the heavens. A prayer of remembering and a prayer for forgetting, a prayer for the living and a prayer for the dead.

This year, with the first frost, there had been a flood at the entrance to the church, and workmen had been called in to raise the floor slab by slab. Now, the workmen had been replaced by the police. Father Avery always put the living first, but the police preferred to concentrate on the dead, and the remains were exhumed and taken away to be examined. Because of the police presence, Iris thought she might be unable to reach St Jude. At this time of year, she liked to light a candle. Iris had done so every year for so long now it would be wrong not to. There was a young policeman at the church door, and she worried she wouldn't be allowed through, but Trevor appeared. He had attended Sunday School and was now a detective. He took her wrinkled hand gently in his and escorted her around the crime scene tape that had replaced the builders' barriers.

'Not that we know a crime has been committed,' he said to Iris reassuringly. 'It's just a precaution, but there's no church record of a body being down there, and the last time the floor was up, was over fifty years ago.'

'Watch your step,' said Iris as they walked together into the gloom of the church. 'The floors are uneven here.'

'Isn't it a bit dark back here, Miss Mackie?'

'Even the obscure and marginal need to be remembered sometimes,' said Iris, and she lit her candle to St Jude.

On the way back through the church, Detective Trevor Cummings invited Iris into the vestry for some tea.

'It's always good, tea, don't you find, when there's something distressing going on,' said Trevor.

Iris did not feel upset; now she'd lit her candle, but she did not want to seem impolite. She sat on one of the mismatched chairs at the old vestry table while Trevor boiled the kettle.

'I hope you don't mind us having a chat,' said the detective. 'But as one of the oldest members of the congregation ... I mean, as you have been coming to the church for so long.' The teabags splashed as Trevor tossed them into the bin, and a dirty puddle formed where he placed the teaspoon back on the counter. 'Um, well, you have been involved with the church for, well, quite some time.' Iris didn't take sugar, but she took the mug of sweet tea Trevor placed carefully on the worn pine table in front of her.

'I wondered if there was anything from that time that you could remember at all?' Trevor said.

Iris looked down at her tea. The much-used vestry mug was one of a number she remembered had been rescued years ago from a church jumble sale. The mug had once been white but had been given a cursory rinse out in the vestry kitchen sink once too often. They were always running out of washing-up liquid. There was a tea-stained chip in the rim. Iris carefully turned the mug and sipped from the side less used.

'Well, have a think, and we can talk again at a later date if you remember anything,' Trevor broke the silence that had stretched between them as he waited for Iris to reply.

As she walked home, Iris thought back. She remembered skipping along these streets with her younger brother, Simon. She wondered if she could still skip. Lift and hop, lift and hop, perhaps not. She didn't want to be arrested. As youngsters, her parents regularly brought Simon and herself to St Mary's. Iris would sit through the long services, still, quiet and good as their mother had told her to behave. Simon would run up and down the aisle, and their mother would have to take him to the back of the church and find the toy box.

'That's a good girl, Iris, nice and quiet,' Iris' father would lean over and whisper. Iris didn't need reminding; she loved the coolness, the music, and the smell of the incense. On sunny Sundays, she would watch the light that filtered down through the stained-glass windows paint the pale slabs of the aisle in liquid blocks of moving colour.

The following Sunday, Father Avery was most apologetic. Iris had arrived in good time, as she always did. She had made her way around the repair work in the aisle to sit in her usual pew and join the small congregation at the front of the church for the service.

'You will have noticed,' Father Avery announced during the notices. 'That the candlesticks are missing from the holy altar. The police, God bless them, have taken them for forensic investigation.'

After the service, as she was leaving, Iris overheard Father Avery talking to the organist, 'Apparently, there's a correlation between the ornamental base of the candlesticks and the crenelations in the victim's skull. It's all a bit distressing.'

Iris noted that the 'body' had become the 'victim'.

When she got home from the service, Trevor was on her doorstep.

'Hope you don't mind if we have another chat, Miss Mackie. We're going door to door. Just in case anyone remembers anything, though it's that long ago now. Have you had a chance to think about whether you remember anything unusual?' asked the detective. 'We're looking at the early '60s. It would have been Father O'Flaherty who presided at the church back then. Do you remember? You must have been quite young.'

'Yes, it would have been Father O'Flaherty,' said Iris, rankled that Trevor should question her memory. She put the kettle on. 'It was he who arranged for the workmen to come the last time there was a flood at the church. It would have been 1962. The year I left school.'

Iris had done well at school, was more academic than her younger brother and had enough ambition to think of going to college. She'd chosen a university carefully, somewhere to take her away from home, somewhere she could be independent and learn to fly.

'Do you really want to go? And so far away from family?' her father said. 'you'll have your grant, of course, but I'm sure there won't be enough to cover travel expenses when you want to come home.'

'We'll have to see if there's a nice local church you could join. There must be a cousin nearby who could advise us,' said her mother when Iris proved determined. Once the idea had been allowed to settle in their minds, her parents relented.

'Thank you.' Iris said. She had always needed to please. Her acts of quiet subterfuge had to be within the expected norms for her own peace of mind.

'She's predicted straight 'A's,' her mother told Father O'Flaherty as they left church that summer. Iris squirmed at her side.

'Now, now,' checked her father. 'Pride comes before a fall.'

'Oh, I'm sure Iris will do very well,' said Father O'Flaherty. 'Iris is very diligent. We will miss her at the church when she goes to university.'

'Iris will be back, Father,' said her mother. 'She's a real homebody. She'll not want to stay away. Will you, Iris? Girls like to stay with their family until they have one of their own, that is.'

'After all,' joked her father. 'Who'd feed the cat?'

'Well,' said the Priest. 'You say that, but children need to spread their wings.'

'Were you already running the Sunday school then?' asked the detective, breaking into Iris' thoughts. He laughed. 'I remember you were pretty strict. Didn't let us get away with anything!'

'No, not then,' she said as she warmed the teapot. 'You know someone had to let you boys know what appropriate behaviour was. We're formed by our experiences, don't you think, particularly when young and the mind is so pliable.'

Detective Cummings was looking around for somewhere to sit.

'Just move that cat off the chair,' she told him as she sorted the cups and saucers on a tray. 'I helped at the homeless centre back then; it was run in the church hall.' All her life, she had helped at the church. When Iris was a child, she had handed out hymn books and, at Christmas, set up the nativity. She had joined the choir as a teenager. So, it had seemed natural to volunteer at the church soup kitchen the summer before she was due to go to university.

Iris passed the detective a cup of tea without offering sugar.

'I can tell you the names of most of the congregation back then, where they sat, and who was in the choir … if you are interested?' Iris started to list the names, occupations, and predilections of all the faces from the past that she could remember.' Detective Cummings took notes. His pencil dryly scraping over his notebook, page after page.

'I have enjoyed our chat,' she said to the detective as he left. 'Do come again if you think I can help with anything else.' Then Iris gave her fine teacups a thorough wash before feeding the cat. They had always had cats, often more than one at a time, but this one would be the last. She thought. He was getting old, and she was too.

Iris remembered what happened in 1962 only too well. It was the first time the pipe had burst, and the floor was up in the church, and part of the central aisle was cordoned off. The work had been finished. The next day, the hole was to be filled, and the slabs were to be re-laid.

That evening, Iris had been helping Miss Watson in the soup kitchen. It had been a quiet night, and Father O'Flaherty had popped in for a chat as he often did when Miss Watson was around.

'Could you close up for the night, Iris? Miss Watson asked. 'I have something I need to run over with Father O'Flaherty.' And Miss Watson had headed off to the privacy of the vestry where it was well known that Father O'Flaherty kept a fine dry sherry.

Iris had washed the plates and cutlery wiped the tables and put any leftovers in the fridge. She was emptying the urns when she noticed the man. She had not seen him at the soup kitchen before. Iris wasn't sure when he'd arrived or how long he had been there watching her.

'We're just about to close. I've tidied up, but I could get you a quick bowl of soup?' Iris had offered. He didn't answer but walked up to her and gently took her hand. She noticed his earthy smell and the grime that rimmed his nails as she looked at their fingers locked together. Her eyes fixed on the everyday detail of their hands entwined as if they were friends. He led her into the dimly lit church.

'Oh, we shouldn't be here. It's closed for renovation.' Iris tried to pull away, but he paid no attention and gripping her hand tighter, he led her to the darkest part of the church by the side chapel of St Jude. Iris tried to free her hands, but still, he held her.

'Shh now,' he said in a gentle Irish lilt. 'Hold still, be good … keep quiet.' She thought about those soft words, her parents, and the sanctity of the church.

Soon, the stranger was ripping into her as he had ripped her clothes.

'That's it, quiet as a mouse,' he whispered in her ear with hot breath.

Iris wouldn't feel the pain. She looked up at the benign face of the Saint that hovered through the gloom above her so she wouldn't see the man. Iris pulled a lingering drift of incense from the burners at the altar into her nostrils, into her being, to obliterate the smell of him. She concentrated on the unevenness of the floor, painful beneath her rocking back. She could hear through his grunts, as though from far away, as though from another world, the tinkling of Miss Watson's high laugh in response to the deep rumble of Father O'Flaherty that rippled out from the vestry.

At last, he was done. It was over. Iris lay on the floor, feeling the chill of the uneven stones rise and enclose her like a shroud. When she was completely cold, a rage filled her, boiling up in her. Anger at the breaking of the sanctity. She clambered to her feet. The man was still in the church. He was kneeling in one of the front pews by the main altar. She went up to him. He raised his bowed head, looked up at her, and smiled through discoloured, uneven teeth.

'Thank you for a delightful evening, my darling,' he said, taking her hand and kissing her fingertips. Then he rose and started down the aisle to the door, chuckling quietly.

Iris looked down and watched a smear of slime and blood slowly trickle down her leg. Without thinking, she turned back towards the altar, crossed through the gap in the alter rail and stepped onto the red carpet of the sanctuary. She took one of the heavy ornamental candlesticks and chased after the man, catching up with him as he reached the front of the church. Iris lifted the candlestick, and as if it had been made for the purpose, as if it were guided by some higher hand, the candlestick had swung in a perfect arch, and Iris had embedded the base of it in the back of the man's head. With barely a sound, he had fallen, rolled, and ended up in the ditch dug for the water pipes that were to be filled in in the morning.

The church was quiet. Iris was very quiet. Gradually, she felt the weight of the candlestick still dangling from her hand. Iris couldn't bring herself to look at the man. She emptied some of the nearby heavy bags of sand into the hole over the body, so she didn't have to look at it. Iris took a breath and then another until it felt easy. As though to breathe was perfectly ordinary. Then she rinsed and replaced the candlestick on the altar. Iris had cleaned up and locked up as she had been asked to do, put on her coat, and went home.

Iris did not go to university that autumn as she had planned. She spent the year at home watching her brother complete his exams, send off his university applications, and receive offers, as she had done the year before. Her parents were jubilant at her brother's modest success. The following summer, Iris got a job at the local library helping in the children's department. Her parents had been pleased. It was an appropriate job. Her brother finished his degree and began a career in the city. Her parents were appalled by his unapologetic defection from the church but impressed by his success and the trappings it brought. Iris stayed at home and helped her father keep house as her mother's health deteriorated. Her brother brought his wife and children to visit. Their parents doted on their grandchildren. Her brother took her parents on a trip to Africa. Iris stayed home and fed the cat. Her mother died a few years later; her father didn't last long after. Her parents were buried in the same plot, behind the church. Iris stayed on in the house. She hadn't wanted to sell even though her brother advised it. She kept her job at the library. Iris worked in the same section until she was asked to retire.

The next day, Iris was dusting in the large front window of the house, trying to reach a fine spider's webs she could see in the low squinting sun when the detective appeared at her gate. By the time she opened the door, Trevor had his notebook open.

'I'm sorry to trouble you again, Miss Mackie, but your neighbour,' The detective glanced at his pad and then continued. 'Mr Jenkins next door, he mentioned that he remembered years ago your father and then yourself, on occasion, digging in the back garden late in the evening.' He glanced at her. 'I'm sorry to bother you with this, but we must follow up on any suspicious behaviour, however tenuous ….' His voice trailed off out into the street.

'Of course, Trevor, you must do what you must, but you'll find it's the cats. My father always liked to give them a decent burial at the bottom of the garden under the weeping willow where they used to enjoy the late afternoon sun.'

The police had arrived prepared, with spades and tarpaulin. Not long after, looking out the kitchen window, Iris saw Trevor squatting down, talking with the lads digging up the flower beds. They were examining something in the ground. Then Trevor slowly rose and walked up the lawn to the back door.

'Can I get you all some tea? It must be hot work in the sun?' said Iris. 'How many cats have you found?'

'It's not the cats we're interested in,' said Detective Cummings slowly. 'Miss Mackie, what can you tell us about the baby?'

At the Edge of the Woods, a Sanctuary and a Mausoleum

On a purple winter's night, just after he turned thirteen, the boy stepped outside to a hushed world blanketed in snow. In the tribal Gheg country of northern Albania, he was surrounded by his aunts and mother and sisters, and though he was a little older now, he still brandished the face of someone who dreamt of sword fights and gogols hiding in the shadows as he fell asleep each night. The boy knew of violence; he was born in the thick of it, amidst a blood feud that spanned generations where the families plucked each male member that stepped out into the world unknowingly or foolishly or suicidally.

The ancient Kanun remained steadfast and unchanged for centuries, its customary laws about protecting family dignity through revenge killings only claimed men since women and children were viewed as less than. They were faultless in their perceived ignorance, and therefore had no choice but to know and accept two things: men's rage at existing and that that they were likely to die before their time.

It had begun with the boy's great-grandfather, whose ghost haunted the family lineage; a disgraced legacy that had stitched itself to their home like a pox, claiming one generation of boys after another.

It had been something about a girl and a broken marriage arrangement, and then another girl and a seduction that evolved into three families embroiled in slander and revenge-seeking, each new male family member shuttered in a tower for sanctuary or hidden away in their home for safekeeping.

Whenever any of the three families worried the last of their men would be claimed, a girl became just old enough to marry and have babies, and miraculously—somehow—always birthed a boy. The girls, if any were to come, always came after, like Fate's afterthought.

Above the boy, the sky was a melon cracked open, its seeds scattered and glowing amid soft flesh, and when he exhaled, he imagined his milky, white breath was the souls of his male ancestors breaking free at last in the cold midnight air.

Though the boy was the oldest of his siblings, he was still young. He understood his sisters had greater freedoms. Twirling around the yard, making faces at him through the window, and bringing him wildflowers in the spring and summer months; a small slice of the outside world—a consolation prize—for someone tethered to the indoors.

Each time he told them so, they smiled a tight-lipped smile at him, never wishing to contradict their older brother. After all, what did he know of female submission? Of short bursts of joy before they, too, were relegated to the indoors, to servitude, to eternal mourning? Be it for their brief youth, or for the parade of men's funerals that would mark their calendars year after year.

When they were little, the children were told bedtime stories, ones that were always rooted in a woman's pain, eventually to blossom into growth, or a cautionary tale, or martyrdom. They were the same stories shared time and time again, and despite the impossible predicaments the characters suffered, the endings spoke to the ultimate fear men harbored: of women never needing them to exit the forest unscathed.

This is why a woman needs a husband, their mother would say. *To be her guide so she never loses her way. To never have to enter the forest.*

Why then does a man need a woman, the boy would ask.

To surround him like a shield because no one can touch a woman, his mother would reply.

The boy nodded but deep down knew that was only half the truth. He remembered a time he spied a burst of outrage from his father against his mother, his shadow on the wall morphing into a wolf; a bear; a hydra.

As he walked amongst his female relatives, the boy thought of his great-grandfather's broken promise to marry one girl while seducing another. Both would have been punished for his selfish recklessness; the betrothed never bound to marry and the seduced girl never to live. One bang from an enraged father's rifle determined a fate of cataclysmic proportions, like a new galaxy ripping through the universe with its repercussions continuing to reverberate birth after birth and death after death, until only old, widowed women were left standing.

The women were shields until they themselves turned into tattered sheets of cloth, punctured through with holes from grief and exhaustion, never having enough fabric to patch themselves up. It's why they came out stronger in the bedtime stories, sifting through the world unaccompanied by man and his taste for respectable violence.

The gray stone house had shrunk far behind him and all the boy could do was look up at the sky as the women shielded him with their arms, shuffling in unison like a flock of old, disgruntled birds. Their heads moved in such a way to indicate they were looking for prey, their eyes black and blinking quickly through the night.

The boy felt his mother's knife's hilt hanging at her side and remembered those stories, of relentless women who quietly persisted against the paranormal and against their husbands. He wondered if their village would one day be rid of the men and leave the women to spin the blood feuds into fabled stories of a long-forgotten history.

Above him, the stars pulsed in no recognizable pattern, barely lighting their path. The boy felt his face go numb and his throat tickle with every inhalation of the stinging air, and he smiled, wanting to slow his pace, and wishing to become rooted in the outdoors, as stagnant and constant as the Accursed Mountains around them.

The kulla—his family's tall, stone tower and refuge—appeared before them like a mythical beast sitting at the edge of the woods, a black gaping mouth ready to swallow them whole. The boy was ushered up to the front door, the women forming a half moon around him. In the cracks of night that appeared and disappeared between the women's pressed bodies, as they moved in and out of rhythm with each other, the boy saw a milky field, white with fresh snow, laid out before him like a sheepskin rug or a glassy mirror reflecting the moon's light back to Her.

The scene furled back up in a moment as the women, now weeping and anguished, crushed back together against each other, kissing his cheeks and his head of curly hair before pushing him through the door—through the threshold of another stone structure for him to seclude into.

Bir i mamit, it's for your own good, his mother cried behind the heavy wooden door. The boy wanted to be brave but instead began to cry, too, and wondered why there was no way out of this treachery.

His sisters had handed him small bouquets of dried-up flowers that sat half crushed in his clumped fist. The petals had long ago fallen off, leaving mostly thick, browned stems pricking his skin and leaving hairline scratches. He wondered how long they had saved them since spring was so far behind them.

He wondered how long they had known.

He imagined them tomorrow—and next month, next year—in their yard, coming indoors and smelling of dandelion root and mint. He imagined them married and mothers themselves, their joy having dried up on their wedding night and becoming a distant memory by the birth of their first son.

He imagined a nephew following in his footsteps, keeping his ghost company.

Inside the kulla, old family portraits hung on the walls, yellowed and faded in crooked frames. A thin, worn rug lay in the middle, and slits for windows sat like narrowed eyes overlooking the scene below. The boy stood there, watching the women—the murder of crows in their black wool shawls and long black skirts—fade into the night, and he couldn't help but wonder if they had been figments of his imagination all along.

Looking around the small, damp room—at what was now his new home far above and away from the family that preyed upon him—he cried some more before sitting down on the rug to eat his mother's fresh bread and cheese. More would come the next day, and again the day after that. His mother or sisters would now come each day to bring him his meals and relay news while he sat captive to his bloodline, waiting for the other families' men to die and take the feud with them.

Outside, the moon slowly glided across the sky until it curtsied to dawn. The boy was asleep well into the morning, unaware of the men walking slowly past the kulla with eyes to the windows, shotguns thrown over their shoulders; unaware of a young girl walking down the path, her eyes inspecting the curious structure, knowing well its purpose and history, knowing well its promise and its curse—to never release who is residing within it.

Leaving the kulla behind her as she made her way home, the young girl spun her own stories of the stone beast that swallowed a boy whole, never to let him go.

First Fruits Sunday

> "Honour the Lord from your wealth and from the first of all your produce." Proverbs 3:9

LONG BEFORE THE SUN ROSE, A FARMER HUGGED HIS EVER-LOVING WIFE, tumbled from his rickety bed, kissed his sleeping children and gave thanks for the most humble of breakfasts. By the yellowy flicker of a well-worn candle he fumbled into his ragged clothes, slung his heavy bag across his aching back and placed his hat firmly on his head to shield him from the elements. Fully aware of his modest estate, he determined to travel far and wide to sow his seed in the best ground he could possibly find.'

Pastor paused. Straightened his back, stretched his neck forward like a quacking duck, widened his bulbous eyes and blinked his mascara coated eyelashes.

'I want you to hear me now.'

He extended his arm to the balcony seats of Sacred Spirit God In Christ One Redeemer Church, his pudgy fist of four fat fingers wrapped in a sausage thumb.

'The seed that fell on the rocky path came to no good. Aww.' Pastor sighed with an exaggerated frown. 'The birds, they came and they ate it all up!' He splayed his fingers sharply for dramatic effect, his arm waving from side to side still in mid-air.

'Oh no!' Constant Faith shifted in her middle seat on the ground floor of the auditorium.

'And do you know what else?' Pastor's chin jutted out, commanding yet challenging his flock.

'What?' The crowd slipped easily into the familiar call and response. Constant Faith leaned in, hands clasped to her chest, eyes shining, a tingle in her stomach.

'The mighty sun scorched the seeds which fell on shallow ground! I said, it burned them up!' Hallelujah!'

'Hallelujah!' Echoed the throng.

'You may ask me what happened to the seed which fell on good ground?' The preacher leaned to one side theatrically, his arm bent, elbow pointing, cupping his ear with his big hand, his eyes sweeping the hall.

'What happened to the seed?' The fellowship obliged with smiles and some laughter.

'Weeellll…' Pastor turned his back to them. Arms expanded towards the band, his bejewelled index finger indicating the percussion section. 'Can I get a drum roll please?'

Sunglasses on, baseball hat backwards, jaw clicking as he chewed gum, the drummer thrashed out a rhythmic set-up to Pastor's punch line.

'It FLOURISHED! Yes church, it grew into a mighty oak which sheltered the village. Its roots provided nourishment to the soil so all the people, these gentle folk, these men and women of God could live, thrive and survive!'

The drummer pounded a rousing beat and Pastor stepped quickly in time, side to side, forwards and back, Rolex shimmering, diamond cufflinks sparkling, his words riding an infectious refrain as the band played hard and the congregation clapped harder.

'And feed their children,' Pastor danced on, 'and tend their cattle and work their jobs and provide for their elders! Oh, lawd ha' mercy!'

Constant Faith was transfixed by the beat stamped out by Pastor's two-hundred-dollar crocodile skin shoes. She sprang up and moved in sympatico, rapid two-stepping on the spot, her head jerking, the electric atmosphere piercing her veins.

'Have mercy Lord, indeed!' She yelled in a strange new voice.

Pastor jerked and swivelled, turning fast revolutions as the drummer beat on, the piano resonated and the guitar throbbed. 'All because one brave farmer went out to sow his seed!'

The music reached fever pitch. All eyes trained on the stage, hands raised to the ceiling, bodies bouncing, pristine white handkerchiefs flicked high.

'I'm asking you! By God's grace, will you be that farmer today?'

A nod from Pastor and the ushers moved in unison to the ends of each row.

'Will you have the indomitable will of that great man and sow your seed for financial gain right now, this minute?' Pastor wiped sweat from his brow and slipped the silk square into the breast pocket of his plus sized navy Italian suit. He left the pulpit to take root at the edge of the stage, arms outstretched as if to embrace the whole assembly.

Constant Faith caught her breath when his eyes skimmed her row.

'God has it all for you.' He lowered his bass tone to a compelling sotto voce. 'Cars, mansions, more gold than you could ever imagine. All you have to do is prove to him that you believe! Will you do that today, here in this church, in this holy of holies? Will you give unto God what he has always blessed you with?'

The choir's honeyed harmonies undulated about the interior, snaked between each row and swelled like a heavenly musical mist over the people who, with hands raised and eyes closed, swayed together now, brothers and sisters in Christ.

'God reminds you that today is First Fruits, when you are required to give to the Lord all your monthly salary so he may bestow riches upon you and in turn you may care for your families and your community and, with these small things change the world! In the spirit of generosity, let the cherished saints say, AMEN!'

'AMEN! Hallelujah.' The saints responded in one accord.

Constant Faith fingered the notes in her bag. £679, everything she'd earned that month after tax. Absentmindedly, she hummed along with the choir, resplendent in their crimson robes with large gold cross embroidered from neck to toe. Pastor raised one arm and spoke in tongues to fresh applause. Constant Faith clapped too, suppressing the flash of an aberrant thought that Pastor, now down on one knee, fleshy face to the ceiling, arms again aloft, was talking gibberish.

Constant Faith had been taught to recognise signs as a little girl in her Caribbean island Sunday School and she'd been witnessing them all week. The supermarket advert on the back of the bus about freshly arriving fruit. A lottery winner and his wife on the local news who'd put his faith in his last pound and won a million. Her co-worker constantly singing "God will take care of you…" And today, Pastor's new shoes, so similar to the beautiful, burgundy, faux crocodile pair with three-inch heels in the shoe shop on the High Street. She'd even imagined wearing them into this very church. Taking pictures of her feet on the plush carpet and Instagramming the images for meagre anonymous likes. A little something to brighten a tough life in a tough country.

God had big plans for her, a unique anointing once she'd proved her faith. She would give before the service was over and before she left to start her cleaning shift at the care home, the only place that would employ her without papers.

She fixed her gaze on Pastor, now standing, gleaning strength to render everything unto God. She prayed for clemency from her landlord who would receive no rent that month. She steeled herself to wake in the dark just like the humble farmer and trudge through England's January snow because she'd have no bus fare.

Being frugal with the small amount of food in her cupboards could help her to lose the 20lbs her doctor said would benefit her diabetes and ease her hypertension, but there'd be nothing to help feed and send her sister's children to school back home, or to call her momma. She'd even have to forgo her cheap salon wash and press, the only way to tame her super thick afro hair.

A rumbling sob emanated from Pastor's belly, bounced around his rib cage and gargled up into his throat. Rivulets of sweaty tears coursed down his cheeks. The choir hummed, the organ wailed, the drums pulsed an anodyne rhythm. The air was charged, pregnant with anticipation.

Guilt tickled the back of Constant Faith's neck and bumped along her spine. How could she be so selfish? Had she so quickly forgotten God would bring all her earthly desires to fruition in time?

White-gloved ushers with sickly sweet grins guided the congregants from their seats to the altar. Constant Faith pushed her shoulders back and set her chin firmly as she joined the line marching to Zion. She inhaled and exhaled, rubbing the notes between her palms, her conviction increasing with every step.

Standing before the Pastor, close enough to appreciate the luminosity of his complexion from forehead to jawline where his Maybelline for Men maximum coverage foundation ended, she closed her eyes, bearing the weight of his hand upon her head.

The Lord would rain down upon her more blessings than she could handle, Pastor promised aloud and then Constant Faith knew. God would make her a successful businesswoman. She would be able to pay her niece's school and university fees. She could call her momma every day from the latest I Phone. She would have driving lessons and buy a car as big and shiny as Pastor's. She'd gussy up in expensive wigs, haute couture and designer make-up just like the church's First Lady and still, more blessings would come.

Constant Faith vowed to write a new list when she got home. A luxurious A to Z of frivolous and fancy, bold and daring wants, needs and desires because she knew she would see the results not in years but in days, and she would be forever grateful God had led her there on this First Fruits Sunday.

The genial usher at her side gestured for her to lift her notes heavenward, higher and higher until without fanfare or announcement the bills were plucked from her fingers.

'Wait! Please!' Anguished cries burst forth from her gut. Her staccato breath lodged in her chest. A tsunami of cold sweat drenched her skin. Her stomach churned bitter throat-scratching bile and she retched as nausea threatened to ripen into vomit. But the choir sang on, the worshippers prayed heartily for their own blessings and no-one heard her.

She flailed at the usher, tried to take after her money but Pastor's chunky fingers stayed rigid on her skull. Her eyes tracked the oversized, overflowing, fast-moving gold-tasselled bucket, to a newly seen side-door where its blue velvet-sequined mass glittered in the spotlight before it was whisked inside and the door slammed swiftly shut.

Pastor ended his prayer and released her. She stumbled but no-one reached out to steady her. The choir hummed their final notes, exhorting followers to take their place within the army of the Lord. The musicians played pianoforte to a close and the brethren turned away from the altar.

A raw icy emptiness bled through Constant Faith's inner core. It clawed at her skin and penetrated her bones. The doors of the church were heaved open and the light of the world pricked her eyes while her feet moved ponderously as if through mud.

Pastor beamed, nodding to his staff at a job again well done. First Fruits Sunday was over for yet another year. The counting was about to begin but he was already assured of his harvest.

In Search of Michael Mouse

The thrill of it looming into view as pungent sea lions fade behind. Across choppy waters a sentinel, peeling, watching over tourists scrambling through lettered blocks, keen for a moment in solitary they can brag about to friends back home. Kite surfers skimming the top of a bottomless bay, stringing air and water together, hauling onwards towards it. No fog today to chill and cloud the vista. It's really there! A gateway, a portal to this city, to my tenderloin. Anchored on two arching pages of this life-sized pop-up book. How can the magnetism of a bridge pull you six thousand miles from home? Others have tried and failed. As a child I was glued to the television as the ancient land of tomorrow celebrated two hundred years with fireworks over its iconic scaffold. Still I have not waltzed with Matilda. Yet this, not red, but 'international orange' majesty of engineering pulls me to the far edge of North America.

Sometimes I think the Golden Gate is my fantasy version of the Severn Bridge. Travelling home on the M4, passing Bristol, cheek pressed against cool pane desperate to be the first one to "see the bridge" - win the title. Teenage sister no longer finding it exciting but joining in for the love of her little brother. The race to the bridge is the race to leave behind the qualifying of being Welsh in an English accent. Of correcting classmates when they try to pronounce my *real name*. Instead face head on the taunts of an ancient uncle calling down the passage "here comes the Englishman!" What does he know, silly old man? The life of a winder, unhearing to all but my most ardent screaming at our boys in red on the tele. Old aunts growing hoarse. Mam's neck throbbing. Great aunt retelling stories of service in London for Doctor Fielding. The doctor's wife hurling a chicken at her head. Me laughing. Everyone laughing as she plays out the episode serious as a Greek tragedy, kettle whistling urgent chorus in the back kitchen. Aunty passing my cosy nook jammed in behind the table, a wink and a wicked grin. All real? Some real? Different to last time? More tea, more dirt in the bottom of the cup, another story aunty! More, more, again, again.

A nation that welcomed the huddled masses on one side of the country, disgracefully tipped out her misfits onto the other shore sixty years later. Whether yearning to be free or desperate to survive a war effort that deemed them morally unfit to serve, they settled. The new pioneers. Carving out a place to call home. Gays atop missionaries. Where are the Ohlone people? Where is their place to call home? Ensnared by the churches, trampled by the forty-niners, almost extinct by the days of Milk and Moscone. A seismic city. Canyons divide as well as protect.

Squeezing out of the MUNI carriage and ascending an outdoor escalator. Holding my breath. Heartbeat raised. Keep calm, it's just another street. Emerging into the twinkle of dusk. Can't stop the smile from widening. Subdued light through the windows of Twin Peaks. A transparent monument to bravery. *Fuck you, we exist, this is who we are. Hey! Don't look too different from you, do we? Why don't you come on in?* Flags of solidarity beckoning. Where to start? Just to be here. My trainers on these pavements, or rather sneakers on these sidewalks. Could I have known? How did they recruit me? Here I stride answering the call to my young homosexual self. A calling to this radical, accepting heartland. The home of happiness. Pulse thumping as men jump from the car and set upon Michael and Brian. A glint of metal. Not here, not in San Francisco! A promontory that promised to protect us. Fiction cutting my teenage self in two. Where is safety if not here? The clang of the trolley, holding at a red as the cable grinds under feet. Lurching as we clatter over the intersection and descend towards the bay, a rollercoaster in slow motion. Trying to remain in 1976. A seat becomes available, offering it up to someone else, instead to ride the running board. A peal of personal fog pushing towards the corner of my eye. First taste of dim sum. Sourdough baking in my nostrils. Sweet nectarines sticky on my chin. The generosity of Atlantis dwellers filling my lungs.

One night to be confused
One night to speed up truth
We had a promise made
Four hands and then away

Cousins soldering circuit boards in Pencoed. Eighteenth birthday, crossing my fingers a Sony CD multiplayer comes up in the staff discount shop. Kaleidoscopic balls bouncing through Madrigal streets. Gonzalez connecting heartbeats. A city cousins will never see. An escape to full colour they won't realise. Freedom cascading everywhere.

My forefathers and mothers were not neophytes subdued by their conquerors. They came to the valleys for survival. These Welsh forty-niners made a home beside the furnace. Generations of miners, lives and language changed by the masters of industry. In my infancy the valleys were littered with steel giants. Dark, imposing, still anchored to the blackened ground. They stood motionless in a forsaken game of musical statues, no longer dancing as colliery men sung.

Nid wy'n gofyn bywyd moethus,
Aur y byd na'i berlau mân:
Gofyn wyf am galon hapus,
Calon onest, calon lân.

I longed for no material gifts as a child. The world's gold or its fine pearls were set in the familial love given so unreservedly. So why, growing inside, a feeling of displacement? My childhood trips revisiting a nostalgia I knew should root me, yet increasingly becoming a source of guilt that life was better on the other side. That within me was a growing chasm to bridge.

An eight-day holiday all my self-imposed emigration could realise. I climb up to the Palace of the Legion of Honour, scene of Norman's unclipping, and watch the cool ocean current fight its way into the bay. I'm equally awed by Rodin's muscular welcome. A sense of disappointment leaches through me as I learn there are many thinkers around the world. This one an original, if not unique. Am I like him? Cast the same, but different? It's cold here today. There's moisture dappling his thighs. How much are we shaped by our surroundings? Am I somehow altered? My uncle with his Englishman barbs. Would his thinker be the same if he'd been at the coal face? An old age of deafness in return for clean lungs.

Sitting in the window of the Washbag ticking off the list. Marina Safeway still there, but just a supermarket. Too early to dance my ass off at the End Up. Saving the steps for the final day as some sort of commemoration. And so boarded walkways call to my feet. These 'streets' so lush with exotic plants I expect them to start singing. I look closely at the branches for a glimpse of the famous green parrots. My aunty Babs once looked after a grey parrot for an owner that never returned. Sullenly confined to a kitchen perch it would occasionally pipe up with messages from a former life. Bethesda and microwaves must have been popular topics in its former home. Filled with meat and potato pie, from Bab's house we'd venture forth, intrepid mountaineers, striding our descent. Sometimes cutting through the mountain mist, the streets below drizzling, unfocused. The valley air quenching an innate thirst. Beyond long rows of rooftops, the terrain scrub-like and spoiled. The gwli tight between terraces, concrete steps leading us towards the shop my other aunty owns and Babs works in. I help serve penny sweets to kids on BMX bikes. Now beneath trumpet-like flowers, the planks beg me to be barefoot. Large purple tinged rubber leaves fence a small vegetable patch. On a luscious stoop a smile from behind a cloud of pungent, cloying smoke. Back then you could still buy single cigarettes. I'd take them from the tin and pass them to newspaper print palms and yellowed nails.

"You chose the perfect weather to visit our little slice of paradise."

His eyes swimming over me. A phoenix rising across his chest. I give some pleasantry in return, my own words catching in my ear, hearing how British I sound. One old lady, not really family but familiar all the same would get me to 'talk posh' for her. Fifty pence my poisoned piece of silver to be gotten rid of as quickly as possible. Chocolate and chews for my sister and me, Croeso i Loegr becoming Welcome to Slumberland.

Each time I'd saved up enough for the next instalment of my imagined family's lives I would start again at the beginning, with Mary Ann calling home. I too would come here and be changed. I was in the back seat, not watching out for the bridge when Jon died. I was seventeen and outside it was 1996. At St. Sebastian's it was a decade or so earlier and those falling tombstones were crushing people into an unforgiving ground. Maybe I'll never have sex. It's too dangerous. I can fall in love without touching.

"Would it be too old fashioned if I bought you a drink?"

"Not as old fashioned as your porn star moustache."

Why hadn't I said that? Nice smile. The moustache suits him. He buys me a vodka and lemonade and compliments my accent. I tell him he's tall. I think he's heard that one before. My leg is tapping out a tune the rest of me doesn't know as he orders another vodka and a something and coke for himself. Whenever he's about to say something silly he looks up at the ceiling first and then fixes me with those hazel eyes. I laugh every time. The music gets cranked. I add tequila to round three when I get a turn at the bar. He eyes me suspiciously when I tell him about hiring in-line blades to go over the bridge but having to take them off before I even got to the first tower.

"Falling over twelve times has to be anyone's limit, right?"

Untangling my shoes from around my neck. Dropping one of them. Seeing it bounce and wobble for a moment before freefalling into another life. He tips his head back and roars at the image of me continuing my pilgrimage, one skate on, one shoe-clad foot pushing. He leans over the table. He's going to kiss me. This is the moment. He puts his lips right up against my ear.

"Why don't we go someplace quieter?"

The glow of the cinema sign sends a thrill through me, only partially helped by the tequila.

"How about that place over there? If we can get a table in the back, we'll be able to hear each other."

He wants to carry on talking to me. He is still interested. This tall American with a moustache and eyes that disappear when he laughs.

"Great. Yeah, sounds good."

Stepping into the road, smooth skin making contact with my left palm. His fingers sliding between mine. Pulling our paths tighter together. Keep looking ahead, at the bar. Play it cool. Hide your smile. What's happening to my breathing? Stepping up onto the sidewalk my hand is being pulled back gently so I turn around, no time to stifle my beaming face. He's bending down. His lips are pressing against mine, parting. I'm too keen, pushing my tongue into his mouth. His hand grips mine harder for just a moment. My tongue is retreating, but his is advancing and playing with mine. My free hand rises to the back of his neck and I'm pulling him closer. Our lips are moving together, tongues dancing in unison. Where did I learn how to do this? He tastes of whisky and salt and better than every Barbary Lane fantasy I've ever had.

Underground, Craig Smith

Underground

We received the all-clear an hour ago. The guard strolled by to say we're safe to leave. But my friend and I remain on this bare wood bench on the Northbound platform, shoulder against shoulder, unable to go. To go is to say goodbye, which is not what I want. And, it seems, neither does she.

Umpteen trains have come and gone. Each train is torture as it sits with its doors wide until I choose not to board. Once I decide to wait for the following train, it buys us five to ten minutes of peace until it arrives. We know we can't stay all night. The tubes will stop running before long. The guards wish to go home. She and I have places to be, but we stretch each moment as far as we're able because we don't know when our next chance to meet will come.

Upon hearing the siren this evening, I ran past four stations in the hope we'd meet. I walked the shrill platforms through crowds of dislocated people until I saw her. She was moving from platform to platform, searching for me. She offered a shy wave; her smile was slow to arrive but, when it did, it was a dazzling half moon that lit the starless night of this bleak underground station.

Our usual spot was taken, so she walked us to this place, where we squeezed onto a bench between an expectant mother and two pensioners with sticks. The expectant mother rocked with her hands on her belly, bent over, promising care to her unborn child. The pensioners talked loudly, oblivious to us. She and I spoke just loud enough to communicate in an alliance borne on whispers. My shoulder brushed hers as we worked into the cramped space, and I closed my eyes to savour the moment.

The back of my hand glanced the knuckles of her fingers, a touch so brief that no one knew, but I knew. My skin still tingles where her flesh touched mine.

And now, everyone has left but us, yet I still need more time. It is never enough. She makes me laugh and she makes me think. She takes my mind on strange journeys that I never thought to take. As for my heart, it does ridiculous dances whenever we meet, the nature of which I'm yet to fathom.

It was her book that drew me, the first time we spoke. She was at the distant end of the Northbound platform, the last person standing before it dropped to the track. We were reading the same book: *Farewell My Lovely*, Chandler. We laughed at the coincidence, then became embarrassed at our laughter. She asked where I'd bought it. Another strange chance: we bought it at Foyles on the very same afternoon. We might have stood in the queue together, unknowingly.

That day, we had nothing to hide because we hadn't yet fallen, but we laughed more heartily than can be justified beneath ground when the bombs are dropping. There were people around us who feared for their homes, for their loved ones. So did we, of course. We had people who might be in trouble at home, but we couldn't stop ourselves. We talked about our gramophones, and the recordings we revere. We'd both discovered The Boswell Sisters. She mentioned Mildred Bailey. Over lunch the following day, I hunted out Mildred's platters, and played them that evening to the complaints of my children. And we talked about the books we loved: Hemingway; Fitzgerald; the poetry of Eliot, Auden and MacNeice. Woolf.

Our second meeting was also an accident, but less so. We each selected the place we previously met, and renewed our acquaintance eagerly. She removed her hairband and shook out her hair, as if she'd arrived somewhere she knew she'd find contentment. We continued our conversation where we left off, as if we hadn't been away, talked of books, music and cinema. She'd finished Chandler and was onto Wodehouse. She showed me lines on the page that made me howl, and she watched as I laughed in order to absorb the full extent of the effect she had on me, as if she'd waited her days in anticipation of sharing those passages. We ate boiled sweets, and our finger ends grazed as we underlined text with the invisible ink of our confederacy, while above us came the boot-stomp of a bomb, and then another.

That patch of platform became our regular spot. One time, the Salvation Army band played to spoil it, right where we meet - cornets, euphonium and thump drum. Another time, two old ladies in bathchairs were side by side, giggling and singing. And twice I failed to find her, and spent the air-raid at the far end of the platform, tempted by the tunnel. I wanted to lose myself beneath London until I could cope.

She asks about my life, and I'm careful what I say. I tell her I'm lucky to be in work. The University department has lost many staff to war. Men are serving overseas. A registrar died in Belgium. Two ladies in the typing pool are working the land. The academics are men in their fifties no longer at risk of call-up. One fought in the Great War, in Gallipoli; I know of men who do not discuss what they saw, but this man speaks constantly of the experience of conflict. He talks about firing a loaded rifle at the enemy for the first time. About how a soldier fell, and how my colleague felt remorse and sat with the soldier while he died, but went on to kill again.

I dread that, next year, my son could be called to fight. I tell her this, and think how glad I am that we do not send women to war, because she's of an age to be conscripted. The thought doubles me up in pain: I do not want to lose this, whatever it is, however long it lasts.

She is so handsome I dare not look at her. I keep my eyes straight ahead, other than glances to glimpse her face. She frowns when she talks, becomes animated and agile and loses herself within her themes and reasons. She speaks self-consciously at first, then freely as she passes the threshold of her shyness, once she's reached an exuberant state and her heart has taken over. Her hands move, shaping the story. I tell her I would know what she was saying just from the pictures she draws with her hands. Occasionally she glances at me as she speaks, wondering if I'm keeping track of where she's going on her excursions into language. I'm with her wherever her mind choses to travel.
I listen as she relates the stacked stories of her wider family, her aunts and uncles. Her erratic cousins. Her hands own more colour than mine, which makes me plain and unappealing in comparison. She has elegant fingers filled with motion and joy. I suggest she plays piano, but she says not, though she writes for work so her fingers are exercised every day. She swears under her breath for my amusement, delicious, sumptuous swearwords that make me smile.

We watch another train go by. The trains are quieter now. People are home already, sitting with their children, eating together. The present is a tube train, hurtling up to the platform then departing for the next destination while we remain here, dreaming, as we stare at the empty track, wondering how long we can let the present slide by.

The sapphire of my wedding ring catches her slacks. I apologise and our hands touch, and for a moment our fingers wrap in a knot. She takes my ring between her thumb and index finger and rocks it side to side, sliding it along my finger, past the first knuckle, past the second. Her flesh is like a feather as it brushes my skin until the sapphire hovers over my unpainted nail. I do not know what she will do. Neither does she, but whatever she chooses, I will let her. Her hand is trembling. She looks at me with sorrowful eyes, and the entire universe pauses underground until we establish the meaning of this moment. I well up. And then she guides the ring back along my ring finger, back to where it came from, back to where my finger meets my palm. 'With this ring …' she whispers. And we release, and I do not know when such a moment will come again.

Whenever we say goodbye, I become bereft. We speak from a distance – three feet, four – as the train door gapes, and it feels like we are shouting across a thousand miles as our voices are fractured by the thunder of the train. I back into the carriage, losing grip like she is falling away from me, or like I'm being dragged into the underworld, never to re-emerge. And the train takes me away, and I see her, tall on the platform, watching me go.

I have been known to walk with her out of the station into the open air, where we see rubble in the street that was once a home. In our blinking liberation, we walk a circuit to elongate our goodbye. In the dark of night, she takes my arm, and for a moment we are promenading along a seafront with the wind in our faces. But she hugs me and leaves, as she must, and we glance back as we go, until we are beyond the strength of our sight. I want to run to be with her, but I never do. Instead, I walk home, sometimes, five miles, claiming the tube broke down. I am close to confessing that I didn't want to go home at all.

She doesn't get to hear about my unhappiness. I edit it from our conversation because there's disloyalty in saying it out loud.

But I am deeply unhappy. I only now realise that I have been unhappy for a long time. I shield her from it because she has helped me see it, and that is a burden too far. She should not be cited in my unhappiness.

We have no control over who we fall for. Nor when. Nor how. Life runs away with us, and our hearts are horses that will not wait. They move to the place that draws them at the pace they choose, and all we can do is run with them. We do not have a choice. And we may call over our shoulder to the ones we leave behind, and hope they do not notice that we are ever more distant, ever less use to them. Even when we sit with them, our mind is with the horses in the far fields, picking at the grass, bewitched. We do not mean to be mean. It is not what we want, it is not how they deserve to be treated. It is not fair that it is to their detriment that our lives are being enriched. But it’s like we have learned to dream again, and our imagination can no longer be contained. We dream and our dream is of horses, and the horses run wild until they find a place to be.

One day, we may walk in daylight with our hands clasped. One day, we may meet in private beneath a blanket, before an open fire, without shame. But I do not have the imagination to foresee the circumstances that would allow that to occur. My bigger concern it what happens when we do not need to hide underground anymore, when the raids are over and we no longer have an excuse to take shelter. I fear I will lose her forever. I shall stand in the queue at Foyles for the rest of my days, waiting for her to return to buy a new book.

Holloway Road, Luke Lewin Davies

Holloway Road

The house that we used to live in was on a long stretch of road between Archway and Finsbury Park – mostly old Victorian terrace houses, four storeys high, with ground floors converted for commercial use.

Ours was the final building along its stretch and five of us lived there. It was a student house and inside it was full of yellow peziza domiciliana fungus, empty pizza boxes stained with grease, and DVD cases lined with traces of 4-methylmethcathinone.

Below the house on the left-hand side was a railway track fringed with thick undergrowth – entangled roots clasping at carrier bags and crisp packets and construction detritus. Hovering above this, mounted against the exterior wall of the building, was a large billboard with a ladder and a small platform just beneath it. A trivision billboard, in fact, with motorised triangular prisms rotating in sync every twelve or so seconds – except that one of the prisms was stuck, so that the advertised images were always imperfect.

On the other side of the building – on its right-hand side – was the burnt-out house.

There had been a fire there, apparently, and inside it was a blackened shell – though you could hardly tell from the front. The only signs of the fire when you stood on the street, or when you sat on the top deck of a passing bus, were the boarded-up windows and the faint streaks of soot above them, like raised eyebrows. As if the house were discretely surprised by the intense heat that had once filled it.

If you went round the back, however – if you climbed over the little wall by the train track and pushed your way along the edge of the overgrowth – it became immediately obvious that the whole building had once been engulfed in flames.

*

I only remember breaking into the burnt-out house one time, around April or May in 2010.

It was like a house in a horror film, unsurprisingly. Peering through the window we could see that the layout inside was exactly like ours – only the floor had completely given way, revealing a skeleton of blackened support beams. We could see, also, that the walls were lined with sooty wallpaper, peeling at the edges to reveal the preserved layers of previous residents' living rooms and bedrooms. Lining the walls, traces of furniture and belongings that had been removed – a pale rectangle where a picture frame had once hung and the shadowy outline of a double bed.

Truly it looked like something out of a John Carpenter film – except that being inside it wasn't scary, somehow. Maybe because it was too sobering an experience. Because climbing into it was like plunging your feet into a cold bath or holding your hand out of the window of a moving car – too complete a sensation for wandering thoughts.

The dampness, to begin with. Anything you touched – the cold exterior bricks, the mortar lined with thick green moss – was wet to the touch.

Then there was the texture of the place. When you placed your hand onto what had once been a functioning window frame to lever yourself across it and into the house, the wood felt soft and crumbly, immediately giving way. Then when you pressed the wallpaper for support as you lowered your feet onto the floor below, the wall was flat and cool like a paving slab or a sheet of glass.

It was as if the house were healing itself from the fire that had led to its abandonment – embalming itself with cold and mildew and earth. As if it were preserving the memories of those who had once lived here.

*

Sometimes I wonder whether the people who live in our old house now, in the house next to the burnt-out house – probably students like we once were, Gen Z kids with star-shaped stickers covering the spots on their immaculate faces – I wonder whether they also occasionally make out traces of our former existence. Whether the house that they live in also sporadically functions as a kind of memorial.

A memorial commemorating evenings spent indiscriminately making out with one another on a bed shoved up against the window to capture the morning light, wrists and ankles twitching from the effects of too much MDMA, or daytime drinking two-for-five-pound corner-shop wine, devouring instant noodles and precooked frankfurters cooked together in our one clean pot.

A mausoleum preserving our most cherished memories – like the time Y. threw an empty bottle of High Commissioner off the roof and K. photographed the police officers who came round to investigate. Or the illustrious occasion upon which I got so fucking high I lay inside an empty bathtub the whole night long, sucking drops of water from a limescale-encrusted tap. Or the tragedy of H. smashing her front teeth on an empty dance floor in Angel on New Year's Eve, forcing her to hide for weeks nursing the broken shards inside her mouth.

Except, of course, that the house remembers none of these things. Unlike the burnt-out house, it has refused to trap these memories in time – leaving the kids who live there now with nothing to remind them of our tragic (but still cherished) noughties transgressions.

And maybe somewhere outside in the undergrowth beside the railway tracks there remain traces of our existence among the cold and the mildew and the earth. A shrivelled cigarette butt; the broken fragments of an empty beer bottle; a slowly disintegrating prophylactic.

But still, objects that if noticed would be nothing to the present.

Nothing to the arresting present currently subsuming the tenants of our old house – a present that, like the burnt-out house, is death to wandering thoughts like these.

Enter, Exit the Ghosts, Robin Luce Martin

Enter, Exit the Ghosts

Brooklyn, April 2020

(We have not left the apartment for 47 days, except for two grocery runs, taking the garbage out, and my husband sitting on the stoop smoking in the middle of the night.)

I mean to wake slowly and look inside my shores to seek out some inner specialty, linger in the bird song, and stand by the window as the sun runs into my eyes—instead, sirens rouse and shake me. Not five minutes away, a mobile morgue awaits Brooklyn citizens turned ghosts. Trumpets of doom wheeze. I sit in bed amid my sea of papers and books, hair shrouding my face. Those phantasmic players from the 1981 production of "Twelfth Night" populate my head, tearing naked across their Laurel Canyon home, where the Monkees had lived—Clown holding a cored apple stuffed with brown sugar in one hand and a bottle of Jameson in the other, swilling with lust and laughter. All followers of Rajneesh, glorious in their outbursts, phenomenally articulate, Shakespearean in their passions, living communally in the big Monkees house where sexual freedom reigned until AIDs corralled and took them.

I throw the covers aside, suddenly hot with sweltering Canyon breezes fanning my mind. I hear the Los Angeles wilderness invade my Brooklyn apartment: hawks, falcons, owls, eagles, coyotes, deer, rats, raccoons, bobcats, and bears meld together into one all-seeing Argos circling the parameters of my room. All the boundaries of my personal history rattle.

I hear Brute, my husband, pacing in the living room and blabbing away in Italian. I imagine him dragging the phone—the landline Princess with a 25-yard curly cord that tangles into a ball. I wonder if he slept at all. We are lucky to have our own rooms like a King and Queen. He spends much of his time talking to faraway friends.

I draw my laptop from under the covers and find images of animals streaming: grey langurs, buffalo, peahens, dogs, civets, wild deer, and a mountain of monkeys taking back their power, strutting on empty Mumbai streets. Perhaps the congruence of these images from India and the evidence of power shifting makes me again think of Clown and his remarkable feat. The clown's name is Feste, but Shakespeare only used it once, so I use Clown. First, he had bucked the London Theater's sanctity, leading a mutiny of actors to form a Shakespearean repertory company in India. Then, seven years later, another feat: the company departs the ashram with Clown leading the troupe to Hollywood.

Would I recognize him if he were to arrive today, not dressed in Rajneesh red but in his ghostly countenance? Look, Clown, it's Nora Finch. Remember me? Viola in "Twelfth Night?"

His blend of Irish and Cockney accents comes alive in my ears. "Darling Nora, how could I forget you?"

I recline and close my eyes as it is impossible for him to have materialized, yet even as I tell myself it's not possible, I begin to laugh. Someone, something, is tickling me.

"Open your eyes, or I'll kiss you."

Go ahead, I think, kiss me, and let me wake from this fucking quarantine! Make it end, Princely Clown. I open my eyes to find him lounging next to me.

(loudly) I scream.

Ah! EEEE! What the hell!

Course, my husband does not hear me as he must have returned to his desk, sunk into the butterfly chair wearing his fancy headphones, and fallen deep into the noir film *Out of the Past*, which he watches over and over.

Clown begins, "Darling Nora, it's time you return to the theater."

"That's unlikely," I reply. "Theater, it appears, is dead. And I stopped acting long ago."

"Don't let appearances fool with you. You will be ready when this pandemic is over and comeback time arrives. Tragedy and comedy are brewing as we speak in kitchens worldwide. I am here to cajole you. I imagine a series of characters confined to bunkers searching for the truth."

"You are such a clown," I say and shake off the nostalgia for theater enveloping my spirit. I quit long ago.

"You'll bring them to life—"The Bunker Monologues"—and emerge from this period with a show and turn back time."

"Why should I listen to you since you're not even actually here?"

"Don't be so sure about that," Clown says, pulling a bottle of Jameson out from under the covers, "Cheers! All the world's a bunker."

I haven't slept well again—incessant sirens. So, as Clown suggested, I decided that the best way to care for myself was to create a series of monologues. Though I have no intention of performing ever. Brute barges into my room and announces that today, April 30, 2020, is the 75th anniversary of Hitler's death, and he will be watching everything Nazi day and night, rattling off a list of films: *The Sorrow and the Pity, Patton, Inglorious Bastards, Judgment at Nuremberg, Schindler's List, Triumph of the Will, Iron Cross*.

"You'll be up all night."

"That's the COVID fun."

"What about *Casablanca*? I'd join you for that."

"Maybe, but the story is really about Sam, the piano player. How he follows Rick through hell to Casablanca and that club. Then Rick just dumps him for the dame. *As Time*

Goes By. It's a white man / black man betrayal story. I want Nazis! But maybe I can fall asleep to it."

Brute's influence grips me, and I decide on the Führerbunker as my first point of departure.

Off I go into Hitler's bunker to become Eva. It is the hour before their deaths, and they are about to get married. History books say he shot himself, and she died of cyanide poisoning. On the other hand, she would do anything for him and pledged not to let him die alone, so perhaps she shot him, placed the gun in his hand, and then took the cyanide.

Monologue Eva Braun

Adolph plays with Blondi in the courtyard, and they walk together. It's always the dog who shares his bed. He caresses Blondi's ears with a tenderness that makes my cunt throb. Severe envy flares here and here, all through my body. I have an idea to give the dog cyanide a test to ensure the pills are potent and not Himmler's trick. I absolutely must make sure we are dead. When I think about falling into Russian hands, a chasm opens in my spine, and the pain is as we learn of eternal hell. My eyes capsize, and all is glaringly white. Surely, God is willing to forgive our suicides.

When the dog dies, Adolph crumbles and his vulnerability is disgusting. I slap him until my hands burn.

Adolph devours kilos of pralines each day. I'm worried about tooth decay. I have a recurring nightmare where he kisses me, at last, and my mouth fills with his rotten teeth. To keep me from screaming, he stuffs pralines into my mouth. The teeth line up, sticking out of the sugary dough like tombstones. To assuage my nightmares, I drink champagne and, on many occasions, bathe in its bubbles. Will he kiss me before the end?

For me, marriage defines legitimacy in the eyes of God, and I am blissful. Eyes that have watched me since I was a little girl, from the bottom of the lake, on the shaded side of our mountain, and at last, within the bunker walls. God stays close to me.

While Adolph's skin has turned ashen, mine is brighter. As he sinks into himself, I am expanding beyond the borders of the body. I close my eyes and recall my family's home movies flickering on the screen. The lake's beauty and waterfalls were overwhelming, yet not nearly as beautiful as me—all that I was and would become sparkling in the eternal light.

The grief I felt upon Adolph's indifference long ago arrives yet again. I don't attempt to turn away. It is in my vulnerability that I come alive. How humiliated I have felt by his hands. The memory of that grief grips my legs and slithers into my cunt, and brings tears sharp as glass. Without his attention, I attempted suicide. Others think this was coyness, but they don't understand the depth of my attachment. Will I never get over how I struggled for his love?

Only 17 when we met, and Adolph, 40, I can still see myself in the shop, the little photographer's assistant. Adolph made a little pantomime upon meeting me. He grabbed his chest, then held his heart out to me, and I could taste it. The gesture haunts me. His hair, slick as an eel, fell in a comma over a forehead as pale as mine. Later, I invoked that gesture when I had to endure his remoteness in rooms filled with others.

I went out on an errand to buy some luncheon supplies. In the store, I twirled around in my Ferragamo high heels and chose the ingredients for cooking Leberknödelsuppe. Liver dumplings were his favorite then, before the potatoes. When I handed the fare to the cook, I wished him a good appetite. A blush colored my face as it forever did in his presence. Our affair did not begin for two years, yet all the while, I pledged my love. I knew our union would become a portal where destiny would find me. Why think of this now, moments before the wedding? How can I marry with the memory of my struggle for his love still scarring me? I must purify myself so that our union transcends memory.

Since he began pledging to kill himself, he cannot fuck. Straddling him, I hang forward, brushing his face and chest with my hair. I twist his nipples until he whimpers like the dog. My dog, I call him. My bitch, he says.

Mein Hund, Meine Shlampe!

The candlelight stabs at his icy eyes, and I think maybe he'll climax—before I die, I want him to shudder.

As a little girl, I swam in icy water and felt its warmth. In death, I will be even more beautiful.

Pledging pure Aryan descent, we are pronounced man and wife.

I am whacked from becoming Eva, as happens to actors. Surrender occupies me. Even the peacock mantis shrimp adorned in clownish psychedelic colors, both beautiful and horribly psychotic, might surrender. The shrimp can see ultraviolet, infrared, and polarized light with perfect depth perception. Its eyes work independently and see nine more colors than humans can imagine. The speed of its punch, faster than the acceleration of a 22-caliber bullet, makes water boil like my husband when he is manic.

"Let's hope sheltering does not trigger mania. That would not be fun!" says Clown as he floats around the room.

"You again! You can hear my thoughts?!"

"Yours forever, Darling Nora. Regarding Eva—Bravo!" he says, exiting through the ceiling.

While I read the newspaper, the sirens boom.

Prisoners on Rikers Island are offered $6. an hour, a fortune, and P.P.E. if they agree to dig mass graves. On Hart Island, off the eastern shore of City Island, there are 101 acres of potter fields with more than a million people buried. Buried and lost by the score, its ghosts stand with open arms, welcoming the vulnerable to the common ground.

Clown suddenly appears on my bed, disrupting my newspaper, jumps up and down, and says, "Remember when you visited our graveyard? Hollywood Forever Cemetery! We were all rolling around in the earth under your feet. Then, finally, you fell to the ground and whispered goodbye."

Why is this happening—this coming and going of Clown?

I wonder if God and Jesus will become references no one remembers. It's possible. There isn't anything sacred or sustainable.

Something is not right. How long has that thought been ignored? Brute's body is taking on the shape of his butterfly chair. Pounds of depression bloat his belly. Though we pretend not to notice. We sit across from each other and know. He won't get a blood test; it is too complicated to get there, warnings to stay sheltered from the plague. Something is more than not right; his handwriting is illegible; his balance is shot; and he trembles so liquids spill and food flies.

I click back to India and allow the viewing of animals to put me in a trance. Eventually, Clown appears. Ragged hair frames his face and curls to his shoulders. Mirth exudes from his eyes as he is fully fleshed in my mind's eye and urges me to prepare a cocktail.

"Here you are, Nora, in the land of plenty! Toast to love! Toast to entrances and exits!"

I sway, sitting on my bed with the play's closing song seeping out; *with the wind and the rain, it raineth every day.* I see all the faces of those lovely actors who died of AIDS. Brute watches Patton again. I can hear George C. Scott's timbre through the wall, not the words but that energy. Something is wrong. I know something is wrong. I go into his room and watch with him for a bit until he rolls onto his side, and it is as if I am all alone.

Spoilt for Choice, Joanna Garbutt

Spoilt for Choice

It was lunchtime but gloomy in there, the only natural light from a few small windows. Strip lighting from the ceiling caused dark patches and light patches throughout the restaurant. The hot plates were also brightly lit with a burning whiteness, so everything had an otherworldly glow, and the vivid colour of the food emphasised its artificiality. The staff hung around, watching and waiting to pounce, like cats eyeing up birds.

The bartender stood cleaning glasses a little way to the left of their table. Sticky cocktail menus in transparent plastic were scattered at intervals along the length of the counter in front of him. The couple sat in one of the booths, a generous seating area each side of them, though the upholstery had been partially ripped and was now held together with gaffer tape. They were the only customers, apart from a few individuals.

'Why did you want to meet here?' she asked.

'I saw some recommendations online,' he said. 'Aren't you hungry?'

'I'll get something in a minute.'

A waiter, a short, thin man with an asymmetrical haircut and a tattoo resembling chains that disappeared up under a shirt cuff, came over and placed a pint of lager in front of him and a fizzy mineral water in front of her.

'I thought they'd done away with stuff like this,' she said. 'Buffets, I mean. I thought they worried about food waste nowadays. And of course, no one could mingle during COVID.'

'Yeah,' he said, wiping his face with a napkin. 'There aren't so many of them about.'

'I haven't been to one for years.' She looked out over the restaurant. 'I mean, it's a weird collection of food, isn't it? I know it's mostly supposed to be Chinese, but there are chips–'

'Chips are cheap to make but filling,' he said. 'I think they make a lot of money from the chips.'

'Okay, okay, but it is a bit of a mix. I mean, chicken nuggets? I think I saw some samosas. And sausages.'

'Sausages are universal. Take slightly different forms but they are what everyone uses to get rid of those bits of meat that no one would eat otherwise.' He laughed lightly as she pulled a face. 'You're the one who mentioned food waste.'

She watched him as he took a bite from a spring roll, dipped in sweet chilli sauce, then put it back on his plate.

'What?' he asked.

'It looks like a dismembered finger, that's all.'

He chewed slowly and looked down at his plate. He smiled and prodded it with his fork. 'You're right. It does have that look to it. In amongst all this rice.'

'I remember once reading somewhere that bin men in New York call maggots "disco rice".'

He considered this, taking another bite of the spring roll. 'I get it.' He looked over at her again. 'You should eat though. I've paid for it now. And to be honest, you look like you've lost weight.'

'I thought that was always supposed to be a good thing, particularly when you get to my age. People are always on at you to stay slim.'

'Maybe. But I always thought you were a lovely shape.'

She took a deep breath. Put her hand out and touched the lip of the plate, as if she was going to pick it up and go and help herself. But she remained seated.

'It's been a tough couple of years,' she said.

'I know. Well, I can only imagine.'

She took a sip of water. 'I'm surprised you suggested meeting.'

'I wanted to talk.'

She looked around. 'I don't think these places are really designed for talking. Everyone getting up and down, helping themselves to more and more food over and over again.'

'Yeah, I suppose so.'

She paused for a moment, taking another sip of water. 'You want to tell him, don't you?' she said.

He stopped eating for a moment. One of the waiting staff was immediately hovering at his elbow, to take his plate. A few grains of sticky rice were all that remained. 'Thank you,' he said, as the waiter took it away.

'I don't know if it's a good idea,' she said. 'I'm a bit worried about what Charlie will think about us but I'm worried about Dave too. How Charlie will remember him.'

He wiped his hands on the paper napkin at his side. 'I think it might be the right time though. Wouldn't you want to know if it was you?'

'I don't know,' she said.

'I never wanted to ask but did Dave know? About Charlie?'

'I think so but he never said anything to me. Never accused me of anything. Though of course, he would have been right to accuse me.'

'Why do you think Dave knew then? If he never said anything?' he asked, frowning.

'Maybe what he didn't say,' she said. 'He never drew attention to the inconsistencies, I suppose. Things that didn't add up. He never asked me about you. Wouldn't really talk to me about you at all, as if it was painful for him. Maybe. I don't know.'

'But you never knew for sure?'

She shook her head.

He took a long drink from his pint. 'I can't believe it's been two years since he died.'

She took her hand away from the plate. 'I know.'

'That place Dave was working at are still looking after you and Charlie though, aren't they?' he asked. 'He told me at the time he'd warned them about that bloody machine, that it was only a matter of time before someone got hurt.'

She shrugged. 'They pay his pension every month.'

'Good. It's the least they can do. Poor Dave.'

'Yeah, poor Dave.' She stared again at her plate.

'Go and get yourself something to eat,' he said. 'They've got some chow mein. You always used to like that.'

Instead, she cleared her throat and looked away to where his plate had been, a slight smearing of grease where he'd put his dirty cutlery back down on the table cloth. 'Don't you worry that telling Charlie the truth would be like erasing the last bit of Dave?'

'Is that what you think?' he asked.

'It's just something that comes to mind now and again, when I do think about telling Charlie. And I wonder if it wasn't for the accident, and if Dave was still about, whether I would ever tell Charlie. At least I would've had the chance to talk to Dave about it first.'

'I think we should tell him but you know best. You're his mum.'

'You never spoke to Dave about it yourself?' she asked.

'Of course not. How could I? I didn't know if you'd told him and I didn't want to get you into trouble. Not when it had all finished years before. I had no idea how Dave would react if I said anything about us.' He paused for a second. 'I assumed he just didn't know as he never treated me differently.'

'He loved Charlie.'

'Oh, you could see that,' he said.

She smiled. 'He is such a lovely boy. Though I need to stop thinking about him as a boy.'

He laughed. 'Yeah. He's fifteen now.'

'Nearly sixteen.' She sighed.

'Do you remember the Golden Rose?' he asked. 'It was one of the reasons I suggested coming here.'

'I remember it well,' she said. 'Is it closed down now?'

'Yeah, years ago,' he said.

'It was a strange place to have a first date.'

'It wasn't a proper first date. You were already married.'

'Even so,' she said. 'I think of it as our first date.'

'So do I, really.'

She laughed. 'Do you remember I ordered those prawns but they hadn't taken the shells off? My fingers smelt of garlic for days never mind how many times I washed them.' She picked up her plate. 'I think I will get some chow mein.' She stood up and turned to go before looking back. 'Anything else you'd recommend?'

'You might have to go and see for yourself,' he said.

When she returned, her plate was only half full with the chow mein. She looked at it for a moment before picking up her fork, stabbing a small mushroom, bringing it to her mouth and putting it in.

'You don't think it would be a comfort for Charlie?' he suggested. 'I mean, Dave will always be his dad but knowing that I'm there for him, to help him. Not a replacement, never a replacement, obviously. But someone else who…' He paused. 'Well, is his dad, technically, I mean.'

She put down her fork and took another sip of water. It was nearly finished. 'I don't know.' She cleared her throat. 'I was never on the pill or anything, you know. We always wanted another but it never happened.'

'I didn't know that.'

'But Dave always said how lucky we were to have Charlie. He was everything Dave wanted. That was why I thought he might have known.' She found another vegetable, a water chestnut, in the grey sauce and brought it up to her mouth. Chewed it tentatively. 'It was just a feeling I had, that he'd guessed. Maybe just to make myself feel better.'

'Do you want another drink?' the waiter asked as he hovered next to her, pointing at the now virtually empty glass. She shook her head quickly and he left.

'It's not very nice. The chow mein, I mean. Tastes more like chicken gravy with overcooked vegetables.'

'It was never that nice at the Golden Rose either, now I come to think of it,' he said.

'It didn't matter then.'

He quickly finished his pint. 'Are you sure you don't want another drink? I might have another. Everything's so salty.'

'Okay, then. Maybe a lemonade. A diet lemonade.'

He walked over and spoke to the bartender. She watched before he turned round and called to her. 'They've got no diet lemonade. Did you want a normal lemonade? Or a diet coke?'

'Honestly, I don't need anything.'

'Another fizzy water?'

She shook her head.

He talked with the bartender and waited while the man poured his lager. She ate some more, for something to do, and watched as other customers came in, including a heavily pregnant woman, who was smiling broadly but keeping her eyes on the hotplates in front of her. Her top wasn't a maternity top, but an oversized one which had been stretched to accommodate her belly, the diagonal stripes disjointed and bulging.

He came back to the table with his drink and sat down. A waiter quickly took her plate away and they were left with no food between them, just his lager fizzing.

'So, what do we do?' he asked. 'We have to agree.'

'Do you want to tell him?'

'I would but not if it's going to cause problems. Do you think it will?'

She looked away towards the pregnant woman who was busy filling her plate. 'Of course it will,' she said.

'Not telling him would be a problem too, wouldn't it?'

The waiter walked past again and went away empty handed.

'Yes,' she said.

He took another long sip of lager and left the table to get more food. She watched him before getting up herself and going over to the bar and spending a while looking at the drinks menu. The bartender stood there waiting, poised and ready for her eventual choice.

THE TEA DANCE, Clare Reddaway

THE TEA DANCE

Miss Gold popped a liquorice sweet into her mouth and sucked hard. The temptation to snap at the child in front of her was almost overwhelming. They had been over this so very many times. The aniseed liquor slid down her throat. Miss Gold forced a smile.

"D major has how many sharps?"

The girl stared at the lines in her exercise book. She chewed the end of her blond plait.

"Imagine you're playing the scale on the piano. How would it go?"

The girl stared at Miss Gold.

Obviously the word imagine was not a concept the child could grasp.

Gormless, that's what she was. Gormless.

"How about C? How many sharps or flats are there in the C major scale?"

The girl stared at her book. Miss Gold ground the sweet between her teeth. The girl had been playing the piano for years and years and years.

"There are no sharps or flats in C major are there Alison."

"No, Miss Gold."

"How about we start again with C. You draw me a nice C major scale on those lines you've got in your book. I'd like some crotchets – lovely round base with a tall strong stem. Off you go."

Alison began laboriously to draw the notes.

Miss Gold allowed her gaze to stray out of the window. She loved her street. Daphne Greenwood's front garden always full of dahlias and marigolds. The brand new red brick houses. Her own brand new brick house, which she lived in with her dear friend Miss Watson. “We’re a couple of old spinsters” she’d trill to the newsagent who nodded with a smile as he handed over The Times and two packets of Benson and Hedges. Sometimes she’d treat herself to a copy of Melody Maker to see what was happening in the world of pop music. Not that she had much time for pop music. Shaking her head at the thought of the simplistic chords she heard blaring out on Top of the Pops, she craned her neck to get a glimpse of the blue sea through the gap between No 3 and No 4. Only the Channel, but still, it was the sea.

Alison squirmed. Miss Gold realised she’d been leaning right over the girl’s exercise book and the page she was working on, with its wonky blotched notes drifting across the pre-drawn staves.

Don’t. Just. Don’t.

“That’s lovely dear. Now, turn the page and let’s try D major shall we?”

Miss Gold could hear the final bars of Bach’s Minuet in G being played in the lounge. It was a light, joyful piece of music but it was neither light or joyful in the hands of Alison’s sister Heather. Miss Gold thought it might well have been most suitable for a funeral. A mass funeral for an entire village wiped out by a sudden deadly plague. She gritted her teeth. The day was nearly over.

There was a ring on the doorbell.

Alison and Heather’s mother. Dot on 5.

Miss Gold opened the door. Angela Freeman was standing on the front path, with her swishy blond hair and those patent white boots. Miss Gold pictured herself in white patent boots, laced up the front. She imagined how sexy they’d make her feel. She shoved the thought down. She was far far too old for such fripperies. And those boots were far far too expensive.

“Can I have a word, Miss Gold?” said Angela. Miss Gold smiled a tight smile. “I’m ever so sorry, but my husband has been having a bit of a review of our ins and outs at home. We're going to have to make some cut backs….."

Her voice continued but Miss Gold didn't listen. She was doing sums in her head. Heather and Alison both had two lessons a week – piano and music theory. That was a loss of four lessons, four lessons! They were barely managing as it was. The mortgage, the bills. Sky-high inflation was hitting them hard. She felt a little bit panicky. She must smile, she must say something, say something nice so that this horrible woman would recommend them to her horrible friends and their horrible children could come to more lessons and she could try to instil even the most basics rudiments of musical knowledge into their dullard –

"Oh, that's such a shame, Mrs Freeman. Heather is doing so well, her minuet is a delight to listen to! I think she has real promise." Miss Gold had not heard Miss Watson creeping up behind her. "And Alison, well I really think that we are nearly there with Alison. She is shaping up to be a good little pianist. And isn't she quite the showgirl."

Miss Gold was amazed to see Heather and Alison's mother beam. Surely she didn't think that Alison could play the piano? Didn't she have ears?

"Do you really think so?"

"I do indeed," smiled Miss Watson. "It would be such a shame to restrict such talent. Perhaps we could come to a temporary arrangement, to tide you over? How about fortnightly lessons? Although that does mean that the rigour of practice can be lost, so sad when they are both at such a crucial point…"

Miss Gold stepped away and leant against the wall. Miss Watson was saving the day. Again. Like she always did with her gentle smile and her warm ways.

By the time Heather and Alison's mother walked her girls home, she was convinced they were on the way to becoming professional musicians. All lessons remained intact.

Miss Watson closed the door.

"Mavis Louise you are a wonder," said Miss Gold.

Miss Watson smiled a vague, amiable smile. Her soft pale face framed by a ghostly fluff of grey hair was as familiar to Miss Gold as her own.

"I've been thinking," said Miss Watson. "That it is time to separate. I think we'd do better on our own." She wandered into the kitchen.

On our own. Miss Gold been waiting for those words. Waiting for them for months. For years. Forever.

She wouldn't cry. What would be the point? A single woman in her late fifties can't afford the luxury of tears.

She'd have to leave this house. It had been her haven. Her refuge. She'd been so happy when they'd moved here, down from London to the coast, to this neat, safe place with its neat, safe rooms and its neat, safe pupils. She wasn't to know that she was not a natural teacher. Or that Mavis Louise was.

Of course, music theory was much harder to teach than the piano. Pupils weren't interested. It was too like maths and they got enough of that at school. Miss Thomas was relieved that theory was an obligatory part of music exams or she wouldn't have a single pupil. Oh, she missed her trumpet, she missed the band. It was different for Mavis Louise. Pianists were rarely in orchestras and performance options had dried up long ago – the days of live music at a tea dance were gone. Promoters had jumped firmed onto the pop music band wagon. Discos! What on earth were musicians supposed to do when courting couples wanted to hurl themselves around to recorded music at discos!

Adapt or die that's what her mother used to say. Adapt or die. Well, she wasn't going to die. She just wasn't sure how to adapt.

Miss Gold went into what was the dining room when Alison and Heather and the rest were not using it as a music theory torture chamber. She started to return it to its natural state, tidying the papers and the books she used to teach, the games she'd invented to inspire them. Who was she kidding. She didn't inspire them. They hated her. She saw them sneaking glances at her hair when they thought she wasn't looking. She liked the black dye, but maybe they found it intimidating. Or ridiculous. It wasn't her fault she needed spectacles. She knew that her manner was sharp. She knew that she was impatient and snappy. It had never mattered when she was a trumpeter, it gave her edge and sass. It seemed to matter now.

Why had Mavis Louise decided that this was the time to go their separate ways, after all these years?

Miss Gold swallowed. She was scared. The majority of the money in the house had come from Mavis Louise, a tiny inheritance that came to her after her mother died. Miss Gold had no such inheritance. Her parents were still alive, although they had cut off all contact. They preferred the company of their asinine son with his three fat children and the sow-like brood mare that he'd married. They didn't approve their daughter's bohemian life with the band, of her friendship with Miss Watson. Her parents didn't understand her relationship, but they sensed that they should find it shocking. There would be no handouts from them. If Miss Watson threw her out, she'd have nowhere to go. Miss Gold used to have lots of friends in London but they'd dispersed long ago, and her new friends in Bexhill, well, would they want her? She'd have to find lodgings, a small room at the top of a boarding house. And she'd be alone. She'd be living without Mavis Louise….

Miss Gold fought down the rising panic. She needed a plan.

It was Saturday afternoon, wasn't it?

Hm.

Miss Watson was making tea in the kitchen when Miss Gold breezed in, smiling and sunny, a jaunty red scarf tied around her neck.

"I think you and I need a little bit of fun," she said.

If Mavis Louise was surprised, she didn't say so and she was ready enough to pop on her outside shoes and accompany Miss Gold as she led them out of the house and down the hill through the town to the promenade.

"Were you thinking fish and chips for supper, dear?" said Miss Watson.

"Not yet," said Miss Gold, "I thought first…" She pointed.

There, outside the pavilion, right on the sea front, was a dance floor. Couples were waltzing to a recording of the Blue Danube, in the open air, under the sky.

"What's brought this on?" asked Miss Watson.

"Nothing. Do I have to have a reason to dance with the woman I love?" said Miss Gold smiled, but those dreaded tears were brimming behind her eyes. She swallowed them down.

"What a good idea," said Mavis Louise.

Miss Gold would be brave, she must be brave, she must not be a moaning minny, she must –

"Do you want me to move out?" the words were blurted out before she could stop them, even though she put her hand over her mouth to keep them in.

Mavis Louise smiled.

"Why would I want you to do that?" she said. "Is this about those wretched girls earlier?"

Miss Gold nodded.

"I thought we might schedule the lessons in separately in the future. That's all."

She laid her hand on Miss Gold's cheek. "I don't want you to move out. I never want you to move out. Surely that's clear by now. How many years is it? Ten? Twelve?"

The relief that flooded through Miss Gold nearly brought those tears back again.

"Fifteen," she said.

"Fifteen years," said Mavis Louise. "And you're still not sure?"

"Of course I'm sure," said Miss Gold. "I was just worried you weren't."

"My dear," said Mavis Louise. "I've never been more certain of anything in my life."

Miss Gold swallowed and smiled a wobbly smile.

"Would you dance with me?" she asked. Mavis Louise smiled back.

"Oh yes," she said.

They stepped onto the dance floor and into each other's arms. Wearing their light summer macs, with their handbags slung over their wrists, they waltzed together as the blue sky turned to violet and the sun set over the sea.

The Meantime, A.M. Gough

The Meantime

This pub used to be one of my haunts, and now, amid the clinking of glasses and the waves of laughter, crammed in knee-to-knee around this small table with my old uni friends, I feel myself relax for the first time in months.

I haven't really missed the pub itself. The beer is cheap for a reason, and I can't help but look around disapprovingly at the crowds of students, even though I was one this time last year. They all seem so loud and immature now, so young, so…samey. My ability to differentiate between freshers and third years has gone, and now all that's left is students and not-students, or at a push undergrads and postgrads. The young and the not-yet-old.

'Seems like only yesterday that we were here,' Jenny says, and I realise that I've missed her, even though we haven't really stayed in touch.

'It was only a year ago.'

'I know, but we were so *young,'* she replies, only half-joking. 'Anyway, Heather, what are you doing with your life?' It's a valid question, but that doesn't make it easy to answer.

'Well, it's been mainly temp work. You know. Arts degree.' There's a murmur of sympathy around the table. "Arts degree" has always been a codeword for unemployability in our group, half-formed as we are of former literature students, historians and linguists. 'Shame my parents aren't quite so sympathetic as you lot, but you can't have everything. I've got an interview lined up, though. Communications. So might be a bit of press stuff, copy-editing, stakeholder emails.'

'Try and sound a bit less excited, someone might think you gave a toss,' says Simon, rather lacking in sympathy since he got himself a cushy grad scheme in the City. I usually appreciate his scathing humour, it keeps me from sinking into self-pity, but that place in my head is a little raw tonight.

'I know. But after the fifty-third…no, wait, fifty-fourth rejection, you start to lose enthusiasm. Is it really that entitled to think that a degree from a Russel Group uni would make me vaguely employable?'

'Aww.' Connor pats me on the shoulder.

'Fuck it,' says Jenny, lifting the mood again. 'Who needs money when you've got alcohol?'

'You need money to buy alcohol,' says Jack, finally finding a point at which to leap in.

'True,' I reply, kindly, because he's not wrong, although the observation isn't exactly hilarious. I feel a twinge of pity as I look over at my shaggy-haired ex-housemate. Jack's a smart guy, but not always witty. He has a tendency to get lost when the conversation sinks into banter. 'So, how's the thesis, Jackster?' I don't think I've ever called him that before, but he's giving me that look that makes me nervous and I want to relieve the tension.

'Well, it's shifted a bit since you last asked,' he replies, and even though that last conversation was months ago, I have a funny feeling he remembers every word I said.

'Will I understand it?'

Jack's a computer scientist, so I won't.

'Nope.'

'Is it going okay?'

'Yep.'

'Cool.' Vital information exchanged, we go quiet. That look is still there in his eyes. The sparkling challenge, the expectation that in a second I'll say something hilarious, that I'll engage with him, smile at him like I used to.

I look away, unsure what to do with it.

'So, Si, how's the new job?' I ask, although I actually see him regularly, so I already know.

'Never mind that, how's everyone's love life?' Connor butts in.

'In other words, Connor's got a new somebody, and he wants to talk about them,' Simon quips. 'Go on, then. Name? Pronouns? Do we like them?'

'Mike,' Connor admits sheepishly. 'I wasn't sure about him at first-'

Thus follows a long-winded, charming explanation of why Connor has become sure about Mike, even to the extent of considering posting a joint selfie on Instagram. A love story for this age.

Jenny got back with her ex from school after they hooked up on a night out in her hometown. Never having met him I can't say if it's a good thing or not. She seems happy. Simon's too busy with the job, and Jack is…well, Jack. No explanation necessary, although a lifetime tied to a computer screen coupled with a general disinterest in people he doesn't already know is a good one. The conversation turns to me.

'Heather. Still single?' Simon asks, holding a pretend microphone up to me.

'Simon. Yes. Of course.'

'Why of course?'

'Because it's me,' I say, glancing down at my plus-size frame with a good-natured grimace. Jack's eyes are on me again. 'Also, what with living with the parents…not much opportunity, and at the moment I don't really know what I'm doing or where I'm going, so you know...' I receive a few pitying looks and realise I'm being a bit bleak. 'Besides which, what do I need a boyfriend for? It just seems like such a faff. You know, dating…emotional investment…people…' my offhand tone brings us back on track and we start laughing again.

'You need to get on Tinder, girly. Start playing the field.'

'I'm honestly not that fussed. I've never been able to understand how some people can go from one relationship to another in a matter of weeks. It takes me six months to work out whether I like someone! I just seem to work on a different timescale to everyone else.'

'You're pretty terrible at being young, aren't you?'

I shrug.

'Meh. There'll be time for love later.' In theory, of course.

***

'I can't believe they lost the booking.' The cobbled streets are shiny and wet, and I have to take care not to splash pedestrians as I navigate the infuriating one-way system.

'Idiots,' Jack says, sympathetically. 'At least they gave you a refund.'

'Yeah. Thanks for putting me up.'

'No worries. Thanks for the lift,' he says, nodding to the messy interior of my car.

'Well, I was hardly going to drive on to your place and leave you to walk it, was I?' I point out. 'If anything I owe you for walking me to the hotel.' He laughs at that, a scratchy, musical sound that I'd nearly forgotten.

'We could've had a race,' he suggests.

'I have an image of you nicking a skateboard from a passing teenager and rocketing down the underpass.'

Another laugh.

'I wish I had an imagination.'

'You've got one.'

'Not like yours,' he says, shaking his head. 'I never know where my conversations with you are going to end up.'

I can't really think of a response to that, so I say nothing. He doesn't seem particularly bothered by my silence. That's one of the things I've missed about him. With so many of my friends, if I can't make them laugh, I feel like I haven't held up my end of the social bargain. There isn't that pressure with Jack. I always feel like he's just glad to have me around.

'It's up here.'

'I remember.'

'Do you?' he asks, sounding a little too pleased. I flip the indicator with a sigh.

***

'Done?'

'Yep.' Pyjamas on, I stuff my clothes into my rucksack.

'Cool.' Jack comes back in. 'I'll take the sleeping bag. You can have the bed.' He wanders around his room, absent-mindedly picking up the clothes strewn across it. 'Sorry about the mess,' he adds. I decide not to mention that the fact he's standing there in nothing but his tracksuit bottoms is making me more nervous than a bit of dirty laundry.

'Don't be daft, I'll take the sleeping bag. You're already doing me a favour.'

'I'm trying to be chivalrous.'

'It's not working,' I say. 'You know me.'

'That I do.'

'A-anyway, we can share. It's a double.' At the moment the dynamic has shifted into 'just-good-friends' so I don't feel uncomfortable making the suggestion. One doesn't usually proposition one's friends when one has just been gifted a view of their dirty socks. He shrugs.

'If you like. D'you want me to sleep above the blanket?'

'Nah, it's freezing in here. I trust you.' Ah, damn. I shouldn't have said that last part. His eyes start to sparkle, my heart goes sideways, and we're back to being friends-except-with-this-unspoken-tension-that-we-try-to-ignore. Damn, damn, damn. I break eye contact and start fussing with the bedsheets. 'You're right, it's a bit of a tip in here, mate.'

'It's okay, I'll take the sleeping bag,' he says, gently.

'I trust you,' I say again, because it's true. My fear has nothing to do with him. He wouldn't so much as tap me on the shoulder without my consent. It's something different, not repulsion or attraction but something complicated, a Gordian's knot at the pit of my stomach that simultaneously makes me want to pull him close and run for the hills, hide in a cave somewhere and wait until I can successfully pass myself off as a crazy old spinster.

He sits on the edge of the bed with a sigh.

'I…' I begin, but I've only started the sentence because I want something to say, and it fades into nothing.

'I get it.' Of course he does. It takes more than a year to forget your feelings for a person, even if it wasn't quite love. Even if it was never mentioned or acted upon.

'That job I've got the interview for is in Cardiff,' I say, sitting beside him.

'Bit of a trek.' He means that it's a long way from my parents, but also a long way from here.

'Yeah. But maybe it'll become home. Home isn't just where you're from, after all.'

'Do you like living with your parents?'

'I've… gotten used to it,' I say, cautiously. 'And I'm not sure that's a good thing. I need to move on again, find my own place in the world. Hopefully this'll be my chance.'

'Are you depressed?'

'Meh,' I say, because I'm not sure that's exactly it. 'It's just hard…you spend years away from home, getting to know the world, and then you're-'

'Back dealing with their version of it,' he finishes, and for the hundredth time since I've known him, I am reminded how much I tend to underestimate him, assuming that all his hours coding have left him part-computer. 'Do you want the job?' he asks.

'Yeah, I guess so. It's good experience…it pays pretty well. I've heard Cardiff's alright. Cheapish.'

'I hope you get it. Let me know if you do,' he says.

'Yeah, of course.'

'And if you ever find yourself back here again-'

'Yeah, always,' I say. 'Though I don't know if I really…'

'If you'd really want to come back. I get that. I've been getting bored of it too.'

'Well, if I end up in Cardiff and you find yourself there-' I say, trying to sound more upbeat.

'Shall do.'

I'm not sure what I was going to suggest, or what he's just agreed to. I get into bed and gesture for him to do the same. He turns the light off and climbs in. 'What do you want to do?' he asks the ceiling. 'Like, if you didn't have to think about anyone else.'

'I honestly don't know. I was always so good at this, you know. Academia. But that's not what I want to do long-term, so I'm…'

'Stuck,' he supplies.

'So, I need to just find something to do and keep moving.'

'Yeah, good idea,' he says, and his confirmation that I'm thinking on the right lines is as warming as the proximity of his body. I feel suddenly calm, as if something inside me that was dislodged and rattling around has found its place again.

'Sorry. I've been a bit depressing tonight.'

'You're alright. I'm always glad to see you,' he says. Glad. That's the right word. Not happy, not sad, or uncomfortable, or excited or nervous. Glad. 'Do you…do you ever miss …it? Here?'

'I miss…the people,' I reply. 'I miss having all my friends just down the road. A city full of people my age, all at the same stage as me. But that's not true anymore, so I can't really miss it here. Did you miss...us? When we graduated?'

‘Yeah.’ And somehow I know he feels it too, that sense of calm with a tinge of excitement at its edges. That thing that I can’t say, because I don’t have a word for it, because it isn’t explicit enough for a word. Because we understand each other without knowing each other.

‘Who knows, maybe someday we’ll be living in the same place,’ I say, but without any particular expression.

‘Maybe,’ he replies, in the same bland tone. Not hopeful, not hopeless, not disappointed. Whatever happens, Jack’s here until he gets his doctorate, and I’ve got to find my place out in the real world. Twenty-three isn’t a good time to be making plans.

‘Do you ever think we’re too clever for our own good?’ I ask.

‘I wish I was stupider. I wish I could just…’ he trails off.

‘Just dive into a thing. Without worrying about the consequences.’ Without worrying about how it could go wrong, leaving us hurt and older and lonelier than before, how it could stop us moving forward right when we need to be free to take on the world.

‘Yeah.’

‘I get it. I’m so sick of being paralysed. Of being so *aware* of everything all the time. What I’m feeling. What everyone else is feeling. What I need. What they expect. How the world works. How it doesn’t. All the different jobs I could do, or not, all the paths I could take, all the choices I could get wrong. All the consequences. It’s all too many perspectives and thoughts, all the time.’

It takes him a moment to reply, and I worry that I’ve been too honest.

‘That’s what you get with an arts degree,’ he says eventually, in the same comfortable tone. ‘Subjective axioms.’

‘I’ll take it over ones and zeroes.’

‘Even with the brain overload?’

'Even computers freeze from time to time. I'll take having all the feelings and getting paralysed to having none of them. But it would be nice if I could just…switch it off now and then. Just long enough to be able to *do* something.'

'You are *definitely* too clever for your own good,' he chuckles.

'It's not fair. What's the point of being clever if you can't answer any questions?'

I hear him shrug in the darkness, and I realise with a sinking feeling that there might not be an answer. Or if there is, it's not going to be out in the world, in Cardiff, or anywhere other than here, in this bed, with a person who, at least for the moment, understands. And there's a very strong possibility that when I go out into the world, I'll lose the answer that was here as well, and I won't know that calm again. The distance will take its toll, the old understanding will fly away on the wings of a new infatuation, and I'll just have to grow up and go it alone and learn not to mind. Maybe this is adulthood, always slightly out of place, slightly uncomfortable, slightly confused. Always carrying on in the hopes that there will be a home around the next corner.

Or I could say to hell with it, reach out and touch him, stake my claim and break everything and make the kind of mistakes I'm supposed to make at this age.

'Well, I'm knackered,' he says, and I remember that I'm a coward.

'Yeah. Me too. Sleep well.'

Youth is wasted on the young.

LONDON INDEPENDENT STORY PRIZE 2023 PROMISING PENS

Have you noticed, Nelly Bryce

Have you noticed

the way children just lounge on each other,
limbs against other limbs,
bodies nestled together like tables,
like leaves stacked together for warmth on wintery pavements,
like drawing without taking your pen off the paper,
like pieces of rock stuck together in a white paper bag but
softer,
like the feel of your tongue resting within your mouth,
like a barely audible sigh of relief,
like the heel of a hand needing just-risen dough,
like the way both hands move to soothe each other after hearing
bad news,
like the way an elderly woman finds your arm in the street as
they tell you what sounds
like the God's honest truth,
like we weren't meant to be forever touching the skin of
another human being,
like we weren't designed to love.

Daffodil, Jennifer Duffy

Daffodil

Divination by daffodil;
a yellow trumpet marches into spring
as I become numb to the changing air.

From my view, looking out the window,
misfortune hangs its' head towards me.
Baneful scents fresh from the banks
of Acheron envelop this

room this

house this

mind this

body. Nausea,
heaving headaches. A wish

to walk in the garden, free
from this mind, this body,
this poison seizing my legs at the front
door. Open

a crack in the night,

as I gather my courage
to gather daffodils;
savouring the spring however I can.
Bringing in the following

afternoon's air as
daffodils rest in a vase, heads turned
towards the sun shining through the window.

After a Storm

Pull up your anchor. The storm has passed.
You have survived the squalls of driving rain.
You have battened down the hatches, bailed out water, faced and fought sea monsters
- a kraken of your own making.
You have felt the sting of salt in eyes, have cowered from the wrath of storms, have navigated whirlpools and strong currents.
You dropped anchor - taught rigging, fighting drift - and held your ground, kept your vessel afloat.
You have battled with the elements, ridden the swell and crash of waves upon waves upon waves.

Pull up your anchor now. The storm has passed.
It rings in your ears still like the shriek of gulls which circle overhead, but the waters will calm, and the sun is rising.
You do not need to resist. You do not need to paddle furiously or cry out above the wind. You will not sink.

Embrace the albatross, not as a burden around your neck but as a prince upon the waves, guiding you intuitively to safety.
Do not frantically look for land on the horizon, nor scan for lighthouses to guide you in.
You need no lifeboats.
But stop, pull up your anchor, and rest awhile.

Look up. Up to skies where white clouds foam and float upon a sea of blue.
Hear the soft ringing of the rigging, the flapping of sails like bird's wings on the breeze.
Feel the gentle roll of waves beneath you -
Trust them to wash away the flotsam and jetsam.

The waters will clear.
Fish will swim.
The tide will still roll in and out, in and out.

Somewhere, on sandy shorelines, are pebbles smoothed by waves and glimmering in sunlight.
A shimmering of something hopeful.

Somewhere, in rock pools or stony coves, are pearls in oysters, waiting to be discovered.
Somewhere, high overhead and beyond the horizon, are birds migrating, seeking warmth and light.
And somewhere, wet feet paddling and rainbow coloured nets in sticky hands, are children collecting shells and making memories.

You do not need to seek them out.
You do not need to forge them from the waves.
You do not need to sail upon treacherous seas in search of them or turn the tide.
You do not need to repair, with rope-burned hands, the erosion of rock and stone.

Let seas be seas and skies be skies.
Pull up your anchor.
Breathe in the air - salt and all - and
just
float.

On Hoy, Emma Williams

On Hoy

Impulsive. To live on Hoy. The biggest decision
I ever made. By steel blue boat we sailed into fog
and craziness. A calm crossing. No portents.
We bobbed and swayed and stepped
through emptiness into a world of ancient light.
Flat lands, three-quarters sky.

We stood in the certainty of granite, trusted the sheer
drops and each other. Looked at *The Old Man*
with young eyes. In the biting wind we held hands
in a hail of gannets, a show just for us, a reward
for adventurousness. On the cliff edge
we hugged through the midges. Anything was possible.

We bought an acre of dry-stone walls and talked ourselves
into a future. Shared the reckless lure of freedom
Took the unspoken test: what would you give up for me?
Everything, everything, everything.
But I had more to lose, I knew the danger of nowhere
to run to. The inescapable bond. The ultimate dare.

Heavenish

Peaceful times my dear
You won't find it here

Stress free times, not a chance
The hustle and bustle does not do much to enhance

Slow-paced living is far from the dream
And the sight, oh the sight of concrete is part of the regime

But it holds dear to my heart, my soul
And it certainly does make me feel whole

In the midst of despair it gives me hope
All of which allows me to cope

When all said and done, and my heart melts
Why would I want to be anywhere else?

The Wooden Coat, Laura Kyle

The Wooden Coat

Nora fiddled with the white cardigan. She'd made it for Cara's baby. There was hope crocheted into every stich, the hope that this baby would be the one to push through. It wouldn't be needed now. She'd put in the sideboard with the keep-for-best glasses and a few bit of her Mammy's wedding china.

'Honestly Mum, you can't stay in this house. You never throw anything away. It's out of

control.' Cara had brought her around a leaflet. 'Sheltered Housing' it said on the front. 'Inspired Living'.

But Nora liked the clutter. It was all memories. Hers, Eddie's and at one time Cara's. There was a photo album on the coffee table. She opened it. A newspaper article was sellotaped onto the first page.

'Mr & Mrs Edward Sheehan are delighted to announce the marriage of their daughter, Cara to James Devlin, son of Dr. & Mrs Jack Devlin'.

'Isn't that lovely?' she had said. 'It was such a wonderful day.'

Cara had rolled her eyes, refused to sit down in case she got a mark on her cream coat. And then she'd left.

Nora touched the photo of her and Eddie at the wedding. She stood up, looked at herself in the mirror above the fireplace. There was space for another person in the old shirt of Eddie's she was wearing. When had she become such a twig of a woman?

She started spinning, like she had when she was a little girl, spinning with grief in the middle of the room until she was so dizzy that she fell down onto the sofa and wept. Cara could say what she liked but no-one was getting her out of here, not until it was time for her to don her wooden coat.

The first of the last goodbyes

Machines beep and whir as I hold your bony hand, trying to ignore the smell of shit overlaid with disinfectant.

"It was nice to see Tim yesterday," I say.

Your eyes flutter open. "When Millie's not there, he's more..."

"Himself?" I'm relieved we've finally found some common ground.

"Don't mess it up for him." You snatch your hand out of my grasp. "He's happy."

I laugh. I've known Tim all his life and he's always been miserable.

"You remember what he was like," you say. "He needs someone."

The drinking; the panic attacks. I clench my fists, my nails biting into my palms. "Not someone like that."

"He's not confident like you."

Confident? That's a joke. I have the feeling, not unfamiliar, that you don't know me at all.

"But she's controlling him. You just admitted it!" The patient opposite looks up sharply and I realise how loud my voice is.

"He likes it."

“Well, I don’t!” I tremble, thrilled and appalled that we’re finally having this conversation. Better late than never.

You’ve been gazing off into the distance but now you fix me with a stare, your eyes as grey and flat as the sea outside the window. “It doesn’t matter how you feel.”

Your voice is quiet but you might as well have bellowed into my face. I realise I’ve always known it, been told so many times without words, and now you’ve confirmed it.

I lurch to my feet on a wave of fury. I could just leave. Then I see your deflated body in the too-big hospital bed; your eyes closed, your breath coming in gasps.

Party, Lucy Lasasso

Party

The other guests scattered nervously around me like sheep sensing a wolf about to pick off a bleating lamb.
The men looked at me slyly in my too-tight dress and too-much make up. The wives looked at their husbands looking at me.
The bravest wife tried to head me off where I stood at the drinks table draining glass after glass of cold pink wine. My stomach boiled up in protest, but I told it to stop whining and be grateful. I was trying to tame my body so it would carry me around like a good soldier, uncomplaining. For this reason, too, I had taken to walking barefoot in the park until the soles of my feet toughened and dirt settled into the cracks.
The wine was sweet, but its coldness dulled the sweetness. It was only when I burped that I could detect a sickly strawberry note.
The brave wife asked me what part of the city I lived in and how I knew the hostess.
I used to copy her homework, I said, and take chocolate bars from her lunchbox.
What a beautiful ring, said the wife, looking past me for a way out.
My boyfriend gave it to me before he found out what kind of person I really am, I told her. He liked me at first, but after a while I noticed he started many of his sentences with "Don't take this the wrong way but…"
She blinked.
Does your husband ever say that? I asked.
Some people find me rude or too direct but I genuinely wanted to know.
I could see her thinking about that one, then she buried the thought a long way down.
Never, she said, and for the first time she smiled.

Out of this World, Liz Gwinnell

Out of this World

She flew to Cloud Cuckoo Land with Flights of Fancy Airlines and paid for it on the never never. It was a strange and curious isle, full of sounds and sweet airs that gave delight; a little, she thought, like the island where Prospero was shipwrecked in *The Tempest.* Or maybe not.

For two weeks, time should still. She tasted pie in the sky and walked on sunshine. In the evenings when cumulus, cirrus and alto stratus vanished into thin air, she tango'd in the night and tripped the light fantastic.

She took a day trip to the village of Cloud Nine where she watched a young hopeful woman stitching silver linings. She thought about buying one but they weren't for sale. She wasn't so sure about the clouds the bartender in the hotel added to her coffee but as a passing stranger in a midnight mood told her, they were a speciality of the island and everyone should live a little. She suspected he was a diamond in the rough.

"We use clouds to store data back home," she told him.
"Don't be ridiculous," he said. "Clouds are just clouds."

When she arrived back at Heathrow, her best friend asked her about her holiday of a lifetime.
"It was out of this world," she said. "Out of this world."
"Oh," her best friend said, rolling her eyes. "Is that the best you can do? Describe it with a *cliché?"* "
"Yes," she said. "That's what happens when your heads in the clouds."

Herding Instinct

At the family reunion, a group of us snuck down the road. Leaned on a fence, and smoked some pot, watching a small herd of cows moving across the field. When the weather started turning, the party broke up.

My cousins from Baltimore had booked a couple motel rooms for the night. The girls jumped in the pool, but I didn't have a suit. I sprawled in a chair, draining a tepid beer, craving more. I knew a place across the highway, could almost see the flickering LIQUORS.

Jimmy offered to make a beer run with me.

Inside the store, a dank carpet snagged at my shoes. Buzzing lights pinged off the cash register, and tiny explosions popped in my periphery. I recognized a guy from high school loitering with the cashier. It was that kind of place, where people hung out.

I said, "Hey," but the guy just glared.

Jimmy said, "He was talking to you."

Jimmy was offended. Protective, in his own way. Jimmy had done some time, had certain rules. I didn't care, I was too far gone. From leaning on the fence, getting high, to now, the evening started tipping toward ugly, like always. We left before Jimmy's agitation ignited.

He drove down a dead-end road, both of us sucking on beers. I wished we had done this years ago. With bottles of Coke, not beer.

They say your cousins are your first friends. But we'd wasted opportunities. Drifted apart. Weathered addictions alone.

The cows had huddled together as the storm approached.

Back at the motel, the girls scrounged up some food. I sobered up some. We pressed together on the beds. Blurry tv, rain running down the window, white noise.

We breathed, our elbows and knees bumping gently.

Instinctively.

Going Out, Grant Wandle

Going Out

On my way to the shop I bump into Bob, who asks straight out if I know where my ex is these days. *Christ!* I am not about to give him her number, and he is a shameless scumbag for wanting to make a move on her now. The silence lengthens, as I compose a suitably unhelpful reply: "She's in small bags in my freezer". I grin.

A pause before he laughs – too loud, as ever. "You're a funny guy," he says. He slaps my shoulder in his mistaken idea of bonhomie. My whole body stiffens. I wait for him to leave.

I hate going out. I spent all morning hugging my knees, rocking back and forth on the kitchen floor, dreading this trip. Hunger finally forced me out, but the crunch of a snail underfoot sent me rushing back indoors. I sang softly to myself until I stopped shaking.

I finally felt strong enough to venture out again and I bump into Bob. Even if I make it to the shop this time I know that the cashier will emit an almost inaudible tut as she rings up each of my purchases.

The world is full of insensitive people, but when I am at home I can lock them all away beyond my front door. I wish I could stock up on food so I didn't have to go out so often, but there is no room in my freezer.

DOMESTIC, Sarah Hill Wheeler

DOMESTIC

She never sees the red roses, shrouded in cellophane, or the note he leaves on her bed. *Love you to eternity and back. Together, forever.* When the nurse returns with a vase, thirty minutes later because of a person incident in the lift, she is alone and already flat-lining.
It's doubtful she ever hears the voice, gentle as a mangrove creek, telling her to hang in there, that everything will be okay. But in the half-breath beforehand, in the amniotic blackness that has become her, memories fall against her sides like breaking stars; if there's a way back, she'll take it. Feverishly, she counts down the accelerando of footsteps, pulling them back to the soft shuffle of crêpe soles, two clicks of a door. *Everyone deserves a second chance*, she thinks, closing her eyes, burying the strobes of pain which Catherine wheel across her face as the light hits her, rolling the metal gurney back to the ambulance, back to the kitchen before the paramedics unfold her, to a time when the Moroccan blue floor tiles are new and her hair isn't matted with blood. *Never again,* he says, *I promise.* But the light is too bright, too white, like the sheets of foolscap he holds above her, laughing as he squeezes the eclipse through a pinprick. *I want you to remember this moment all your life.* On the 49th parallel, waiting for time to unfurl, she smiles as he reverse-slips the band off her finger and returns it to its heart-shaped box. *Will you?* he asks, rising up from his knees, but that moment too slips into the future, behind her; all she feels now is the glass shard in her leg, the sun burning her edges like paper, and she realises none of this can ever happen again.

Coat

I couldn't live there anymore. Creeping about on eggshells, amidst white-wash walls and sparkling granite. I longed for an oozy sofa I could spill curry on. Squirrelling suitcases, I left your parents' house in Highgate, for the squalid streets of Brixton.

I said I needed space. We both knew it was a lie.

I moved into a basement flat with an obese recluse. Her cats pissed in my wardrobe, and when they shat, they made sure I was present so they could look me in the eye.

You stood in the windowless kitchen and stared at the litter tray. I drank too much and when you left, you turned on the stairs, face sickly in the glare of the bare bulb.

We could get somewhere together?

I don't want to. I said, and realised it was true.

I watched your beautiful halo-face crumple in the half-light.

The slam of the door.

I went to Edinburgh to forget. I spent a month blinded by bright lights and festival nights. I laughed and drank and soared and sank. I discovered the arrogance of men, the shocking thrill of their bitter semen.

Yours was always so sweet.

One night I found myself alone on an unknown street, the wind wild. It snatched at bins and kicked tins along the pavement. I looked at road signs. I searched the night sky. Nothing made sense, not the signs or the stars.

I shivered and realised I had lost my coat.

BAGATELLE, Philippa Howell

BAGATELLE

Sofie was staying with us that August. I had spent Easter with her family in Munich, preparing for "O" level, and in my schoolgirl German I explained that "O" stood for ordinary.
"O is for Oral," Sofie whispered, later.
Her father wrote: "*all arrangements are satisfactory for Sofie's journey to Wales, but we are having trouble with her back passage*".
I remember my father sniggering when he read the letter to us at breakfast.
Then suddenly she was there, succulent in her blue bikini. I noticed my father studying her as she lay stretched out on the sand, legs slightly spread. A trail of soft down lead from her navel to the darkness under the blue.
My mother shoved the dinghy towards the sea. "Come on Alistair, your turn to crew" she commanded.
Alistair rose shakily. My brother jumped up, concerned for his friend. "All right?" he asked. Alistair nodded, zipping up his lifejacket.
"The tide's going out," remarked my father. It was a statement of fact, not a warning.
The wind was getting up and the dinghy shot away from the beach, leaving the rest of us standing in a row, towels flapping. We watched till it became a dot.
When it vanished, my brother ran to the beach café to phone for the lifeboat. Sofie held my hand. My father shivered convulsively, but did not speak.
Two months later he left my mother for his PA, twenty-nine years his junior. Everything fell into place, like the silver balls that slide into slots on a bagatelle board. We had one at home. It was made of balsa wood, light and easy to tip.

Hammam, Scarlett Sangster

Hammam

The room is warm and the air is damp and busy. Cramped with peppermint, salt and orange. Opulent, distracting. Though not enough to hide the bitterness underneath. The smells clash against the tiles, tracing silent tears down the walls, collecting on the floor. I glance over at you, but your eyes are closed, led with your hands on your stomach, your face empty as the words I cannot say.

The door cracks open and whispers enter with bare feet and wooden bowls. They kneel by the taps and let the water crash over their hands, waves over tiles. They rub their hands in sweet-smelling salts, floral and woody, soft and hard, attempting to scrub away the parts of us that shouldn't be – the bitter thoughts that have seeped from our pores, stained our skin. Sweat and ink. Anguish and blame. They scrape our arms and legs, across our stomachs, over my breasts. I try to imagine myself brand new, fresh skinned. I imagine the light bouncing off my skin, that it might illuminate like opal in the desert, that my eyes might shine bright enough to enchant you once again. To help you forget – or remember.

Once they've scrubbed the dead weight from our bodies, they fill their bowls and dowse us down. The water runs over me like oil. And I wonder, what do I do if it cannot clean me? If I cannot be restored?

The whispers retreat, leaving us in the silence that isn't silence, pools of bitter-sweet tears on the floor. The air has broken now. No longer close and suffocating, but tepid, and free to move around. I could, but I do not look over. Cannot bear to discover if the hammam has taken us back to the beginning, or solidified the end.

We Haven’t Eaten

We bought the house on a quiet street like a deep sigh. Children played kickball. There was a sign that said slow down.
She planted the rose bed first and over the years put fish bones and bone powder at each of their bases.
“The calcium helps them grow,” she says, holding a flower by the stem so as not to prick herself. She puts down a fish, an offering, at the boneyard.
We haven’t eaten fish in a hundred and eighty-five days.
She puts the bones over the deep, dark mulch in early fall and I have no idea where they ever come from. I don’t love her anymore, but sometimes when she says she’s about to go, she kisses me on the cheek, and I miss the woman she was more than when she’s even around.

MONICA, Rohit Singh

MONICA

It was suffocating. To stand and smile in front of people, when all she wanted was to run away screaming; to hold hands that promised "Now and Forever" not a long time ago, that were caught red handed caressing a stranger's body just now. All Monica felt was a rush of emotions, as if the logic had faded away like faded memories of childhood.

She felt a shock, despair and her veins going numb, all at the same time. She kept spiraling back to the sunny day when she thought her "Happy Forever" moment had arrived with the love of her life. Did she miss noticing something she should have noticed? Did she rush the decision to wear the ring? Was there any way to undo what was already done?

"Pull yourself together Monica. Remember when those bullies in school said you can't swim, and you captained the school team later that year. You will come out of this phase as well.", Monica thought.

"This was all my fault. I should have looked for some signs. I should have done something. I should have been patient. How could I do this to myself", another voice inside Monica's head questioned her.

While many versions of the treacherous night kept playing in her head like a constant reel of a single movie, she heard in some distance "Monica, would you like to share something? Monica? Are you with us?"

Monica realized it was time to try and find solace amidst strangers by sharing the lies that drove her to struggle with alcohol just like the others in the room.

After the Shine Wore Off

The light when they broke up was her favourite kind.

As they walked along the cracked pavement, not quite side by side, the autumn sun reached around the Victorian terraces, turning maple trees into blazing beacons, puddles into sheets of polished amber. The light made what was ordinary seem urgent and romantic. Even the litter. Even the potholes. Even him.

He clapped his gloved hands together. “Come on, it’s cold.”

They passed an alleyway leading to the railway. The sky at the horizon was a serenely pale blue, but the clouds above were orange with a dusting of pink.

Their first date, six months before, had been similarly luminous. In the warm haze of the pub he seemed sweet, shy. Listening while she talked. Then on the walk to the station, a downpour drove her beneath his umbrella, the fog of her glasses transforming the streetlamps and headlights into shimmering orbs. She leaned into him, finding his solidity a refuge when all was wildly elemental.

Had she mistaken the rush of sensation for attraction? Had it been an error from the start?

There followed a picnic in the radiance of a coming thunderstorm. There followed dimmed coffee shops, strip-lit noodle bars and twilight walks. There followed fumblings in the dark. But she still did all the talking, and lately, she’d run out of things to say. Today, at his flat, there would be no candlelit dinner, only the glare of the TV.

She slowed to gaze at a spider’s web hung with pearlescent raindrops.

His feet scuffed the tarmac. “Let’s go.”

“But the light.”

If they couldn't share this moment of wonder, what were they but parallel beams travelling on their own paths with no hope of intersecting?

"The light," she said, and with rolling eyes, he turned away.

THE AFTERNOON TEA, Kathrine Bancroft

THE AFTERNOON TEA

The table is set with your best china. Champagne glasses too.
One each and chipped with the memories of other afternoon teas.
Of other lips.
But there is no champagne today.
Just tea and a chocolate cake.
I watch your hand trembling for a second slice, your gaze still glittering with life.
I sip my tea and try to imagine all that you've ever seen– the faces and the places of a hundred years.
The tea is bitter strong, and stone cold.
You've forgotten to boil the kettle.
But I don't mention it. I let you enjoy your cake in peace.
On the mantel behind you sits an old ceramic mug.
And I remember when you first placed it into my hands.
You'd carried it out of the camp whilst the wind howled against you.
You'd marched with it next to your chest, on and on, through the blizzarding snow,
through the bullets, and the blood, and into Berlin.
For mile after mile, you'd carried it with you.
Miles that had led you back to this London street and back to this London house.
Miles that had finally led you back home.
You finish eating and sit back in your chair.
You look around your living room, an Englishman surveying his castle.
An Englishman taking his leave.
You tell me that the few clothes you're permitted have been labelled up with your name, and your new room number - so they don't get mixed up with all the others in the wash.

'Just like one of them posh schools' you say.
And we both do our best to smile.
Because now there are no more words and no more stories and no more miles.
Just tea and a chocolate cake.
And a hand that comes to rest upon mine.

Breathing, Karon Alderman

Breathing

When I woke up this morning I was one of two children. When I went to bed, I was one of one.
I get the blanket off your bed and pull it over my face and try not to breathe. I can hear Mum sobbing in her bedroom. And the sudden groan of the floorboards as Dad walks up and down. Like he's still waiting for news, pacing the corridor in the hospital; or measuring a cell, trying to work out how long he'll be waiting, waiting, doing time.

But at least he's moving. Mum stopped moving when they told us. Dad had to carry her to the car. Driving home, windscreen wipers beating time on the windscreen, 'Mum,' I said. She didn't reply in words.

The crying grows louder, grows quieter, but never stops. I put my fingers in my ears. But I can't keep them there forever, can't block it out. I wrap my body in your pale grey duvet, my whole head in your blanket. Slide my head under my pillow. I am cocooned. Like I'm bandaged head to toe. I hold my breath.

But it's hard to stop breathing when you try. It seems like it only happens when you're not watching, your head turned away as you laughingly look back to see if your brother is chasing you and he is and you keep running with your head turned away, as you fall through the glass door and

stop breathing.

She told me it was just one time…

She said it was a mistake. I shouldn't care so much, especially as I'm the bloke in the relationship. She stood ten feet beneath me, belaying me. With black painted fingernails, she held onto the rope I was hanging from: a handful of ellipses. Nail polish was the only girl-thing she permitted herself. I was trying to reach new heights in the gorge. Her weight was my anchor. But I was too much for her. She couldn't hold me if worse came to worst because I was getting heavier. I was hardening to stone.

Water trickled down the rock face like tears as it started to drizzle. Mud marked it like scars. She said she'd slipped up, that it would never happen again, and the words circled my head like squawking seagulls, looking to swoop in and pick me apart. When I stretched from foothold to foothold, trying to get a grip, I felt my hands calcify, stiffen. My joints fused on the side of the cliff. She shouted: 'you're too sensitive', 'you should just move on, keep looking up and stop looking back.'

I pushed through, bone grinding on flinty bone. I came to an impasse, a muddy overhang that a boulder like me shouldn't get over. I hung on by my bitten fingernails. She shouted that if I couldn't get over it, then I shouldn't bother. I stared down at her. Nodded. She seemed so far away, so insignificant. She had one hand resting on her head, and only one finger hooked onto the rope that bound us together: a full stop of nail. She wasn't even trying to hold on to me.

I unhooked my carabiner and didn't look back at my mistake as I climbed up and away,

holding on,
to me,
for the first time.

CRUMBS, Molly Lanzarotta

CRUMBS

My father circulates at this party, but he is not convincingly alive. Each facial expression, every gesture: still dead. I maneuver so that buffet tables and a fruit tower remain between us.

My brother keeps withholding information. I try to get it out of him. He says, no, we need a private place to talk. We're attending a large outdoor reception on a farm in Minas Gerais and the passed appetizers look exquisite but keep passing me by.

I try to find out what my brother hints at—our mother stashed money in a closet? She is hiding a bruise?—and it's then that my brother gets angry at me for not dividing my ginger snaps. We are adults, still fighting over the cookies.

In all of the cosmos, there will never be enough dessert to share: real, imagined, alive, dead, on this continent or any other. At each table confections rise on tiered crystal platters, but my brother desires the tangy biscuits that he knows I carry in my messenger bag.

I shove snaps into his mouth. We have shut ourselves in an old Chevrolet Brasil we discovered in a barn. Windows rolled up, we are sealed away from all the color and music and vitality and my brother still won't tell me a thing, just ridicules me with his sardonic laugh, spitting ginger crumbs.

I am clever, protect myself, deflecting his crumbs with a shred of the cookie bag. My resources have been nothing but scraps all along, a lifetime of employing flimsy shields against an onrush of generational chaos.

It won't matter how long we both live or if he is still refusing to speak to me after we die. My brother will hang on to whatever information is so crucial he thinks I shouldn't know it.

Mire, Patricia Mullin

Mire

Jude's regular route was cut off. The ponds, home to the rare natterjack toad, had flooded, engulfing all paths. Navigating through the gorse which snatched at her clothes and pricked her skin, she raged at nature and at Otto who'd cut her adrift. Why did he taunt her like this?

'This isn't unusual; you're newly bereaved,' Doctor Khattar had explained. 'It *will* pass.'

Draugr or Revenant? Jude almost asked but sensing that Doctor Khattar was speaking from personal experience she felt reassured.

Jude startled awake. The roof? A tree?

'Otto,' she cried. On the edge of the bed, her husband calm and silent smiled, then releasing her hand he slipped from the room.

The following day she chose to walk safer lanes where she witnessed lakes forming in fields, spoiling the tender crops. She shivered, though not from cold.

That night Jude woke and opening the window found she was all at sea. The saltwater slapped and lapped at the windowsill and on a bludgeon wind spume cast itself high into the air then frothed and fell in a camera–caught blur. Full, yet fractured on this inland sea, the moon cast seductive milky shards. From his boat Otto called urgently beckoning her to come to him. Reaching beyond the fragmented moon Jude stretched — but too far — tumbling down and down she descended into the chilling watery mire.

A neighbour called Doctor Khattar; and the Detective arrived.

'Suicide?' He queried, and then, 'She's drenched?

'Nothing obvious,' the doctor responded. 'Her late husband has been visiting her.'

'*Late* husband?'

'Vivid hallucinations,' the Doctor added and snapping her case shut she stood and sighed.

He crouched down and prised some vegetation trailing from Jude's clasped fist. Baffled, he looked up at the Doctor.

'Bladderwrack.' She stated.

'Seaweed? *Six miles inland?'*

FOUR STOREYS… ONE ENDING, Julian Cadman

FOUR STOREYS… ONE ENDING

The Georgian townhouse is as beautiful as it is deceitful… loaded with treasures but weighed down by a secret. It's every little girl's dream. A house where wishes may come true. A house covering four floors… but home to one flaw.

She loves watching her daughter play in it… whilst he's playing away.

Acting out made up games… whilst he's making up excuses.

Watching her daughter put the plastic beakers down on the tiny table, she finishes her second glass of pinot grigio, putting it down on a faded family photo coaster. Her daughter giggles as she sets the table, and it's joyous to hear a house full of warm laughter. And not the coldness of loathing.

Her daughter's miniature house, where everyone is welcome, serves to magnify the reality of her townhouse that no one enters. A little house full of innocence, versus a big one brushed over in a Farrow and Ball makeover of money fuelled deceit.

Peering in, she shakes her head at the little bed with its pristine white sheets. Her own bed sheets replaced by darker ones keeping secret the bloodied stains of their marriage.

She smiles at her daughter playing happy families. The smile snapping like a frozen twig, when her daughter snatches at a figurine with her tiny fingers. Mirroring how he'd grabbed her neck last night with talons of venom.

Then she recoils as the plastic figurine in his dark suit whacks the porcelain doll, sending it flying across the kitchen.

Her daughter hadn't learnt that from a Punch and Judy show… no, she'd seen it on the Mummy and Daddy reality show.

And, in that moment, she knew it was time to make the call.

The call she should've made when it started.

The call that would change their lives.

THE HITCHHIKER

While ambling along that quiet west-country lane, I listened to their measured, out of sight, around a bend, behind a rise, overtaking approach. At first, just a clippety-clop sound, like a pair of coconut shells being struck together—before the sound of cartwheels on tarmac became audible. When a comforting, pleasant horse smell came into range—without glancing back—I stuck out my thumb. The horse brayed, pulling up beside me.

A proud-looking horse. Big fella—bay coloured with fine, straight, silky white hairy calves. He turned his long, lean white face to scrutinise me with his substantial eyes from under his straight fringe—I swear the horse winked at me. He then whinnied and tossed his long-combed mane.

His human made a throat clearing cough to draw attention to himself. He was driving a colourful gypsy caravan—reins in hand. He, too, was a big fella; with a reassuring smile under his thick black moustache. His was a round face topped off with long thick unruly hair. His dress: mustard yellow cravat, red waistcoat, dark green shirt, chocolate brown corduroys, black heavy shoes. When he asked the usual questions of a hitchhiker—his was an unexpected gentle voice: a Welsh accent; he spoke at the speed he travelled: slow. I climbed up beside him, and holding out my hand, introduced myself.

He softly shook mine with his massive hand: 'Folks call me Horse.'
'And the horse.' Said I.
'Socrates.'
The horse nickered, seeming to snigger.

'We are travelling to Socrates's favourite festival—Big Green Gathering.'
I questioningly pointed up to the long poles wrapped in canvas that projected over my head from the caravan roof.
'Tipi.'
He removed his leather tobacco pouch from a waistcoat pocket, offering it to me.
'Don't smoke.'
His left-hand index-middle fingers were nicotine stained.

Shotgun

"Back home we call them 'shotguns'," he said, standing on the street in Wellington where narrow houses sit an arm's length apart. The streetlights wove the shadows of tī kōuka fronds against wooden walls. The local ruru called to its mate, a mournful plea to return to the nest.

"Everything's guns with you people," I said. The front door of the cottage framed panels of stained glass, liquid-looking red and gold, back-lit by a family's Friday night. I'd stopped to look because it was so beautiful. "Riding shotgun. Shotgun weddings."

"The hallway runs front to back," he said, "to create a breeze. So if you open the doors you can shoot right through the house."

"They're workman's cottages," I corrected him. Built a hundred years ago, one storey high, one room wide, close to the railway and the port. A little patch of garden out the back. Just enough space for a man, alone, stopping for a few years to make a living, not a life. But the city's changed and the cottages have been renovated and now they can fit in a mum, dad and kid, living the Kiwi dream. "They're worth over a million."

"That's crazy," he said. He told me that night he'd bought his ticket back to America. His working visa was expiring. He wanted to go home. "C'mon, it's late."

But I stood longer to look at the glow behind the glass.

Lisbon is yellow, *Rachel Makinson*

'Lisbon is yellow'

The walls are canary-coloured and the trams are yellow like custard. And the golden custard filling of the Pastel de Nata is charred like his arms, the rest of him golden, too, in the evening sun.

We take a boat up to the Belém Tower with our hands cradling paper cups that are refilled with amber-green wine. My hair flails in the breeze and catches my eyes and I catch him smiling at me. And later that evening, once the boat is tired and our stomachs are flip-flopping with booze, we share a cod fish cake — only a flickering tea light between us.

Did You Go A Nice Colour?

The tan spreads across my limbs like fireplace warmth. We buy a watermelon-shaped rubber ring and spin each other over crystalline waves. We pad barefoot, laughing, fingertips tangled. Collapse on a threadbare towel.

The next day, the sun carves lines in my shoulders, unstirred streaks of coffee and cream. I wear the dress and heels you bought me. The straps rub my ankles raw, but when I slip on the cobbled hill your arm is there, strong, ready.

The tan evens out, flowing across the valley of my back while I lie on velvet sand. You head into town, hunting for cigarettes. I scroll shakily through your phone, hunting for proof, ammunition, a reason. A message to a friend reads, '*if she doesnt come on this holiday im done with this bitch i swear.*'

I turn walnut-brown, shining, sore. We throw back daquiris and I watch you flirt with the barmaid. A group of lads with baby pot bellies and Hawaiian shirts do the robot. You spin me round the dancefloor to Tina Turner.

I'm glowing deep red. We stumble back to the hotel room. In my eagerness to kick off the shoes and flop into bed, I don't close the door properly. You let me know by slamming it into the frame until the wood splinters. Later that night you hold a kitchen knife to your wrists. I wrestle it off you. It glows silver on the night-blue grass outside.

We fly home together. The tan peels, turns mottled bronze and rose. Tina wasn't even her real name; Ike gave it to her, believing that naming a life allows you to possess it. A week later it comes off in flakes, leaving fresh, raw skin beneath. You tell me you will kill yourself if I leave.

I leave anyway.

The Dance of My Parents, , August 1946, after My Father Gave His College Sweetheart a Ring and a Promise, Then Left for Philadelphia, Where He Cut the Rug at Justine Belson's Party , Lee Reilly

The Dance of My Parents, August 1946, after My Father Gave His College Sweetheart a Ring and a Promise, Then Left for Philadelphia, Where He Cut the Rug at Justine Belson's Party

1. What Nancy Noble Thought When She Saw Mulligan Jitterbugging with Justine's Little Sister
    Wound tight like a snake (thought it, and said it too).

2.What Justine, the Hostess, Thought
    Nancy's just bitter because her boy's still in the Pacific.

3.How Simon Saw It, as He Grabbed a Lamp before It Fell
    Mulligan better not drop Justine's little sister.

4. How Justine's Little Sister Felt during That Last Swing between Mulligan's Legs
    I'm in love.

5.When the Room Changed and Why
    The girl by the window stored her glasses in her purse, pinched her cheeks, and moved next to Simon.

6. What Simon Thought
    What's she doing?

7. What Justine's Little Sister Thought, Still Swooning from Dancing with Mulligan
    What's that girl doing?

8. What that Girl in the Glasses Not Wearing Her Glasses Knew

She was beautiful Florence Baker, fresh from a broken engagement with an agnostic from Harvard, and she didn't need glasses to find out if Mulligan was Catholic.

9. What Mulligan Knew as He Took Her Hand

He was a catch who'd never been caught.

10. What the Girl Not Wearing Her Glasses Thought as Mulligan Whipped Her into a Hip Lift

Is this safe? This doesn't feel safe.

11. What Mulligan Noticed

Whoa. That was close.

12. What the Girl Not Wearing Her Glasses Almost Said But Didn't

What? Not again?

13. What Mulligan's Sweetheart Back in New Jersey Knew

Catholic—and wound tighter than a major league pitcher.

Farfaphus, Russell Heywood

Farfaphus

'Welcome to those of you who've chosen to become human.'

Arthur winces at Merlin's briefing. They always sound like fiction to him.

'For those of you who've never done this before' says Merlin, 'it may be difficult to believe you'll forget everything. But I assure you, nobody remembers who they are after birth on Earth. Your initial job is to awaken.'

Arthur's been unwell. He can only recall the odd event from centuries of previous lives amongst the humans. But he's sure awakening starts with glimmers, half-dreams, voices whispering the truth in the early years after birth. You grew up thinking you were human though, and only later the full transition might occur.

The doctors have told him to stay at home, and he's happy viewing things from the distant safety of the gallery. From up near the vast lilac domed ceiling, he listens to Merlin's pre-mission talk and feels sorry for the gullible rookies as they stand there like flames of naïve hope flickering in the expanse of the mothership's central hall. Their hopeless plight triggers a memory from his last journey to Earth. At which point, he's overwhelmed with anxieties that he misinterprets as a sense of duty and destiny. Arthur forgets his orders to stay at home and marches downstairs to join them.

Moments after arriving, he realises his error and tries to edge back from the line of twenty recruits he's now standing in. Their mauve humanoid heads turn one by one to observe him. He sees their trusting eyes are like children experiencing their first day of school. Arthur points behind himself in a professional manner, to suggest he's forgotten something in his room. His feet stop moving though, despite his intentions, as

Merlin says, 'Without you, they will wipe the Earth out.' Again, a gut-wrenching feeling of alarm or responsibility, he's no longer sure which nails him to the spot.

He wants to tell these recruits that wave after wave of lies will drown them until they repeat the enemy's stories as if they were their own.

'The main thing is to stay positive and calm,' says Merlin. 'The Earth is a classroom, where you'll learn a lot.'

It's worse than you admit, Merlin, Arthur thinks. *Earth is about death, taxes, madness and being forced to work until you die of stress. Don't forget to mention disease, drunken aggression, train delays, poverty, and the subjugation of nature. In Sweden, there is a plague of self-assembly kitchen units with the wrong screws. Farfaphians have failed to help the humans evolve. The enemy always wins.*

Merlin looks over at Arthur and abruptly holds up her hand.

'May I remind you we all hear your thoughts,' she says, waving to someone in the distance for help.

'Sorry,' Arthur replies politely.

'Each of you will transform negative emotions, similar to those Arthur is now demonstrating,' says Merlin.

Arthur had tried to heal on his home world Farfaphus for a couple of months, walking for hours in the harmonic garden amongst the trees, flowers and rocks that soothed his emotions. He met Farfaphians from his childhood, in purple crystalline spheres that had been home to his principal group of 150. A community free of money, war, or crime. Now, he couldn't even hear himself think.

Millenia ago, Farfaphians had been exploited by a world with more advanced technology. Travellers from other worlds had then helped them evolve beyond their oppressors' grasp. They learned to use telepathy, so nobody could lie or hide their thoughts. Only one thing remained from their primitive past - a purple earflap that twitched when you felt something was wrong. It often embarrassed them. Your ears twitched whether you liked it or not. Farfaphians couldn't understand why the flaps hadn't disappeared when they were not needed anymore.

'Just as we Farfaphians can move between worlds and dimensions,' says Merlin. 'The humans will also one day be free.' Merlin smiles. 'Our state-of-the-art training gives you the key tools to fight the enemy.' She looks over at Arthur. 'But all that training will be close to useless unless you wake up.'

Arthur had to stifle a laugh when she'd said state-of-the-art training. The human birth simulator is still a joke for a start. You get covered in gel and put in a giant artificial womb with an intense heartbeat echoing in your Farfaphian auditory holes. You wiggle down the birth canal, which is more like the horizontal end section of a water slide at an Earth theme park. It flashes bright lights in your eyes as a small crane, shaped like a human arm, grabs you by the feet and holds your body upside down. There is a lack of screaming, drama, or danger. No moments of beauty and joy. And when you arrive covered in slime, a few Farfaphians dressed like humans start talking to you like a moron.

'Hello,' announces one of the Farfaphian staff as she enters the central hall in a blue, medical style tunic and strides across the vast floor towards the group at its centre. Arthur stares at her and notices she seems familiar. Her large bright oval azure eyes have a fleck of purple like his own and her emerald lips seem more sensuous than most Farfaphians. He watches her long, shining dark hair, as waves of light move over the surface of her translucent mauve skin. And as she gets nearer, Arthur senses her eyes are focused on him. He also notices the flaps of skin under her ears as she pushes her hair back. They are twitching.

Guinevere reminds him of someone, although he can't remember ever seeing her before. She still looks uncomfortable. He guesses she must be here because of his problems. The Farfaphian doctors tell him it's a result of overwork, the low moods that make everyone seem fake and the loud thinking that makes everyone scared. Given one thought-free moment, he might get a grip on the compulsive thinking that's being shared with everyone in the surrounding area.

We're all going to die down there, thinks Arthur.

'How are you?' asks the member of staff.

'Are you here to look after me?' asks Arthur. 'Or to shut me up?'

Arthur suspects she's far too healthy to understand him. She doesn't know what it's like when you cannot hear the minds of those around you. Arthur's thoughts rush this way and that, like they're trying to protect him from her and everyone else.

'I haven't lived your life. I'm not here to judge,' she says. Her medical tunic seems threatening to Arthur. 'Do you recognise me?'

'No,' replies Arthur.

Arthur tries again to recall where he's seen her. One well-meaning, upbeat Farfaphian who's never worried about their sanity looks much like another, he guesses. But he can't stop wondering who she is, as her eyes search him like they're old friends.

'My name's Guinevere.'

Guinevere smiles again and beneath it Arthur senses even more intensity in the way she observes him, almost like she's checking for danger in a forgotten memory deep within his mind. He decides her uneasiness must be a kind of primal revulsion because he's what she fears; a living example of what happens when they can't sort you out. He senses a wall between them, keeping her safe from something she doesn't want to catch.

Arthur shrugs and says, 'Glad you'll be safe on the ship.'

'I may be closer than that,' replies Guinevere.

Arthur can still remember awakening as a Farfaphian in his last life on Earth. Born in 1914, he'd become a psychiatrist and walked the wards of a mental asylum in East London during the 1950s. He'd attended to the inmates in that grubby old Victorian building, while refusing to remove parts of their brain. In World War II, he'd served in a front-line hospital for wounded soldiers and was still seeing the faces of those whose arms and legs he'd amputated or stitched ten years later. Blown up bodies appeared when he closed his eyes to sleep each night. They had moved him into psychiatry to help those who hadn't recovered.

He'd been miles away at first, before the Farfaphian agent contacted him. Everyone had been watching the new black and white television in the hospital. They'd gathered around to see Queen Elizabeth's 1953 coronation ceremony. He'd felt like a new era was beginning. The world was changing. And he'd been changing as well. For weeks, he'd dreamed of escape and being liberated into something he couldn't quite see or imagine. He just knew he needed to transform his life. Another person was deep inside him, waiting to emerge. Now those vague intuitions had grown stronger. His existence so far seemed like someone else's story, an accident of birth or history. He didn't belong here. He just needed to hear himself above the noise and find the reason he'd been born.

'It's the frontal lobes, I'm sure; he needs immediate surgery,' the young doctor with cropped brown hair had said to him in a sharp voice. They'd stood in their white coats with their notes, staring at the man lying in one of the thirty shabby beds. It wasn't Arthur's ward, but they had asked him to give his opinion.

Before them that day was a bone thin man who'd spent a decade wandering between jobs. His records showed they'd found him homeless. He claimed to have worked as a clown and musician in the war. His face was smooth, perhaps because someone had just shaved off his long beard. In his late thirties, there was an older tiredness around the eyes. He looked quite close to death and like someone who'd surrendered to that fact. Arthur watched the serene half smile on the man's face as the younger, brusque doctor discussed his future. He'd thumbed through the scant medical records. Wounded in the war. The man said it was during a stint entertaining the troops in India.

'How are you today?' Arthur hears himself asking the Farfaphian, who would help him awaken in that life. He hadn't replied at first and just smiled at the young doctor, who was pushing his hair back, with fingers spread and half clenched like a claw.

'Similar to cases reported in America,' the young doctor said. 'I'll show you.' He provided a professional smile. 'Where are you from?'

'I'm from Farfaphus,' replied the man lying in the bed.

'A full-blown alien,' the doctor explained.

Arthur had gazed into the patient's eyes. Just as now, he glares into Guinevere's on the mothership.

'Farfaphus,' Arthur asks the patient. 'What's it like?'

'Our minds are open, and there's no war.'

Arthur remembers, he felt the man was telling the truth. A sudden sense of loyalty arose in him. The young doctor laughed and said, 'It gets worse. They reproduce through mental transmissions of energy.'

'I think we need to keep him under observation for longer,' says Arthur. 'I want to run more tests; the medication may be wrong.'

'But' said the younger doctor, looking horrified. 'I can't be responsible if he's not operated on.'

The next day, Arthur had gone to see the patient alone. He'd enquired further about Farfaphus.

'It's where you're from,' said the patient. 'We travelled here, many of us. But our missions alter, things go wrong.'

'Where are your friends, then?' Arthur remembers the slight cynicism in his voice.

'Dozens of Farfaphian casualties are here.'

'Maybe it's better to keep quiet about them for now.' Arthur remembers himself smiling and patting the man's hand. He'd looked deep into the patient's eyes and felt only kindness coming from him.

'Our enemy is destroying everyone,' the patient replied in a calm voice.

Arthur had laughed, saying, 'I often think like that.' The patient didn't laugh though and instead reached out with his right hand and touched Arthur's arm, sending a pulse of energy through him that spread throughout his body.

'What was that?' he'd asked, trying to pull away but finding himself unable to move.

'We will see now,' said the patient. His eyes brightened and glowed. Arthur felt himself expanding with light and joy. The radiant patient leaned forward, grabbing both Arthur's hands. 'Farfaphus,' said the patient. Arthur sensed more energy surging into him, as the patient transformed into a beautiful mauve humanoid creature with long, glistening red hair and azure oval eyes. 'We only use the human bodies to live on Earth.'

'I'm unwell,' Arthur remembers his human mind thinking as waves of information about Farfaphus entered his consciousness.

'What are you telling me? Who am I?' he'd asked.

'We have visited many times,' said the Farfaphian. He'd held Arthur's hands tighter. 'Let us see more.'

'What am I?'

'A Farfaphian,' replied the patient. He placed his hands on Arthur's shoulders. They'd floated out of their human body's into the starry night. 'There are frequencies of joy and other planets where terror lives.' Arthur saw a world of heavenly beings, then turned to see a world with half-human and animal faces, mouthing silent screams inside steel cages, as robots with electric saws chopped them like logs. 'We're connected to almost infinite dimensions. But this energy form is difficult to maintain. The enemy found me before I could stabilise. We must return now.'

Arthur tried to rationalise what had just happened when he was alone in his office. The patient's delusion must have taken him over. It had been an extreme case of transference. But that night, he dreamt about Farfaphus. He saw himself growing up in beautiful gardens, where wise tree beings helped him discover the interrelatedness of all life. Beneath a pink, hazy sky with two lemon suns, delicate indigo Briallian flowers, shaped like giant snowflakes, blossomed. Their petals vibrated with tranquil, rhythmic melodies. Luminescent green, white, and blue trees answered them with gentle hums and whispering songs. He'd seen his childhood home, inside the crystalline sphere where a sense of care and wonder pervaded every room. Inside an orb made from pure energy, he'd glided over the blue and white rolling hills of Farfaphus, marvelling at the sparkling, clear oceans abundant with life.

The next day, Arthur realised many other inmates at the hospital were agents from Farfaphus. He worked every hour to help his new friends. The mothership never arrived; it'd been down to him. He'd got as many of the agents released as he could. Unfortunately, he'd not been able to hide his activities from the other staff and one day, the enemy found him.

'Dr Hythe's arrived to see you,' the nurse had said. 'He's brought several colleagues.'

They were polite at first. Then, he was questioned for two days about irregularities in his procedure. Officials checked his files and asked the staff about his behaviour.

'The findings are quite clear, and we are unanimous,' Dr Hythe had said. They were in a large Victorian room with an old grandfather clock. A panel of doctors watched him, like he wasn't quite human anymore. He sat alone on the other side of the long mahogany table. Dr Hythe said, 'It's unfortunate, but it seems there's no way back. Rigorous care is the only option. The man you were is lost.' Arthur had ended up as a patient himself, silenced.

The Farfaphian doctors say his nervous system was so overloaded in that last life, it will take years to heal. After he'd become a patient, he kept working. More galactic agents had arrived. But without authority, it was tough. Any glimmers of hope were crushed. He'd lived amongst those broken and flattened daily. Soon, nobody was left to notice. Arthur died inside years before he left that body, pumped with pills, staring at people too shattered to tell their tale. He wasn't able to keep his sense of Farfaphian identity. But when all connection to himself and others disappeared, he'd kept repeating stories, memories from his childhood growing up on Farfaphus that had once seemed true.

After he left Earth, he kept waking up in sweats. One night, he must have become convinced he was still an overworked psychiatrist. He'd got out of his white, floating cocoon bed in the rejuvenation centre and gone to the harmonic gardens. He'd been found there, sleepwalking. Several carers were called to help him home as he was spotted carrying a laser needle, attempting to administer injections to passers-by. Today, as he faces another journey, another body, he tries to keep up appearances for the newcomers, but feels worse than a wreck.

As he stands staring at Guinevere's fraught face, an armoured warrior appears in his mind being killed with a sword in some mud filled hell hole. Arthur can see the Farfaphian recruits looking, mostly with pity. A part of him doesn't care if they can hear the horror and confusion inside his mind. Another part of him is terrified he's forgotten how to be a Farfaphian.

The Escalator

I join the queue for the down escalator, pushing back the hood of my raincoat. The lights seem duller than usual and two strips are blinking randomly. A small child on her father's shoulders lets out a little screech in time with the lights. Off, on, off on, eee, silence, eee, silence. Between cries, she grins, high above the crowd, a cloth monkey clutched under one arm. A loud electric buzz fills the air, and there is a final, fractionally longer black-out, before the lights come on properly. The little girl dances the monkey on her father's head.

A young woman – short and blonde with a half-moon tattoo on her cheekbone – glances at me. I smile at her. We won't have to wait in the dark, we are saying, or take the stairs. But she isn't looking at me, she's looking at a man in front of me, at his back, his t-shirt. It's covered in tiny letters, words I can't read without my glasses. She can, obviously, and the message makes her frown.

I edge forward with the shifting crowd, still yards from the top of the escalator. I lift my toes inside my trainers, adjust my shoulder bag. Others have their bags on their backs. Matching yellow rucksacks for a cluster of French-speakers ahead. A canvas khaki thing to my right, bulging with odd shapes over a young shoulder. A few inches in front of my nose is a neat padded rectangle perched high on someone's back. I could undo the zip right now and slip out the slim, glossy laptop that's certainly inside.

I tighten my armpit over my bag. My laptop is old. My office shoes – a pair of cheap pumps – are tucked down one side, a tube of hand cream on the other. My book is a second-hand paperback – an okay romance with a woman in a sunhat on the front. Nothing I'd miss. But my insides contract at the idea of being robbed in such a public way, at a stranger poking into my life and my possessions, while people look the other way. I pull my shoulders forward, pressing the side pocket of my bag against my tummy, making it a shield.

Mother's always telling me about my posture. Don't stoop. Push your shoulders back. But I feel tall enough already. She's always been petite, and straight as a ramrod. In her eyes, I still need correcting. Do you really need a second biscuit? Your elbow's on the table and I've not finished eating. Don't turn out your feet like that. Seventy-four and she does yoga in front of morning TV every day, priding herself on her flat stomach and slim ankles. Lilian – my friend Anthea's mother – is much older in herself. On my weekly visits, I rub cuticle oil into Lilian's dry, ridged nails and then she holds my hand and chats on about the past. Anthea and I played netball together at school. Decades ago. Now, I phone every Friday night to give her an update on Lilian's health, though I often have to leave a message.

The girl with the tattoo has her backpack resting on her front, like a baby in a papoose. Long ago, I thought I'd wear my newborn like that. Dad thought baby slings were a great invention. 'I'd love to have carried you in one of these,' he'd said, pointing to a picture in the catalogue. 'But your mum always wanted to use the big pram.' He'd grinned. 'Now's my chance, eh? I can be cool Grandad.' I was only a few weeks along. It was too early to buy anything.

There's an announcement over the PA system but the sound is distorted. I can't make it out. A delay? A station closure? A jumper on the Northern line? It's usually the Northern line. Like this one, it has some of the deepest platforms. Perhaps that's why people choose them, as a match for the depth of their despair. Or for the sense of privacy. In fact, I found out, those platforms are often the safest, because of the drainage pits. A pit under the tracks reduces the chances of dying by about 30%.

I look sideways for the girl with the cheekbone tattoo, to see her reaction to the unintelligible message. But the crowd has pushed her ahead, or behind. Her place by my side has been taken by a Black man, a navy suit jacket draped from one finger over his shoulder. He's nodding, eyes half-closed, to whatever is playing on his headphones. I drop my head and see that they're plugged into a Walkman clipped to his belt. The little plastic door is scratched and there's a sticker on it, slightly off-centre. It's a genuine 80s relic, by the looks – not some modern retro remake. I had one just the same – a birthday present from Dad when I was fourteen. Fifteen. He made a tape too. Fleetwood Mac and The Beatles and Stevie Ray Vaughan. All the songs he loved to play in the car when he drove me to swimming on Friday nights, listed in his tiny capital letters on the insert card. Between some tracks there was a crackle and a tiny thud – the lift and drop of the needle. His record-player sat in pride of place on the cabinet in the lounge.

Another few shuffles of the crowd and I am standing square in the middle of a metal panel. Near my left toe is a lever, folded flush. A service door. I imagine someone, down there, trying to push it open. I think of him every time I pass this place. He's chunky and solid in his grey overalls, and his faded hard-hat tips backwards as he reaches up, pushing, calling out. He spends his days down there, in the network of tunnels. The underground of the underground. There are lights – I imagine domes studded at intervals along the walls that emit an eerie glow – but at his feet it's dark. Rats scurry and try to gnaw through the thick cables clamped in place. That's what the man does all day – checks the cables. Sometimes I wonder why he tries to get out now, at this busiest time? Then I remember he's not real.

The man with the little ballet girl is right in front of me. She's on his hip now, head resting on his shoulder, one hand gripping the cloth monkey tail at his back. Finally, the heads of the crowd are dipping as they step onto the escalator. This escalator is one of the longest in the city. The platforms far below are tiled in toilet-white. The air that blows through with the trains is cool and stale. There are no buskers or vending machines. The hoardings aren't often refreshed so their adverts are old, but still ungraffitied. It must be too much trouble, to go down there with the spray paints.

My right foot slides forward on to the first moving stair and I feel a familiar lurch of attention to my balance. Will I stumble? Will I sway and press into the body ahead or behind? I'm carrying a few middle-age pounds. If I topple, I'll start a cascade, a domino effect. I picture them – the French-speakers, cheekbone tattoo girl, the man in the suit, the toddler in her father's arms – all struggling to stay upright, just managing, righting themselves, tutting, looking around to see who to blame. I plant my feet firmly, gripping the black rubber of the handrail. Mother wouldn't. She'd grasp her own forearms, the short handles of her stiff handbag tucked in the crook of one arm. The tube is a key battlefield in her lifelong war on germs. She carries wipes everywhere and opens doors with her elbow if she can.

A long line of posters slides by. West End musicals. Serious drama at the National. The summer season – dates long past – at The Globe. In a few weeks, there's an exhibition by an artist I don't know at the Royal Academy. I went there once. Not inside, only to the courtyard – the meeting point for me and a boy I knew. Our second date. It was a freezing day – a nose-running, lip-chapping wind was blowing and I pushed my mittened hands together as I waited at the edge of the square. 'See you at the statue,' he'd said, but I felt conspicuous there, in the middle. I was far too early. I was eighteen and his name was

Adam Burke, which made Mother smirk. 'Burke by name, berk by nature,' she said. I met him through Anthea. He went to her church. When he arrived, I was so busy retying my scarf and pulling down my hat that I didn't realise he was going to kiss me and I missed it. He put one arm over my shoulders as we walked, and the only way I could step evenly beside him was to thread my arm around his waist. His anorak made his waist bulky – there was nothing to hold on to or wedge my hand in place. My arm ached with the effort of keeping it there. We walked through Trafalgar Square to Covent Garden where we stood to watch a unicyclist performing for the winter shoppers. I was relieved to take back my hand, which was numb even inside my mitten. I remember the fake wobbling of the cycling man before his triumphant finale, and even the hat he passed round – a tatty red bowler, a clown's prop. But I don't remember what we talked about, Adam and me, or the name of the pub where we went to warm up.

He laced his fingers through mine as we sipped half-pints of cider.

At Christmas, I think, I'll go to Covent Garden with the girls from the office – it's what they do every year. Maybe we'll pass that pub, or the girls will push their way through a door and I'll recognise the bar and the corner table where Adam and I sat.

I never go in pubs on my own.

On the up escalator is a man with greying curly hair. A leather coat is folded tidily over his arm. His ears are prominent, his forehead broad and friendly. Could that be Adam? Slim, with just a bit of a belly. My Adam was skinny – his frame bony against mine on the few nights we lay together on his bed. We never progressed past kissing. His hair was curly too, black and always wet-looking. His ears stuck out in just that way. Mother had said, why would a boy with such large ears want to draw attention to them by having one pierced?

It can't be him. Nearly ten million Londoners, the paper said last week. What are the chances of passing just the one I was thinking of, at just this particular moment? I let my gaze follow the man, and as he slides away I see his shirt is untucked at the back. Then he's gone.

I don't even know if Adam's still in London. The last I heard, from Lilian, he'd married a woman from Romania, or Albania, or somewhere. They lived south of the river for a while. She was a nurse and he was in sales. They didn't have any children so the divorce was relatively easy.

The RA poster has made me think of Adam Burke every day for the last month.

I am nearing the bottom of the escalator, and the people ahead are levelling out. I concentrate when it's my turn, watching my feet again and the narrow grooves in the metal as the step ahead of mine disappears under the yellow lip. Passengers peel away through tunnels to right and left. I speed up, dodging a man in a long woollen overcoat, a small dog under his arm. A woman with a smart, swinging mac is pulling a hat off and running a hand through short hair. A man with a reddish beard is wrestling himself out of a waterproof. I veer round him and someone barges into me.

'What the fuck?'

'Sorry, sorry,' I say. A young man in sporty clothes, hood up.

I step – this way, that way – but he does the same, so that we are dancing stupidly in the space we've made. Then a glare and he is gone.

I watch his white trainers disappear, thinking of the story he will tell – a dowdy woman stepping blindly in his way.

Did he hear my apology? I turn left, through a narrow linkway, and left again.

I know Dad left London. He sent a few postcards, at first. Scarborough. The Lakes. The Isle of Arran. 'Beautiful place. Raining of course! Love you, Dad.' Mother would leave the cards on the mat and we never discussed them. They'd not been happy for years, but when he supported me over the baby – that broke the marriage. From the moment I told them I was pregnant, Mother could barely look at me. Her purse-lipped whispers travelled like a bad smell through doors and floorboards. Dad's replies grew quieter and quieter, and then one day when I came home from work, he was gone. I booked myself into the clinic the next week. I dreaded the waiting room, but it was all right. Tight smiles all round and gentle lift music. The receptionist had a soft voice.

That first tape Dad made me was already a decade old. I wore it to breaking point, pressing the rewind button again and again, listening to those tiny in-between moments over and over.

On the next escalator, I hear a deep voice behind me and, turning, I see the little girl with her dad. She is standing next to him, dirty pink ballet pumps turned outwards, her hand gripped in his, her arm slightly over-stretched because he is tall. She gazes up at him, nodding big-eyed at what he has just said.

A tiny sob rises in my throat and I look away.

I blink, looking at my hand on the moving rail, the faint hairs catching the light. My hand is Londoner-pale, squarish, ringless. Like Mother's. She hasn't worn a ring since she took off her wedding band, the day Dad left. A long time later, letters came. 'Karen and I have found a flat. We're redecorating and we move in next month.' He invited me to the wedding but it would have killed Mother if I'd gone. In his last Christmas card, he included an email address and a mobile number. There's been no news for years now.

My platform is quiet. I sit alone on a bench that is three plastic seats welded together with a metal mesh. A handful of people are waiting, far enough away to be only shapes of grey. They don't know each other but they know a train door will open there, where they stand. The train comes – one of the new ones, shiny blue and white with red doors. Not mine. Three schoolboys tumble out in front of me, all black blazers and laughing faces. The grey bodies step aboard.

Once the train has gone, I stand up. Ballet child is jumping nearby. Her little feet are almost graceful in the air, but her baby-body imposes itself each time she lands – with a slight wobble, crouching, sticking out her bottom. On the electric sign, yellow letters spin and flicker, spelling nothing. The darkness where the next train will come from is silent and empty. A mouth, or a cave. Somewhere monsters live. I look away. I hear a train rumble. The tracks are shiny ribbons against black stones. There's no drainage pit here.

When the next train comes, it isn't stopping. My body feels sucked forward. My breath whips away as carriage after carriage strips past, making the wind race. I want to scream into the white noise. I hold on tight with both hands to the strap of my bag. The air that's left behind settles slowly. My ears adjust to the silence. My eyes focus on the hard black lines of the tube poster, punctuated neatly with a small, regular circle for each stop.

My ballet baby is at the edge of the platform, right at the edge, her toes in those soft shoes almost curling over the concrete lip. Her father has his phone to his ear, listening. 'That's right. Look, the plan is . . . ' Listening again. She is looking down, sucking her thumb, the tail of her monkey dangling from the fist at her mouth. She is suddenly tired, I can see. She sways. When she drops the monkey it lands, half-over the edge, head flopping. I move fast, not thinking, seeing its balance shift, seeing it fall way out of reach to the littery darkness below – but I grab it just in time.

The child has stepped back of her own accord. Still crouching on the edge, I hold out the monkey and she takes her thumb from her mouth and pushes both hands out in front of her, almost flat. I lay the toy on them. She nods at me, eyes wide and serious, turns and runs to her father, burying her face in his thigh. He's seen nothing. He strokes her head and ends his call and lifts her to his hip in one movement. The monkey is folded into place at his back once more.

I stand and walk away from the tracks. I pass my plastic seat, take the first escalator, and the next. Nearing ground level, I take my hand from the rail, unzip the inner pocket of my bag and fetch out my phone. It takes a while to find what I'm looking for.

I am going to be late for supper, but when I reach the street, I don't call Mother.

THE DEATH CAFÉ IS CLOSED, Rosalyn Huxley

THE DEATH CAFÉ IS CLOSED

At first, the *Death Café* met in a real café. People dropped in to discuss death and dying over a latte or chai tea. But even if Suzie was brave enough to share existential anxieties in public, she'd been too busy then. Elite nannying was full-on, and when she wasn't serving rich people and their babies, she was keeping her parents alive. Doing their admin, keeping them safe and stimulated. Like nannying, but without a wage. Only the cat needed a light touch.

Then the café, the real one not the Death Café, transformed into a restaurant and the . the Death Café participants formed small groups that met in members' homes. Like book clubs, but without the wine. Suzie thought meeting in a private space would be easier and plucked up the courage to phone. But none of the groups had room.

"It's partly practical, our homes are too small for more than five or six to meet," explained Maria, the coordinator. "And partly spiritual or, if you like, psychological. Too heavy a burden to support a crowd as they pop off the mortal coil. I'll put you on the waiting list."

It took three years before the pandemic culled a space for Suzie. Covid didn't kill them (pneumonia and urinary infections did that), but she had to give up her job because she couldn't bubble with babies and her parents. When the vaccines arrived she'd already inherited her parents' bungalow and buried the cat in their garden.

As a nanny, Suzie was well-versed in saying goodbye. You got close to a family, helped them flourish and, after a while you moved on. Sometimes you were glad to leave. It was different when the family was your own. She missed her parents. She did not want to go back to work. She did not need to.

Suzie started renovating the bungalow. She didn't mind that tradespeople and materials were in short supply. Waiting for plumbers or glaziers left time to try the many pleasant activities available for non-working people who want to keep active and stimulated: walking netball, poetry appreciation, and the Ramblers. She enjoyed the casual exchanges and easy conversations that these groups offered. She got fitter, let her hair turn silver.

When she joined the leisure centre, she used her full name to signal that she was, finally, a grown-up. But *Susannah* was a mouthful to shout across the netball court and her teammates shortened it to *Suze*. Which seemed even sillier than Suzie.

Retirement was enjoyable. She was in good health and her parents had paid off the bungalow's mortgage years ago. But every now and then, fears for the future and the losses she'd experienced in the past, felt overwhelming and Suzie yearned for a deeper connection, somewhere she could find answers to the big questions about growing old and dying. The national Death Café network, like everything post-pandemic, had online groups, but discussing funeral plans or reincarnation on zoom felt ridiculous, and Suzie pretended her broadband was too weak.

At last, Maria phoned. Long-covid had taken a member of her group. "We've changed our name but we're the same. Come next Wednesday for a taster. If it doesn't work for you, we won't be offended."

"What's the new name?" asked Suzie. She'd grown fond of *Death Café*. Macabre but comic, like dancing skeletons she'd seen in Cancun when a family took her on holiday to Mexico.

"We wanted something more attractive. Joyful. Positive." Suzie hummed an assent. An interesting conversation already. "*Ageing Graciously*," said Maria. "Less passive. A verb, not a thing. Look forward to meeting you, Suzie."

"It's Anna, actually," said Suzie. This is a good moment to launch a version of Susannah that was both short and mature. "I've changed my name too."

Maria lived in a Victorian cottage on a quiet road on the eastern side of town. The front garden brimmed with birdfeeders and bamboo. A windchime swayed above the front door.

"Welcome. Help yourself to slippers." Suzie-Anna followed Maria into a warm conservatory filled with house plants and coloured glass. "Let me introduce you to Stephen, Allison, and Carlos. Everyone, this is Anna."

A pale, thin man rose awkwardly from the cane sofa to extend a swollen-knuckle hand. "Anna, a perfect palindrome in a name," he smiled. "Stephen Shanks-Smith. Good to meet you."

"And a perfect name for this group," said his tanned, well-covered neighbour. "Anna, from Channah, the gracious one." He lifted a fleshy hand and silver bracelets rattled. "Salut Anna. Carlos Jones at your service."

"Welcome Anna, I'm Allison," said a woman in a headscarf. "Come and sit by the log burner."

"I'll get the coffee," said Maria.

The morning was over too quickly. Anna buzzed. The members shared a wide range of health, family, and finance problems. Everyone listened intently and only offered advice when it was asked for. Then they watched a YouTube video about a drone service that scattered ashes in hard-to-reach burial sites. Next, they discussed Allison's Power of Attorney forms and finally, Carlos read a poem in memory of the member who had died. Apart from Maria's teary recounting of a telephone row with her daughter, there had been no drama, and nothing felt awkward or embarrassing. When Stephen invited Anna to share, she did. It all tumbled out, her parents, the cat, the bungalow. Allison passed the box of tissues and Carlos handed a plate of figs.

Maria phoned the next day. "We'd love you to age graciously with us, Anna." It was affirming, like being chosen for the netball team.

"Thank you. It's just what I need. You are all so welcoming and it is such a relief to discuss these difficult things."

"Humans are the only animals that think about the end of life," murmured Maria.

"Right," said Anna, eyeing the purple crocuses where the cat was buried.

"We're going on a day trip for the next meeting," said Maria. "To *Green Endings*. Help Allison choose her spot. Bring boots. It can be muddy."

The *Ageing Graciously* group kept things fresh, alternating between contemplative sessions at Maria's and days out to death-related attractions. Carlos's camper van had an excellent sound system, a mini-fridge, and plenty of room for Allison's wheelchair when it was needed. They packed cans of kombucha and took turns curating the music. They visited a heritage willow centre where eco-coffins were made, compared notes on the three crematoria within a forty minute drive, and, at midsummer, Carlos drove the group to an older people's circle-singing workshop where Anna danced barefoot till dawn.

Anna told the group things she'd never shared with anyone and with every revelation, she felt lighter. Shedding the heaviness of her previous life. She grew literally lighter too; the fat that coated her for half a century, turning into muscle. The walking netball team made her captain.

The videos they watched when *Ageing Graciously* met at Maria's were the education she'd always wanted; Stephen's selections rooted in science, Carlos's in culture, and Allison's yo-yoed from Quakerism to witchcraft depending on her chemo cycle. Nothing was mocked and no one's opinions dismissed. Between meetings, the group emailed links to each other for further reading or viewing. If Anna couldn't download something (the bungalow's broadband really was poor) then Carlos made a hard copy and brought it to her door.

Maria managed the group well. Graciously even. When busy with refreshments or Allison's increasingly complex medical care, she still monitored every conversation, tactfully intervening if the videos were too long or incomprehensible.

"Shall I summarise?" Maria asked after a dense lecture by a Canadian psychologist that left Allison asleep and Anna feeling stupid. Everyone nodded. "The Buddha says we don't respond to what happens, we respond to our perception of what happens. Our minds create the world." Everyone nodded again. Maria passed polenta cake. Graciously.

Carlos started delivering more than printouts; books of poetry, jars of homemade dipping sauce, and fresh-cut flowers from his allotment. He dug a vegetable plot for Anna in (far from the cat's burial site) and when the clocks went back, and Maria ordered winter logs Carlos began to warm Anna with a passion she had never imagined was feasible.

The others pretended not to notice the *Ageing Graciously* romance but when it was clear that Allison would not be leaving the hospice, Maria created a rota for visits, putting Stephen on mornings which fitted in with the buses he now required, herself on afternoons, and Carlos and Anna on nights.

The couple sat either side of Allison's bed in the warm, softly lit room. Carlos read poems and sang low, melancholy songs in Spanish and Portuguese. Anna could only remember lullabies for babies but when Carlos harmonised with her the words seemed more profound and the sound was soothing.

Allison's final breath came at three. They'd been singing "Hush little baby don't say a word" and stopped for a moment to hold hands and gaze at the harvest moon. Anna opened the window and Allison slipped out.

Allison's passing prompted Maria to mend the rift with her daughter. She spent more and more time away so the *Ageing Graciously* meetings moved to Anna's bungalow and now it was Anna who lit a fire and baked polenta cake. The group knew they should introduce a new member, perhaps two, but Maria had the waiting list, and she was preoccupied with her daughter's divorce.

When Stephen fell in a Megabus and broke his hip Carlos and Anna sprung into action. Stephen was frailer than anyone had realised and the many steps and stairs in his cluttered home were impossible to navigate. The bungalow's spare room had a garden view. They hired a mobility bed and Stephen watched Carlos digging and weeding while Anna cooked soup and sat by his bed reading aloud from the medical and science journals he adored. Stephen only interrupted when she struggled to pronounce a chemical or condition. She was still learning.

"I am in a state of grace," whispered Stephen when Anna hugged him goodbye before a walking netball weekend tournament. "Marked by your kindness and courtesy."

"And love," said Anna. Another thing she'd never said to anyone before.

They buried Stephen a few meters from Allison at *Green Endings*. Maria returned for the funeral and recited the verses Stephen had selected many *Ageing Graciously* meetings before. It was the moment to discuss which new members to approach but Maria said she was selling her house to live permanently with her daughter and Carlos and Anna couldn't face getting to know three new people, watching the same videos, organising more trips to green burial sites, and then having to support the new members as they reached the end of their lives.

"The Death Café must find new owners, Carlos," said Anna as they polished the camper van for a trip to Cornwall. "I have never felt so alive."

"And you have never looked so beautiful, my graceful *Su Sann Ha*," beamed Carlos. "We don't need new members. We will be there for each other. Like we were for Allison and Stephen." He touched her eyelids with his lips in the way she loved.

It took a few months to complete the probate tasks for Allison and Stephen. Anna used the time to train up a new captain for the walking netball team and put the bungalow on Airbnb. By midsummer, a year after they'd all danced barefoot, Anna's vegetable plot was bursting with strawberries, raspberries, and redcurrants. Anna learned how to make jam and stored the jars next to Carlos's chilli jelly at the bottom of the camper van's wardrobe. Her jam was a deeper red than his jelly, but both tasted delicious. In different ways.

When Maria emailed photos of her first great-grandchild, and reviews of the bungalow had pushed it to the top of the Airbnb listings, Carlos persuaded Anna to upgrade from the cold beaches of Cornwall to the warm Mediterranean.

"We'll journey through France, to Spain and Portugal, then onto Morocco and, who knows? We have only ourselves to care for. We'll follow the sun and eat jam and chilli jelly every day. With the best local coffee and bread we can find."

Susannah touched his mouth. "I'm glad to move on this time."

Carlos nodded. "The Death Café is closed."

Terracotta Lavender, Karen Storey

Terracotta Lavender

Flowers. You're kidding, right? I'd laugh if I could. Never thought I'd see the day when my father gave me flowers. I guess a father might do that for a daughter, but for a son? Although hey, you know something? They're pretty damn cool. Who would have thought that a terracotta lily would sit so perfectly against a lavender rose? I'm not being facetious. It's clear you put a lot of thought into these.

They actually surpass the enormous bunch of roses you pressed to your mistress behind the office block. Yeah, I heard about that. Mum found out when your receptionist slurred it at your office Christmas party. I can also see how you put more thought into my flowers than the pretty clutch of peonies you gave to your third wife the day before she left you.

Don't worry, I'm not judging you, just stating my observations on the flowers. And yeah, as I look at these again, the reaching out of the lily petals and the way the roses are still opening, these flowers are, frankly, awesome. Reaching and opening, those are actions I can appreciate.

I appreciate other things too. Like the futility of manufactured silence. When I look at the times we didn't speak, do you know those months would outnumber each of these flowers here that you'd carefully chosen? In fact, take this incredible bouquet and add to it. Add to it some more until each flower that nestles against the other stretches on through the length of this aisle, covering every floor tile. Add more flowers still, perhaps half a dozen leaping into the hands of every person standing here behind these wooden pews.

The days we didn't speak would still outnumber those flowers.

I didn't show it enough when you came to break the silence. I wanted to thrust my fist in the air. Instead, I clasped my trembling fingers while you sat in the chair opposite me.

Do you remember that day? It was a week after my birthday. I gave you a hint of my cheer when I joked with you. You didn't smile. My appearance shocked you. I could tell.

I had lost so much weight since you'd last seen me. I asked if you remembered I'd celebrated a birthday a week ago. Forty-seven. You'd forgotten. I grinned, letting you know it was okay, expected even. I said how funny it seemed we were always reversed in life, like the numbers of our current ages. You were seventy-four to my forty-seven. I asked if you got it. You didn't smile at the coincidence, your eyes instead fought against the tears that glistened.

I wondered if you'd been remembering, like me, how our roles would often reverse. The Sunday morning when I was seventeen. I found you at the breakfast table with an empty vodka bottle. Your shoulders slumped forward, the side of your face stuck to the plastic tablecloth. I absorbed the role of my mother, whom you had abandoned two years before. I shook you awake and made you coffee. Me, the weekend guest, the part-time son. I insisted you have a shower and dress before your girlfriend came and saw you like that.

Oh and then, do you remember the time when I was twenty-two, and you got me a job in your office? I sat next to you in a client meeting, frantically scribbling notes for you, giving you the answers to the client's queries. You hadn't prepared, having just come from a more intimate meeting with your personal assistant.

When you last came to visit, I wanted us to laugh at that crazy scene, but I didn't bring it up. You see, even though I'd reached the point where I saw how the past between us no longer mattered, you weren't there yet. I decided not to worry too much about that. I figured one day you'd simply catch up.

And you did.

Today.

The flowers.

I can feel how incredibly hard this is for you. The curling and uncurling of your fingers into your palms, like you're trying to crush the guilt you're holding. Just let that drop from your hands, okay?

This? This is nothing. Just the last episode of our twisted journey, that's all. One where our roles merely got reversed again. At forty-seven, my illness made me feel like a seventy-four-year-old. You, with your energy for new experiences, your passion for women and for partying, you are forty-seven.

You will always be young.

I will never be young again.

If there was a way I could tell you, I would say I am grateful, Dad. For the love that we hid from each other, that got a bit tangled like the trailing ivy on the arrangement you purchased for me today. You must have spent hours at the florist choosing and fretting, determined to get it right. I get it. For you, finding the right flowers would help me see the love in your heart.

I see it.

How you chose two flowers so different with colours anyone might assume would clash. Yet put together, you can't imagine any combination more rewarding.

The bright terracotta of the lily beside the lavender of the rose sits so perfectly against the dark wood of my coffin. I promise you this, Dad, you'll see these colours together again. Perhaps in a butterfly or on a clothes mannequin as you pass a shop window. That will be me, telling you I got it. I saw that love in your heart and I'm sending the tenderness that lived in mine right back at you.

You see, death is not the end of love. I promise it continues to blow softly between the veil of your world and mine. It takes on momentum and flourishes, picking up our memory fragments of happiness. Fragments of delight and love.

You know, it's not unlike these roses and lilies picking up fragments of sun through the church's stained glass. Their petals expanding, opening still. Think about it. Someone cut the life source away with their roots, yet the flowers continue to reach out, not in fear, but in gratitude, for another moment of the sun's love.

I bet if you held out your hand, you could touch it. That invisible energy that flourishes between the sunlight and the terracotta lily that sits beside a lavender rose.

Woman Is Stone, Michael Pearson

Woman Is Stone

From stone they're born,
with necks that grunt.
Here to mourn
by headless hunt.
Deceased desire
that flesh begets,
bequeath your wants
and do not fret.

The Gol will not come.

…

Villagers darted left and right with muddy garments and irrational minds. Anna couldn't look away. It was like watching roadkill. But Anna had never seen roadkill. She'd never left the village.

The sight was enthralling. Everyone bounced from house to house and body to body, not knowing where they were running from or to. But they all knew what they were running from. Anna knew. The Gol were coming to take their heads.

She hadn't even noticed the splinters pushing into her fingertips as she grasped the window frame and pulled her head through the open curtain. Her eyes stretched open as her breath slowed to near silence. Take the whole dammed village she thought. Take them!

…

Five hundred crunches under foot are often more accurate than the path we can see. That was the distance to the Gol Stone. Texture was language in the forest and Anna knew to walk the distance with her eyes closed. With arms extended sidewards, she felt for leftover leaves and bare branches in case the sprites tried to tease her off path. But they seemed to guide her straight there. The change in the air on her skin let her know she'd arrived. It was humid. Tactile. Something ancient breathed there.

Pulling her garment too far above her knees, she knelt on the ground and opened her eyes. It looked like no other stone. This was made of many stones folded one over another to form a single mound. A thousand streams had made its surface smooth. It stood eleven feet tall and arched forward, looking down with a crooked back so it could cherish the heads below.

On the floor lay a pile of berries. It was the season of The Turning of the Sun and like every turn, the village gave the Gol Stone every berry they harvested in return for patience and protection.

Anna licked her lips and yearned. For years she'd wondered what they tasted of. These juicy gifts that faded into the ground until they vanished without attention. No, she wouldn't let this happen anymore. She couldn't suppress this urge. She sunk her hands into the mound and scooped upwards. Berries bounced off her mouth and cheeks as juices squirted red, pink and purple. This was a taste she never thought possible and worth a thousand bowls of porridge. More and more she shovelled until nothing remained but pulp and dark stains.

She realised her breathing had stopped and gasped to rectify the situation. With two fingers, she adjusted her bonnet and looked at the Gol Stone. Her eyes trailed up and up and up until they landed on the lurching tip. It looked at her. She was sure. She squinted and stared back, waiting, sneering

"Come on you cowards! Come get me!"

With disappointment and dirty clothes, Anna left, alone.

...

When people run back and forth on mud it just gets muddier. Whipped like chocolate frosting and turned into brown clouds. Of course, Anna didn't know what chocolate frosting was. But she delighted nonetheless. She grinned at the rows of lost boots, sunken in their trenches and flailing their wet, skinny arms. Flicks and spots flew into the air, hitting fleeing faces like bullets.

"Your bonnet! Where is your bonnet?!" The elder roared and spat as he grabbed a villager's collar, shaking them like a ragdoll. Anna winced as her skin tightened and recoiled from her back, up to her bruised neck. On the floor her bonnet sat in an ugly pile. It peered up with two purple fingerprints for eyes, begging for retrieval. She grabbed it and picked at the line of grey, wooden buttons that imitated stones. The fabric refused to stretch as she pulled until the skin on her knuckles screamed.

...

The floor is surprisingly heavy when it hits you. There's a precise moment when you're thrown that gravity flips and the ground seems to fall on you. Of course, Anna didn't know what gravity was. But that didn't stop her feeling it.

"Pick up your bonnet. Now! Or the Gol will come to take your head!" It wasn't the Gol she feared. Her bonnet was back on before she'd even realised. Messy, red hair fell out of one side and purple blemishes were already pushing through the skin on her throat. She held his eyes with hers as she scurried backwards with practised agility, never breaking contact. Holding this line of sight was vital.

"A girl? A girl?!" He walked side to side as his thick heels drummed the wooden floor like a war cry. "You disgusting little..." Her fingers clutched and scrapped the surface of the floor to anchor her body. But nothing came. He turned and a single tear shined on his cheek like a slug trail. His eyes retreated into their dark sockets. His creased forrid buried every year of innocence. "You will curse this family, Anna. The whole village. Mark my word, you'll make the Gods sob." His thick finger swung like a cane. "Don't ever, ever tell anyone of this. Tomorrow, we will find you a match, and you will be matched for the rest of your life. To a man."

...

Screams are not unlike bird calls. Not the nice kind. Not melodic and subtle, but forced and shattered. Alerts to anyone that can hear them. They're broken songs, torn to pieces and scratched with claws.

Anna's bonnet lay on the floor in two. The tips of her fingers were red and joints aching. Each scream faded one by one, shot from the air. At first a morning chorus and then a desperate few. Almost as quickly as the chaos had started it had stopped.

The last call she recognised. A disgusting call. It echoed and gurgled in the bile of his stomach so deeply it made Anna wince. But this was a tone she quickly grew to enjoy. She smiled at the fleeting idea that she would never see her father again. She wouldn't see anyone. Guilt became a snigger. A snigger became a laugh. A laugh became tears.

When the silence thickened, she grew curious. She pressed her scarred forehead against the window and the glass steamed like a footprint. She saw no one. The villagers had gone. Her shoulders sank and the tension in her neck fell like autumn.

Something moved in the foliage. Behind the hut adjacent, in the bushes beyond, she saw the leaves and branches shift. They swayed and bounced and played with the sunlight shimmering in-between. To the right, to the left, the stirring spread. Arms, legs and torsos appeared. But no heads. A row of grey-skinned figures blindly marched into the opening, hissing from their grieving necks. Anna's hut lay ahead and she knew they were coming for retribution.

…

Children are cruel and kind and neither all at once. They're unbounded in their love and hate, and their experience of one or the other and everything in between makes an angel or a monster. Neither of which they have much control over.

"You can't play with us! You're a girl!"

"I don't want to."

"Why are you so weird, Anna?!"

"I'm not weird."

"Go play with the girls weirdo!" THUMP. Anna sat in the mud, rubbing her swelling lip as the boys ran and laughed. She squinted tightly and used her eyelids as dams.

The mud felt silky and cold between her fingers so she pushed them in further and squeezed her eyes as hard as she could. The texture was telling her it's been a rainy summer. THUD. Laughter erupted in the distance and blood trickled down Anna's forehead. She tried to focus on the fleeing children but her vision blurred. Sitting still, the dirt soaked into her clothes and red drops landed on her lap.

"Are you ok?" Elizabeth stood at the edge of the mud looking down, frowning.

"Yes, I'm fine."

"Are you sure Anna?" She held her hand out, delicate and pale. Her fingers were short and skinny but reached forward decisively. Anna took Elizabeth's hand and mud squelched between their palms like glue.

"That looks painful." Elizabeth dabbed Anna's forehead with the edge of her sleeve, the blood passing from one to the other, bit by bit.

"It's ok. I'll be ok. I'm going to be fine." Anna smiled.

...

Secrets are never really so. The body and mind gives what it wants, whether we know it or not. The Gol had been listening from the moment Anna devoured their blessings. To them she was as transparent as the air they barely breathed. They knew her. And Anna knew what they wanted. She'd betrayed them and the whole village and hey knew she didn't care. Not a bit.

Anna retreated back into the hut as the Gol approached. She wasn't scared. She was excited. This was the end of everything.

The silence turned to murmurs as they reached the wooden door. Heavy breathing and asthmatic choruses announced their arrival. The door swung open. The first stepped in, gargling from the open hollow in its neck. The second. The third. Countless others entered and approached. Arms outstretched and creaking.

She closed her eyes and unexpectedly saw Elizabeth's face. Her chest itched, ached and burnt all at once. A hand startled her and clawed at her collarbone, climbing to her neck with exploring steps. She gasped with the shock of hot skin and gentle fingertips. Another grasped her wrist, her ankle, her calf. Cracks appeared in her dry lips as she grinned and waited to disappear.

Like air, she floated up. Elevated above their torsos, she opened her eyes and saw cobwebs and rotting rafters.

The Gol proceeded outside, coughing and moaning from necks, expelling air like dusty trumpets with Anna atop. She bounced as they stepped in unison, splashing mud and singing to her with lost-lips. She rubbed her neck half-expecting her head to be missing. But for now, it persisted.

"A...A..." They grunted.

"A...na..." They chanted.

"An...na..." They urged and pleaded. She stood firm on their wide hands as they balanced her frame with a delicacy she had never experienced. Her arms stretched and reached into the empty air, whilst she filled the sky with her smile. In their grips her feet began to turn grey, followed by her ankles, her legs and all that remained. She felt their voices coursing over her skin and heard there commands deep in her gut. With her hands on her head, she pushed. She pushed it all away. The guilt, the shame, the pretence. She pushed as hard as she could and felt her head click and crunch and dissolve into the hole in her neck. And then it all made sense. A head can wear no mask if there is no head to begin with.

"An-na...An-na...AN-NA!"

They hailed and they sobbed.

The Magnets, Kate Arnold

The Magnets

'I can't see what the problem is,' you say. 'You want to go over there at midnight, you go - I'm not stopping you.'

You do this every year. You know damn well you do. You watch her flounce into the kitchen. She was right: her arse looks great in those Lift and Shape jeans you were frogmarched into Next to buy so she could wrap them, put them under the tree with a tag that says, 'To Dot, love Santa'.

Bit old for being cutesy now, you think; but she knows what suits her. You'll give her that.

'Well, maybe I don't want to go on my own again this year.'

Her words bounce off the stainless-steel sink, lurid with a tension she has only recently allowed to escape.

'Maybe, just once…'

She'll start scrubbing at stuff furiously in a moment. Her favourite way to make you feel guilty.

'…it'd be nice not to have to go on my own …'

And there it is. The belligerent smell of bleach. You hope she doesn't get any of it on those jeans, not at that price.

'…not have to explain away to the neighbours why my 'husband'…

No need for quotation marks drawn in the air.

'…is being such a miserable fucking git yet again this year. I might as well be single.'

You let that go. 'Tis the season to be jolly.

But, come on. New Year? Just the plus one of Christmas. It bungees in on the last of the tinsel, all jazz hands, with its diets and its revisions and its 'everything's going to be different'.

Nothing's going to be different. Nothing's ever going to be different. You don't understand why no one has clocked that yet. New Year? Nothing more than a human construct of time. You'll go to bed with your John Niven at eleven as every other night, shrug off the midnight assault of fireworks that sputters like typewriter keys through the carbon paper of your sleep. The smug morse code of missing out.

And yet.

A memory shimmies across the backs of your eyes.

'Ten! Nine! Eight! Seven!'

'Come on, man. It's midnight – just go and snog her, will you? Put us all out of our misery!'

'What a gentleman you truly are, my Davo. Snog who, anyway?'

You'd started at lunchtime, and were nearly ten pints in, drinking yourself to a clarity that steered your disingenuity. You glanced down at your Adidas Gazelles, then back up at her through your floppy fringe. Your signature move.

'Fucking Dot! You've been circling each other for months!'

'Have we fuck. We're just gig-buddies. Friends.'

'Five! Four! Three!'

'You've got enough friends, dude. Mate, she's looking over. Now go…go!'

'Two! One!'

You were shoved from behind. The crowd parted like clouds. And there she was, under a violet light, in her docs and her Menswear tee, with her waxy belladonna bob; shoved too by her friends, laughing, holding her hands palm-up in a shrug that said something which looked a lot like 'well, come on then - let's get this over with'.

'Happy New Year, Dunster.'

She kissed you.

She kissed *you*.

And it wasn't just a drunken New Year snog, like the ones going on all around you. It was a butterfly that chose your lips on which to dry its wings. A conversation begun.

Six hours later, you watched your father die.

*

Right. Time this tree came down. Manky artificial shit, taking up the spot where your cherry red Gibson SG usually stands. You'd pull the lot down on Boxing Day if you could.

You wonder who it's for these days. Certainly not the kids. All that effort—mainly from Dot, granted, but you'll be paying for it—and they've been upstairs now for nearly a week, lit up like twin Zoltars by their new phones. You didn't even get to choose their presents this year: you just fulfilled the orders. They only shoot from their rooms when they're hungry—synchronised cuckoos from clocks—to collect the trays of food she makes for them.

You wonder what happened to the tantrums over whose turn it was to be held up first to put the star on the top of that same tree. You wonder what happened to spangled woodland advent calendars with pictures, not chocolates; bellowed renditions of *Away in a Manger*, a headband stretched over a tea towel, tinsel wrapped round a coat hanger halo; a mince pie left out for Santa on Christmas Eve, a carrot for Rudolph. You wonder what happened to sneaking into their rooms, pissed on Hot Buttered Rum, to lay crackly stockings at the foot of each bed, before having hushed and giggly sex against the wall underneath the mistletoe in the hallway. Oh, the traditions that somehow stole away into the night.

You pull off a knackered bauble, wonder what happened to your own childhood. A faded Santa, hand-painted and smeared with glitter in a long-ago classroom, dangles now like a suicide.

And, just like that, you're ambushed.

Twenty years. It's been twenty years.

You are forty-four.

*

'Right. So, we're taking the tree down today, are we?'

The snap of her Marigolds—as if she'd just completed an appendectomy—flings you back into the room.

'You couldn't even wait until midnight?'

You wonder when it began, this ennui that drips rankly from the walls behind the pegged-up Christmas cards. You used to thrill each other. You did.

My Dark Pixie: the song you wrote for her. With her mannequin make-up, the back pocket notepad of observations she would transform into small-hours poetry, it suited her. Hair a shiny brillo of frustration, a joint dangling from her skinny lip, she would ransack her soft thesaurus, listening for how a word would taste on her tongue, how it would tremble the bell of her ideas. You were transfixed from the first moment you saw her - at a poetry night you had stumbled into enroute to the bogs in the back room of your local, where none of the jester-trousered hippies were listening to a single word she said. She was your Dot. Your full stop. There was never going to be anyone else.

And she was transfixed by you. She was.

You are the shock to prod my dead frog's leg.

She wrote that in a letter, taping a match to the bottom, so you could burn it, blow the ashes to the wind. Goth, but you knew what she meant. She was as affected by words as you were by music: a wrongly placed apostrophe would wound her for a week.

Now she's Teflon. The only thing she reads out these days are sappy memes from Facebook; all she writes for you is a list of stuff to do. Yesterday, you found the car radio tuned to Heart FM.

Then you wonder: did you do this? Is it your mood that drives her daily to the furnace of the gym where she forges flush her once guitar-shaped body? Sometimes you turn and catch her—under a lightbulb of astonished horror—observing you as if you were an insolent fly still wringing its inky hands on a windowsill; a Marlboro Light she can't stub out. You wonder if she's seeing someone else; what she tells her dip-dyed, gin o'clock friends about him. You know you're holding her back. You just hope she can wait until the children are gone.

*

So, yeah. Twenty years since you've seen your father's face.

The funeral? Just polaroids now.

The mottled midriff of January. An empathic chill to explain away your tears. Icing sugar puddles; albino breath. Your mother's face stiff as a shark at the plummeting elevator of shock. Every skeleton finger of every tree furred like arteries with frost, as the stately black car—the nearest you were ever going to get to a stretch limo—snorted up the steely drive of the crematorium.

The shabby pall bearers—you, Davo and the rest of your band—had practised, pissed, with a bass cab the night before. It was all just another gig to you. In your black skinny tie and jeans and your pork pie hat; still half-cut, weren't you, when you read that poem, the one about death being nothing at all? Twenty years now says he's not just in the next room.

At the wake in the village hall, long after the aunties had fled, Dot stood up to read from her notebook.

'*He has made you fearless,'* she began, *'but not in the way he meant to.*

He has made you adventurous, but not in the way he thought.

He has made you resourceful, but not in the way he wanted.

I think because he knew he would leave you unfinished.
He who would never conceive of a job half-done.

She paused.
No time now
to find some kind of common ground,
an overlap in the Venn diagram.
Oh, the magnets that men must pull apart.'

She was right then. But she was wrong. You know this only now.

Frank was a shy man; a silent man.

Seventeen—just a year older, it occurs to you today, than the eldest of the standing stones upstairs that you call your children—when he began the milk round that provided for your mother and the burgeoning belly that tented you. No colleagues, no pub after work, no football on a Saturday. Friends? They just got in the way of the garden, he said. Frank's afternoons, evenings, and every weekend were for building with his red reptilian hands a safe house around you both; the house—now worth at least half a million—that cloisters your mother still.

Wood, steel, glass, brick: that was the language of his love.

But twenty years ago, the language of your love was Ecstasy, Poppers: anything with a buzz. A blowjob against a transit, illegal warehouse raves. The only thing you ever constructed was rage at the boring loser who had fashioned you the gift of being so fireproof.

Oh, the slamming of all the doors he had so carefully hung when he heard you'd tapped your gran for money for a scooter, dared to question how you intended to pay her back. You throttled off; moved into a spiteful bedsit in the roughest part of town, refusing his offers to help you make it nice. Spent every night in a sleeping bag on a bed made of pallets, didn't you, a rancid old armchair shoved up against the door, quaking at the fights on the stairs. You never spoke to him again.

What was he even doing out on his round on that New Year's morning twenty years ago? Would it have hurt his customers to go to the corner shop for once? They found him collapsed by a lamppost, heart like a bronco, a charging pair of Rottweilers –enraged as politicians—ramming again and again the gate his trembling fingers had only just managed to buckle shut. He never came round.

You crashed the Vespa, drunk, two days later.

He was right, of course. You never did pay her back.

*

'Another one, Dunster?'

Davo's face was already double-edged with JD, as Dot sat down to table-banging applause. 'Come on, man - it's what he would've wanted.'

Davo with both his parents intact. Davo with no idea what the flying fuck he was talking about.

No, you had seethed to yourself as you staggered home under tumbling streetlights, runny-nosed and alone: what Frank would have wanted was not to have been hacked down by a heart attack at forty-four, leaving his wife in your vain and shoddy, lilywhite hands.

What he would have wanted—you never really stopped seething, you realise this now as you fling bauble after bauble to the floor—was to have been at your wedding, got to know your kids; witnessed the cheeks of Time blow white feathers into his wife's temples. To have had time, finally, to unearth a life outside of his round. Outside the moods of his self-centred waster of an only son. Tapped at your new walls. Shown you how to fix it with Dot.

'I can't do another year of this,' she fires over a bristling gym bag. 'We'll talk when I get back.'

You remove the star, fold the tree into its box.

Shoulder it back into the loft.

The Empty Quarter

We often wonder what we saw that day. And once again, I recount the details here not to convince you that this happened, but to remind myself that it really did.

We had hoped to cross the desert by sunset. We had made similar journeys many times before, though admittedly, never to Rub-al-Khali, the Empty Quarter. But how different could one desert drive be from another?

We set off early, the road cutting through the orange ground, the landscape brightening as the sun rose. The sand stretched into the distance, soft dunes undulating, punctuated periodically by grey rock formations, some solitary stones, others grouped like families.

The car sped on, filled with chatter and music, my hand light on the steering wheel and my foot relaxed on the gas. Bilal, beside me, kept up a supply of kebabs rolled in flatbread, nuts and water. Tariq in the back was following the map, but since there was really only one straight road to follow, he had given up and was googling facts about the area instead.

"Rub al Khalil covers a quarter of a million square miles. It receives just 1.2 inches of rain a year and this year not even that! No wonder it's considered the most uninhabitable place on earth."

"But why would anyone even want to inhabit this area?" Bilal commented, rolling his hands in circles to indicate the endlessness and emptiness of the desert around us.

"There was once an ancient city here," continued Tariq, "Iram of the Pillars. It says it was 'a land of grand buildings and high monuments.'"

I remembered a reference to Iram from the Quran, "'Hast thou not seen how thy Lord dealt with Ad – the tribe of Iram, possessor of lofty buildings, the likes of which have not been created in these parts.'" I recited. "Iram was destroyed by God when the people strayed from the teachings of Prophet Hud. The city and all its people perished in a sandstorm, buried under the sand. That's what I recall reading."

"What I can never understand about these stories is why punish the children?" said Bilal. "What do they know about sinning and straying?"

"Only Allah knows what is hidden in the heavens and the earth!" I replied, and though my tone was light, wanting to change the subject, the mood had turned grim. And in that instant, we all felt the sands shift, and in their rise and fall and light and shade, they took on the shape of a bustle of people, that with a squint became a procession of camels, and after a rubbing of the eyes became distant watchtowers.

Bilal turned up the music to ease the discomfort.

"More water please, Tariq." Bilal extended his hand over his shoulder to take a new bottle.

But the water had finished. The two last bottles which we thought were full were actually empty. Perhaps the tops were loose and the water had dripped away, but there was no sign of any leakage.

"Not to worry," I said cheerfully, "We will be out of the desert in three hours, and back to civilisation and bottles of water."

However, the more we tried to put the empty bottles to the back of our minds, the drier our tongues became. I started swallowing faster and more frequently trying to moisten the back of my throat. Bilal licked his lips compulsively. Tariq tried to stifle a recurrent cough. We turned the music off and continued in silence.

The sun journeyed with us and in the late afternoon the desert was aglow - a vast canvas, amber against azure - and our jeep, a black dot moving through it. In the distance there appeared to be a breeze stirring the sand into a cloud, catching the light in sparkles as it swirled. We watched it closely, trying to determine its distance and the direction it was taking. We did not want to drive into a sandstorm. But suddenly the sand dropped, the sky cleared, and a shimmer of water appeared on the horizon.

"It looks like there's water ahead," I said cautiously, "Maybe it's an underwater spring that comes to the surface here."

Tariq checked the map. "There's nothing shown on the map," he said, "But it's in the same direction we are headed, we may as well take a look."

I drove on faster, sending the sand scattering under the wheels, and surely and gradually, the shimmering stretch grew larger and became a lake. Patchy scrub grew along one side and soft dunes curved along the other. I pulled off the road and along a dirt track, slowing down to park several feet from the edge of the water. Tariq was out of the car even before I had stopped and Bilal and I watched him quickly striding towards the lake. He had hardly taken a few steps when he suddenly stumbled and lurched forward awkwardly, landing on his knees and outstretched hands. We laughed, but our smiles faded when we realised he couldn't get up, and when he tried he was almost knee deep in the dry but evidently swampy ground. He wobbled and fell on his back.

"Stay on your back," I shouted, my voice thin in the heat and span of the desert. "You won't sink if you stay on your back."

Bilal retrieved the tow rope, tied one end to the jeep, and threw the other end to Tariq, and as I reversed, we gently pulled him out. Tariq was coated with a thin film of sludge that quickly turned to powder and fell away. And when we looked out to the spot where he had fallen, there was no lake to be seen, only an expanse of wind-rippled sand and scrappy bushes scratching against the rocks.

This diversion had cost us dearly in time and in cheer. We should have been almost out of the desert by now, nearly at the end of the straight line of road, getting closer to the highway, and to our hotel rooms where we would lie down and smoke and call our wives and tell them about the day, exaggerating a bit the heat, and embellishing a little the dangers of the journey.

But here we were instead. Dusk was rapidly darkening to night, the dunes dissolving at the edges, and stars appearing at the borders, until soon, above, and below, and all around, was one big blackness.

We turned the music back on and up, shone the full beam of the headlights onto the road, and sliced steadily through the night. About an hour had gone by when in the distance I noticed a glow, a little way off the main road, almost throbbing, pulsing, into the darkness.

"It could be a town, or a small settlement," I guessed. "We could stop for water, or even stay the night if we need to."

Tariq checked the map on his phone. The Wi-Fi signals were long gone, but the map still worked on GPS.

"There's nothing marked on the map. Nothing for miles in fact."

"Maybe it's a camp," ventured Bilal, though we all agreed the light was far brighter than one would expect from a small camp.

"As long as it's not another mirage!" I laughed nervously and turned off the main road onto a smaller one. Under the headlights, the sand here seemed to take the shape of a dried-up river bed, and the narrow road curled alongside the furrowed trench, into the desert, and eventually moved away and upwards to the place from where the light emanated.

Sometime later we reached the top of the hill and found ourselves at the rim of a shallow bowl of similar dunes, their sides sweeping seamlessly down to what appeared to be some sort of settlement at its centre, glimmering and flickering in the darkness. We continued downwards and soon reached the outskirts of a small village.

The village was built in a square grid, with a main road running down the middle and several smaller roads branching from it and ending a short way in. The roads were bordered with clusters of houses, each arranged within their own compound, shaded by trees, and ornamented with geometric shapes cut into the low boundary walls. The houses were almost identical; single storeyed, with verandahs running along the front and around one side, onto which a double-leaf wooden door opened, painted red, or green, or yellow, and three shuttered windows, one on one side of the door and two on the other. The gates of each compound were wide open. The doors of the houses stood agape. The shutters of the windows were pulled right back against the wall. And light, brighter than any light we had seen from any lantern or bulb, streamed from the doors and windows, revealing what lay behind them – the paraphernalia of ordinary life – rugs on rough floors, embroidered blankets pulled over bed frames, plain cabinets holding crockery and steel cups, books stacked in corners, carved and beaded toys strewn over the tables.

And from each house emerged young children, dressed up in traditional clothes, their hair combed neatly, as if ready for some party. The children congregated at the corners of the lanes, their houses standing open and empty behind them, and then joined up in groups and walked down the main road we were driving along. They interacted animatedly, the boys jostling each other playfully, the girls linking arms, skipping and giggling. The whole atmosphere was one of festivity, gaiety, life.

But we could not hear a single sound.

And we did not see a single adult.

And not a single girl or boy turned to look at us.

We drove like this for ten minutes, through the light spilling into the streets, side by side with these silent, yet animated children, transfixed by their merriment, bewildered by their oblivion.

Eventually the children fell behind, and the road continued out of the light, blurring momentarily with the darkness, and then into the night. The glow of this mysterious village grew smaller and fainter until we could no longer distinguish it from the stars that twinkled around us as we drove out of the Empty Quarter.

We often wonder what we saw that day. Did we cross into another dimension? Just as the land has a topography of heights and depths, time too has its topography of moments, some that are imbued with significance and some that pass without distinction. In the desert, the topographies of place and time converge, and at these points there is a meeting of realms, the veil between them so thin, one can pass through and pass back. Did we chance upon such a concurrence, that took us through a space folded away into the sands of time? I believe so. You may not. But as I said, my purpose is not to convince you that it happened, but rather to remind myself it really did.

A Trip Into Town

My personal challenge each day is to make it out of my house without being spotted by my nosey neighbours. Why they're so interested in my comings and goings, I've no idea. They have their own lives, their own issues. All that arguing makes me wonder why they stick at it. Small things, too: his car leaking oil on the driveway; her leaving washing on the line, days after it has dried, only to be rained upon.

I vary the times I come and go, but I have appointments like anyone else, places I have to be. Today, it's the ophthalmologist wanting to follow up on my cataract surgery. What a blessed relief it was to get the procedure done and no longer be dependant on glasses. Forty years of wearing them, my hand still goes to push them up on my nose, still searches for them on top of the bedside drawers when I wake.

There's hardly anything in the cupboard or fridge, but I don't eat much these days. Tea and toast gets me through until mid-afternoon. I may have more tea, or coffee with a plain biscuit later. The pension is barely enough to live on. But I have to live on something, so I make a shopping list, run a comb through my hair, and check the neighbours' house.

I know *her* routine well: out by seven o'clock, home about four, Monday to Friday. He's difficult to pin down, and there are days when he seems not to leave the house at all. I see him on the back verandah, drinking beer, looking at his phone. He'll stand suddenly and go inside. Sometimes he looks over my way. I've thought about going over and demanding that he stop. I've thought about going to the police, claiming psychological warfare.

Today, there's no sign of him. To be honest, I'm in such a good mood about my eyes that it wouldn't bother me if he were to knock at my door wanting a cup of sugar. I gather my purse, keys and a shopping bag.

It's a blustery day. Unpleasant to be afoot. The crepe myrtle in the front yard shakes wildly. I find gloves in the pockets of my coat and put them on as I head down out the gate. Turning the corner, I see the neighbours' garage door rolled up, the man crouched over a lawnmower. On the concrete floor are tools and oily rags. Some men relish this kind of activity. He looks over his shoulder. I wasn't making any noise and realise that he was waiting. The lawnmower was just a ploy.

'Morning, Rosie. Need a lift?'

What happened to respect for your elders? The last person to call me Rosie was my husband, Guido.

'Where're you off to?' he asks, persistent bugger.

If this isn't harassment, I don't know what is.

'None of your business.'

He laughs and says, 'Suit yourself.'

I storm down the street to the bus stop, cursing the day I bought the house. On the hard bench, waiting, I realise I've left my shopping list behind. No matter—it's just a few items. I wouldn't give him the satisfaction of walking back. A young woman with a baby strapped to her chest and a child clutching her hand amble toward me.

'Hello, little one,' I say as they get closer.

The woman has a ring through her nose. The baby is nestling into her chest, its tiny legs poking out of the carrier.

'Can it breath alright, like that?'

She looks down and cups its head.

'Yeah, he's fine.'

'How old are you?' I ask the child who I now discern is a girl.

'What's your name?'

She's mute.

'Go on.' The mother nudges her with her knee. 'Tell her.'

The girl says something. Garbles, she does. How am I supposed to understand?

'What? What did she say?'
'Annabelle,' the mother says loudly.
'I'm not deaf. I'm old but I'm not deaf, thank you.'
The girl—Annabelle—pulls at her mother's hand, urging her to sit on the bench. I move along to the edge. The mother gestures that it's not necessary, settles her daughter, and sways from foot to foot, looking away. I wiggled a finger along the bench, like a worm, hoping to amuse the girl. She's not immediately amused, so I touch the frill of her skirt and retreat quickly, as though burnt. She whimpers and the mother looks down and frowns.
'That ring,' I say and tap my nose. 'You'll want to be careful.'
'*What?*'
'With children. They may not mean to, but it could get yanked out. Caught on a sleeve or something.'
I wince at the thought.
'Yeah,' she says and shakes her head. 'Whatever.'
Her insolence is infuriating. I get up and stand, looking resolutely ahead until the bus arrives.
'Morning, Mrs D'Angelo,' the driver says. 'Mind your step.'
'Good morning,' I say and tap my card on the electronic pad.
He waits until we are all seated before pulling out. Some of them don't. Some of them take off and send you careening down the aisle. The driver greets each passenger, addressing a few by name. It takes me back to my youth, when this was the norm. When people weren't too busy to talk. When people were, basically, decent.
In Sydney, as a young thing, I caught the Manly ferry every morning at 8:00 am, heading over to Wynyard Secretarial School. The men wore hats and tipped them when they saw a young lady, and even offered their seats. We sat together, chugging along, those without newspapers read the pages of those who did. When we disembarked at Circular Quay, I fell in step with my fellow classmates, and we chatted about our homework, our boyfriends, our hair, tugging our gloves off as we streamed into the dull brown building.

'Ladies,' the school's principal said loudly. 'Ladies! Ladies!' I suppose we were making too much noise, or not showing enough decorum.

'Lady?'

'Mrs D'Angelo?'

I become aware that the bus has stopped and people are looking at me.

'Mrs D'Angelo?' the driver calls over his shoulder. 'Your stop, right? Mrs D'Angelo, you okay?'

I get up, flustered. I apologise, laughing that I was taking a trip down memory lane. He tells me to have a good day and to mind the step.

Standing on the street, I am utterly discombobulated. I could smell the salty air and hear the waves slapping against the hull of the ferry. I was nineteen years old and pretty and full of hope.

Taking a deep breath, I look around to get my bearings.

Right, I tell myself, I'm on the main street. The ophthalmologist's office is on the second floor, above a place selling cameras, two streets down. I head off, rubbing at the stiffness in my back that happens after sitting for a time. Best to keep moving, these days. The two flights wind me a little. An electronic bell sounds as I open the door. Four people are waiting and glance at me as I enter. The waiting room has been refurbished since I was last here—landscape prints on the walls, deep crimson-coloured carpet, large ferns.

'Rosemary D'Angelo for Dr Koopman,' I tell the receptionist. She's a beaky little thing with enormous glasses. Not a great advertisement, in my opinion.

She scans the screen in front of her.

'For Dr Koopman?'

'Yes.'

'Today?'

'Obviously.'

She tightens her lips into a line and jabs away at the keyboard.

'It's a follow up on my cataract surgery, if that's any help.'

'And he *asked* you to come in?'

'No, I woke up today and decided it. The appointment is for 10 am, and here I am at 9:50.'

I leave her to do her job and find a seat next to one of the plants. There is also a stand with shiny brochures and pamphlets explaining all manner of eye-related ailments. The receptionist talks in a low voice to her colleague and gives me evil looks. A woman appears from behind the closed door to the consultation rooms.

'Jeremy?'

The teenager with lank hair and a smattering of dandruff on his shoulders—that's how good my vision is now—gets up and strolls over.

Over the course of the next fifteen minutes, two others, Alicia and Giorgio, are also called. That leaves two of us. I inspect the other patient, a man some years older than me. He must be almost ninety. The reception staff have abandoned their post.

'Excuse me,' I say as I shift one seat closer. 'What time is your appointment? Are they running late?'

'Koopman at ten. They're always behind. But it's not as bad as the place I go to for my feet.'

'Who's your podiatrist? I see Dr Eckman. She's out at Thirroul. Nice woman. Professional.'

'Eckman? Mine is to blazes down at Lake Illawarra. Have to get my grandson to drive me each time.'

'How annoying.'

We fall into talking about our complaints, commiserating the way old people do.

'Phillip? Mr Duncan?'

The woman smiles at him and looks warily at me.

'Sorry about the wait. Come through.'

He jumps up—a sprite ninety-year old, that's for sure—without giving me a second glance. I go and stand at the reception desk, looking for a bell to ring. There's nothing, so I stand at the entrance until Miss Goggly-Eyes appears.

'You've double-booked. That man and I have Dr Koopman at ten. Now, I understand mistakes get made—I was in the business world when you were in nappies—but this is unacceptable. Not only has there been no apology, there's been—'

'Stop yelling at me,' she says. 'I don't have to take this.'

'Excuse me? I'm not yelling.'

'You are. You're raising your voice.'

'There's a big difference between raising your voice and yelling, and I'm not doing either. For God's sake, can you please get your co-worker, or *some*one—'

'Rosemary. Mrs D'Angelo.'

Dr Koopman is suddenly behind me.

'I hear there's been a mix up.' Such a kind man. 'Can you wait a little more? Are you in a hurry?'

'No, I have time. That's not—'

He guides me to a seat.

'Perhaps our exciting range of pamphlets about diabetic retinopathy will help you pass the time.'

He winks and is gone before I can think of a reply. The reception staff have absconded. I'm alone until Jeremy comes out, pays—Lo! She appears!—and goes. Alicia, too. Giorgio is told to sit and wait for about twenty minutes until his pupils are fully dilated. He takes a pair of sunglasses from his backpack and puts them on and jams a pair of little white speakers in his ears. Everyone wears them these days. It's as though they have been mandated. It's as though people don't want to hear anything around them anymore, not birds, the wind through the trees, not even each other.

Dr Koopman pokes his head around the door.

'Come on through, Mrs D'Angelo.'

Finally!

Beyond the door, there's another doctor in one of the consultation rooms. She's on the phone at looking at a computer.
'I've already tried that,' she says. 'Yes, I went to system preferences.'
'We're having a few internet problems,' Dr Koopman says to me. As though I care about that.
I sit in a chair and he sits opposite me.
'Well, now. A follow up, is it?'
'Yes. You said four weeks after the surgery, even if nothing is wrong. So, here I am.'
He nods his head.
'My eyes are perfectly fine,' I tell him.
He nods again.
'Aren't you going to check them?'
'Yes, of course.'
He leans toward me and performs a perfunctory examination.
'Look up…to the left…down…to your right…up again…'
Sitting back in his chair, he informs me that my eyes appear to be healing well.
'You don't need to use one of your little devices? Machines? For a more thorough check?'
'That's not necessary,' he says yet still sits there looking at me.'Everything else alright? Getting enough sleep? Exercise?'
'As well as can be expected for a seventy-eight-year old woman. I hope you're not going to charge me for this. It seems—'
'No charge.' He waves his hand. 'It's good to see you on the mend.'
'It's good to *be* on the mend.' I get up. 'Thank you, Doctor.'
He walks me all the way to the front door and watches me descend the stairs. If he's so worried about old folk falling, he should have an elevator installed. Or move to more suitable premises.

The mall is an unwelcoming place—I prefer walking along streets looking in shopfronts—but I fancy a reward for traipsing all the way into town. There's a food court on the top floor of one of the department stores. A few young people occupy the tables, looking at their phones. Some business-types sit with their laptops. It's shocking that people are eating fast food at this time of the day. I find a place that does a decent cappuccino and treat myself to a large slice of carrot cake. Once upon a time, I would've walked on by, hearing the voice my friend, Edith, saying, 'You're getting a bit broad across the beam, Rosemary.' Now, I can't seem to keep any weight on my bones. There are less people sitting in an area which is akin to an conservatory. They've made an attempt, these city-planners and architects, to fool us into believing we are outdoors when we are indoors. I hide behind a large spikey succulent and look down at the people coming and going on the street below.

My mind wanders back to Edith—how odd that it should do so after all these years—*Edith.* The woman I called my friend purely because she was there and the only white face among all the Italians in the street where Guido and I finally bought a house. She was the only one who, like me, didn't speak Italian and had no fondness for eating dinner after 7 pm. Unlike me, she was not married to an Italian. Her husband was a reticent newsagent called Arthur, who, whenever I was there, greeted me politely and then left the room. It was as though I were tainted, somehow, being married to one of *them.* Whenever she deigned to walk across the street to my house for morning tea, she entered timorous as a cat. I'd show her through to the kitchen, and her eyes would be wide with amazement—as though my house were all that different to hers. We sat on chairs at a table like anyone else.

'Is the man of the house here?' she'd ask.

It strikes me suddenly that Edith was quietly lusting after Guido all those years. Her own Arthur—as plain and interesting as a biscuit—was nothing compared to my husband's sparkling dark eyes and obvious liking for women. Why did I not see it? I could have used it to my advantage. Certainly, it would've given me the upper hand with her condescending remarks. 'Broad across the beam?' I could've said back to her. 'This is because Guido likes bottoms. He likes to clutch my fleshy buttocks in his hands while I ride him, you stupid, insipid woman.'

I laugh and go to finish my coffee, but it is gone. So is the cake. A few crumbs remain, and the coffee's bitterness lingers on my tongue so I know I drank it. There is a woman in an ill-fitting uniform clearing the tables, so I can only assume she took my empty plate and cup. How deeply I disappear into my own thoughts these days.

The lunchtime crowd will be swarming in soon. Best to get back home and continue with the day. At the bus-stop, I'm surrounded by noisy teenagers in school uniforms. It's odd that they should be here at this time of the day but schools are not as regimented as they were in my day. Students are allowed to come and go. We were locked in like prisoners, the nuns our suspicious wardens. I am offered a seat on the bus which arrives almost full. At the next stop, more school children get on and I have to suffer through their yelps and guffaws and blows to the side of the head from their enormous backpacks. The driver has the radio blaring and the godawful cacophony of noise that passes for music these days is interrupted by the afternoon news report.

Afternoon?

I stagger out onto the street when I arrive at my stop. Slowly, I make my way towards home, barely registering that *his* car is gone and *her* car is in its place. I could head directly to the beach for my usual walk, but I'm wearing my good shoes and need a wind cheater.

The back door is open and I'm presented with my neighbour's rear end sticking out of the cupboard under the sink. I know it's her because of those dreadful leggings she wears. They're stretched so tight I can see the floral pattern of her undies. On the counter, is a shopping bag full of groceries.

'What in God's name are you doing?' I demand.

This is it. They've gone too far now.

She withdraws her head and torso from my cupboard, banging her head in the process. I hope it hurt.

'Oh,' she says and flicks hair from her eyes. 'Hey, Mum. Just putting down some new cockroach baits.'

Until Death Do Us Part

The Mazda's parked in the disabled spot outside Home Depot. The heat hits me like something solid and I spy Frank slumped forward onto the dashboard. For a moment everything is bleached to a bright grey and I think he must be dead, his neck bent like that. Behind me, a voice on the public address system, its message lost in the depths of the air-conditioned store. I'm gripping the hammer, my only purchase, like I could use it right now.

"Frank!" I yell, yanking the passenger door open.

"Jeez Rosemary. Gave me a fright," he mumbles, wiping his mouth on the handkerchief he keeps clutched in his hand.

"You fell asleep," I shout, like he's an infant, or hard of hearing.

He has his hand on the breast pocket of his plaid shirt, which is always a precursor to him saying something like, 'you shouldn't go around scaring people like that Rosemary.'

I slam the door and walk round to the driver's side. By the time I'm seated he's done grumbling and put his belt on.

"Seven ninety-nine. Before you ask. The hammer Frank! The hammer!"

I reverse out as he turns painfully in his seat to tell me to watch out for something that isn't there. The Mazda's gears grate if you're not at a complete stop before finding first. Frank always used to say he preferred a stick, but he hasn't driven in years and I want an automatic.

He'll be wondering what's for dinner. Or whether I've seen the school bus pulling out. Or wanting to comment on the heat. Fifty-two summers we've spent in Texas but he still never tires of talking about the heat. Half a century of flat dusty nothing, three kids, long gone, decent jobs, a pack of dogs, but he wants to talk about the weather.

Days like these I long for Colorado. Roaming the hills with my twin brothers, playing games, trying to slot in beside them and their secret world. My teenage years, wild and free. I miss the green, the air, but Frank never liked my brothers and we've only been back a few times. To bury them, one after the other, in the plot beside mom and dad.

Frank jams his foot on an imagined brake on his side of the car. Like a cartoon on the TV, it's ridiculous. I signal and pull into the outside lane, accelerating away from the mess of fur and blood on the highway.

"Deer," Frank announces, like he's an expert on roadkill. Like someone's listening.

I don't mean to bully him but nowadays he pisses me off. He repeats things, fusses all the time, pretends he doesn't hear. I've given up being gentle and I'm not sure whether he's hurt or if he's even noticed. I'm not an angry person usually, but in the airless heat of the Mazda, I can feel my fury like poison in my blood.

We're out on the highway and with the windows down I can only hear wind and the rush of trucks heading east. Frank's eyes are on the road.

It's less than ten minutes to our turn and we pull onto the drive and I park under the carport. Frank doesn't like me parking here as he says the structure's unsafe. He should know. He built it. It's a wooden frame and he reckons termites have gotten into the uprights. I grab the hammer off the back seat and leave him sitting there.

Inside it's shady and cool. I left the air conditioner on in the kitchen and with the doors closed it offers a moment of calm, of stillness. There's a bottle of Pepsi in the fridge and I pour a large glass and drain it in one, stifling a burp. By the time Frank's shuffled in, I've got bread, margarine, cheese and tomatoes out onto the counter.

"You fixing a sandwich?" he asks.

"You were asleep back there. Why don't you go lie down? Take a rest?"

He's crowding me at the bench.

"You wanna sandwich Frank?"

"What's for dinner?"

"Why don't you go watch TV. Quit bugging me."

If I let him, he'll pretend to be outraged that I'm eating in the middle of the afternoon. I know he'd like a slice of cheese but instead he's itching to mention my weight, how the doctor said I should only eat at mealtimes. I cut him a thin piece, but he's already turned away, mumbling to himself.

It never used to be like this. Not so long ago we got along fine. He kept working and now I think that it was his job that preserved him. He had so many clients and he said he didn't want to let them down. Small businesses, mainly. Accounts, payroll. But when everything moved to computers, he was left behind and within a couple of years nobody wanted him anymore.

My cousin Coral who calls every Sunday says I'm in mourning. That I've lost the man I loved and now I share a house with someone different. I thought about that a lot recently.

On our wedding day he wore a blue suit that matched his eyes and I thought he was the most beautiful man I'd ever seen. I was the luckiest girl and I pretend to myself that that was the happiest day of my life.

He was a good dad to the kids too. Better with Dan and Marlon who he'd gotten into all kinds of projects out in the shed. I don't think he knew what to do with Annie. She was smart and read books and he didn't know how to handle a girl. But he was always good to her and we got her through college and her law exams.

He's already asleep in the armchair and I have no idea how he does that. I used to think it was an act. To avoid having to listen to me. But now I'm sure he just sleeps, whenever and wherever he likes. Sleeps, eats, watches TV.

"What's the point of you Frank?" I shouted too loud in the back yard a week ago.

It was a horrible thing to say but I'd only asked him to cut back some of the dead foliage on the bleeding hearts that run along the trellis. He's perfectly capable but he seems to have lost the will to do much of anything.

I had him checked out when he turned seventy-five. I was almost willing the doctor to tell me he'd had a minor stroke or that his heart was failing or his blood pressure dangerously low. Something that might explain his general decline. But he's fine. Whatever he's lost isn't something a doctor can find.

I make an effort to remember the man I shared my life with. Some nights I pore over old photo albums, spending hours studying every detail. My finger traces Frank, and the kids, and it's like I can conjure something of that moment again. There's a photograph of Frank reversing a friend's boat on a trailer into Lake Travis. It amazed me, that he could do that. His shirt off, leaning out of the window, one arm on the wheel. The trailer disappearing into the water until the boat was floating free. Back then he never failed to impress me.

And now I stand over him and want to prod him awake. I imagine a knitting needle jabbed once, twice, below his ribs. Or a large glass of iced water, right in his face.

This feeling scares me. That I could do this to the man I love. The man I loved. I hate the idea that I could be so cruel. That I have this thing inside me that's grown unchecked over years. Layers of accreted pain and hurt and something else that might be boredom or my hormones or the wires in my brain.

He's dribbling and I return to the kitchen to get the other half of my sandwich. I'll call Dan, our eldest, in a bit. He'll be finishing work in Baltimore soon and I can catch him on his drive home. It's an hour in the car and he says he understands, about Frank, about how I might need some help. I imagine him sitting in traffic, listening to me talking about his father like it's some dull radio call-in.

I worry that I'm going to catch what Frank has. That if I let myself succumb, I'll be like him in no time. All my ambition, my get-up-and-go, shot to pieces. I see him and I see a geriatric. We're the same age but you won't catch me sleeping in the day or stumbling around the house in my slippers. Frank's let go, given up, and I'm nowhere near ready for that.

I'm scared of the rage that's built up inside me, just below the surface. Frightened of what I could unleash. And that I too might be reduced to falling asleep in a chair just before four in the afternoon.

The man in the other room is no longer recognisable to me. I know I stood facing him in the huge church on Congress Street and I said that I would love him in sickness and in health. But that was fifty years ago and now I wish that I hadn't. That I'd spotted that clause, asked for it to be amended, requested something different in the knowledge that one day things might get like this.

I told Dan last week that I didn't think his father had long left. I heard the blast of a car horn as he pulled onto the side of the road. I'm not sure why I said it now. Wishful thinking perhaps. Dan had said he would come visit, and I'd backtracked saying I didn't think it was imminent. That things hadn't gone that far.

Frank sleeps in Annie's old room down the hall. I hear him in the middle of the night, rattling like a radiator that needs bleeding. It's beyond me how he can sleep through that racket. One time I walked into the room, switched on the light and stood over him.

"Why do you do this to me!" I shrieked and he just kept going, like he was daring me to grab a pillow and press it over his face. I imagine doing that now. One of the cushions from the couch. It'd be all over in a minute, and I convince myself it would be doing us both a favour.

"He has quality of life," says Coral, on the phone. "He still has all his faculties. Doesn't he?"

I think about all the things he used to be able to do. Reverse a trailer. Build a carport. Manage the finances. Piss straight.

I bought the hammer because I want a bird box in the cedar in the backyard and Frank couldn't find the one in the garage. I weigh it in my hand, the rubberised grip is just right in my palm, and I let the head swing.

There are hummingbirds at the bleeding hearts on the trellis and I open the bottle one handed and wash the pills down with a glass of water, unable to let go of the hammer. It'll be twenty minutes before I can start to relax, before the muscles in my jaw, my wrists, get loose.

From the other room I hear him snoring loudly and then it stops abruptly, and I hold my breath too. It's silent in the house and I dare not breathe. I tell myself that if he makes another sound, I'll take the hammer and swing it against the side of his head. I don't think about the mess it would make or any of the consequences of such a violent act. I just know in this moment that if he breathes, I could do it.

The air conditioning hums and, far off, the sound of a church bell.

Barren, Karen Browne

Barren

The waiting is excruciating, but I won't unlock the door until Paul stops shouting. Teddy is nestled in beside me as we sit on the cold tiles of the ensuite floor. His ears are pricked to the volatile anger consuming the bedroom and his nose is twitching as he smells the blood trickling from my nose.

Ten minutes goes by before silence descends. I get on my feet and Teddy moves into position beside the toilet, knowing that he can't budge until I say it's safe. The bathroom cabinet holds a stash of cheese flavoured treats and I give him two, but he's far too stressed to wag his tail.

The key must be turned slowly and gently which takes patience and practice. All remains quiet as I open the door a little bit at a time, my heart pounding in my ears. I can't see the bed from this side of the ensuite door so If I want to know what Paul is doing, I must be brave and look around the edge of the door.

'I told you to get out of my sight Kate.'

He's sprawled on the bed with a look of absolute fury, probably unable to stand. His left hand grasps the neck of an almost empty vodka bottle, and his eyes are half-closed. His speech was slurred so he must be on the verge of passing out. I'll risk a few more steps.

'Are you deaf?'

He throws the vodka bottle at me, and it smashes off the wall, inches from my head. The air smells of alcohol and drops have settled on my forehead and on my nose. The smithereens are like glitter on the bedroom carpet.

I'm frozen to the spot, quivering all over with silent tears rolling down my face, but Paul has passed out. One small mercy and given how much he's had to drink at least four hours of peace and quiet. His body looks strangely contorted as drool dribbles from the corner of his mouth onto the pillow.

The moment the adrenaline rush subsides I run back to the ensuite. Teddy is exactly where he should be, but he's shaking all over and whimpers as soon as his eyes meet mine. I pick him up, feed him more treats and hold him close until my eyes run dry and his whimpering stops.

Even though it feels like my entire body is shaking, I'll keep him in my arms to protect his paws from the broken glass as I tiptoe through the bedroom.

Due to a broken hinge, the bedroom door can't be fully closed without banging it so I close it as much as possible and whisper to Teddy that everything will be okay. By the time we're downstairs, his shaking has stopped.

I collapse onto the sofa and Teddy snuggles in beside my leg. The only disturbance is the occasional loud snore emanating from the bedroom. The living room curtains are open, and all the moonlight can show me is the dying acer which forms the centrepiece of a barren garden. Barren like me.

We tried so hard to be parents, but the IVF failed, and tempers got short. Five years ago, Paul closed the bank account we used to save for fertility treatments and spent the meagre balance on a puppy. He told me that caring for Teddy would ease the grief of being denied a family, but not a day goes by that I don't wish a very different little creature was slumbering in a cot.

I'm racked with grief, and it's compounded by every punch to the stomach that's rooted in Paul's loathing of my barren belly. The familiar sting of tears has returned. I weep for myself. I weep for the baby I never had, but most of all, I weep for the life I never had.

Running my tongue over my teeth, I can still taste blood and one of my molars feels a bit wobbly. I better rinse with salt water to avoid an infection.

While I'm waiting for the kettle to boil, I catch my reflection in the polished stainless-steel door of the fridge and see that tonight's tears have washed my face clean of foundation. I have two black eyes, a cut lip, and a jaw that's black and blue, but at least my nose isn't broken. The rest of my body is a canvas of bruises, each one a different colour and in a different phase of healing.

The kettle clicks off and I dissolve salt in a mug of water and rinse my mouth even though it's scalding hot. My eyes are watering, and my nose is burning, but at least this is pain of my own choosing. I spit out the bloody brine and watch the once wobbly molar go down the drain.

Teddy is gently snoring on the sofa as I tiptoe upstairs to open a door that's always closed. When we bought the house, this room was going to be the nursery. It's painted in a gender-neutral colour, but the stencilled cartoon animals are a stark reminder of what never happened.

There's something hidden in the wardrobe that I need and I'm confident it's there because Paul would have put me in hospital if he found it. I reach in behind stacks of blankets and feel for the strap, which comes free with no noise. This backpack feels like treasure as I run downstairs.

Shaking off the dust brings back painful memories of all that I've endured since packing it. Staying put seems like an act of madness now, but I wasn't ready before. I was still clutching on to the hope of a future pregnancy making everything right. I know now that day will never come and the only thing I might meet here is an early death.

Everything inside is exactly how I remember. A couple of jumpers and two pairs of jeans that Paul has never seen me wear. A week's worth of socks and underwear and new toiletries as moving my toothbrush and soap would make him suspicious. There's also hair dye, a hat, and scissors. A small zip pocket at the back has my passport and a debit card linked to a bank account he knows nothing about.

I'll change clothes now so that Paul will give an inaccurate description when he calls the police to declare me missing. That gives me one set of clothes to take with me and more room in the backpack. I'll leave the old clothes in a pile on the floor. God knows how his hangover will interpret that.

As I'm putting on my jacket, I'm wondering if Paul will be able to describe it. Probably, but it's from the high street and unremarkable in every way. What witness ever noticed a woman in a black jacket? Then it dawns on me that the state of my face will attract attention and my only option is to redo my foundation.

The tube in my handbag is empty and the only other make-up is in the ensuite. All I have to do is grab it and run back downstairs. Just in case Paul has one eye open, I'll take the jacket off. My heartrate is climbing as I grab the banister and head upstairs.

My palms are clammy as I push open the bedroom door and see Paul in the same position on the bed snoring. I duck into the ensuite to grab my make-up bag, my chest tight from anxiety. I take a long look in the mirror and promise myself a better future before going back to the bedroom.

'Kate?'

My right foot is just beyond the doorway. Should I pretend I didn't hear and keep going? No, that would only lead to more trouble.

'Go back to sleep Paul.'

I glance over my shoulder and thankfully he's still lying down.

'Where are you going with that bag? It's always beside the mirror.'

I better turn and face him and hope he's still too drunk to notice my shallow breathing.

'I need to sort out what's in it and I'd be making noise if I did it here, so I thought I'd do it downstairs before bed.'

'Okay. Sorry about your face.'

He closes his eyes and I leave the room. I'm tempted to slam the door good and hard, but one beating is enough so I do the usual gentle closing and run back downstairs with everything in the bag rattling because my hands are shaking so much.

It takes more than a few minutes for my hands to stop quivering, but once they're steady, I sit at the kitchen table with a small mirror and turn my face into something that will blend in with the crowd.

As I'll have more bruises in the coming days, I put the make-up bag in the backpack, wondering why it didn't occur to me that I'd need it in the first place. I put my jacket back on and zip it up with a sense of purpose.

My engagement and wedding rings could be used to identify me, so I take them off and put them in the zip pocket of the backpack where they'll be safe until the time comes to pawn them.

I plait my long red hair and tuck the braid under a black hat. Not so much as a strand can be seen and I'll keep it that way until I'm in another city and have time to dye it brown and cut it.

Teddy is still snoring and every part of me wants to say a proper goodbye to him, but I can't because that would be cruel for us both. I have no plan and no concrete idea of where I'm going other than away from here. When I've gathered my strength, I'll come back and take him away from this place because he's the child I couldn't create. Until that day, the countless photos on my phone will have to do.

There's only one person who knows the extent of the abuse in this house, my only friend, Lauren. She calls here every morning to make sure I'm still alive and we go for a walk. I'll message her that I'm leaving and will be in touch when I've found somewhere to stay. That's the least I can do to repay her for all her support. She won't tell a soul that I contacted her and if the need arises, she'll give Teddy a home.

I'm leaving through the back because if Paul comes round and sees I'm gone, the first thing he'll do is open the front door and walk up and down the street. I'll have to jump a wall to get to the alley, but I know I can do it because I practiced the last time I thought about leaving. The patio door slides open nice and quietly. I'll leave it open a bit, let the cold give Paul a shock when he wakes to find me gone.

I jump to grab the top of the wall and haul myself up. Just as I'm sitting, I hear a whimper and look down to see Teddy's eyes full of questions about where I'm going without him, but no lights on in the house.

His big, dark eyes are full of worry and if I disappear now, he'll bark loudly, and I won't get very far. I shudder to think of the punishment I'd face for an attempted escape. I climb back down and as soon as I kneel, Teddy climbs into my lap.

As I stroke Teddy's eternally soft black and white coat, my mind is gripped by one question. If Paul can't beat me, will he continue to spare the dog? I can't take that chance.

It takes all my nerve to go back into the house to put some dog food into a zip lock bag and grab Teddy's leash and harness. Once the lights are off, we make our way back outside.

'It's just you and me now Teddy.'

As space is at a premium, I wrap the leash inside the jumper and the harness inside the jeans. There should be just enough room if I put the dog food and make-up bag in the front pocket. I pick Teddy up, sit him into the backpack and carefully zip it up so that his fur isn't caught, and his head is sticking out comfortably. He looks confused and who could blame him. At this moment, I couldn't be more grateful that he's a small dog.

'We are going to survive.'

The instant I'm wearing the backpack, Teddy starts licking the nape of my neck. I clamber up and over the wall and run through the alley as soon as my feet hit the ground. Never again will we return. I am finally unburdened and free to carry a weight of my own choosing.

The Painting

The little girl ran as the screams echoed through the house. Her friend upstairs would help. She always did, despite an encroaching bitterness, a sinister resentment that bled into the atmosphere whenever her savior dispensed advice or comfort. The air, electrified by anxiety and fear, came dangerously close to igniting from the earth-shattering vibrations that came with each squeak of the stairs she climbed. But the little girl's secret was her salvation. Whenever the house suffocated with an anger so stifling that even opening the windows in her room overlooking the bay could not help her breathe, she had somewhere else to go.

In her eight short years of life, the little girl had become well versed in the performance as she observed her parents' capacity for tremendous love and great resentment. Today, the first four acts had already occurred, which meant that the finale would be upon them shortly.

Act one, in which their mouths spewed vile words as she sat quietly as witness, once again questioning her parents' marriage, was over as quickly as it began. Her father cried as she handed him tissues. Her mother embarked on a bitter tirade. Her husband did not truly love his wife; he took her for granted – and she was stupid enough to allow him to do so. The little girl felt obligated to listen.

In act two, the ice followed the fire. The laptop keys clicked in her father's office as he threw himself into his work to prove his worth. Sated for the moment of her need to vent, her mother used her silence as a weapon against her father and retreated into herself. It was the only power her mother felt she had.

Act three started as it always did, with a seemingly innocuous discussion on what had occurred between her parents. Then her mother made a comment, innocent to her, inflammatory to her daughter. Or perhaps – did her mother know what it would do? The little girl had learned to steel herself, to manage her emotions so her mother could not get what she wanted from her. A fight. Someone else to blame for her feelings but herself and her father. She often felt sad for her mother.

With act four the flames were reignited. Her father entered, whimpering pathetically, supplicating himself at her mother's feet, promising both his wife and daughter that he would change, swearing that things would be different, that he was sorry, that he loved his wife more than anything. The little girl knew he wanted these things to be true. But she suspected they were not. Love was not enough. Not for them. The little girl often pitied her father.

Now they found themselves in the last scene of the fourth act, her mother freezing her father out a while longer, desperately clinging to the little power that she had. The little girl sometimes wondered if her mother enjoyed fighting because it was the only scenario in which she could honestly face the life she hated.

The old Victorian house echoed with mute resentment, every creak of the wooden floors laden with danger. Each sound held the potential to break the quiet home, releasing the hatred and self-loathing. She continued to creep up the stairs to the attic, ignoring the deafening silence of her mother in the family room and her father his cramped little office, both desperately trying to prove that they were the one the other needed more.

The girl entered the attic which, unlike most others, was barren – no junk from their family life cluttering up the space. The only things they held on to from the past were their resentments.

But the girl knew better. In the far corner by the window, she picked up the loose floorboard and removed her treasure: a small painting of a young girl playing the piano.

"Hi."

After a moment's pause, the girl in the painting began to move. Within its confines, she turned her head and grinned, warmth entering her brush-stroked features.

"Hello, Leila. It's nice to see you again."

Leila folded her legs as she sat, a sad smile etched on her face.

"I'm sorry I haven't visited you in a while. My parents were going through a good time. I couldn't sneak up here. But now I could."

The girl in the painting smiled wider. "That's okay. I'm just happy you're with me now. I don't know what it's like to have a family and friends outside. You're lucky."

Leila sighed, picking at the hem of her pants. "I am, but I don't have anybody to talk to when my parents are fighting. It's not good to tell people outside the family when your parents are fighting."

"Did your parents tell you that?" the girl in the painting asked. With fluid movement, she turned the rest of her body on the piano bench to face Leila.

"No. But they pretend they're not fighting when we go out. I get sad when we have to come back home because I know they won't pretend to be happy anymore and I'll be alone again."

"You have me. You shouldn't forget that."

Leila smiled. "Yes. Thank you for always listening to me."

"I'm glad you keep coming back." The girl stood up from the piano bench. "I know what it feels like to be lonely. I've never talked to anyone else."

Leila gaped at her friend. “But other people lived in this house before we came. Haven’t you had any other friends?”

“No.” The girl in the painting gazed with an intense loneliness at her right hand. “I’ve never even touched another person.”

Leila glanced down at her own hands, suddenly overwhelmed by the parallels between their situations. “Do you think you could feel me through the painting?”

The girl in the painting looked up at Leila, hope and guarded anticipation illuminating her features. “Maybe. I don’t know. I’ve been too scared to try. What if it doesn’t work?”

“I’ll still be your friend. And I’ll still come talk to you. Every day,” Leila vowed. She would never again abandon the person who cared for her, who only listened and never judged.

Wordlessly, the girl in the painting nodded, a curious expression painted onto her face. She held up her left hand and Leila reached out her right until their palms touched. A spark of warmth and a flash of bright red light fried Leila’s senses, and she let out a wordless scream. Her world became dark.

Light slowly emerged and with it, a view of a piano.

“Finally.”

“Leila!” Her mother’s voice rang from downstairs. “Come to the kitchen please. Come. We’re all going to watch a movie together, and you can choose it.”

Leila tried to call out, but her lips were frozen. Panic bloomed in her chest. She could not move a muscle, not even her eyes, to see the girl formerly in the painting, now in Leila’s body, tuck the painting under her arm. As she ambled down the stairs with a now trapped Leila, she whispered to her.

“I had to listen to your incessant whining every time your parents fought. You stupid girl, you never learned to live. You have parents, you have a life, freedom. Had. You never appreciated it. I’ll do that for you. And now you’ll watch the world go by. I will make sure of it. And who knows? Maybe your – sorry, *my* – parents won't fight as much anymore now that I'm their daughter."

All smiles, the girl formerly in the painting strode into the kitchen and set the painting with Leila down on the counter. "I found this upstairs in the attic. I thought it might look good here."

Leila's father smiled. "Yes, it's very nice."

"You can leave it there," Leila's mother added. "Let's go watch a movie."

"But first, family hug," Leila's father announced.

Leila's parents and the girl formerly in the painting embraced tightly, so lost in the moment that none of them noticed the movement in the painting. One of Leila's fingers slowly, torturously, pressed down on a piano key. Act five had always ended with a feeble, contrived return to normalcy. This time, Leila determined that the finale would look quite different.

Drive Carefully, Mum

Big Bear Lake glistened between the pines. Angie slowed the car for a clearer view, and a deer bolted across the road. She slammed on the brakes, and in a reflex action put the car in neutral. The deer vanished into the trees.

When she learnt to drive nearly forty years ago, changing gears had felt unnatural: she had wanted to perform the action with her right hand. But driving from LAX had been instinctive, confirming her suspicion.

She'd lived on this earth before. In a country that drove on the right hand side of the road.

"You can rent a cabin in the Lake District, Mum," Martin said. "Why go to America?"

If she'd lived before, and driven on the right, likely her home had been America, because she had no aptitude for European languages. Angie had her reasons for travelling to California and Big Bear Lake.

The cabin sat beside the rocky lake shoreline, water shimmering below the golden San Bernardino Mountains. Inside, a kitchenette, living area, and bed linked the open-plan space. The fridge whizzed and popped, and there were pictures of eagles on the walls. Angie collapsed into a blue leather sofa, held out her legs and rotated her ankles.

Sixty-three was a preposterous age.

Is the cabin nice, Mum? Martin messaged. He'd programmed her phone to relay GPS coordinates every five minutes, following her trip on his computer. *I googled. There are bears. Be careful.*

Angie went outside to fetch her belongings from the car, smiled awkwardly at the couple sitting on wooden recliners by the neighbouring cabin.

"I'm Emily," the woman said. "This is Mort."

Angie lifted her groceries from the back seat of the car.

"Need a hand with your bags?" The man's paunch sagged over his trousers as he shifted to stand.

"I'm fine."

He sank back into the chair.

"Are you alone?" Emily asked. "Where's your husband?"

"No husband," Angie said. "I'm fine. Thanks."

"I don't know how you feel safe alone," Emily said. "Isn't she brave, Mort?"

Angie's hand brushed the phone in her pocket. Martin was right. She wasn't safe. She took the groceries inside. Unpacked the bags, placed the milk in the fridge.

Men don't make you safe. Look at Marjorie Brooks, romanced in her fifties and coerced into signing over her pension for better returns. Now she lives with her sister, and sleeps in her nephew's bedroom.

Angie went back outside for her suitcase.

"We're going fishing on the lake tomorrow," Emily said. "Join us."

Angie set her suitcase on its wheels, extended the handle. "Thanks, but I've got plans."

The next day, Angie drove to the local history museum.

Martin didn't like the twisty San Bernardino Mountain roads. *Drive carefully, Mum,* he messaged.

The museum was a converted settler church. An old clapboard shed with rusty ploughs and scythes stacked against the walls. She parked beside the only other car. Angie had emailed Francine, curator of the museum, to arrange a meeting.

"You wanted the recent history section?" Francine asked.

"Yes." Angie unfolded a piece of paper from her bag. "I'm interested in seeing this photograph and others from the same collection."

"We keep those photographs in the back." Francine winced apologetically. "People are more interested in the settlers."

The museum was dark, the windows partially covered by blinds and dirt. Angie squeezed between displays of cups and clothing. Gold panning equipment, and small glistening nuggets, locked behind glass. Dust coated her tongue, gritted her teeth.

"We used that photograph in our anniversary exhibition." Francine crouched and opened the door of a blown chipboard cupboard.

In the weeks after her mum died, Angie sprang awake every few hours during the night, used to being needed. She found the picture on the internet when she couldn't sleep. It was a photograph of VJ day, 8th of August, 1945, taken in Big Bear, California. A parade, floats, flowers. In the foreground, a young girl, with ringlets, hugging a woman's neck, clasping an American flag, a tear on her cheek. Across the street was a woman. She wore wide hipped trousers, and a pale shirt with an exaggerated collar.

"I'm interested in this woman."

Francine turned from the cupboard, glanced where Angie pointed, nodded, looked away, twisted back, and studied Angie.

"She sure looks like you."

"Do you have photographs you didn't post on the internet?" Angie asked.

Francine placed a thick black photo album on the table. "The picture you've seen is in there." She pushed the folder towards Angie, pulled five more from the cupboard. "This is our collection from that era."

Angie sat at the table and opened the folder, her hands shaking. Must seeped into her nose and mouth as she turned the pages. She found photographs of the parade first. The young girl. Then the woman.

Enjoy the museum, Martin messaged.

She had found the photographs from Big Bear Lake, California, through a process of elimination. If in a past life she'd lived in America, it had to have been before her current birth date, 1959. And if she'd driven, then likely she'd lived in the 40s or 50s. Maybe she'd learnt to drive in the war. So she searched for photos taken in the US during this period. Individuals posted photographs hoping to find old friends before it was too late, or local history museums advertised exhibitions.

Angie had followed the clicks until she fell asleep, her tablet falling from her hands onto the sheets. But one night she found herself in a photograph of a parade, in Big Bear Lake, California.

For an instant, her heart stopped beating.

"Would your parents or grandparents know this person?" Angie asked.

"My family's from Portland," Francine said. "I moved here for the job."

Angie studied the photographs from VJ day, isolating every face for a glimpse of her neat, dark bob across her cheekbone. Francine brought her a sandwich for lunch.

Must be an interesting museum, Martin messaged.

She broadened her search to photographs from that year, then the war era, through to 1950. She didn't find herself again.

"We close at five," Francine said. "But I've consulted our records, and Maisie Prout donated those photographs before she went into the care home. I think she's still alive, well into her nineties now. I could ring the home, see if she'll talk to you?"

Outside the cabin, Mort and Emily were barbecuing fish on an open fire. Evening crept down the mountain and over the lake. Reflections of the pier lights floated on the water.

"Join us," Mort said. "There's plenty. I caught them myself."

The gutted fish carcasses lay on a grill, their iridescence skin dancing in the firelight, their smell strangely metallic. Martin had warned her against eating fish from the lake because of the mercury.

"I'm tired." Angie pointed to her cabin. "Goodnight."

Two days later, Angie drove to Maisie Prout's care home. The large white house sat in manicured grounds, a lawn dropped toward a pond, willow trees planted to block the road. Residents sat in twos and threes, chatting in the morning sun.

She registered at reception. The house didn't smell of old age or disinfectant. Nothing like the places she'd viewed for Mum, ubiquitous communal living areas and overbearing TVs. She should have looked harder, found her mum professional care.

Maisie sat at a garden table on the back terrace, her face shaded by a wide brimmed straw hat.

"This is lovely." Angie sat beside her.

"You're Francine's friend from the museum?" Maisie's voice sang. "She'd said you'd be visiting. You want to ask about my old photographs?" Her skin enveloped her sparkling eyes in soft, deep wrinkles.

There were thirty years between them. Angie had grown, had love affairs, married and had Martin by the time she was thirty. Maisie was a reminder. There was time.

Angie took the photograph from her handbag.

"I'm interested in this person." She pointed to the woman. "Do you recognise her?"

Maisie smiled at the photo. "I remember taking that picture. I thought I was Alfred Stieglitz, took photographs of everything, even my food. Do you know Edward Weston's work?"

Angie shook her head, felt her heart beating as if it were separate from her body. "Do you know that woman?"

Maisie lifted her glasses from around her neck and balanced them on her nose.

"That's young Patricia Morgan." Maisie pointed to the girl in the foreground. "She's passed now, four years ago, more. And only a few years older than my own kids. Funny how life works." She took off her glasses, glanced across the garden. "Keeps some of us, lets others go."

Maisie raised her arm, and a nurse appeared. "Iced tea, please," she said.

Angie gripped the seat of her chair. She believed the elderly had the right to make you wait; they had less time and should dictate its use.

The tea arrived. Maisie sipped through a striped paper straw. "That woman looks a lot like you."

Angie ran her finger around the rim of her glass.

"Do you have family here?" Maisie asked.

Angie shook her head. Her family had lived in Worcestershire for centuries. And she didn't share their features; Angie's mum and sister had the same round face; hers was long and drawn.

Maisie replaced her glasses and studied the picture again.

"Is that an Army uniform?" Angie asked. If Maisie could give her a name, she could research war records.

"Back then I was nineteen," Maisie said. "Gracie was eighteen months. Do you have children?"

"One." Angie clasped her phone, and it buzzed.

Why are you visiting a care home, Mum? Is everything OK?

Angie looked up from the screen. "He wants to know why I'm visiting you."

Maisie closed her eyes. "I don't recognise her. I'm sorry."

Angie put the phone in her bag, tried to close the zip, but it caught in the lining.

"I can tell you she wasn't local. Probably passing through. It was VJ Day. Everyone was celebrating, everyone was in transit. Except me."

Maisie pointed out friends from the picture. The grocer and the postmaster. Angie watched two old men playing miniature golf on the lawn.

Her brother and sister hired a nurse when Mum deteriorated. Three days, and two nights a week. Angie hadn't been the favourite child, or the preferred daughter. "Why don't you visit more?" Angie had asked.

"We can't all live on alimony," her sister replied.

Her brother paid the bill.

Mum wouldn't have recognised them if they had visited, but maybe they would have brought her comfort. They had time to attend the funeral.

"Is there anyone else who might remember her?" Angie scanned the grounds for residents of a likely age.

Maisie delicately brushed Angie's cheek, her fingers powdery and soft. "If she had been local, I'd know her. I'm sorry I can't help you."

Angie's chest contracted. Her mum loved sitting in the garden. Even when she couldn't remember who she was, Mum recalled the names of flowers.

Angie drove around town, stopped for coffee and then dinner, ordered a burger, sour with pickle, and a root beer float.

Be careful driving in the dark, Mum. Martin messaged.

Back at the cabin, Emily and Mort were outside, beside the open fire, a cooler of beer at their feet.

"We've got s'mores," Emily said. "Please, have one."

Angie glanced at her cabin door, wanted to crawl under the duvet, wait for tomorrow, and her flight home.

Mort held out a marshmallow on the end of a toasting fork.

If she'd ever lived in America, likely she'd eaten s'mores before.

"I don't know what to do." Angie dragged the recliner from her cabin.

"First you melt the marshmallow," Mort said, holding out the packet. Emily provided the roasting fork.

Angie squeezed a pink pillow from the bag, much larger than they sold at home, pierced it with the fork and held it over the fire.

"Careful, not directly in the flame, you don't want to burn it," Mort said.

Emily placed two biscuits on a plastic plate, broke off squares of chocolate from a bumper sized bar.

"When the marshmallow's melted, you make a sandwich with the crackers," she said.

Angie scraped the melting marshmallow onto the biscuit and added three squares. Mum chastised her for eating too much chocolate and she considered returning a square to the wrapper.

"You have to wait until the chocolate has just melted," Mort said. Emily laughed.

Angie moved the s'mores towards her mouth, the toasted marshmallow faintly acrid.

"Not yet."

Laughter tickled Angie's throat. "When?"

"Not now," Mort said. "Now."

Angie woke at five am. She'd organised a late checkout. Her flight was at eight that evening. She put on her swimming costume and left her phone in the cabin so Martin would think she was sleeping. The sky foreshadowed the sun over the mountain, a soft baby blue, feathering to darkness. Birds cawed from the tree line. She sat on the end of the pier, dipped her feet into the water, shivered and pushed herself in.

The water tugged at her body and she twisted, floated on her back. Watched the stars fade. Slowly, the pain and cold became indistinguishable from warmth and comfort.

"Where are you, Mum?" she whispered.

The Hazelnut Tree

June 2009, Babaji, Helmand Province, Afghanistan

In Helmand Province, Afghanistan, there's an arterial road in the green zone, a disturbed landscape in the chalky delta perforated by the crimson papaver heads of the opium crops. Kev's been embedded there for almost three months with B Company, sweeping Improvised Explosive Devices from the moonscapes of the old silk route. The nightly bunk bantering with the lads keeps him almost sane, when the day's excess adrenaline is a lit blue touch paper sparking his nerve endings and leaving his skin grit grey and filmy with sweat. On his shoulder, he wears the badge of The International Security Force, which Jenny had sewn onto his desert combats the day before he left. He thinks of her in that moment, her spidery legs crossed on the worn carpet of their Penicuik quarter, her dark hair falling into her black eyes, swollen with the secret tears she'd shed when she'd thought he couldn't see.

"You don't need to sew it on, pet," he'd told his wife gently, the night before he'd deployed. "They taught me how to sew back in Army Cadet College in Harrogate."

"I bloody know that!" Jenny had roared in frustration like the lioness that she is. His soft tone had unnerved her, and she'd furiously swiped at the treacherous tear glittering hotly on her cheek. Kev had smiled but he'd been careful to turn his face away. She'd ballsed up the stiches, and he knew he'd have to rip it off and sew it on again sitting at Brize with his muckers, waiting for the trooper to transport them out the next day.

That was the most challenging part, those forty-eight hours before deploying. Jenny had been struggling to see the stitches, even though you couldn't miss them from space. She'd always makes him leave his kit bag in the airing cupboard upstairs until the very last moment before his departure.

"It looks like a body bag, and I keep falling over the bastard thing when I get up to the boys when they're crying in the night," she'd said.

Whenever he got to where he was going, he'd find that she'd stuffed ripped up pieces of paper amongst his kit. Notes telling him to take his vitamins, to clip the hair inside his ears, which she hated, and that she loved him so much and would miss him every moment. These tiny pieces of lined paper are nailed to the wall above his bunk. They're curled now and dried out by the desert heat, but to Kev they are everything.

Kev's been holed up in Kandahar airfield for the past few weeks, but now B company are on the move, crammed into massive twin-rotor helicopters, swamped with their kit. They're heavy with weapons, ammunition, and rations to last twenty-four hours. With the regular seats stowed away, the Jocks sit on the helicopter floors, their rifles, rocket launchers, and radios entomb them. These helicopters are in short supply. He should feel grateful that the Americans have lent them this one, but he doesn't.

The rotors gather speed, and the cabin lights dim – it's dark except for the anti-missile flares exploding from the side of the machine. The Chinooks lift away from Kandahar, like giant beetles, towards the irrigated farmland and the blood-red poppy fields held by the Taliban insurgents. They're waiting until tonight to start the operation – according to the Ruperts, the plan is simple. They will flood Babaji, forcing the Taliban out of the villages.

Over the past few weeks, Kev's been playing with the local children. They are arresting and dark eyed their faces full of wonder and laughter when he pulls out the miniature dinosaur jigsaws and sticky packets of lemon sherberts he keeps in the leg pockets of his desert combats. Military jargon calls them Consent Winning Goods. He doesn't have a name for giving the local kids some treats, but irrationally, he doesn't want them to think badly of him, to see him as the bogeyman with a gun. He'd asked Jenny to send them over for him, and he takes them out on every foot patrol - that and his rifle, his Glock and his hand grenades.

"Do you wee ones want to play Head, Shoulders, Knees and Toes?" he asks them, and although they don't understand what he's saying, they recognise the father that he is in the twinkle in his eyes, and they laugh and scream with delight as his lanky frame twists and contorts into ridiculous shapes. Women fetch water from the canal; their long linen dresses are loose and cool, and their bright colours and mirrored skirts are prisms of light in the dust. Their chadors shimmer and flutter in the light breeze, and Kev is reminded of Jenny back home in Edinburgh, who's been tie-dying the boy's old grey Y-fronts for a school project on a book about pants. Children play and water their goats. Life looks simple when you're observing it from a distance down the barrel of a cat's arsehole of an SA80. It doesn't feel a million miles away from the lives of Kev's Highland ancestors.

But Kev tries not to think of home. For a moment, Jenny and the boys feel like a distant memory; something smudged behind thick glass. His stomach churns with the fierce acid of homesickness, and he stops for a second to wipe the sweat from his face and something which feels like a tear from his eye.

On their last night in the FOB, after their oily dust-covered burgers and chips, B Company had sat shoulder to shoulder and watched a tribute to Rob McLaren projected onto a massive screen on the wall. They'd found photos of Rob arsing around with his mates, washing his socks in the Helmand river. There's a photo of him flying a rainbow kite above the compound's walls, his 19-year-old face laughing up into the Afghan sky, but the only image that Kev can see now is the one of his union flag-draped coffin waiting to go home to Scotland, carrying what's left of Rob wrapped in his Rangers football shirt.

The Chinooks drop them onto Babaji, north of the Forward Operating Base at Lashkar Gah. Three hundred and fifty of his battalion in a wave with 30 seconds' notice. With the leftover particles of Pte McLaren floating around in their brains, the men weighed down with weapons, ammunition and the rations that would sustain them for the coming 24 hours. Kev spends the first and the second day searching the ground and making it safe. He and his company come under fire from rocket-propelled grenades. The enemy don't have the weaponry to win, but the IEDs haunt them with every potentially fatal step they take.

They walk and check, walk and check.

Captain Shep-Shepherd and his bomb disposal dog, Clive, walk ahead with the detector. Kev knows it's the loneliest job in the world, They're clever, the insurgent bastards; they're out there now watching Kev and his mates. They only need to be successful once. Shep and Clive need to win every time. The Green zone is densely populated and perfect for ambushes. The patrols kick up clouds of dust which can be seen for miles. Gravel tracks fall sharply away to the canals, and the desert stretches out for miles. The enemy is hidden, embedded in bushes and abandoned compounds; most of the Black Watch boys don't see their targets; only the snipers and the soldiers monitoring the drones can see the whites of the eyes of the insurgents.

The locals had been tipped off and fled the night before the Black Watch arrived in the town. Their compounds are locked and silent, great grounded ships dark on the edges of the lush, irrigated fields. The opium crops have been harvested, sold, and smoked – the origins of poppies are little more than some faded flowers in the dust alongside the discarded glass heroin pipes.

On the third night, there's no question that the remaining people in the mud-walled compounds are militia. But Kev's gunner finds a head in a field when a missile is launched in an aerial assault. The head is that of a young girl, perhaps 12 or 13, her hair long and plaited. The force of the explosion had flung her body out of the building. Why the fuck was she still here when the others had left? Was she a wife, a servant, a soldier herself? Who did she belong to, who had loved her? Did she matter to anyone? Life here is cheap. It's the arsehole of the world and Kev has new material for his nightly horror shows.

A group of insurgents are dealt with, and British drones spotted them carrying a belt-fed anti-aircraft machine gun."Serves them fucking right. They weren't out doing the shopping, were they?" says a voice in the darkness, watching through night vision goggles. Kev is grateful for the pathos and the military humour. "Can we get a brew on now?" says the voice.

"Fuck that for a game of soldiers," replies Kev, "Crack open the Buckie." The Jocks laugh, remembering the fortified wine they got shit-faced on as teenagers. Some are still teenagers, and some are still virgins. Some still cry out for their mammies at night.

Eventually, they find cover and rest against a tree, settling for what's left of the water in their tin bottles. Kev lifts his night goggles and sees his platoon on a wide street strewn with rubbish and lined on either side with concrete alcoves. In some parts of Helmand, the white flags of the Taliban fly above grocers, tailors, and pharmacies with morphine and dressings, but tonight, Babaji is deserted. Kev is chin-strapped from walking across the fields of poppy stubble and irrigation ditches, he just wants to get back to the FOB and swim in the canal under cover of darkness. Then Kev hears a noise up ahead – a teenage boy is foraging for stale bread, and when he's captured, quickly and without a struggle, the interpreter tells the

Platoon Commander that he thinks he's a dicker. The boy's story doesn't stack up, so he is probably a watchman.

They're not far from the FOB now, the young prisoner in tow, when they come across an elderly man with a long grey beard in traditional Pashtun robes and a Lungee turban with a wool Pakol cap on top. He's sitting on a small bench under a hazelnut tree. Kev knows he's an elder, a wise man, a Malik. They are men of great power and wield influence over their communities. The little hazelnut tree is outside a tiny mud-brick home the size of two telephone boxes, and the malik seems to be the only one who's been left behind. His rickets have probably prevented him from joining the exodus with his family. He's seen the wars before and watches the soldiers passing him with a weathered eye. They barely glance in his direction.

Kev is reminded of his Granda Shuggie and imagines if the tables were turned, and they'd had to leave Shug behind. Kev remembers the ten-pack of Benson and Hedges in his bicep pocket and slows to the back of the group.

"Keep walking Corporal," the Platoon Commander barks, sensing the change in Kev's pace. But something shifts in Kev, as he thinks of the old man, so he ignores the Captain and heads back to the Malik, he knows he's breaking all the rules. He lowers his rifle and reaches into his pocket with his right hand. Shuggie's in his mind, sitting in the smoke-filled bar in the west end of Glasgow, shouting instructions to Kev on how to feed the fag machine with 50ps. Kev smiles, his Granda is close by, and he'd approve of this gesture, a small act of kindness in a fucked-up world.

The bullet from the British Glock, hidden under the Malik's robes, is too fast for Kev, to slick for them all. The shot cracks out across the night, the intensity of the pulse in the sound wave reverberating off the mud-walled compounds. The soldiers react, but already too late, and Kev is already dead when his helmet bounces off the ground and face hits the dirt of the deserted village street. The Malik holds the pistol to his own temple, tight against the cloth of his turban.

“Allahu Akbar”, he shouts, his mouth wide, no teeth in his head, his eyes raised to the sky as he pulls the trigger.

*

June 2009, Redford Barracks, Edinburgh

It’s three months into Kev’s third operational tour of Afghanistan, and Jenny is scrubbing at the yellow sticky patches of misfired boy piss from around the lino in the corner of the tiny downstairs loo. She covers her face with the rubberised ski mask she finds buried under the coat mountain at the front door. Kev’s combat jacket sits at one end. His Greens. It’s one of Kev’s Army ski team things, and she snorts aloud, thinking what he’d say if he could see her wearing it now. Despite being used to living with her four blokes, the smells they produce still turn her stomach. Previous soldiers’ families haven’t been so meticulous,the stains round the loo indicate and she wonders how many boys have peed on these pieces of plastic before hers.

Archie sits in his highchair watching Holly and Phil on This Morning. Holly laughs throatily at herself and Phil’s slapstick innuendos. Holly is showcasing her ‘funny ejector dress’; if she breathes out, the belt pings open. Jenny momentarily kneels back on her heels, the bleach overpowering her, sweat trickling underneath her greying bra, and visualises marching into their TV studios and slapping them both very hard until they stop their jovial antics.

Her third-born son is nine months old, and he is the colour and size of a healthy young piglet. His appetite and the dimples in his cheeks are pure Kev, and already, he doesn’t take any shit from his two bigger brothers. Archie contentedly dips batons of carrot and his cherubic face into the smashed chickpeas, swirling his patterns and smacking his lips and humming to himself.

A sharp knock at the UPVC front door is the signal that Jenny's life is about to change. Archie hears it from his highchair and knocks his chubby fists on the tray table too. But the knock is terse and startles Jenny and she crashes her head upwards in surprise against the cistern of the loo.

"Coming!" she yells, peeling off her hole filled marigolds. What is it with Army wives and greetings cards, Tupperware, and idiotic Pampered Chef cookware parties? It's probably Suze from Trafalgar Street with the Phoenix cards she was guilted into buying at the community centre last week.

"What have you done, little chonk?" She laughs and points at Archie, mock horrified, his fists caked like plump chicken drumsticks. She wipes her hands before heading to the door, but the second knock stops her in her tracks. The staccato force of the knock is wrong. Archie has fallen silent; his knocking and drumming has stopped, and he can smell his mother's alarm. A carrot baton falls to the plastic sheet on the carpet. Jenny watches it, mesmerised, afraid to move her eyes away from it.

She snaps off the TV and Archie's eyes follow her as the air around her changes shape. The third knock almost splits the safety glass of the Army issue door. Archie's eyes widen, and his chin begins to wobble. It's not a game anymore. Jenny snatches him out of his chair, her blood thumping hard, a drumbeat in her ears. She breathes in Archie's smell, closes her eyes for a moment, and as she opens them, sees through the wobbly glass of the front door that standing there are her worst fears.

Islay Carmichael, The Patch's Families' Officer, his short square silhouette familiar to her, particularly during the months the men are away

"Open the door, Jenny," Islay says softly but firmly. His voice usually soothes her; the melodic lilt of his Hebridean accent sounds almost more Irish than Scottish to her,yet is distinctly different to both. Hearing it now her stomach is glacial.

"We need to talk to you. I can see you; I know you're in there."

Jen knows that because it's Islay, and she can see he's in his Number Ones and not his combat pyjamas, and that someone else in uniform is standing next to him, that he is here with the very worst news.

Archie starts to whimper, and Jenny is whimpering too. An Officer, a tall man, has been delivering the blows to her front door.

Two men. Uniforms. The knock at the door.

No, it's not her turn. She'll not have it. For as long as she doesn't answer, she can stop them from talking, from saying the words she cannot hear.

"No," she whispers; the word scratches her throat as it escapes. Islay is bending down now, peering through the letterbox.

"Jenny, we have a key; we're coming in, darling. We need to come inside."

She thinks she could run to the door. She could heave her whole weight against it, jamming her shoulder against the lock, her flesh draining of blood until she turns to heavy, impenetrable stone. They won't be able to come in then.

The key in the door is clicking and turning, rotating round and round like an antique clock winder. Time slows and stops as she plays out the scene in her head, and after what seems like a millennium, Archie whimpers again. She hears him moan and then realises the sound is coming from her. Her legs dissolve with every turn. She is sinking into the terrible brown polyester of the Army-issue carpet, Archie clasped too tightly to her body, a reminder of her old life, a strange place now to which she will never return.

*

June 2020, Helmand Province, Afghanistan

A scrawny cow stands beside the road under a hazelnut tree, a chicken pecking at her hoof. A tiny girl, her brown eyes watchful pools, her dusty dress glittering with Pashtun mirrors and sequins, rattles a dry opium pod back and forth, a toy, an instrument, a flare of despair.

A widow, their mother, plants vermillion poppies in front of her mud baked home. She's trying to attract buyers so that her six children can eat. Her husband is lost to the war, and her brothers are lost in their haze of opium addiction. The little girl doesn't go to school anymore; she's confined to the compounds now, the charred spines of her textbooks discarded on the road, burned in a terrible poetry of heat and light. The air is cloying and sweet with the smell of iron blood, and amongst the debris of opium and violence, a boy flies his plastic bag kite to the sound of static on an old military radio he finds lying at the side of the road.

Mr Greenlee does not visit anymore.

It all went wrong when I murdered Mr Greenlee, it was fine until then. I should have realised when my sewing needles went missing, again. I knew the miserly mice had mithered them, away, because of the waistcoat, the waistcoat that the tailor was designing. I mean to say, if you are going to do something do it properly. Now those saucy silly mice are going to try and fix his mistakes. I hear them at night, squeaking away, under the worn scuffed floorboards, they keep me awake.

'Don't be so nasty old woman, they squeak, he's not well.'

As Mandy Rice Davies said. 'He would say that, wouldn't he.'

I tut tut to myself, but it can be frustrating when characters, tumble, out of my neatly piled up books, gradually sneaking out into Pear. Let me tell you about Pear because this is where it all happened. it is a very interesting story.

I live in Pear Tree Cottage, which I refer to as 'Pear.' It once belonged to a little old wandering washing woman, who left to live in her Dr Martens, I know mad isn't. So, when I retired, I moved into Pear, when wandering washing woman moved out, taking all her snotty sloppy kids with her, thank goodness, because they were so naughty. A good spanking, they could have done with, but of course that's illegal in Wales.

Now some saucy unsavoury characters, walk or run, depending on how mad they are, to the other side of the Severn bridge, making sure they avoid the Tripping Trolls Traps, watch out for these they're all over Wales. The Trolls set up rollie pollie hills, where kids roll down, and then land plop into waiting Trolls Traps. Lots of kids have gone missing this way, their parents are still searching for them, to this day, so be careful, be very very careful.

Back to what I was saying, about saucy unsavoury characters, so, they find themselves in England and clip their kid's ears, where it is perfectly legal to do so. There is always a lot of howling scowling screams in England, or so I'm told. I never go there, it's far too full of people, and far too fast and furious for me.

But there we are, they have very strange laws there, at least in Wales kids are not getting their ears clipped, so it's a lot quieter in Wales, in fact, though we like to keep it to ourselves, the valleys are as peaceful as the Church mice, who very often chew the bald bandy bishops', vast violet velvet vestments. Anyway, let's get back to the beginning of our conversation. Pear is where I live, with my dog who is called Pipkin, Pip for short.

Pear is the prettiest place you are ever likely to see. It is a teeny tiny two up two down cottage, with soft white stoned walls, a small squared crooked red brick chimney, all glimmering together in the suns smile. The soft white stone peeps out from rambling red, pink and orange roses, who entwine and knot among themselves, in the glossy emerald, green ivy, all scrambling for supremacy.

Now, as you probably have heard, Queenie only likes red roses, so I very often make sure the pink and orange roses are painted red, which took forever, until I met Mr Greenlee, the gardener, but more of him later.

Queenie liked my roses so much, that she would visit quite often, her red shiny soft satin dress, ballooning out over the white wrought iron legs of my garden chairs. Her little red velvet pumps, with their pink oversized bows, peeping out from under the dress. There she will sit, puckered painted bow red lips, smoking her lemon flavoured vape, yellow smoke encircling the blue heavens.

'And whoooo doooo youuuu think youuuu are?' she used to say to me.

Removing myself from her rude comments I would bake jam tarts and sit in the yellow smoke and sunshine, until the sun waved goodbye. Queenie, always got sozzled on the white wine, thankfully leaving, before Mr Greenlee arrived. She would lift her skirts, revealing white ruffled petticoats, and then proceed to topple tipsy turvy, knocking the garden furniture over. It usually needs the wise wide-eyed owl to carry her off into the night sky. I am always glad to see the back of her, I must be honest.

Anyway, back to the pear, Pip and I were very happy there, oh I better tell you a little bit about Pip. He is the sweetest kindest black Labrador you are ever likely to meet. I would be so lonely without him. We talk throughout the day; well, I talk he wags his tail and listens. Our favourite time of year is Christmas when he can talk.

On the Eve of Christmas, we sit together, me drinking chardonnay, and Pip scoffing treats, and we talk all the moons away. He always tells the reindeers off for making such a noise on the roof.

'Hey what's going on up there,' he says. 'Some of us are trying to have a quiet night here you know.'

The reindeers then make more noise and between Santa laughing and booming out 'MERRY CHRISTMAS EVERYONE,' it can be quite a chaotic night. I usually fall to sleep by the crackling fire and leave them all to it. In the morning Pip is fast asleep as quiet as Mary's little lamb.

Anyway, let's get back on track. As I said I'm retired, no longer a member of the real world, thank goodness, so the days and nights are very much my own, to do as I wish. I have no friends as such, except for Mr Greenlee, the gardener, who visits every day, here he comes now, down the winding lane, hear him. Clip, clop, clip, clop, yes, you are right, he has a dear old black shiny horse, named Darkie. Darkie used to be a pit pony, but he is retired now, when you stroke him, black coal dust floats into the glowing glimmering sun rays.

'Hello there Dorothy.' 'The grass is wild and overgrown, it must be rushing in the breeze of the summer, and then flattened by the pouring rain.'

Mr Greenlee writes poetry, so can be quite poetic with his prose.

I ushered him into Pear. 'Yes, I know Mr Greenlee it's a disgrace isn't, I was just going to tidy it up.'

He would sit doffing his green tweed cap, smiling, and rolling a spliff in his nicotine-stained fingers. 'No, my deary, Dorothy, let me do it for you, it's no trouble, I insist.'

And off he went, and before I knew it, he had chopped and cut down every ruddy, thing, no more red roses, let alone white ones, no more entangling glossy emerald, green ivy, they were all shorn and sorrowful, drowning in their own tears. I knew Queenie would be mad, so taking the chainsaw, I promptly chopped Mr Greenlee's head off, telling him to never return to Pear. He was upset. It was so swift, he was still smiling as he progressed to heaven, which I knew was where he was heading, beheaded, because he always attended church.

And I know this because I had attended his confirmation, just a few black moons ago, wearing my long black velvet dress, with a silver crucifix necklace, finished off with a black satin headband, which held my curly windswept hair, at least, in some resemblance, of trying. I certainly looked the part. It was a wonnnderful day.

The church was in its usual darkest depression, its melancholy mournful self. Its tearful stained-glass eyes looking on. I stared at them, the forever old Christian stories, etched out in a rainbow of ruby red, citrus orange, and heavy black leaded glass. Mary stood to the side holding the baby Jesus, I smiled at her, but she did not smile back, she was as usual in deep thought, well I suppose Jesus was a huge responsibility.

It was then the balding bandy bishop floated down the aisle, his white satin robes reaching to the cold parquet floor. I could not see his feet- maybe he doesn't have any. Balancing on his little bald head, was a hat of golden satin, shimmering in beams of sunlight, gaily bouncing off the well-polished mahogany pews.

Then coursing through the skylights of his heavens, the silence was shattered by the soaring singing choir. 'He's got the whole, world in his hands; He's got the whole wide world, in his hands…' I'm not a great lover of this hymn I must be honest, I much prefer, how great thou art, now that song can soar, but I suppose Mr Greenlee did have the whole world in his hands being a gardener and all.

As I slowly step, by careful step, walk out of the church, I glimpse a crowd of black bat cackling crows, but when I was nearer, I saw they were waiting in the queue, the death queue. They were all cuddled up together, the very elderly people, smelling of stale pee and lavender, sweet and sour all at the same time. They nodded, and their holes for mouths smiled eerie smiles at me. I walked a little quicker, I am not ready for their time, not quite yet. Queenie was already flying high as the clock chimed nine, when I got back to pear.

'Helooooo Dorothy, 'isn't it time we took Mr Greenlee out of the freezer? he's taking up so much room.

I poured myself a chardonnay. 'Don't be stupid Queenie, he's far too heavy for us to carry, I've tried, he's frozen solid.'

'Well, we must get help then. We need the witches help; we'll throw him in the river. She stopped for a minute to puff the vape before continuing the conversation. 'We must stop crushing the eggshells we throw out after our breakfasts. Now listen to me Dorothy, as you know, we only crush the eggshells so the witches cannot use them as sailing boats. But now we need their help, so what I propose we do is to fill the recycling bin with eggshells that are not shattered, are you listening Dorothy I'm not going to say this again.'

I saw smoke billowing out of her ears, so I stared at her and spoke. 'Yes, Queenie I'm listening, here have a chardonnay.

So, I did as she said and very soon, we had a recycling bin full of eggshells, which were quite whole, except for the small opening, where we had dipped in our hot buttered toast soldiers, who by the way are always complaining, with-

'Flipping heck my heads boiling.'

Now, it was a quiet, soft, white, snowy morning when I heard the recycling bin rattling, even though it was not the day for the recycling to be taken. I jumped out of bed, pulled on my pink furry dressing gown, fell over Pip who was about to go outside, so we squeezed through the dog flap together, and then I saw them.

A very large cackling bunch of witches, who were headfirst in the recycling bin. Their hairy scrawny black knee-high socked legs, dangled over the edge of the bin. They were screeching and giggling to each other.

'We could get to Timbuktu in all these sailing boats. 'Timbuktu yooo whoo

Timbuktu here we come, two by two, Timbuktu, tumm tumm Toooo'

They cackled and screamed until even Pip put his paws over his ears. I just stood there unsure really on what to do. I mean what do you do when you see a gang of witches? They carried on for a time, throwing the eggshells into black sacks that they had strung around their humped backs, until finally, the sacks were full. They plopped all to the floor together, brushing themselves off with a satisfied-

'Whew, all done girls, well done girls. Eee Eee Eee, Ooo Ooo Ooo,Timbukto, here we come, and remember girls whatever happens in Timbuktu, stays in Timbukto.'

Then they saw me.

'What you are looking at, gobby mouth,' one of them creaked.

'Oh hello, I'm Dorothy, pleased to meet you, I'm sure, I had heard this in a film so thought it was appropriate.'

A squeaky, creaky voice spoke. 'Pleased to meet us, pleased to meet us, well you won't be when we've finished with you.'

A tall lanky one, came towards me waving her broomstick.

'Wait,' a fatter one said. 'Wait let's not be too hasty, after all, we are in this person recycling bin, where's your manners, Florence.'

So, to cut this short story short, they all climbed through the dog flap, and came in for breakfast., this is when I asked them for their help to get rid of Mr Greenlee. This, I said, would be in exchange for the eggshells. They agreed, so with their help, Queenie and I dragged frozen Mr Greenlee down to the river.

Mr Toad was fuming. Sullying mustard pond,' he said.

Queenie told him to,' mind his own toadying business.'

'Who's that silly fat frog', Florence creaked.

Toady soon retracted his words when she swung her broomstick.

'Oh well what will be will be,' he croaked. 'I suppose, some things must be done.' The witches screeched and laughed as he flipped flopped back to his picnic on the riverbank. We watched as Mr Greenlee eventually sank to Davy Jones locker, never to be seen again. We were soon back at Pear. Queenie was mad when she saw the roses or the lack of them. I promised her it would never happen again; but she was pleased we had fed Mr Greenlee to the feisty silver foil fishes.

Over the coming months, the painted roses and glossy emerald, green ivy grew back, they began taking over the soft stone white walls of Pear. I was a little wary because I remember Mr Greenlee warning me of Pear becoming engulfed in the overgrowth, however, Queenie insisted, they should all be left to grow as they wished, so I let them.

At first, I was quite happy to pop out now and again to buy food, after all I had all the company I needed at Pear. However, one day, as I was trying to make my way past the rambling red roses when the emerald, green ivy, reached out grabbing my ankle. I fell with quite a bump, only just managing to drag myself back into Pear.

I found it difficult to walk following my fall, so I began ordering online food, and anything else I needed. There all sorted, or so I thought then one day I received a phone call it was from the post office.

'Hello is this, Dorothy?

'Speaking.'

'The postman cannot post your mail anymore, because your cottage is a danger zone, an hazard, a no-go area, an health and safety issue.'

'What do you mean, what are you talking about.'

'Have a look Missis at your outside. Your painted red roses and emerald, green ivy has completed entangled themselves around your letter box, around your house in fact. One of our postmen landed up in A and E, all his face and hands scratched to, pieces, furthermore there were no ambulances available, so he had to get there on his old rusty rickety battered bike, and then when he got to A and E, there were no beds, no nurses, or doctors either, or so they tell me.'

'Tell him to try the dentist then,' I said, and slammed the phone down. I knew full well dentist were as rare as red squirrels, I thought they had a bloody cheek, but I told them to keep my post it was usually spam mail anyway.

After that we were generally left alone, except for nuisance calls. Someone once pretended to be Mr Greenlee and kept ringing to ask how I was, so we unplugged the phone. So, there it was, Pip, Queenie and I were doing fine, we didn't bother anyone keeping ourselves to ourselves, until one day the silence of Pear was shattered…

'Hello, anyone there, Dorothy I need to talk with you.'

'What about?'

'We heard you had fallen, over the roses and ivy, Mr Greenlee, is worried you don't answer his calls.'

Pip and I cuddled closer. 'I don't know what you're talking about, and yes, I did tell Mr Greenlee to stay away, we did not want him here. Now please all go away, we are fine.'

'We're coming in Dorothy, stay where you are.'

First there were the roaring chainsaws, followed by the sound of the roses and ivy screaming, traumatised, as they were chopped and teared at, until they fell in shattered piles to the floor. I heard the front door being kicked in. I looked into Pip's soft brown eyes. 'Oh well Pip, no more need for your dog flap.' And there we all hid, behind the green stuffed duck feathered sofa, shivering in fright.

'Dorothy, where are you. It's me Mr Greenlee, we not here to hurt you, we've come to help you.'

It took them quite a while to climb through my boxes of books and belongings, but when they did find our hiding place, it was too late. Only Queenie was there. They managed to find a nurse at A and E, and Queenie was questioned rigorously. She sat there, as cool as an icecube, puffing away on my vape. My shiny red soft satin dress, ballooning out over the white wrought iron legs of the hospital bed. My red velvet pumps, with their pink oversized bows, peeping out from under the white ruffled petticoats.

There she still sits, as far as I know, smoking my lemon flavoured vape, the yellow smoke encircling the blue heavens. And what came of me and Pip? Well, we are making our way to Timbukto, with the witches in eggshells. Well, that's what Queenie tells the nurse.

The Vietnamese Pot Belly and the Middle White

On the day the female went into labour, Gilligan didn't interfere. He remained outside the breeding quarters and tended to the weeds in the potato patch. And when he heard her cries grow louder, he hoed, forked, and turned the earth with greater vigour. Not until those cries ended and were replaced by the sound of a new-born's squalls did he approach the breeding pen.

The sound of the two women's excited, high-pitched voices was replaced by silence. From the bed where the mother lay in the birthing chamber, clutching now a new life in a bloody towel, and her companion and midwife seated next to her, they watched Gilligan approach. Their body language he understood – creased eyes, curled lips and raised shoulders. He stopped inside the door, his cap removed from his head and in his hands. He told them that he wasn't there to upset them or interfere. He just wanted to see his son.

On the faces of the women - smiles, which weren't really smiles. The mother looked at her friend. The two nodded together. The friend lifted the new-born from its mother's side and placed it at the foot of the bed. She then gently unwrapped it from its swaddling.

Inside his head, Gilligan felt that terrible familiarity of tiny feet scampering about behind his eyes. In his nostrils a smell like cat's piss – his own stink. He stared hard at the naked child. A girl.

The second woman had now picked up a vase from the bedside table, and was threatening Gilligan with what she would do with it if he came near them.

Gilligan tasted a sourness surging from his throat into his mouth. He ignored the woman's threats, hardly heard them, and, with his head shaking from side to side, backed out of the room.

The construction of the compound had been the initial project Gilligan undertook when his sons Robert and Dale first went away. But, like many other projects, the original idea had now changed direction. His plan to hold onto the offspring as a replacement for one of the boys was no longer an option. A female child was of no use to him.

Separating the females from each other wasn't going to be easy. And attempting to do it so close to the child's birth could prove foolhardy. A female with its newly born young was as dangerous as a bull strayed from the herd. He considered roping them and trusting them up, but decided it too drastic a solution. Traumatising the females might cause the Vietnamese to injure her unborn offspring. Finally he settled for the tranquiliser dart gun he kept for the horses and cows, but seldom needed to use. The dosage required for the larger animals he halved, but then quartered.

Gilligan waited a few days. Got them accustomed to him arriving at the same time each day. And then, when they weren't expecting it, he made his usual call at breakfast time. The dart gun, which he produced from under his long coat, he aimed and fired first at the Vietnamese, striking her in the heart. Without removing the butt from his shoulder or his eye from the sight, he shifted and shot the middle white next to her. As an experienced hunter and marksman, he knew the risks involved with using such a method on smaller livestock. He could hit vital organs by mistake. Or the dosage he'd carefully measured out might still prove too much and lead to a fatality. But that was a risk you had to take sometimes.

While the women clutched at their chests and squawked and thrashed about, their eyes wide and their mouths twisted, he told them to *go easy*. And that it was only a tranquiliser.

"Sit you down there now the two of you," he said, waving the barrel of the gun at the couch. "Don't fight it. You'll be out in no time."

"The baby," the middle white said. "Jesus, my baby," her arms extended before her to the baby asleep in the wicker basket on the floor.

"Go right ahead," he said. "Go get her."

With the child in her arms, she quietened and worked her way back to the couch and sat next to the Vietnamese potbelly. The woman put their arms about one another, the baby nestled on its mother's lap.

Paying little attention to their pleas and cries, Gilligan twisted his wrist and looked at his watch. A good thirty minutes or so and they'd be out cold. He sat down in a plastic chair, placed his gun across his lap, and waited.

Before the half hour was up, he pushed to his feet. His eyes he had never taken from the two women. Stepping close to the couch, he first extended his weapon and prodded one of the middle white's large breasts. No response. He then slipped the cold steel of the gun's barrel under her top. Nothing. Using his hand instead of his gun, he checked the Vietnamese in the same way. As a final check, he blew into their faces, mostly about the eyes. Neither flinched. Only then did he remove the infant from its mother's lap.

Entering the compound over the next few days, he had already decided, would be reckless. Working all his life with large beasts had taught him to avoid unnecessary provocation of animals in specific conditions and circumstances.

Getting rid of the unwanted offspring was the next issue.

A supplier of wholesale animal stock, Gilligan had neither experience nor interest in locating buyers for individual creatures. But he had plenty of contacts in the business who had and were. And there was one trader in particular who had a reputation for getting hold of anything the market demanded.

Based in the north of the country, he specialised in the illicit trade of exotic birds and rare reptiles. But was also known for smuggling dusky-skinned housekeepers sought after by bachelors and widowers.

In a phone call to the Bird Man, as he was called, Gilligan told him he would be up in the north on the Saturday. And with him he would have something in which the other might have an interest. Both parties understood the importance of vagueness on the phone.

On Saturday afternoon, Gilligan arrived at the Bird Man's holding.

"What were you looking for it?" the man said to Gilligan when he took the baby carrier from the Pajero.

Gilligan pinched his nose and stared at the man whose face revealed neither surprise nor curiosity. "Five thousand."

"I'll give you three," the man said.

"We'll split the difference," Gilligan said.

"Done," he said. And he spat into his palm.

"Good man yourself," Gilligan said, likewise spitting into his own palm.

The two slapped their hands together and sealed the deal.

Although she had failed, this time, to provide him with a male offspring, Gilligan, the man of integrity, recognised that the mother of the female, had nonetheless more than contributed to her upkeep. She wasn't responsible for the gender of her child. So he exempted her from breeding purposes for a while. Until he was ready.

The second pregnant female turned out to have a phantom pregnancy. Practical farm manager that he was, Gilligan ensured he got her pregnant right away. But the nine months gestation period he decided was too lengthy a time to distract him sufficiently from his terrible loss. That's when he decided to take up the offer of the old man on the neighbouring farm. Known for as long as he could remember as 'the old man', his St. Bernard bitch had recently thrown a litter of pups. He'd been extending the offer to Gilligan for weeks, most recently when they'd bumped into each other in the hardware store over the weekend.

A puppy was exactly the distraction Gilligan needed to occupy his distraught mind during those long months until the next birth in the compound.

The Phantom State, Daniel Wade

The Phantom State

District of Gjakova, Kosovo, 1999

There was a reek of cordite somewhere, pungently apparent just as the mortar round's echoing thud died down. Accompanying it was the stinging bite of shrapnel, hideous bullpup ripples and automatic fire muffled by nearby ruins, still carried on some rogue breeze. Clouds of dust geysered upward, like burnt offerings to some genocidal god.

Phil's eardrums raced.

He knew it was pointless shutting his eyes against this onslaught, for this inner film reel had its own soundtrack, too, in full nerve-shredding surround sound: a cacophony of AKM blasts, deep-throated scrape of a tank wheel, the agony-ridden bellows. Fuzzy commands were barked through the radio. Tanks trundled in for the kill at full speed, engines reverberating for miles. The noise burrowed through Phil's skull like a pneumatic drill, chewing his brain.

The guns roared in his ear. The IEDs kept ringing.

Part of him was glad it had finally happened that the explosive torrent of rubble and dried mud was now over. The entire village seemed gutted by the blast and still shaking as shards of rubble plummeted from the sky less than thirty meters away, landing in a grass field, already scorched black from a long-forgotten IED.

If it wasn't a hidden ambush, you could be sure it was a roadside bomb, cobbled together from whatever ignitable materials were nearest to hand and timed to detonate right at the very moment Phil and the rest of the K.FOR† lads trundled past in convoy.

Phil's nerves fizzed.

He was crouched in the upstairs of a shelled two-storey house near the village's southern end, his Steyr AUG assault rifle cradled just below him, the iron musk of blood faintly brushing his nostrils. Though it was early winter, raw wind bit through the streets and mountainside roads. From here, his view was nearly panoramic.

Through his rifle sights, he saw nothing but shrapnel and limbs everywhere in a pulsing, digital throb. His VHF buzzed with incoming situ reports and radio traffic, overlapping in staccato updates and estimates. They could have warned of anything: cluster bombs, hangovers from the airstrikes in off-road terrain, cessation of hostilities, even.

He had to push from his mind how strangely beautiful he found it: explosions blossoming from the damp folds of earth in plumes of dusty amber, its smoke mingling with the heavy fog shrouding the valley, the dull, distant thump of a mortar hitting the ground like the conclusive recoil of a cell door slamming home; from the remote Serb-held towns, phantasmal wails of air-raid sirens, main signals to take cover, echoed in a continuous, blaring ululation, the volume floating for miles around.

Phil had little choice but to wait for the smoke to clear. If he squinted, he thought he could glimpse dark, humanoid shapes dart and surge through the blur, whether civilians or guerillas or his fellow K.FORs, he couldn’t tell. Useless now to even call out for his platoon sergeant, Tommy Kinsella, and no doubt bellowing orders somewhere above the chaos into his handset.

He scanned past the village’s squat Orthodox church spire, burning steadily, silhouetted against the sky. There were no more shapes in the shadows.

The radios could be faulty in a mountainous region; if they weren't careful, the comms picked up bad signals. Worse still, as was the case for all the K.FOR lads, Phil's company did not know what route, destination or coordinates they’d be moving with. Not even their commanders knew until departure time. If their radios short-circuited, they were on their own. Thank fuck for his spare batteries.

Phil grabbed his rifle, levelled it, tried to ignore the screams kicking up around him; putrescine or cadaverine stung his nose as tracer fire scorched the sky. A burst of bullets was already in slick flight, ripping the earth.

The bodies before him were now a tangle of smoking flesh, bone sliver and gristle falling about him in warm, wet lumps. The soil was harvested with steel tubes and flares now, sprays of blood spattering the door and window of the truck; Phil's mind was a blueprint blotched with the bidding of nations, and the sight of the limbs. Under the sun's searchlight glimmer, his bones clinked beneath taut layers of flesh.

He was able to look at them now only with mild curiosity.

His platoon had been passing through, trucks and drops vehicles laden with supplies for the villagers. A livid gleam of sunlight lit up caterpillar tracks clawed into the road's argillaceous soil by the APC up ahead. The horizon was clear and steely, the roads narrow and snaking. They became increasingly riddled with scorched patches of clay from the UXOs and cluster bombs, the further inland Phil's convoy drove. The fields were speckled in the first dewy glitterings of frost, hardening the dust and grime into black sludge. Phil had wondered how long it had been since they'd last been tilled.

Their orders were simple enough. Dispense chocolate, smokes and medical supplies from their pack-rations to whoever in those remote, war-scarred hamlets needed them, climb back into the jeep and be on their way. When Phil had arrived in Kosovo for the first six-month tour of duty he was to undertake, his very first overseas, driving from village to shabby village made him feel like a knight in a flak jacket instead of armour, charging mightily in on an armoured chariot to help deliver the people, who now watched his convoy lurch down their grass-fringed main road and into the square with wary resignation. Not even Kinsella, with all his straight-talking elan, had warned him about this; no amount of news footage showing burning corpses and gutted border towns could prep him for it either.

There was some meagre consolation in mid-afternoon; "all the horrible shite kicks off after dark," Kinsella had warned him. He'd forgotten the name of the dull mining village they pulled into. Only that it was clearly one step above demolished as it came into view from the grass plateau and hardly worth rescuing. The UNMIK checkpoints out this end were a joke.

Phil was surprised the place was still inhabited; abandonment seemed natural. Dusk was still a few hours away, but the site's interlocking shadows seemed to gather and congeal atop each other, obscuring the rutted dirt track where no civilians dared to wander in daylight.

He willed his face to impassiveness as they neared; in return, the Kosovars' hollowed eyes seemed to peer neither at him nor his mates, but to flick past them, at some fatally sunless vista beyond. Even the youngest of them, younger than his brother, even, seemed rapidly aged: their matted hair and pale, soiled flesh, bare feet caked in ash and mud, their clothes' coarse, mismatched raggedness, all seemed to say: "fuck-all you can do now, bud."

The heaviness in the assemblage of eyes he now surveyed struck him most. He envied Kinsella's clinical ease in marching straight up to what was presumably the place's main leader, an emaciated man with a pewter beard, and confer with him in a low voice about the state of play. In its helmet and four-tone DPM camo, Phil's uniform suddenly felt obscene, a mockery shawling his limbs, despite blending in with the grim streetscape around him. Even the children had it, staring at the soldiers with ghoulish indifference.

New snowfall would soon be upon them; the Kosovars wordlessly took the cigarettes and sweets Phil and his convoy dished out to their cracked, open hands, and retreated to the frozen sanctums of their homes. Phil forced himself to walk the full ruined gauntlet of the place until he was out of drops.

Snow began to fall as soon as the first bomb went off, a soft onslaught of flakes strafing in all directions. The screech of shellfire and rifles burst sporadically around him, as he expected it would. The entire street seemed to tremble. Phil glanced over his shoulder, saw his men had scattered into different cover positions and pressed his face hard into the rubble as the screech of a shell filled the air.

He glanced at the corner just as the silhouetted spire of the village's sole collapsed church came crashing to the cobbles in a shower of dust and fiery, fragmented stone. Heat seared through the damp air, blackening the ruins. Phil rechecked his optical sights, still unsure where to aim; though, anyone watching him amid the chaos would have thought he had his target already lined up.

A hideous pounding of bullets sprayed the alley just sidelong below him as unseen guerillas made their AK rounds, answered by scattershot return fire from the K.FOR lads. So far nothing came close to hitting him. Screams were interspersed with each heavy convulsion, and the air-raid siren's benumbed wail knelled amid the smoke.

Orders were being barked from a radio somewhere, fuzzy staccato chatter, amped-up on stats and adrenalin, and drowned out by the pandemonium. Phil stayed on his chest, forcing a few dry coughs out as the smoke whirred past. There really was no telling how long this attack would go on for.

Groping his Steyr closer, he moved fast, a blur of olive camo ducking and diving through a macabre obstacle course of rubble and scorched corpses. His eyes could barely scan and register the faces. People - kids - he'd dished out smokes and sweets to only moments earlier lay still as ragdolls, bullet holes raking their flesh red-raw and smoking. Their clothes were even more ragged from the blast, and their eyes were as hollow in death as they appeared in life, staring into some illusory void.

Once he found cover, Phil sighted his Steyr up. His lens became a forensic little Eye of Providence, surveying reality with glassy, mathematical precision. A tiny black ring filled his vision, enhancing the world beyond it into a stark rendition of itself, a shimmering extrapolation of the village's layout based on its distance and depth. Phil lined up the Steyr's barrel at a dead angle and prepared to fire.

Through its crosshair reticle, he managed to spy a patch through the smoke and scanned the street opposite. He placed the stock against his shoulder and did the waiting routine, with no set target to pick. Not for the first time, he was relieved for the Steyr AUG; its fire rate and ergonomic feel were reassuring in tight situations.

The Serbs would have to show themselves; eventually, he knew, as faceless man-shaped blobs inching through the rubble. Another explosion, another hellish shriek from an inbound missile, and a quick burst of muzzle flashes might light them up or send them diving for cover.

As was his habit, he pushed from his mind the very good possibility that he was exchanging fire with ex-Crvene beretke, probably some of the hardest bastards in Europe, and tried imagining some of their faces. Plenty were scarred, battle-stained, and most had definitely already endured enough bullets and shells that any morsel of youth they had left was souring fast. Most of them would be bearded, ragtag, cradling bargain-basement AKs and worn fatigues, driven by a brute urge to kill as many of their targets as possible, with scant regard for tactics or strategy. The women would be beautiful, even with their flesh rich with scars and scalds. All would be bare-faced, and very much at ease with the weapons they carried. Most of them, men and women alike, would be young, easily around his age, while the others might share a birthday with his dead brother.

As was also his habit, Phil wondered if harbouring such thoughts made him a bad soldier.

He fired, knew the bullets had ripped through the smoke in seconds, and tore large crimson holes through the man's shoulder and ribs.

Another scattershot flash of gunfire strafed the wall below him. He managed to place his chin on the concrete, clenched teeth. He thought he heard Sgt. Kinsella's voice. Phil thought he yelled something in reply, but his voice sounded otherworldly.

A hand roughly grabbed his shoulder, and he turned slightly, still stunned. Kinsella had managed to get to him, uniform a mad battle standard of grenade pouches, binoculars and buzzing Motorola handset, eyes bulging like those of a mad prophet, the veins in his neck and forehead a sweaty mesh of pulsing blue worms, his uniform smoking, wild-eyed but not wounded. His being there told Phil that Toner, their Company captain, had been either killed or injured. Kinsella immediately returned fire and managed to ward them off before dragging Phil back to his feet.

Phil and Kinsella stepped behind the broken door after confirming the street was clear, scrambling and cursing in the haze, Phil following his sergeant's lead, silently cursing the smoke and the bumpy texture of the road, his feet barely steady as they grazed spasmodically along the bloodied cobbles. The two scuttled through the flame, billowing smoke like prisoners had just broken free. Not even five minutes had passed since they had first arrived in the village.

So far, they'd managed to keep out of sight, peering around corners, dropping back behind the edges of doors, their guns' cold, steely weight keeping them grounded as they scrambled forward in fitful stops and starts.

Kinsella ducked into an alleyway just as a fresh spasm blasted through, Phil at his heels. They kept to a crouch, Phil sprawled slightly, supercharged now with adrenalin; the shouts of guerillas had taken on a more frantic air down the road. He could stare at a volley and watch it puttering up the street like a swarm of rapid-fire locusts. He was down to only two magazines; vigilance was sorely needed.

He pressed the Steyr to his shoulder and pulled the grip; five quick bullpup rounds sent the guerillas running. They were intended as warning shots, sporadic and brusque, fired with nothing more than to drive them off for a moment. He saw at least two bodies drop like ragdolls, hitting the cobbles as crimson banderoles fluttered and splotched the street, just as Phil dodged back behind the wall. Kinsella was crouching next to him, clicking a new magazine into his rifle's as it, eyes still on the corner as he made the necessary movements.

"Wait'll I tell yeh to move," he grunted. "It's DEFCON fuckin' 1 here."

"No bother, Sarge," Phil sputtered in response, reloading.

Kinsella was on his feet first, sidestepping past the wall, his goggles now drawn down to avoid the smoke that now fumed in their direction. Phil's lungs were clogged with the taste of burnt things, scorched grass and flesh; he retched a cough as he followed his sergeant back toward the drops vehicle, pace for fraught pace.

The truck was still where they had left it on the pavement, speckled with bullet holes, but still functional. The windshield was cracked, a jagged spiderweb mesh, but the tyres were intact. Only when Phil and Kinsella got closer did they see that yet more salvos had torn through the driver's door and ruptured the dash. A grenade had gone off nearby, missing the vehicle by mere inches, having slapped lightly off the armoured casing just before detonation, but it had left a sizable scorch hole in the ground a good thirsty yard away.

Phil stared past the razor-sharp barbed wire that had somehow escaped the burning. The remnants of their platoon were huddled between the camouflage, still-solid corral formed by the trucks, their Steyr AUGS already mud-caked; the more able-bodied had managed to grab whatever lumps of concrete and debris they could find and busily stacking them up in the gaps between the vehicles. The rest were crouched in the turrets. None of the trucks' engines were left idling or even on.

As well as the platoon, the few sobbing civilians who'd managed to evade the blast were huddled at the far end, some left inside the open carrier doors. Some were prattling to each other in their language, panicked. Even further back were several of the lads he recognised, their uniforms blood-smeared and their limbs unmoving.

He'd guessed right; Capt. Toner was indeed among them, a scarlet starburst bejewelling his cranium. The platoon, or what was left of it, was in Kinsella's hands now.

A few medics were doing their best to rush among them, one or two shouting into their portable satphones for medevac. Phil couldn't blame any of them for beating a retreat here; the entire village seemed beyond gutted.

"Stay where yis are!" Kinsella hissed as loudly as he could without shouting. "Keep down while yis're able!"

Phil knew that the hollering in the distance from the guerillas would only get louder. How many of them there were, he couldn't have guessed. They may come surging down the street towards them, grenades primed, voices at fever pitch as they lobbed the ballistics into the side of the trucks, erupting their chassis into burning metal and all the people they shielded. Or else they'd converge and swarm over the trucks and set them alight from within, flaming bottles bursting in random supernovae of white heat and diesel, washing over them in a baptism of hate, a funeral pyre.

Phil was in no humour to think of either outcome. He tried to stay where he was, wincing from the ragged ache in his lungs. Kinsella was crawling on his stomach among the last of the platoon, urgently murmuring orders under his breath.

One of the operators desperately tuned into whatever frequency he could find; inchoate chatter buzzed and crackled from his headpiece. It was growing in volume too, united with the guerillas' approaching bellows as…

*Arkan's Tigers: a Serbian volunteer paramilitary group established in 1990 and disbanded in 1996, led by Željko Ražnatović AKA Arkan, and also colloquially known as Crvene beretke ('Red Berets'). They were responsible for numerous war crimes during the Yugoslav Wars.

†K.FOR: the NATO-led peacekeeping force in Kosovo, established in 1999.

Reunion, Lisa Johnson Mitchell

Reunion

Patrick wanted to melt into the dirty, plaid industrial carpet in the La Quinta ballroom. That, or vomit—the smells were hideous, a combination of overcooked roast beef, body odor, and sulphur. He didn't like the people in high school then, those who were nested around him now, and he wondered why on earth he thought he'd want to see them again, especially Alison, who he'd run into at the pasta bar. It was as if she was following him.

"So catch me up on you," Alison said. A short bespectacled woman with a frizz of red curls, she stared at Patrick with a strange gleam in her eyes and slurped her martini as it waterfalled over the sides of her glass.

Patrick gave her a quick up-and-down glance. *She's really blimped out.* Guilt coursed through his corpus. *Bad Patrick.* A picture formed in his mind of Alison years ago marching along with the flag corps on the AstroTurf with her cohorts in what looked like a policeman's uniform. In the mists of Patrick's memory, she padded along, high-stepping and clad in culottes and knee socks, instead of the usual heavily starched pants the guys donned. His lips tried to conceal a snicker.

"Do you talk to Thom?" she said in a loud, grating voice.

Patrick's stomach tightened and he folded into himself. "Nah."

An ample, brunette woman in a green pantsuit waddled onto a small stage and positioned herself in front of the microphone.

"Really?" Alison said.

"Sssshh," Patrick said.

"Good evening Wolverines!" It was the class president, Nadine, who was now a dentist. In back of her hung a large sign that said, "Welcome Wolverines Class of 1988" trimmed in black and red balloons.

“If you haven’t signed in with your phone number and email, please see Donny at the front door. Let’s give it up for Donny!” Donny, a slim Jewish guy dressed in overly formal clothing, a tux, jumped up, and flailed his hand and shouted something unintelligible.

“First off, I want to thank everyone who showed up. We weren’t sure if all you rock stars would want to come back to our little gathering, but so glad you did!”

Patrick surveyed the expressions of his classmates around him. Most were as blank as paper bags.

“I thought we’d kick off the event by having the cheerleaders come up and lead us in a cheer!”

A flurry of limbs, arms and legs in motion, hands over mouths in mock embarrassment, merged into a string of girls who push-dragged each other up to the stage. Patrick’s stomach twisted. He knew those faces, faces who’d mocked him in high school for being Mr. Wolverine, the mascot, and the same faces who spread vicious rumors about him.

Why did I buy into the crap that people at work told me, that the nerds like me were the ones who everyone would be jealous of, that things would be different? I mean, heck, I’m the CEO of Plant Town! I have over 30 direct reports!

The cheerleaders formed a line. They pulled down their too-short sparkly dresses over their enlarged thighs and swung their hands around and clutched their wine glasses like prizes.

Patrick was gutted by the way he saw himself in high school: a big, jiggly dork. He was struck with the unassailable truth that he’d made a mistake coming, so while the girls were chittering he skulked away.

“PATRICK GODFREY! COME BACK! WE NEED MR. WOLVERINE!” the voices were shrill and overlapped.

Patrick’s legs stopped and cemented into the carpet. The lure of their compliments, compliments he wanted to believe, paralyzed him. As if led by Svengali, he wheeled around and trudged toward the stage.

"Yay! Patrick!!! Woot, woot!" A few whistles rippled behind him.

"Okay, okay," Patrick said. He shooed them away, deflecting their adulation.

"Grrrrrr, Grrrr!" Patrick growled, fist-pumped into the air and jogged to the stage, drenched in an intoxicating brew of fear and exhilaration. He stumbled up the main step—his new boots were wooden and hurty. The crowd still roared.

Nadine was bent over a box wrestling with something inside. As she turned, Patrick saw it in her clutches: his Wolverine head.

"Put it on!" Nadine cried.

Patrick's face flamed. Every cell revolted. Senior year, he'd left it in the gym and hoped to never see it again.

"Where did you—?"

"I saved it."

"No, please, no. I can't."

"Oh, come on!"

Patrick heaved a sigh, wriggled his head into the paper mache, furry helmet, zipped it up the back, and there he was: Mr. Wolverine.

Everything from high school came back to him: the unsteady weight of the head and small eyeholes. The air was tight, but by gum, he was going to give it his all.

"Let's go Wolverines, let's go!" Clap, clap. "Let's go Wolverines, let's go!" Patrick shouted. The cheerleaders joined in his revelry and swayed back and forth. One of them who wore conspicuously high heels performed a hurky and landed perfectly. Her blonde, shellacked hair helmet didn't move an inch.

As the stage emptied and the crowd dissolved, Patrick floated off the stage. He started to unzip his Wolverine head, but got distracted. *Looking good, Patrick! You're awesome, man! Rock it, Patrick!* Glimpses of toothy, wide-mouthed smiles and compliments kept coming his way as he made his way out of the ballroom. What once was borderline embarrassing, being the mascot, now seemed to be a status symbol. *Guess my work peeps were right.* All through the night, people seemed to be glad to see him. The head cheerleader even said to him, "You were *popular*." Popular? He wanted to believe it was true, but in a muscle lodged somewhere near his heart, a belief thrummed: it's all a lie.

In the distance, Patrick spotted Alison elbowing her way through the crowd towards him, so he picked up his pace to escape her, but someone patted him on the back.

"Dude!"

It was Thom.

Thom stepped forward, and extended his hand and they shook. Patrick was surprised to see Thom clad in khakis, a business shirt, and navy jacket, primed and ready for the top 2%. In high school, he was all Dead Head t-shirts, Birkenstocks, and whiffs of patchouli.

"It's been a while." Patrick's neck and cheeks grew warm, his body stiffened.

"Yeah, how 'ya been?" Thom, who was one of the track stars, ran his hand through his sandy, surfer boy hair, eking out a half-smile, an impossible dimple on each side.

Filmic squares of them smoking a joint in the parking lot with a druggy dream pop score invaded Patrick's mind. Cut to a basketball court, where they were shooting hoops, Patrick winning for a moment. Cut to the playroom in Thom's house, the lights low, Pink Floyd playing, the parents gone for the afternoon, nursing their Jack stolen from the liquor cabinet, them shoveling Doritos in their pieholes and pondering the mysteries of the String Theory.

"I'm doing okay" Patrick said. "Gawd, let me take this thing off. Come with me."

As they reached the hotel lobby, Patrick tugged once more at the zipper of his Wolverine head.

"There you are!" A waifish, blonde woman slinked up. "I'm Megan."

"Right, Megan, this is Patrick. An old buddy of mine," Thom said.

"Nice to meet you," Patrick said. He continued to wrestle with the zipper.

"It's stuck!" Patrick cried.

"What?"

The giant globe muffled Patrick's voice so he raised the volume. "IT'S STUCK!"

"Let me try." Thom said. He jimmied the zipper. No luck. He pulled harder, causing Patrick to falter.

"Hey!" Patrick yelled. "Watch it."

"Sorry." Thom hands rested on Patrick's shoulders

"You gotta help me."

Thom turned to Megan. "Hey, listen, I need to help Patrick. Would you mind just hanging out here then head over to Flannigan's, you know, the bar down the street? This won't take long."

Megan smoothed her poured-on, pink dress. "Oh okay, no problem." She grabbed her shiny bag from a nearby table, gave Thom a peck on the cheek, and sashayed away.

Thom ushered Patrick across the parking lot and informed him about curbs and any upcoming obstacles. When they reached Thom's car, he opened the door and helped Patrick navigate the passenger's seat of his Smart Car. Patrick's fuzzy dome seemed to be a little too big for the space.

"You and your DUMB car," Patrick said.

"Ha! Funny as you ever were. Here…" Thom giggled as he guided Patrick's head, but it banged against the roof. "Tilt it a bit." Finally, he was in.

"What about my car?" Patrick said.

"I'll drive you back when we get that thing off of you."

"So…that Megan is a cute number."

"What? Can you speak up?"

"MEGAN! Are you WITH her?"
"Oh, please."
"Didn't think she was your type."
"What do you want me to say?"
"If you could see my face, you'd see I'm giving you an automatic eye roll."
The silence between them grew and was filled with the lonely putter of the small engine. As they drove along, Patrick's stomach churned and a bit of the pasta began to make its way up his esophagus. "Oh god, I'm gonna hurl."
"Oh, dear," Thom said.
Patrick detected a note of disdain in his voice. "What?"
"Nothing."
"My stomach really doesn't feel right." Patrick swallowed to suppress the sharp stomach juices that were gathering at the back of his throat. *I hope I don't throw up inside this thing.*
Thom slowed down, his headlights shining a few feet in front of the car, but just when it seemed he was home free, hit a pothole. Patrick jerked forward.
"Ugh! Man!"
"Sorry!" Thom grimaced. "Can you make it home?"
"Yes," Patrick whispered. "Please hurry."

#

As they inched into Patrick's apartment, Thom led the way. The walls were bare except for a few dusty photos. A large front window was lined with fluffy palms. Nearly every surface held a healthy, verdant plant. On his dining table was a spray of Gerbera daisies. Patrick rushed to his desk, tugged open a drawer that rattled a terra cotta pot full of ivy.
"Wow, it's a veritable jungle in here—" Thom said.
"Cut if off." Patrick handed him a pair of scissors.
"Really?"
"Really."
"You'll never be able to fix it."

"CUT it off." Patrick's throat tightened: more of the pasta rested at the back of his throat.
Thom placed the blades with surgical care at the base of the Wolverine skull. "Don't want to hit a jugular."
"You wouldn't care."
"What's that supposed to mean?"
"You know."
"No, I don't."
Patrick pivoted and drew close to Thom. "Let's get this thing off and we can talk."
"NO, I want to talk now. You're making me very uncomfortable."
"*You're* uncomfortable?" Patrick twisted the head. He tugged and turned it. Thom grabbed at Patrick's hands, but they eluded him, seizing and fluttering like hummingbirds.
"STOP!" Thom said.
Patrick's fists flailed and curled into tight circles. Thom clutched Patrick's wrists and held them still. "Calm down."
"Get it off, for God's sake!"
As Thom snipped, the Wolverine's hair was slippery, unwieldy. He tried the zipper again, but it remained stubborn.
"Any luck?" Patrick's innards were cooking. His breath heated up his face and the head became an oven. Sweat poured from his hairline. Moisture pooled in his eyes. He placed both hands on the side of his noodle, pulled and yanked, tufts coming off in his hands.
"Aaaaah," Patrick roared. He tottered to a kitchen cabinet and returned with a hammer.
"Here."
"I can't do that. I could hurt you."
"You can. And WILL."
Patrick bent over the couch and braced himself. "Go ahead."
Thom whispered, "Be very still."
Patrick figured if he got a concussion, so be it. At least he wouldn't be imprisoned in hideousness anymore.

Thom slammed the hammer into the head. Nothing. He slammed harder. A small crack peeked through. He slammed again. The fissure expanded. Patrick dug his fingers into the hole and pulled—the material tore a smidge, but not enough.

"Do you have any cuticle scissors?" Thom said.

"I'm not a manicurist! Make the pair I gave you work."

Thom hesitated, then shoved the blades inside the furry mess.

"OUCH!" Patrick felt a small jab at the back of his neck.

Thom thrust his paw in the now-widened hole and *riiiip*, the head split in half. Patrick wrested himself from the offending object's suffocating grip. He threw it on the floor so hard it caused an end table to wobble. He began to choke, then went to the kitchen and downed glass after glass of water.

"You okay?" Thom grasped Patrick's elbow.

"Sure." Patrick's face was glazed over with an icky film like plastic wrap and he stunk. He felt his stomach start to pretzel. "Be right back."

Patrick fled to his bathroom and inspected his face in the mirror: he was puffy and white, like he'd been filled with helium, not unlike the Pillsbury Dough Boy in the Macy's Thanksgiving Parade. He turned on the shower, gingerly stepped in and shivered. He tried to vomit, but somehow he couldn't. He pushed back the curtain, leaned out to pilfer through his medicine cabinet. *Tums! Yes! No, it's empty!* He hesitated, stuck his fingers down his throat and vomited. The shards of cheese pasta and crimson of his multiple Sea Breezes swirled towards the drain.

But then he saw them: skins of tomatoes. *So THAT was the red stuff in the pasta!* He was allergic to them, horribly so.

Even though his purging was warranted, and he was truly sick, he hadn't succumbed to forcing himself to vomit in a while. The fact that he'd made himself upchuck felt worse than the actual upchucking. Shame covered him like cream gravy. He assumed he was over his eating disorder, but perhaps it was still there. *That pasta was irresistible. Guess I need more therapy. But do I, really?*

Patrick gargled with mouthwash and emerged from the bathroom. He turned on the kitchen faucet and filled up his glass. He ran his tongue over his teeth. They were bumpy like pimples.

"You okay?" Thom leaned against the fireplace mantle and fiddled with his watch. "You were in there a long time."

"Yeah." Patrick exhaled. "Want something to drink? Ginger ale okay?"

He poured them each a glass and crept towards him, his water and bubbly beverage threatening to spill.

Thom sipped the soda, then placed it on the fireplace mantle. "I owe you an apology."

"I trusted you," Patrick said.

"I led you on," Thom whispered.

Patrick plunged his hands into his front pockets and peered into Thom's eyes. "I'll never get over Alison walking in, the look on her face when she saw me walking out of the bathroom without my pants, and you all buck naked sprawled out on the sofa. I suspect she started the scuttlebutt, though she swore she wouldn't tell anyone. Did you see her tonight? I swear she was on my heels and I couldn't seem to ditch her."

"No, didn't see her," Thom said.

"Can't believe she had the gall to talk to me. She never apologized."

"Actually, everything, the whole snafu, was my fault. I left the playroom door unlocked."

"It was my fault because I loved you." There they were, those three naked words. They circled in the ether.

"I did care about you."

"Care is for puppies."

Thom gazed out the window. "I'm sorry, I just didn't know who I was then. Maybe it was a phase."

"Are you still in the phase? What, with Megan?"

"I'd be disowned." Thom's face greyed.

"You're safe with me."

"We connected. All our inside jokes. You got me."

"And you got *me*." Patrick shifted closer.

Thom tipped his head down and brushed the carpet with his toe. "Spray painting, barely evading the cops, and running over that stop sign."

"Guilty! I didn't know how to drive a stick shift. I told you that."

"I know, I know." Thom's mouth formed a tender gasp Patrick knew well. "We had some good times."

"We did." Patrick leaned in, their lips met, and his pulse quickened. He unswaddled a familiar, ragged part of himself, a place that he thought was forever lost. The glue was there. It was if they'd never parted.

Thom lingered, then pulled away. His eyes found the floor. The silence was thick.

Patrick stroked the back of his neck and massaged the place where the scissor had nicked him, then examined his fingers. "No blood. Guess I'll be okay."

"Do you still have that thing where you purge?" Thom said.

"Mostly no." Patrick stirred. "But I did throw up in there because I ate tomatoes."

"Oh, gosh," Thom said.

"I feel better now," Patrick said. "You were the first person who knew about me, what I did."

"I always thought you looked great. You didn't need to lose weight. You look pretty fit."

"Thanks, I try." Patrick's skin prickled, as if it had been stripped away.

Thom picked up the two half-shells of the Wolverine head. He examined them as if they were precious, ancient artifacts. "Really did a number on this."

"You can have that. It'll be your souvenir," Patrick said.

“Right.” Thom placed the broken halves together. “Maybe it can be repaired?”

“I’ve got a better idea.” Patrick retreated to the kitchen and returned with a dark green Hefty bag. “Toss that thing in here.”

The Hanging Tree

Alice stood on the remote hilltop, staring at the lone tree which crowned it. Above her, the ominous grey sky threatened snow. A foreboding fluttered in her heart and shivered across her skin as if ice already fell. The craggy, bleak moorland soared and dipped while violent gusts flattened and lifted the long grasses and spiralled Alice's hair into wild, black flames. The old oak leaned heavily to one side – for many lifetimes it had been lashed by an untamed wind from the west and today was no different. Alice studied its thick, naked branches. The bony, crooked tips pointed at the frozen air like accusing fingers. She was acutely aware of this place's history and that, centuries ago, another woman who bore her name had once stood in this same spot.

The past Alice had not been alone like the present day Alice. Instead she had been surrounded by a hoard of jeering people in a summer long gone. The crowd had watched her like modern day folk might view a film in a cinema except there had been angry shouts instead of the rustle of sweet papers and the crunch of popcorn. Alice from hundreds of years ago had been dragged to a stack of wooden crates, above which a rough rope had been looped around one of the tree's sturdy arms – a noose dangling from it.

This long-ago foremother had resisted being led to what the locals called The Hanging Tree. She'd cursed her audience, wishing deadly plagues on them, clawed the muscled arms which hauled her on top of the makeshift platform and spat at the hard eyes of the men who tried to wrap rope around her throat.

Her cursing had unsettled the gathering who urged for the woman to be dealt with quickly. 'Hurry, hurry,' they chanted, 'give her back to the Devil and save us.'

The battle lost, the coarse rope encircled her neck – a bristling, harsh collar of death but the doomed Alice still shouted.

'Damn this tree, damn this hill, damn this land. Damn all of you.' The stack of apple boxes was kicked from under her clogs and she wordlessly dropped to her destiny. Her legs convulsed behind her unadorned smock as her neck snapped. She swayed back and forth, her white cap framing her sightless, sage eyes. The vibrant green foliage trembled as her face glowed from within it – a pale rose caught in the sun's ambivalent caress. Tangled, black hair fell past her slackened shoulders, dark rivers glistening in golden slants of light. Still alive, the roots not yet understanding their fate.

The crowd cheered. 'The witch is dead, we are safe.'

The woman was dead but they were far from safe.

***

Twenty-first century Alice knew this land was where lots of Alices had lived. She could almost sense the spirits of the many women and girls who'd gone before as she stood by the bent tree. The oak had lived through centuries and had watched numerous gatherings on this hill. Its branches appeared benign, harmless, but many a last gasp had been taken from its unyielding boughs. The tree was an unwitting accomplice to death.

What must it think of us? she mused. We come and go so quickly; hating, hurting and dying. Life just a whisper for us but a slow, deep-rooted melody for this being of the earth. Our steadfast companion, a patient, quiet witness to our savagery, our ignorance. A link between our past, present and future. The tree might wither but every spring it's renewed. It endures while we just die, or do we?

Drawn to it as if she could sense the secrets and regrets pulsing through its core, she touched the rough exterior. How many palms had been placed on its gnarled surface? How many tears had soaked into its dark limbs? How many cries had reverberated through its rigid heart? Did the dead still come back to its sprawling, veined roots and beg for breath to wake their sleeping bodies? Or did they come back demanding justice or vengeance? Did their wronged souls blow the furious, bitter wind, bowing the tree into its subservient posture?

The sun broke through the gloom and lit up the day, making her shade her eyes from the glare. The outline of the tree darkened. A shadow danced from behind the huge trunk and Alice blinked as the form disappeared. Her heart stammered for a moment thinking she might be in the presence of the dead.

Silly, of course there were no ghosts. Only the ones created in her mind. Alice had a healthy imagination and could visualise women in long skirts and aprons, going about their chores. Plucking fruit from orchards, filling woven baskets with blackcurrants or heaving pales of water from wells. Trees – integral to life – earth's lungs. Yet, they also surrendered their timber for our work, our homes, and they warmed our hearths and nurtured our bodies with their varied bounties. Funny to think that over many thousands of years, nothing much had changed in this valley. Apples, plums and pears still ripened every summer and winter berries still burnt bright on the bushes. The undulating hills would have appeared the same to the eyes of her predecessors. They too would have seen the sun dipping behind the rugged horizon and rising from the same jagged contours in the mornings. The days death and birth, a perpetual rhythm, the inhaling of dark and the exhaling of light.

The sun was smothered again and an icy wind whipped Alice's wayward hair into her ruddy cheeks. She decided to leave the ancient tree in peace and retreat to the comfort of the cottage she'd rented. Carefully, she made her way down the uneven, boggy terrain. Heavy rains had caused cracks in the land and small rivulets of water dashed down towards the stream in the valley bottom. The creek, running through the holiday home's back garden, had gushed so loudly it had kept her awake last night. Yet, apart from the muddy fractures, the hill was still a verdant green even though it was mid-January. This landscape was alien to her but also strangely familiar. Like an old fairy tale from childhood, she found the rolling countryside comforting. The dips and swells gave her a warm sensation as if she'd been drinking sweet tea or holding a hot water bottle to her stomach. She had never been somewhere so remote, so isolated, so dark at night but, she'd never felt so at ease.

The village was a tiny hamlet and didn't even have a shop or a pub. She'd seen only one person since her arrival yesterday; a bow-legged man in blue overalls, wellies, and a flat cap. He'd said *Afternoon* as he'd herded baaing sheep down the lane in front of her cottage. The greeting was returned but she'd noticed he'd given her a rather quizzical glance. She guessed they didn't see too many strangers in these parts.

Alice reached the oak front door of the whitewashed house and stared at the date carved at the top of it, 1600. A pentagram had been etched at either side of the number and to the left of the door was a brass plaque inscribed with a short history of the building's most famous inhabitant:

This was once the home of Alice Nuttall who was hanged on the above moors after allegedly performing witchcraft. Alice was one of many women in the county accused of being a witch in the middle ages. Below are the words she asked to be recorded before her execution in 1618.

'They drown us in the rivers, burn us on their bonfires and hang us until the air is squeezed out of our lungs. They will not rest until our spirits are forced from our bodies. I am a woman of the earth and a healer. And God knows how I've tried to help those around me but there is no healing this world of men.'

Present day Alice shuddered. She gazed again at the surname – Nuttall – which also belonged to her. All through school she'd endured a stream of awful nicknames: fruitcake, squirrel, the nutty one, mental case and so on. She'd not known, until she'd recently come across the story of Alice, that she shared her name with an alleged witch. Just as well, as she might have been tempted to hurl a few curses of her own at her school-yard tormentors. Fascinated by the plight of the condemned woman, Alice had searched her own family history and discovered she was indeed a blood relative. Having lived in Portsmouth with her elderly parents for most of her thirty years, with no other family to speak of, she was thrilled to discover this new branch of northern ancestors, even though they were long dead.

She ducked as she entered the cottage. Inside, the low ceilings had dark beams dissecting them and Alice had to remember to bob down at all the door frames. She removed her boots. Even through her thick socks, the cold of the stone flags rose up through her feet and made her tremble. She darted to the rug by the inglenook and lit the kindling she'd set earlier. Flames licked at the wood and she imagined the previous Alice staring at the same grate, the same fire. The soot of millennia had blackened the stones inside the fireplace. She thought again of the noose, the burnings and the thundering rivers. Alice knew the so-called witches had most likely been the pharmacists of their time, skilled in using herbs and spices to create medicines and poultices to cure ailments. She visualised cauldrons bubbling with potions over the fire, pungent flora scenting the air, steam turning to water and rivulets dribbling down the thick walls and small windows. The room seemed to envelope her in its history and a strange tingling sensation ran up her spine. Could this place at last remedy her loneliness? It seemed ridiculous that she felt less alone in a village inhabited by so few than she had in a city of hundreds of thousands. Her parents were gone now, her anchors removed. Love, marriage and children had not found her but she didn't desire them, all she craved was somewhere to belong. Just six more nights and then she must return to her dreary flat and her drearier role as an employment officer. Although she rarely found anyone jobs they actually wanted. She sighed and traced her fingers over another five-sided pentagram that had been scratched into the beam above the fireplace. She knew what each point of the star represented: spirit, water, earth, fire, air. The words of the condemned Alice filled her head again.

...there is no healing this world of men.

The sentiment laid heavily on Alice. Why were women persecuted? Why had her ancestor really been killed? Was it because men feared the power of the feminine? The knowledge and wisdom of her sex was ancient and primeval. Women were the key to life and they instinctively knew how to nourish and protect it yet they were not valued. Instead they were vilified and murdered and were still being killed by men today. What a perverse world she lived in and yet, even though things had undoubtedly improved, she longed for the simplicity of days gone by. What would it have been like to belong to a big family? Have sisters and aunties? Live through the seasons in this wild, beautiful county? Concoct beverages or crush potions? She envisaged the villagers coming together in order to harvest the crops. And afterwards, sipping cider under trees which the liquor had come from while lazing on sun-soaked bales. She could almost hear the laughter, the camaraderie, and smell the delicious feasts created from their endeavours in the fields. Then she remembered the microwavable cheesy pasta in the fridge and her mood plummeted. She was no better off here than in her flat. The dead couldn't talk, walk or cook. Yet, she felt something in the stillness of the air, in the quietness of the rooms – a presence. She listened intently and closed her eyes as she stood in front of the fire. Wood and the crack of it splintering, was all she smelled or heard at first. But as she allowed herself to sink deeper into her mind, other things could be detected. A tap running in the kitchen. A window scraping open. The faint smell of roasting meat. Floorboards groaning as footsteps moved above. A door creaking somewhere upstairs.

Her eyes shot open. Electricity heightened her senses. The house was silent again but the air was thick with expectation.

She cautiously gazed around the room. Nothing was out of place. The cream settee sat demurely in the centre of the space. A dark wood coffee table was still positioned in front of it, with its scattering of 'things to do' leaflets. She left the warmth of the fire and went into the kitchen. The butlers sink had no water gushing into it and neither tap dripped. The pine table was as she'd left it – her empty mug of tea and toast-crumbed plate, still in situ. Through the closed window, the hill and the tree that adorned it called to her. She moved closer to the tiny panes and peered out. There were no dancing witches circling its crooked girth while practicing Pagan rituals. She returned to the front room and hurriedly climbed the stairs which protruded from it. At the top, she checked the three bedrooms and the bathroom but found no brooms or women in black cloaks and pointed hats. Bizarrely disappointed, she plonked down on the rose patterned duvet of a double bed, still crumpled from her restless night, and gazed out of the low window. Sheep were passing, the same old guy was with them. He glanced up at the bedroom and doffed his cap. Her spine went rigid. He shouldn't be able to see her, she was set back in the shadows of the room, not stood at the window, looking down.

Cold air rushed through her and she heard footsteps stomping down the stairs. Her muscles tightened as the front door banged. She jumped to her feet and hurried to the window, expecting to see someone running from her cottage. But her garden path was empty. Her heart spiked as the front gate opened and closed. The air seemed still but the wind must have blown it open and shut. The farmer, who had walked past the cottage, stopped and turned around as if someone followed him. He doffed his cap again at some unseen entity and Alice saw his mouth move. She opened the window and listened as the strange, little man spoke.

'Can I help you, Miss Alice?' he asked. His face appeared to crease into an uncertain smile.

Silence as of course no one answered.

'It's a small village,' he said, 'and everyone knows everyone,' he continued as if responding to a question. He laughed. 'Why Miss Alice, you do like to joke. You visit so often, we all know your name.'

More silence.

'Miss Alice, you know very well what I mean. Now I have to get on. I'll get the Rev to come and have another wee chat with you. I'm not so bothered, but the others don't like you talking to them, they don't like it at all.'

Another pause.

'Why don't folk want you talking to them? Alice, you've been dead for some four hundred years, the locals don't appreciate it when you make them jump by appearing out of nowhere.' He looked up at the holiday cottage. 'Don't you go scaring that poor lady visitor either. Let her enjoy her break in peace. Though it's uncanny, she could be your twin.'

The old man waved up at the window again and the very much alive Alice hesitantly waved back.

The farmer shrugged his shoulders and turned his attention back to his herd, once again making his way down the lane.

***

The present-day Alice, still at the window, shook her head. Maybe the old guy was lonely too, or maybe he was a little cuckoo, she thought, watching him become more distant.

A knock sounded on the front door, though she hadn't seen anyone walk down her path. Alice made her way downstairs to answer it, noticing her boots had gone.

She threw open the door but no one was there, though her boots were now on the doorstep. She reasoned, she must have taken them off outside but of course she knew she hadn't. A breeze blew into the house, warming her as if the July sun carried it. The smell of stewing fruit and cinnamon flavoured the cottage and Alice tasted the sweet, tangy produce as if it were in her mouth. She swallowed the delicious air, salivating and felt both ancient and new. An essence vibrated through her, awakening dormant, hallowed knowledge – flooding her with centuries of learning. In a heartbeat, she decided to sell her flat and offer whatever it took to secure this cottage as her home.

Future Alice would roam these hills and tend this land, guided by whispers and unseen footsteps owned by a shadow from the past. Together, they would imbibe the spirits of the trees, water and earth just like their ancestors had. They would be a force to be reckoned with, a source for good, helping their neighbours while respecting and permeating the land with their wisdom. The world of men might be damned but past, present and future Alices would do their best to protect this valley with its splendid harvests and sacred terrain and woe betide anyone who tried to thwart them.

City Walk, Marianne Dugdale

City Walk

Every day of the past ten months, since his son died, his daughter-in-law has phoned at seven thirty, and so at seven ten Gwyndaf Bevan raises himself up to speak into the silent room. His voice needs warming up before it will be audible over the telephone. He recites scraps of remembered Welsh hymns from his youth to the blank wall.

It is a Friday in the middle of September. His bedroom window faces almost directly North. The only sunrises he watches now are in the striated light through the panes, never the event itself.

Outside, the woman next door will be on her patio in dressing gown and slippers for her morning cigarette. The children in the apartment upstairs can be heard through the ceiling in an early morning argument about whether school is really necessary.

The telephone beside his bed rings and he lifts it.

"Good morning dad, it's Clarisse."

"*Bore da*."

"Did you sleep well?"

"The same, thank you *bach*." A moment's silence between them. Despite warming his voice up, it still seems thick with sleep. His Welsh accent has never faded, and always sounds harsher against the soft tones of hers.

"Well, as long as you're alright. I'll come over at lunchtime, okay? I'll bring the paper. *Le Parisien* maybe? So you can practice?"

"The *cymraeg*."

"Dad, they don't have a Welsh paper."

He harrumphs at her, and she sighs heavily. He can picture her, pinching the bridge of her nose in frustration with him, pushing her glasses up her forehead.

He has known her for fifty years. The night his son Eifion brought her home for tea was the first time they had spoken English around the table, their common second language. A fancy French exchange student, from Eifion's college. Gwyndaf had borrowed Pam from down the street's car to drive her back to the family she was staying with, his son in the back seat and nobody speaking.

"I'll see you for lunch, dad." The line goes dead and crackles in his ear.

He knows about the paper, of course. He just wants to remind her of what he lost when she moved him here.

He twists a little to reseat the phone in its cradle, and then slowly begins to stretch out each skinny limb, finally swinging both feet onto the floor. His ankles crack softly as he walks to the door and puts on his dressing gown.

He spends the morning in his pyjamas, sitting in his customary armchair. The heating comes on automatically now and so the sitting room is already cosy when he shuffles in and picks up one of the novels stacked beside his chair, all in Welsh. He is reading *Harri Potter a Maen yr Athronydd,* bought for him by his teenage great-grandson, several years ago. There are a few French novels Clarisse has bought him on the bookshelf, undisturbed.

After a while he begins to doze, chin dipping. He fumbles for the control attached to the side of the chair and presses it to recline the seat. The movement wakes him slightly, but it is comfortable, so he continues to read for a few minutes until his mind begins to drift.

He must have fallen asleep properly, because the hallway clock is now chiming ten. He should get dressed before Clarisse arrives, he thinks. She loves to see him still in his pyjamas when she breezes in. It is her proof that he needs looking after.

The book has fallen on the floor. His page is lost. He will start again tomorrow.

He makes his way down the hall, pausing halfway to stare at the photographs on the wall. They used to hang beside the stairs, in the house where his son grew up. They aren't even straight, Anwen would have scolded him for it, but his shoulders are too stiff to reach up and correct them. He could ask Luca to do it, if he visits anytime soon.

This apartment is very strange to him. He inspects a photograph on the wall. It shows him, with his son, grandson and great-grandson. It seems to have been a birthday, from the cake and banners in the background. The baby is on his knee, arms in the air. Everyone in the photograph is looking at the baby, Gwyndaf realises. This was years ago: it is years since they all got together like that. He shakes his head to clear the sleep still hanging around him and continues to the bathroom.

Once he is dressed, he feels restless.

He decides to stand outside for a while, to get the fresh air. It takes twenty minutes to find where Clarisse has decided he keeps his keys, but eventually he starts out, his stick in his hand as he walks down the echoing communal corridor. The soil spike crunches in the gravel along the short path, and then slides awkwardly on the concrete pavement. They bought him an expensive new one at Christmas, but he doesn't like it. This one fits his hand, he is used to its weight. He does understand it isn't practical – there is no need to walk across fields, here. There is hardly need for him to walk at all. But he is used to it, and anyway, now he has left the house, and spent minutes concentrating on turning the key in the lock, he cannot go back to find the other one. Everything takes too long to do any of it twice.

It is colder than he expected.

He stands at the side of the road and looks around. Since the move, he doesn't leave the house much except for appointments. He resents this –back home, *yng Ngymru*, he could go anywhere, as and when he fancied. He lived in Llanfihangel his whole life. If he had ever been in trouble, well, someone would have known him. The older he got, the more recognised he was. Everyone knew each other, but he was the man nobody could remember the place without. He did the same things every day, from the day he retired. He never fell asleep in the armchair midmorning. Even when Anwen died.

Clarisse says she worries that if he goes out alone he will fall, that he will get lost, that nobody will understand him even if he does ask for help, which of course he's too stubborn to do anyway. She calls him *épineux,* mutters it under her breath every time they argue. It is the only French he has looked up in the dictionary she bought him, though it took a few guesses at spelling.

Gwyndaf thinks privately that none of this would not have been a problem, if he had stayed in his own home. He thinks she only needs him to fuss over because her own children have grown up, moved away to the city.

Once a week she takes him to church, but he struggles to follow the service.

The breeze is fresh against his skin. He is out here now, and Clarisse will not come until at least half past eleven. He has an hour.

Grasping his stick tighter, he checks his pocket for a few coins, though he is not sure how much anything might cost here. He is sure he saw a corner shop just a few streets away, when they drove past in Clarisse's car. He can walk that far, surely. He could buy his own damn paper.

As he begins to walk, he thinks about his son. Eifion was seventy-six when he died – not a bad age, perhaps. People were surprised, at the funeral, to meet Gwyndaf – they had not expected to meet Eifion's father. He wonders how Clarisse had felt, having lost her husband, to then see that strange interest in him, the hundred-year-old father of the dead man. They had been Eifion's peers mostly, all a similar age, and they looked at him as though desperate to ask for his secret. Not that he could be sure what anyone had said, of course. Their French was so fast, and the day had been a blur in any case.

Halfway down the street, he feels breathless and sits down on someone's garden wall. There is no real garden on the other side, though. He is sure Clarisse sees him as provincial, and so he has not asked too many questions about the place he lives now. It is where she lives. But the gardens seem wrong to him – designed not to need time or attention from the residents of the houses. The greenery outside his own flat is tended by a management company. When he first moved in, he wondered if he could be useful by pruning and watering the flowers, but was told it wouldn't be allowed. Something to do with *responsabilité* and *l'assurance*. Perhaps he can ask Clarisse to get him a window box. To go in his bedroom.

He misses being surrounded by growing things, wild things. Everything he can see has been designed, not grown. It all matches, too well.

A young mother is walking towards him, jabbering low, rapid French into a telephone wedged between her ear and shoulder, the sort of native speaking which makes it hard to distinguish separate words from each other. She one-handedly pushes a neon pram which is almost the width of the pavement. Two little ones sit side by side, looking bored and haughty.

Gwyndaf wonders how old they are. It's so long since there was a baby in the family. He's out of practice with how different ages look on small children. When did they start to hold up their own heads? He knows that when Eifion was born, he used to have the baby's head in the crook of his elbow and bum in the palm of his hand. But was that as a newborn? And how long did it last?

The woman stops just before she passes him and starts shouting into her phone. He watches spittle land on her cardigan. The babies push at the straps holding them, faces crumpling, and it is natural to waggle his fingers and to smile, to pull a face and distract them. Their mother finishes her phone call, hissing, and turns to see him with a thumb on his nose, fingers splayed, sticking out his tongue, and her babies open mouthed and placid. She shouts something fast and unintelligible. The little ones start crying as she marches them away.

He starts walking again, rounding the corner, taking things more slowly. A man his grandson's age comes out of a house opposite, with a handsome Dalmatian on a short lead. He's wearing sunglasses and a fitted mackintosh, walking boots which have never seen a speck of mud. The dog is just as immaculately clean. Gwyndaf wonders where the dog walking spots are. He is surprised to see a dog at all.

The shop is in his sights now. He can see the sign hung above the door, bright red with white letters reading *Bonnet – Presse – Tabac.* There is a bench nearby, next to the bus stop, where he sits to catch his breath again. His legs feel sore but good. He hasn't walked this far in months.

He walks into the shop and breathes in, smells tobacco. A man with thin grey hair and three chins sits behind the counter on a bar stool, a newspaper open in his lap. One arm is twisted behind him, holding a lit cigar out of a tiny, cracked window.

"Bonjour," he says in a bored voice, turning the page without looking up.

Gwyndaf potters down the aisle to the paper stand, fumbling in his pocket to count his change. He will get himself one that Clarisse has never brought him.

L'Humanité. La Croix. Le Monde. Le Figaro. Libération. Charlie Hebdo. L'Express.

Beside the stand of black and white papers is a small shelf of comics, brightly coloured. He recognises the name *Asterix*. When his grandson was young and Eifion and Clarisse would visit, they brought stacks of these to keep the boy entertained. He starts to laugh. Yes. This will do.

He takes the comic book to the counter, where the three-chinned man mutters a number and holds out a hand for the money, dropping it coin by coin into the till.

"Salut." He pulls his receipt from between thick outstretched fingers. The man taps ash out of the window.

Gwyndaf clutches the comic in his hand and starts to walk again. He moves faster now, energised by his purchase. He is keen to get home, to try and read it. Eifion could speak French, after all.

There had been another service, back in Llanfihangel. People still gave Gwyndaf sympathetic looks. There was a photograph in the paper, of a young boy, captain of the rugby team, Eifion's moment of local fame. On a normal Sunday, the service had been in his memory, without Gwyndaf ever asking for it. It might have done more for his grief than anything else, if it hadn't been the day Clarisse delivered her decision.

She arrived in the afternoon, her hair tied up in a haphazard way he'd never seen before. He was reclined in his chair, asleep when she walked in and made him jump. Her accent got stronger, and his got stronger in response, until they might have well both spoken in their native tongues for all each could understand the other. She muttered *épineux*, and she called her son, who on the phone said that honestly, this would be for the best, Grandpa. Didn't he want to see more of them? Clarisse looked distraught already. He agreed. He regretted it.

He is standing breathless on the pavement. His chest hurts. He grips *Asterix* hard.

A car honks behind him, he hears it pull up, and then Clarisse is there, her hand tight on his shoulder.

"Dad! Dad, what are you doing!" she is shouting, the way he used to shout at Eifion as a little boy, found doing something dangerous. "Why are you out? You aren't supposed to-"

He grasps her shoulder with his free hand and leans on her. He tips his head onto her shoulder and squeezes his eyes closed. A low whine comes from somewhere in his throat, his lips stretch. He realises that for the first time in many years, he is crying.

"Okay, Dad." Clarisse pats his back, straightens him up and leads him to the car. "Let's get you home, alright? And then you can explain what's going on."

He sits in the car and breathes. Watches the street pass.

Clarisse walks oppressively close beside him all way up the path, all the way to his armchair, her hand firm under his elbow. Once he's sat down she fusses, tucking him into a blanket, tilting the chair back and offering him a hot wheat bag for his knees. He nods. She leaves the room, and he can hear her on the phone with the doctor, making arrangements. Likely, there will be a visit this afternoon.

When she comes back into the room, he asks her to help him read the comic.

Biographies - Rising stars

Jessica Adrews writes fiction. Her debut novel, Saltwater won the Portico Prize in 2020 and her second novel, Milk Teeth was shortlisted for the Royal Society of Literature Encore Award. Her work is translated into seven languages. She is a Contributing Editor at ELLE magazine and she writes for the Guardian, the Independent, BBC Radio 4 and Stylist, among others. She was nominated for the ELLE list in 2020, shortlisted for the Women's Prize for Fiction Futures and longlisted for the BBC National Short Story Award in 2022. She co-runs literary and arts magazine, The Grapevine and co-presents literary podcast, Tender Buttons. She is a Lecturer in Creative Writing at City University, London.

Francesca Duffield is a writer and artist originally from the Midlands now living in East Sussex. She has worked as an illustrator and art lecturer, and taught English as a Second Language. She has had poems published in anthologies by Artemisia Arts and Bourne to Write, and in Ingenue Magazine.

Truly Johnston lives and works in South East London and is mixed heritage Sri-Lankan / British. She writes poetry, short stories and children's fiction, was part of the Penguin #WriteNow programme and won the 2022 Bath Children's Novel Award. Truly is represented by Lauren Gardner of Bell Lomax Moreton.

Emily Tsang: At the age of 10 and 11, she was the youngest winner of two prestigious writing competitions in Hong Kong. Her command of the English language is evident in the publication of her prose in the Rabbit Hole magazine, and her writing and codirecting of a 120-minute surrealist play Decameron.

Michael Salander was shortlisted for the Bridport Poetry Prize in 2015 and the Bridport Prize for Flash Fiction in 2022. He has since had his work published in over six anthologies. He is currently working on a novella-in-flash.

Danielle Todd is a poet and short story writer. She was born in Auckland, New Zealand, where she studied journalism and literature. She was shortlisted for the Sargeson Prize in 2020. Her work has appeared or is forthcoming in titles such as Ink, Sweat & Tears, Oscen, Foxtrot Uniform and Little Stone Journal.

Suzanna Fitzpatrick (she/her) has had poems on BBC Radio 4 and widely published in magazines and anthologies. She came third in the 2023 Shepton Snowdrops Competition, second in the 2016 Café Writers Competition, and won the 2014 Hamish Canham Prize. Pamphlets from Red Squirrel Press, UK: 'Fledglings' (2016), 'Crippled' (2024).

Andrew Boulton is the author of a bestselling book on copywriting and a children's book called Adele Writes an Ad. His stories have been published in journals & competitions including The Bridport Prize, Retreat West, Lunate Fiction, Tiny Molecules, Spelk, Reflex, Bath Flash Fiction anthology, Cranked Anvil and Storgy. He lives in Nottingham with his wife, daughter and a chubby cat.

Alex Reece Abbott - A New Zealand Irish writer, Alex writes across genres and forms. Honoured with the Flash Frontier Summer Writing Award for a body of work, her writing is a Penguin Random House WriteNow finalist and Irish Novel Fair, Northern Crime, Arvon, Crediton, Pulp Literature and HG Wells prize winner. *www.alexreeceabbott.info* / @AlexReeceAbbott

Sarah Masters (she/her) lives in York and teaches English for Speakers of Other Languages. Her tiny stories have appeared in Full House Literary, Flashflood, Shooter Flash, Pure Slush, and Chewin' The Fat.

Frances Dalton has been writing flash for several years. She has been placed in several competitions including the Fiction Factory, Craft Literary and the London Independent Story Prize. She's been published in Reflex Press's flash anthology, Beguiled by a Wild Thing, and the 2023 Bath Flash Fiction Anthology, Dandelion Years.

AJ Morris is London-born and uses most of her writing energy at an ad agency. She writes about interpersonal relationships and one-shots that might have happened. She won the 2021 CWIP Flash Fiction Prize and was shortlisted for Tortive Theatre's FlashFiction101. She's currently working on her first poetry pamphlet.

Emma Burnett is a researcher and writer. She has had stories in Radon, Utopia Magazine, MetaStellar, Milk Candy Review, Elegant Literature, The Stygian Lepus, Roi Fainéant, The Sunlight Press, Rejection Letters, and more. You can find her @slashnburnett, @slashnburnett.bsky.social, or emmaburnett.uk.

Rebecca Douglas is an Australian writer of fiction, essays, and feature articles. Her work has been published by The Sydney Morning Herald, The Australian, Kill Your Darlings, Overland journal, The Big Issue, ABC The Drum, and various other lovely places.

Pierre Perera works in the civil service, which gives him lots of food for thought but less time for writing than he'd like. His story, 'Excuse me, what are your opinions about the end of the world?' was chosen as the overall winner at the 2022 Write By The Sea Literary Festival competition.

Annie Bien has published three poetry chapbooks, won a LISP competition, been finalist in flash fiction and poetry, and nominated for the Pushcart Prize. She translates Tibetan Buddhist texts into English, teaches Buddhism and meditation. Forthcoming is a historical novel on the Sixth Dalai Lama, co-written with Robert Thurman. http://anniebien.com

For the past decade and a half 1988 Barry University Communication Arts graduate **Marc D O'Brien** has been using fiction to artistically describe sensitive material. From "Peter The Peteeatrick Panda's Playground" to "The Final Fence: Sophomores In The Saddle" he hopes his reader will understand facing adversity.

Guy Ware is the author of the story collection 'You Have 24 Hours to Love Us' and four novels. His stories have been anthologised and listed for many awards, including the London Short Story Prize, which he won in 2018. His new novel, 'Our Island Story', will be published in March 2024.

Pippa Wildwood is a multidisciplinary artist. Her background is in theatre and she mainly wrote for stage and screen before turning to fiction and poetry after being affected by chronic illness. Her work has been published by Spread the Word, performed in theatres and developed into short film.

Elizabeth Hewes is a writer, voice actor, and translator. In 2022, she got an Undergraduate Creative Writing Diploma from Oxford University with distinction. She lives in the Beaujolais near Lyon.

Joanna Adam was born in Edinburgh and lives with her husband near Milton Keynes. Now that her children have left home, she has time to write. During lockdown, Joanna took an MA at Manchester Metropolitan University in Creative Writing and has finished her first novel, Kept, which she is preparing for publication.

Nikoletta Gjoni is a fiction and creative nonfiction writer living outside of Washington, D.C. Her work has been previously nominated for the PEN/Robert J. Dau prize, Best of the Net, and Best Microfiction. She is at work on her first novel.

Ava Ming's short stories have been featured online, in print and on radio. She was BBC Radio Drama Writer in Residence and writer and coach for English Heritage. She's had three stage plays produced and lives in Birmingham, apart from in her mind where she's all over the place.

Ieuan Wyn Williams has a Celtic heart and an English accent. He has a BA in Drama from Aberystwyth and an MA in Creative Writing from Roehampton. During the twenty years between those degrees, Ieuan messed around backstage in theatres listening to great stories before finally committing to telling some himself.

Craig Smith is a novelist and poet from Huddersfield. His work has been published by iamb, Fairlight, The North, Writers Rebel, Mechanics' Institute Review, among others. He was a winner of Poetry Archive Now WordWise 2022. @clattermonger clattermonger.com

Luke Lewin Davies is a writer based in London. His writing has appeared in the Times Literary Supplement, The London Magazine, Literary Review, The Los Angeles Review of Books, and elsewhere.

Robin Luce Martin won the Tennessee Williams Festival Story Prize, the Eyelands International Novel Manuscript, and the 3Rock Residency Award, securing a Greek translation of *Lizardmaid*, November 2023. *Out Like a Lion* was shortlisted for the Dundee International Book Prize and Del Sol's First Novel Prize. She co-founded the author series #YeahYouWrite. www.yeahyouwriteevents.com www.robinlucemartin.com

Joanna Garbutt's stories have been broadcast on BBC Radio Cambridgeshire and published in 'Literary Mama' and 'Porridge'. Her novel-in-progress was longlisted in the 2022 Bridport Peggy Chapman-Andrews First Novel Award. She is also a researcher and has a PhD in Applied Linguistics where her research focused on police-suspect interview discourse.

Clare Reddaway writes short stories and plays. Recent highlights include being long-listed for the BBC National Short Story Awards, short-listed for the Bridport Prize and a pamphlet publication by Fly on the Wall Press. Clare's debut novel Dancing in the Shallows will be published by Fairlight Books in 2024.

A.M. Gough is a London-based writer and translator. She has previously been shortlisted for the 2018 Exeter Story Prize, the 2022 Parracombe Prize and the 2022 and 2023 Wolverhampton Literature Festival poetry prizes. She came second in the 2021 John Dryden Translation Competition. She is working on her first novel.

Biographies - Promising Pens.

Nelly Bryce is a writer, poet and mother of four from Manchester, UK. She published her first book of poetry, Motherhood Minus the Medals in 2022. She describes herself as a, 'journaling addict,' writes a blog called Journaling Wild and is rarely found far from decent coffee and a huge slice of cake. Probably chocolate.

Jennifer Duffy is a writer based in Edinburgh, Scotland. Her work explores themes of neurodiversity, mental illness and witchcraft. Her poems have been published in t'ART Press, Wildfire Words and the Poetrygram Anthology: On Hunger. When she isn't writing, Jennifer can be found reading fantasy novels and tarot cards.

Kirsty Woods' writing has appeared in anthologies 'Songs of Love and Strength' and 'Lullabies for New Mums', and in magazines 'Gypsophilia' and 'Gingernut'. In 2022 she performed her poetry at the Southbank Centre, and realised that her desire to share her work is greater than her nervous inclination to hide it.

Emma Williams is a novelist, short story writer and poet. She previously worked in the NHS. Her first novel The Tortoise was published in 2021 and her second Nothing but the Truth in 2023. Best Served Cold won the 2021 Segora International short story prize. She lives in Shropshire, UK.

Paul McGilton Paul is a hardworking Special Educational Needs English teacher with a passion for poetry.

Laura Kyle is an Irish woman who lives on the beautiful island of Jersey. She was a finalist in the LISP in 2021 and 2022. She is currently working on her first novel, Banshee and just about to complete an MFA in Creative Writing.

Madeleine Armstrong is a journalist covering the pharma industry. She has had stories accepted by Flash Fiction Magazine and LISP, and was longlisted for the Henshaw Press Short Story Competition in 2023. When she's not reading, writing or working, she runs for the mighty Croydon Harriers.

Lucy Lasasso is passionate about Adult Education and started writing short fiction after taking creative writing courses at Morley College and City Lit. She lives in East London, which inspires many of her stories.

Liz Gwinnell lives in Wiltshire where she works as a prison law solicitor. In her spare time she enjoys spinning wool, looking after her bees and trying to control two unruly but delightful cats.

Steve Saulsbury resides on Maryland's Eastern Shore. He became intrigued with flash fiction in early 2020. His work has appeared in The Yard, Loch Raven Review, South Florida Poetry Journal and Cosmorama, among others. His story, "Driftwood Days," won first place in the 2021 Rehoboth Beach Reads contest.

Grant Wandle loves the power and impact of very short fiction. In competitions, his stories have been long-listed and – on a good day – prize-winning. In addition to flash fiction, he is keen to explore oral storytelling. He lives and works in London.

Sarah Hill Wheeler: Erstwhile lawyer, writer, frazzled mother, and multi-tasker. Prose winner Urban Tree Festival 2021, currently working on an MA in Creative Writing at MMU. Sometime Londoner and Francophile, returned to my rural Wiltshire roots. Now often found outside, with a double expresso, talking to hens. Website: www.sarahhillwheeler.co.uk

Letty Butler is a multi-disciplinary writer and performer from London. Her first non-fiction book was published in January and her debut novel is out on submission. She won the Fish Short Story Prize and a Northern Writers Award earlier this year, and is now working on a new play.

An RAF nomadic beginning saw actress and now writer **Philippa Howell** settling on the border of the Peak District and Sheffield. She spends her time walking the hills, cooking for friends, and spoiling her two Cretan cats. As well as working on short stories and flash, she has completed a feature film adaptation of Philip Larkin's A GIRL IN WINTER, and is developing a novel set in 1930s Cairo.

Scarlett Sangster is a writer and novelist from Somerset, UK. She is currently seeking representation for her novel In Search of Peter Pan, following Jen as she comes to terms with love, loss and heartbreak while chasing the Kate Bush tour across Europe in 1979.

Christopher Bowen is the author of the chapbook We Were Giants, the novella When I Return to You, I Will Be Unfed, and the non-fiction Debt. He was a semi-finalist in the 2017 Faulkner-Wisdom Novella Competition and honorable mention in the 45th New Millennium Writing Awards in the non-fiction category.

Rohit Singh is a full time service employee in an MNC. He actively writes on reflections and various aspects of life. He has also published his poetry book Ripples which is available on Amazon across all countries.

Amy Ferguson always has a story (or three) on the go and is working on a novel. She has won the Writers' Forum short story competition, advanced to the second round of the Bridport Prize, and been longlisted and shortlisted for contests including Masters Review, Craft and Fish. Twitter: @Amy_M_Ferguson

A former television producer, **Kathrine Bancroft** now works as a communications consultant. She holds an MA in English from Birkbeck and is a City University Novel Studio alumnus, where she began her recently completed first novel. She is also a creative writing volunteer at The Ministry of Stories.

Karon Alderman is a writer and teacher living in Newcastle upon Tyne. She writes novels for children and short stories for adults, published in a range of magazines, including Under the Radar and Gutter Press. Her children's novel, Dark Flood, won the Hachette Prize 2022 and will be published in 2024.

FJ Morris is an award-winning writer and Director of the Oxford Flash Fiction Prize. Freya's collection 'This is (not about) David Bowie' was published by Retreat West and received a special mention in the Saboteur Awards for Best Short Story Collection in 2019.

Molly Lanzarotta was awarded second prize for The Moth Nature Writing Prize 2023 and has been a finalist for numerous other awards. Publications include The Rumpus, FlashFlood, Crosswinds, Cutthroat, About Place, Terrain, Vestal Review, Cimarron Review, Carolina Quarterly, Southeast Review; the Bath Flash Fiction anthology Snow Crow.

Patricia Mullin: A graduate of Central/St Martins and Writing the Visual MA, Patricia's concerns in writing are perception (flawed) and moral ambiguity, using ideas sourced from art, objects, nature, the half–remembered and the unwittingly disclosed. Gene Genie, her published novel, and short fictions have been included in anthologies and literary journals.

Julian Cadman took up creative writing as a hobby eight years ago, when joining a local creative writing class. He particularly enjoys writing flash fiction and short stories.

Robert Young grew up in New Zealand and is a retired architect and London tour guide. Due to his dyslexia, he had always lacked the confidence to write creatively. In 2020, he joined a creative writing class and has been writing ever since.

Mary Francis lives in Aotearoa New Zealand. She writes flash fiction and short stories and has been published by Takahē Magazine and several short fiction anthologies. In 2023 she won First Place in the Te Tauihu Short Story Awards and the Writer's Digest Short Short Story Competition.

Rachel Makinson is a UK-based writer and editor, with a BA in English Literature with Creative Writing from Newcastle University. Her work has been featured by several magazines and journals, including Otherwise Engaged Literature and Arts Journal, Marrow Magazine and Tabula Rasa Review.

Natasha Derczynski is a writer and teaching assistant living in SE London. She has an MA in Creative Writing and a BA in English with Creative Writing from Brunel University. Her work can be found in Queen Mob's Teahouse, Montana Mouthful and the Bombay Review. She won the NAWG 100x100 prize and came second in the QuietManDave prize.

Lee Reilly writes about women, marriage, and the intricacies of family, identity, and care, and is working on a novel-in-flash about her grandmother. Her work has appeared in Smokelong Quarterly, Hippocampus, London Independent Story Prize, Dorothy Parker's Ashes, and elsewhere, and she's earned support from Barbara Deming Fund, Ragdale, and other arts organizations. The author of Women Living Single and Teaching Maggie, she hosts Shannaghe, a residency for writers in Maine.

Russell Heywood has been a teacher in the UK and abroad. This story emerged out of a PhD, and he's had an academic/fictional article published by University of California Press. Russell now lives in Brighton UK.

Jane Branson is an educator and writer living and working in East Sussex, where she advises schools on reading and literacy. A published author of fiction and non-fiction, her first job was as a library assistant – she has been in love with books as long as she can remember.

Rosalyn Huxley lives on the Jurassic Coast and graduated with distinction from Exeter University's MA in Creative Writing. After lockdown she left her job as a charity fundraiser to write, walk and enjoy nature. She is editing her comic novel set in a retirement complex. She is obsessed with ageism.

Karen Storey is an award winning fiction writer. Her short stories have been published, placed and listed in several international competitions. Originally from New York, she lives in Warwickshire with her British husband and has written articles for American in Britain magazine. She is currently working on two novels.

Michael Pearson is a psychotherapist, life-time mental health professional, columnist and multi-published author of fiction and academic work and was featured as one of the most influential LGBTQ+ people in 2023s Pink List. He writes horror, psychological thriller, opinion pieces and academic work on mental health and LGBTQ+ experiences. You can find Michael on Instagram at @michaelpiercewrites & mental_healthy_with_mikey

Kate Arnold is an Undergraduate Creative Writing student at the University of Gloucestershire. Her poetry has been turned into the spoken word/ beats project, Dead Anyway, who have been featured on BBC 6Music and radio stations worldwide. She also writes drama and prose and is working on her first novel.

Frida Khan works for the United Nations and divides her time between her work in Jerusalem, her children in London, and family in Lahore. She is a development sector professional and wishes she could be a writer. Being in the LISP anthology 2023 might be the first step!

Sue Brennan is an Australian writer published in ACE - Contemporary Stories by Emerging Writers, Meniscus, Meanjin and Verandah, and in the USA in The Peauxdunque Review and The Blue Mountain Review. In 2022, she won the New Feathers Anthology prose award. She can be found at www.suebrennan.net

David Micklem is a writer and theatre producer. He's recently been published by The London Magazine, Litro, STORGY Magazine, Scratch Books, the Cardiff Review, and Lunate, and was shortlisted for the 2022 Bristol Prize, and the 2020 Fish Short Story Prize. He's been long listed for the 2023 Brick Lane Short Story Prize.

Karen Browne lives in Galway, Ireland writing short stories, novels and creative non-fiction. Her work has featured in Feels Blind Literary Issue 8 and Roi Faineant Press. She is currently working on her debut novel. She can be found on Twitter:@Karen_Browne, Instagram: @karenm_browne

Neaka Mohtashemi was born in San Mateo, California to Iranian immigrants who raised her on stories ranging from Persian literature, Aesop's Fables, Disney classics, and beyond. She believes there is a little magic in everything even if it isn't immediately obvious, and that anyone can find it if they try.

Jessie Payne writes novels, short stories and flash fiction. She is on the editorial team at Retreat West, and is an associate editor at RUBY.

Jilly Carrell was originally from Edinburgh and is now from everywhere. 18 years as an army wife, her husband's operational tours of Afghanistan, and the impact of the conflict on military families provide the inspiration for her story. 2023 She graduated with an MA (distinction) in Creative Writing from Bath Spa.

Julie M Watkins was born in South Wales. She began writing in 2018. Julie was a LISP short story finalist in 2022. She describes her stories as, magical, with dream like qualities, taking you to surreal worlds. Many of the characters in her stories lead very strange complicated lives.

Steve Wade is a fiction writer and English language teacher. His short story collection 'In Fields of Butterfly Flames and Other Stories' was published by Bridge House Publishing in 2020. His fiction has been widely published and anthologised. He has won awards and had work recorded for radio.

Daniel Wade is a poet, novelist and playwright from Dublin, Ireland. His most recent books include the poetry collections Iceberg Relief (Underground Press, 2017) and Rapids (Finishing Line Press, 2021), and the novel A Land Without Wolves (Temple Dark Books, 2021).

Lisa Johnson Mitchell's work has appeared in X-R-A-Y, Fictive Dream, and Cleaver, among others. One of her pieces was a Finalist in the 2022 London Independent Story Prize Competition. Another placed in the Top 10 of the 2020 Columbia Journal Short Fiction Contest. She holds an MFA from Bennington College.

Karen Milner lives in Lancashire with her husband and two sons. For many years she worked as a reporter in local radio and is still haunted by some of the crimes she covered. Karen writes to try and understand life and to explore what it is to be human.

Marianne Dugdale is a writer and tutor who lives in Staffordshire with her husband and two young children. In 2023 her writing has featured in Mag North and Mutter Magazine, and her review of Death of a Bookseller won the NewWriters.org book review competition. She is currently writing a novel.

LISP

LONDON INDEPENDENT STORY PRIZE

2023